MUSIC CITY MURDER

A Justice Sisters Novel

LEKECIA BARCLAY

Arlington Street Publishing

MUSIC CITY MURDER

ACKNOWLEDGEMENTS

Writing a book is a labor of love, harder than I thought, but worth every second of every minute. With writing comes a rollercoaster of emotions- excitement, trepidation, joy, self-doubt and absolute terror but it's one ride I never want to get off. Being able to bring my characters to life in words is a reward in and of itself. Writing has always been a passion and finally putting my work out into the world has brought me the greatest joy.

This book wouldn't be possible without the patience and understanding of my family. I must start by thanking my wonderful husband, Paul, for giving me the time and the space to craft this novel. I want to thank my awesome children, Tarquis and Keriana, for being my inspiration to always push myself further. Without you, I would be nothing. A huge thank you to my closest friend and confidant, Brittania Stewart, for reading drafts and providing feedback, your input was invaluable. You've been my ride-or-die since first semester law school. I am eternally grateful for your friendship.

CHAPTER 1

Evoni

Evoni knocked loudly. "Amar, I need my keys." Silence. Evoni shouted. "I know you hear me knocking. Don't make me act a fool out here on this front doorstep!"

The door opened. Amar stood there looking delectable in nothing but a towel. "I thought you were gone, so I went to shower."

"Why? Did you need to wash our sex off you so that ho can come over?"

"Look, Evoni, I am not trying to hear that right now. I told you that was a one-time thing and that I was sorry. Damn baby, everybody makes a mistake, so why don't you come back in and go to sleep?"

"Negro, are you crazy? You will never feel this body next to you in bed again. I was your fiancée, which meant that I was the only one you were supposed to be sleeping with. Instead, I find out you've been screwing some chick with three kids and two baby daddies. Fucking unbelievable. And you're telling me to come back in and go to bed. I feel like I'm on an episode of Maury fucking Povich."

"Evoni, it was only once."

"If it was only once, then why the hell is she calling you at 2:30 in the morning?"

"What I have is addictive, you know that," Amar quipped.

"Oh, so you think this is funny, huh? Let's see how funny it is tomorrow when my brothers come through."

"See, why you gotta go there? This is between me and you."

"This stopped being about me and you when you brought another woman into our relationship. Now move so I can get my keys and go."

Evoni brushed past Amar. "I don't have time for this shit."

Evoni grabbed her keys from the kitchen table and turned to leave. Amar grabbed her hand.

Evoni's reflexes kicked in. "Get your damn hands off me," she yelled as she kneed him in the groin and raced out the door.

Ten minutes later Evoni pulled into her driveway. As she was getting out of the car, her cell rang. It was Amar. She ignored it and went into her house. Once inside, she crumbled on the floor and burst into tears. She had held on as long as she could. She couldn't believe Amar would do something like this to her. He was her life; he was the reason she woke up every morning. He was the first man she had ever trusted with her heart, and he had broken it.

After about five minutes, Evoni wiped her eyes and got up. She would not let this destroy her; she was a strong independent woman. She would get through this just as she'd gotten through every other hurt in her life. Evoni looked down at what she was wearing and chuckled. Here she was dressed in red lace boy shorts with a matching bra and whip cream still between her legs. Don't even ask.

Evoni showered and hopped into her king size bed. Her silk sheets felt so good against her skin. Better than Amar's hands ever did.

Evoni opened her eyes and saw the sun streaming through her window. She rolled over and looked at the clock. It was 12:30. She had missed the morning service at church. Damn Amar for ruining her night, her morning, hell her life.

Since she had missed the morning service, maybe she would try to catch the evening service at her church, Greater East Nashville Baptist Church, of which she had been a member since she was seven.

Evoni's phone rang. She glanced over at the caller I.D. and saw it was her mother, Gloria. What did she want? Probably to remind Evoni yet again that she was over 30 and still hadn't given her any grandkids. Evoni loved her mother, but they were like oil and water, they just didn't mix.

Evoni contemplated not answering, she really wasn't in the mood. "Hello, mommy dearest. What a pleasant surprise."

Her mother ignored the sarcasm and asked, "What did you do? I just got off the phone with Amar, and he told me you called off the wedding. What's wrong with you? Are you losing the little bit of sense God gave you?"

Evoni wanted to scream and curse. "Well, Mother, if you would take the time to hear my side of the story before jumping down my throat, you would know that I have a good reason for calling off the wedding."

"And what could that possibly be?" Gloria asked cynically.

"Well, let's see how about this for starters. Amar is a trifling good for nothing Negro who has been creeping with somebody's baby mama behind my back," Evoni snapped.

"Don't raise your voice at me, young lady," her mother retorted. "I will not tolerate that kind of rudeness. And I'm sure you just misunderstood the situation. I'm sure Amar has a plausible explanation. He's a good man and you know how hard it was to find him, don't sacrifice a good thing over such nonsense."

"What!!!!" Evoni shouted angrily. "A good man doesn't cheat on his fiancée with some skank and then lie about it. I hate to inform you but sitting at home cooking and cleaning while your husband is out whoring went out in the 50s," Evoni shouted pressing the end button.

Her mother could be so infuriating. *Why can't she take my side just once?* It was like her mother took pleasure in berating her. No matter what happened, in Evoni's mother's eyes, she was always the bad guy.

Evoni's phone rang again. *Please don't let this be my mother again; I would hate to have to curse out my own mother.*

"Hey, girl," Evoni said. It was her best friend, Bri.

"What's up, girl, why weren't you in church? Amar wore you out last night?" Evoni's best friend Bri asked while giggling.

In that moment, the last thing Evoni wanted was to rehash what happened with Amar. So, she did something she rarely did with her best friend, she lied. "I'd love to tell you all about it, but I am swamped with work. One of the senior partners handed me a last-minute assignment. I have no idea how long this will take but let's schedule lunch for next Saturday at Mama Bee's," suggested Evoni to get Bri off the phone.

"Bet, girl you know I love me some Mama Bee's. Remember make the money, don't let your money make you," said Bri quoting a famous movie line.

Evoni laughed lightly and promised to do just that. After hanging up, Evoni debated going back to sleep but realized she really did have some work to do. As a lawyer, there was always work to do.

Evoni worked diligently for the next few hours, only stopping when her stomach began protesting the lack of sustenance. Evoni headed to the kitchen where she made herself a can of tomato soup, a grilled cheese, and a very large glass of wine. It was just what the doctor ordered. While eating, Evoni perused the news on her phone. The local news sites were obsessively covering a string of murders in the city. It was being suggested there was a serial killer in Nashville preying on unsuspecting women and strangling them to death. The killer was suspected of posing as a police officer to ensnare his victims. So far, all the victims had been middle age and blonde. The blogs had nicknamed the killings "The Music City Murders."

Evoni noticed the stories tended to focus more on the possible killer than on the victims. Hopefully the perpetrator was caught soon, and the victim's family received some kind of justice and closure.

Evoni's phone rang interrupting her reading. *Damn, who could this be calling now?*

"Hello, Evoni speaking."

"Hi, Ms. Singleton. This is Joe Bradford calling from Krispy & Klean Auto Repair. I'm calling to inform you that the piece you ordered has arrived."

Damn. Evoni had forgotten all about the gift she ordered for Amar. As a wedding gift, she had finally located a place that had the part needed to complete the renovations on his 1930 Bentley Grand Prix. She'd looked everywhere for that part, and it had cost a pretty penny. *What the hell am I supposed to do with it now?*

"Oh, hi. How are you? Um, thanks for calling, I will be there Monday evening to pick it up," stated Evoni.

"That'll be fine, just remember we close at 7:00 on weekdays."

"I'll be there by 6:00, again thank you for calling."

"No problem, you have a blessed day. Good-bye."

"You do the same, goodbye." Evoni clicked off the phone. Finished with her early dinner, Evoni went to take a shower before returning to finish her work. Feeding her soul would have to wait until next week.

CHAPTER 2

Bri

Miles away in her home in Belle Meade, Bri Montgomery stood in her bedroom watching Harold, her partner for the last three years, sleep. As she watched the man she loved, Bri's mind took her back to the events from the day before.

After finishing lunch with Evoni, Bri decided to head over to her mother's and pay her a long overdue visit. She hadn't seen or spoken to her mother, Francine, in over a month. They'd had a falling out at a family picnic about her living with Harold. Her mother thought it was indecent for a woman her age to date and live with a man who was old enough to be her father, even possibly her grandfather. Bri had defended her relationship with Harold and told her mother that maybe she was the reason why Bri gravitated towards old rich men, since she had done the same thing in her early twenties, including with Bri's father, a married doctor, who was a good 30 years older than her mother. Only after meeting Bri's stepfather, a wealthy businessman her own age, did Francine stop dating men old enough to be her own father. It's funny how hypocritical a person can become after they've changed their ways.

Not one to air her "dirty laundry" in the streets, Francine slapped Bri across her face for putting her business out there. Until that moment, no one other than Francine's sisters, mother and closest friends had any inkling of who Bri's natural father was. All they knew was that it wasn't Francine's husband, Eugene. Bri's mother was so upset with her that she called her a "gold-digging tramp" and Bri retaliated with "I guess the apple doesn't fall far from the tree." Since that eventful day, Bri's mother had refused to speak to her. Bri felt bad about speaking to her mother that way and had tried to apologize several times, but her mother wouldn't accept her calls or any of the gifts she sent.

When she pulled into her mother's driveway, Bri noticed the curtains moving and she knew it was her nosey ass Aunt Deidre. The lady should go work for the CIA as a spy; Bri was sure she would have found Bin Laden within hours. She seemed to always know when trouble was brewing and exactly where to find it. Before Bri could ring the bell, the door flew open and her aunt was standing in the door with a smirk on her face, looking like an uglier version of Lil' Kim. No matter how old the woman got she still insisted on dressing like a two-dollar whore. She was dressed in an orange Lycra halter top with a purple mini skirt and fishnet pantyhose. She had black and orange microbraids and enough makeup on to supply all of Sephora's customers. She looked like she had stepped off the bus from clown school.

"What do you want, haven't you caused your mother enough pain and embarrassment?" sniped her aunt. "Why can't you just leave well enough alone?"

"Hello to you too Aunt D, could you please step aside and allow me to enter *my* mother's home? Thank you," said Bri while brushing past her aunt.

"Humph, I know Frannie raised you better than that, but then again, you probably got that attitude from your no-good daddy. You look just like him so you may as well act like the bastard too," squawked Bri's aunt following her into the kitchen where her mother was busy directing the housekeeper on how to properly cook lamb. Bri waited until her mother had finished up with the housekeeper before approaching her. Bri knew how much her mother hated being interrupted and Bri didn't want to do anything else to piss her off.

Not wanting to make the situation with her mother any worse, Bri ignored her aunt's comments and proceeded to speak to her mother.

"Hi, Mother. How are you? Have you been ill, locked up, or kidnapped? If you weren't a black woman who would never be caught in a blonde wig, I'd be worried you'd become a victim of the Music City Murderer."

Turning to stare at Bri, Francine gave her an exasperated look. "Oh, Bria knock it off. Joking about a serial killer is never appropriate. Why are you being so ridiculous?"

"Well, since I've been calling you for weeks now and the housekeeper always tells me, your own daughter, you're unavailable; I just assumed something had to be wrong. Otherwise, why would my own mother disregard my phone calls?"

"You know good and well why I haven't spoken with you, so don't come in here with that nonsense. You embarrassed me in front of my friends and family, not to mention Pastor Davis."

"I'm sorry for the things I said to you, Mother, but I've asked you time and time again to stay out of my relationship with Harold. What we do is none of your business. I make him happy, and he makes me happy and that's all that counts. So why can't you just be happy that I found a good man who takes care of me and provides a fantastic home and lifestyle for me?"

"Honey, that sounds good, but I know that there is no way a woman your age could really be happy with a man as old as Harold. As you so eloquently pointed out at the family picnic, I used to wear those same shoes you're wearing now, so I know first-hand that what's making you happy isn't Harold but rather his money."

"Mother, I am happy with Harold. He treats me better than any man my own age ever has or could. He's kind and gentle, and he respects me. I'm not going to lie and say I don't love the lifestyle that he provides for me, but there's more to our relationship than that."

Her Aunt Deidre butted in. "What more could it be? It damn sure can't be the sex. He probably needs a stand to prop it up."

"Aunt D, this a private conversation between my mother and me so could you please stay out of it? Besides from what I've heard, you need to be worried about your own home. It seems Bruce has found his way into many a bed lately. I wonder why that is? Maybe because you're too busy butting into everybody else's business instead of taking care of your own," snapped Bri.

"You two stop it right now. Deidre could you please give us a minute?" asked Francine.

Glaring at Bri, Deidre barked. "I'll give ya'll more than a minute. I can tell I'm not welcome here right now, so I'll just leave you two alone. Besides, the air in here is really beginning to stink," Deidre stated while turning her nose up at Bri.

Fighting the urge to pull those ugly ass braids out of her aunt's head, Bri counted to ten, walked over to the fridge and grabbed a bottle of water. When she turned back around, her aunt was gone, and it was just her and her mother in the kitchen. Thank God for small favors.

"Bria, I don't understand why you can't get along with your aunt. The bickering between you two has to stop. She and your sisters get along just fine."

Trying to refrain from saying something smart, Bri just shrugged her shoulders and ignored her mother's comments. "Are you really still upset with me?"

"Well, what you said wasn't very nice, but I know that I probably provoked you. So, let's just let sleeping dogs lie and pretend like it never happened. It's water under the bridge."

Smiling softly, Bri reached over and hugged her mother. Although she and her mother loved each very much, the fact that they were just alike often caused issues between the two, like this recent episode. Maybe one day they would learn to co-exist without the constant arguing, but until then, Bri would try her best to avoid any more confrontations with her mother.

Now Bri watched Harold nap. Usually up at 4 a.m. and out golfing by 7 a.m. on Sunday, it was a rarity for Harold to take a mid-day nap, but he hadn't gotten home from a business meeting in Orlando until around 2 a.m. Not wanting to wake him, Bri eased out of the room and headed downstairs. Noting the time, she gave Evoni, her best friend, a call to needle her about missing church. Evoni seemed preoccupied and

Bri wondered why. Had Amar upset her? She would find out at lunch on Saturday.

CHAPTER 3

Evoni

Evoni peered out of her office window, wondering why men were such asses. Not just brothas either, but all creeds and colors. She had dated white men, a guy from Nigeria, a few Hispanic guys and even an Asian guy in college, and they all had one thing in common, they thought with their penises and not with the peanut sized brains God gave them. Just then one shining example walked in her office, proving her point. Standing in her doorway was Jeff Johnson, fifth year associate and complete pain in the ass. He made a point to come by her office and make inappropriate statements to her. Today was no exception.

"Hey sweet cakes, why don't you let me take that fine as wine ass out tomorrow night? Let you get a taste of this white chocolate." Cringing, Evoni prayed for patience, so she wouldn't curse this fool out. She was definitely not in the mood for Jeff's ignorant comments.

Unfortunately, Jeff was one of those white guys who somehow became confused at some point in life and now pretended to be a "brotha." And Evoni had the good luck of having to deal with him every day and to make matters even worse, his father was a senior partner at the firm.

"Jeff, how many times have I told you not to refer to me as sweet cakes, cupcake, or any other baked dish? I am not now, nor will I ever be your sweet cakes. Don't think that just because your father is a senior partner, I won't sue you for sexual harassment."

"Whoa, whoa, now. Why all the hostility?" Jeff asked with a slight smirk on his face. "Damn who pissed in your soup? There's no need to get all upset. You know I don't mean anything by what I say. I just think you're a fine chocolate specimen, and I'd like to get to know you better."

"Yeah well, Jeff, referring to me as a specimen is not helping your case. How about you set your sights back on the usual bimbos you date? You know the ones who are impressed by the size of your bank account and your fancy car? The ones who probably can't count past twenty and wouldn't know what a corporate attorney did if their lives depended on it? A strong intelligent black woman like me is too much for a little man like you. So, stick with the bimbos and airheads please. Today is not the day. I am not in the mood for your BS; I suggest that you take your cheesy little pickup lines and exit my office."

"Damn, so now you're going to diss my lady friends? Evoni, you are one cold sista, but one day I'm going to have the opportunity to warm that ass up," quipped Jeff as he turned to leave.

"The odds of you even remotely getting close enough to me to "warm" me up are about as likely as Al Sharpton getting rid of his processed hair. It's never going to happen. So, if you would, please leave now so I can do some work. Unfortunately, my daddy isn't a senior partner; so, I don't have the luxury of walking the halls and doing nothing."

"Ouch. Alright, already. I can see my services are not welcome here. I'm leaving now. Just remember Evoni, not everything sweet comes in chocolate. Peace." Watching Jeff walk out the door, Evoni couldn't help but roll her eyes. The guy was a real life "Deuce Bigelow." How any woman could put up with him for more than five minutes was mind boggling. Feeling the onset of a headache, Evoni began to massage her temples.

She had a meeting with her client in forty minutes, and she needed to be on top of her game. She had assigned one of the firm's private investigators to surveil her client's ex-wife, and she was hoping he found out something that would end this bloody custody battle. Evoni couldn't fathom how any parent could put her children through agony and pain out of selfishness and anger. Drug addict or not, no woman worth being called a mother would ever use her kids as a pawn in a game. Evoni just hoped her P.I. had enough dirt on her to make her want to run back to the trailer park where her client found her and never want to lay eyes on her kids again.

Evoni knew her thoughts were bad, but this case was wearing on her nerves. She didn't know how much more of this lady she could take. As Evoni readied herself for her client meeting, her intercom buzzed. "Ms. Singleton, Mr. Jacobs is here to see you."

"Oh, great, Mari, could you please show him in? Thank you."

Hopefully the P.I., Linc Jacobs, had some juicy information. As Mr. Jacobs stepped into her office, Evoni couldn't help but gasp lightly. No matter how often she saw the man, it never ceased to amaze her how damn sexy he was. Yet, he didn't seem to realize the effect he had on women. The man was 6'2", with arms and it appeared abs to die for, the color of Indian sandalwood, with hazel eyes and a dazzling Morris Chestnut smile. He carried himself with an irresistible air of confidence. Evoni's hormones went into overdrive just sitting there. At that moment, she realized that Linc Jacobs was the man from her dream the previous night. Evoni couldn't help but wonder if he was half as good in bed as she had dreamt he was.

"If I can put a smile like that on your face just walking through the door, I can only imagine what type of response I might get from the information I have for you."

If Evoni were a shade lighter, she knew her skin would be beet red. She hadn't realized her thoughts were so easily expressed on her face. If only he knew that he really was the reason she was smiling. "Mr. Jacobs, nice to see you again. I was daydreaming. I take it you have some good news for me?"

"Have I ever disappointed you, Ms. Singleton? You know I always deliver."

Damn, if only he knew what effect those words were having on me. Trying to focus on the subject at hand and not what was standing in front of her, Evoni began speaking. "Um, Mr. Jacobs please sit and fill me in on what you found out. I'm excited to hear what you have. Hopefully, it'll be enough to put an end to this matter."

"Oh, believe me. This information is more than enough to win your case. This will send your client's ex running back to whatever hole she came crawling out of."

"Well, don't keep me waiting any longer; lay it on me," stated Evoni before realizing what she had just said. "I mean please tell me the info you have," stuttered Evoni.

Chuckling softly, Linc wondered what was wrong with Ms. Singleton this morning; she was usually so cool, calm, and reserved. This was so unlike her. Deciding to keep his eye on her, Linc began to recite his findings. "Well, first off, Ms. Jessica French has a criminal record as long as my arm. Starting in 1997, at the ripe age of 20, Jessica's criminal record begins with arrests on multiple occasions for theft and prostitution. In fall of 1999, she served 2 years for aggravated assault of a co-worker at the local Qwik-Stop she worked at back in Murfreesboro before she got the job as a shampoo girl. She was also charged for, get this, distribution of a controlled substance back in October 2002. However, the charges were mysteriously dropped. Here's a copy of her arrest record for you."

Smiling gleefully, Evoni thanked him and urged him to continue, she couldn't wait to hear the rest of it.

"Continuing on. It seems Ms. French has been keeping an even bigger secret from her family. After a lot of digging back in Memphis, Jessica's hometown, I finally found an old-timer who remembered Jessica French, formerly Sims, and who was willing to talk to me. Apparently, her parents and younger sister died when she was seventeen in a mysterious fire. The authorities couldn't tell if it was arson or not, but Jessica was the only survivor."

"Wait, wait, wait, Mr. French told me that his wife was an orphan and didn't know who her parents were. That's part of the reason he was attracted to her, he wanted to bring love and stability into her life. Why would she lie about something like that? What kind of person is she? Did you find out anything else?"

"Not in Memphis, but my surveillance of her here in Nashville turned out to be worth it. Take a look at these."

Grabbing the photos off her desk, Evoni couldn't believe her eyes. Here was Ms. French and a young man buying what appeared to be drugs from some hoodlum off the street. "Who is that with her?"

"Oh, man. You really won't believe this. That young man with her attends the same school as her oldest son and is seventeen. If you continue looking, he's more than her drug buddy."

"What the fuck!!!" Evoni knew she shouldn't be cursing at the office let alone in the presence of another, but what she saw before her was unreal. Ms. French was in an alley with the young man on her knees giving the young man a blow job and doing something that was probably illegal in the State of Tennessee with her hands. The other photos contained more sexual acts being performed between the two. What kind of twisted individual was she? When Mr. French found out what kind of woman he had married and fathered children with, he would be devastated. "I'm sorry for my use of profanity, but these photographs are disturbing to say the least."

"No need to apologize, if only you knew what came from my lips when I had to witness that. The woman is sick and possibly a murderer. I hope this is enough to get her out of those kids' lives permanently."

"Trust me, this is more than enough. When I'm done with her, she'll regret ever meeting Marc French," Evoni declared venomously. As the words left her mouth, Evoni thought about the French's kids. They would be in court, and she didn't want them to have to hear and see such filth about their mother. No, she had to settle this another way. Those kids had been through more than enough already.

Sensing her distress, Linc calmly walked over and began to massage her shoulders. He hoped she wouldn't freak out; it's just that he hated to see a woman stressed when he was around. "I'm sure you'll handle the situation and get those kids back to their father. You are an exceptional attorney, and I can tell you really care about the welfare of the children caught in these custody battles. So, just relax and breathe slowly. I have total confidence in your ability."

God, his hands felt good. Evoni knew she should stop him since technically he was a subordinate employee, and this would definitely be deemed inappropriate behavior by the partners, but she couldn't. His hands were magical and the words flowing so sweetly from his lips sounded so sincere. Why couldn't she have a man like this in her life? Instead, she had to deal with assholes like Amar. The thought of Amar broke the spell over Evoni. "Thanks for the massage and the kind words, but I think you should stop now. This is quite inappropriate," Evoni stated slowly.

"Yes, you're right. I'm sorry, please forgive me. You just looked like you needed it."

"Believe me, it was greatly appreciated, but I would hate for someone to walk in and get the wrong idea."

"And what idea is that?" Linc asked playfully.

Seeking to avoid answering, Evoni tried to change the subject. "Thank you again for all your hard work. I'll be sure to tell the powers that be about your exceptional work. Maybe we can get you a bonus for this project. I have a meeting with my client shortly and need to prepare, so if you'll excuse me."

Feigning hurt, Linc slowly turned to leave. "Wow, you sure know how to cut a brotha off at the knees. I can take a hint though, Ms. Singleton. Just let me know when you will be in need of my services again," Linc said with a hint of seduction in his voice and turned and walked out the office.

Damn. Am I dreaming or did Linc Jacobs really just flirt with me? If only she wasn't fresh off her break-up with Amar and he didn't do work for the firm, then she would definitely consider taking him up on some of his services.

CHAPTER 4

Evoni

Evoni watched patiently as her client slowly processed all the information she had relayed to him concerning the conduct and actions of his ex-wife. The longer Marc sat in silence, the angrier Evoni became at his good for nothing, trailer park trash cunt of an ex-wife for putting this man and his sons through hell. Evoni couldn't imagine causing someone she loved, let alone her own children, such unrelenting heartache and pain; to do so was completely and utterly irreprehensible.

Being a family law attorney with the biggest firm in the state, Jennings, Kaplan, and Craig, had its perks but also some major drawbacks, like long hours and unappreciative bosses. This case, in particular, was really getting to Evoni. Her client, Marc French, the father of fourteen and eight-year-old boys was fighting for full custody against the boys' mother. He sued for full custody after his fourteen-year-old son, Ashton, informed him he'd seen his mother using crystal meth and she often left them alone for days at a time.

Her client was a wealthy investment banker who had met his ex-wife while visiting his grandmother in Murfreesboro, where his ex was working as a shampoo girl. He liked what he saw, so he brought her back to Nashville and married her. It would seem this case was cut and dry, but the mother denied the drug use and accused her client of domestic violence and counter-sued for full custody. So far, the hearings had been extremely contentious and the judge none too happy. Evoni knew she had to make sure her client came out the victor for the sake of her job, but most importantly for the sake of his children.

Breaking out of his trance, Mr. French slowly began to speak. "Ms. Singleton, I want to thank you for all your hard work. I am eternally grateful for all that you have done to help me get custody of my sons. My boys are my life and to think that they were subjected to live alone with this, this bitch for this long is unforgivable on my part. I have failed as a father. What kind of man would allow his children to ever live with such a vile, manipulative, hate filled drug addicted, possibly murdering whore?" questioned Marc French as his voice began to crack slightly. "I loved her so much and only wanted to give her a better life."

Detecting the hurt in her client's voice, Evoni broiled inside. What could she do to ease this man's pain? "Mr. French, please forgive me for being blunt, but there's a saying that 'you can't turn a ho into a house-wife' no matter how hard you try. You are a good man, and it is evident that you love your sons very much. You are a great father; a lesser man couldn't have stood strong against the lies and accusations that have been publicly made against you. You never once faltered or questioned that you were doing the right thing by seeking custody of your sons. You know there are a lot of kids out there who wish they had half the man you are as a father. So, whatever you do, don't ever doubt that you are a wonderful father. You have sacrificed your reputation and standing in your community to save your sons from a life of hell, that alone proves you are a great father and there is no doubt in my mind that your sons feel the same way."

Not knowing how to respond to such kind and thoughtful words, Marc French did something that took him and Evoni completely off guard. He stood, walked over to Evoni, and hugged her. "Thank you so much for your kind words. You are such a kind soul. I don't know what I could ever do to repay you; money is not enough to repay you for the peace you have brought me."

Evoni smiled softly. "Your gratitude is more than enough. Just knowing that you sons will grow into healthy, happy young men under your wings is more than enough repayment for me."

"Well, if you ever need anything, please don't hesitate to call me. I am eternally indebted to you. Now, I must get back to the office."

"It has been my pleasure serving as your attorney. After I confront your ex-wife and her attorney with the evidence we have gathered, I'm sure she'll be more than happy to drop any claim to the boys and relinquish all parental rights. There should be no need for you to ever have to see your ex-wife again."

"That makes me more than happy, because if I see that cunt again, I swear I'll kill her," Mr. French stated with a cold glint in his eye as he turned to leave.

Feeling mentally and physically exhausted and it was only 11:00 a.m., Evoni decided to take a quick power nap on her sofa before that afternoon's monthly senior associates' meeting. Just as Evoni curled into the fetal position and closed her eyes, her intercom sounded. *Damn. What the hell is it now? I don't have another client meeting until three o'clock.* Rising reluctantly, Evoni went to her desk. "Yes, Mari, what's so important you had to interrupt my nap?" questioned Evoni.

"I'm sorry, Ms. Singleton, but I assumed you would want to know that Bri called while you were in your meeting, and it sounded like she had something important to talk to you about."

"Thanks, Mari. I'll call her now. And Mari?"

"Yes, Ms. Singleton?"

"Please hold all my calls and wake me in an hour so I can prepare for the attorney's meeting this afternoon."

"Sure thing. Will there be anything else?"

"No, Mari, that's it for now. Thank you."

Picking up the phone receiver and dialing Bri's cellphone number, Evoni wondered what Bri wanted and hoped it was worth interfering with her nap.

"Hi, you've reached the voicemail of Bria..." *Oh well*, Evoni thought, *I'll catch her later*. It was probably about a shoe sale or something knowing Bri and her obsession with shopping.

CHAPTER 5

Bri

Bri couldn't believe it. She was getting married. She had waited so long for this and now she could have the fairy tale wedding she dreamed of as a little girl.

The previous evening, Bri returned home after a visit to her hair stylist to find a really hot stranger leaving. He passed by Bri and gave an appreciative look. Clearly, he liked what he saw. Bri wondered who he was. She soon found out.

Bri entered the house and called out to Harold. She didn't receive an answer. She went looking for him and found him in his study, closing his safe. Weird. What was Harold putting away?

Harold turned to her and gave her a kiss. "Hello, darling. I'm so glad you're home. Can you do me a favor and meet me upstairs in the bedroom in ten minutes, but not a minute before?"

Bri perplexed, agreed.

Impatiently waiting, Bri practically ran up the stairs once the ten minutes had passed. When she entered their bedroom, the sight stopped her in her tracks. There were bouquets of camellias, her favorite flower, everywhere she looked.

Shocked, Bri was speechless. What was going on.

At that moment Harold approached her holding two glasses of champagne. Handing her a glass, he grabbed her free hand and led her to the bedroom sitting area where a feast was laid out. It was all of Bri's favorite foods.

Harold taking advantage of Bri's speechlessness, dropped down to one knee. "Bria, I have loved you since the first day I laid eyes on you in the elevator of my office building. Little did I know the impact you would have on my life. You are the best thing that has ever happened to me and though I know I've made you wait longer than you would've liked, would you do me the honor of becoming my wife?"

Bri looked down at the ring in Harold's hand. It was gorgeous and the size of a small boulder. "Yes, yes, yes! I will marry you," she said with tears of joy streaming down her face.

Once Bri calmed down, she found out the hot guy who she had seen leaving was a private investigator by the name of Jackson Jameson. He'd been hired by Harold to find his ex-wife, Natasha, who'd disappeared over five years ago without a trace. Harold, worried about her well-being, had hired several private investigators to find her. They'd all failed, until now. Even though Harold loved Bri, he refused to get married again without knowing what had happened to his ex.

Jackson, after months of searching, had finally located Natasha outside Las Vegas working at a bunny ranch. She'd changed her name and her appearance. Apparently, there were things Harold hadn't known about her, like she was in hock to some very bad people and after finding out Harold wasn't a feeble old man she could fleece, she ran.

As soon as Harold found out from Jackson that he'd located Natasha, he began planning his proposal to Bri. In a matter of hours, Harold had everything setup.

Now, the next day, Bri was still slightly in shock but giddy. She had so much to do, but first she needed to tell Evoni.

After searching forever in her pink Fendi bag for her equally pink diamond encrusted iPhone, Bri speed dialed Evoni's work number.

"Jennings, Kaplan, and Craig, Evoni Singleton's office," came a firm but otherwise friendly voice over the phone.

"Hey, Mari. How are you? It's Bri. Is Evoni around?" Bri loved Evoni's secretary. They had become quick friends.

"Hey, girl. How's it going? Ms. Singleton is actually in a meeting right now, but I'll have her call you back as soon as she finishes. So how have you been? I haven't seen you in a while. When are we going to hit the Blue Note again? I had so much fun the last time."

As much as Bri loved Mari, she also knew the girl could talk for days and she wasn't trying to get into a thirty-minute conversation with her right now. "I'm doing fine, Mari. I'll definitely call you next time I'm going out. If you can have Evoni call me as soon as she gets out of her meeting, I would appreciate it. Tell her it's urgent, okay?"

"Will do. Is there anything wrong or anything I can help you with?"

"No, no. Everything is fine. Just have Evoni call me, okay? You're a doll. Talk to you later," Bri said hurriedly and hung up before Mari could get another word in. She had a lot to do and idle chit-chat with Mari wasn't on her list. Bri had to tell someone about her impending nuptials before she burst and since Evoni was busy, the next best person was her youngest sister, Monique. She was the closest to Bri, and Bri could trust her not to tell their mother.

Waiting for her sister to pick up, Bri wondered what color her dress should be? She'd never been a big fan of white; it wasn't the most slimming color.

"What's up, Bri-Bri? What are you doing up so early? I thought you didn't rise until 2:00," joked Bri's sister upon answering the phone.

"Ha-ha, real funny, Moni. Anyway, I called to tell you some exciting news. You're going to freak when you hear this," exclaimed Bri cheerfully.

"Whoa, now. I haven't heard you this excited since Harold flew you to Milan to shop. What's going on, you receive a new bauble from Harold?"

"If you'd hush and let me talk, I'll tell you why I'm so excited. Last night Harold proposed! Your sister is about to be a married woman," squealed Bri happily into the phone.

"Wow, that's great, Bri. So, can I be the maid of honor and when can I start officially begging for a new car? I need to know now, so I can start checking out the dealerships," Monique said humorously. "No, no, on a real note, I'm totally happy for you. It's about time Harold's old ass stopped getting the milk for free. Although you've never really been free, have you? Anyway, what brought this sudden change of events on? I know you've been trying to get Harold to marry you since six months after you guys met."

"Well, it's a long story, but I'll fill you in over lunch tomorrow. My treat. Promise me you won't tell mother? Let me do that when I'm ready."

"You know I don't like to get in the middle of you two's drama, so that will not be a problem. Just tell me where to meet you tomorrow. A sista could use a good expensive free meal," joked Monique.

Bri laughed out loud, finally realizing what she must sound like to Evoni whenever they met for lunch or dinner, always looking for a free meal. However, given her sister's situation, Bri was more than happy to oblige. Her sister had just broken up with her piece of shit ex-husband, Stephen, who had taken everything and left her damn near penniless. She was living off a schoolteacher's salary in a one-bedroom walk-up while her ex was living in their Palisade Heights home, one of the wealthier communities in Nashville. Her husband, the fucking jerk, entertainment law attorney to most of the famous country stars, was a real piece of work. Monique had given up an opportunity to pursue her master's in education to support him through law school and then about a year ago, he came home and said he wanted a divorce. Unbeknownst to Monique at the time, her ex-best friend was the reason behind the divorce. The trick had been sleeping with Stephen, and it wasn't until after the divorce was final that he trotted the two-faced heifa out in public and had the audacity to announce that they were engaged.

All hell broke loose. Bri, Monique, and Aiden, their other sister, opened a can of whoop ass on Stephen's trifling butt and that skank. Thankfully Harold's influence kept them out of jail and the incident off their records.

"Alright, I'll call you later today with lunch details. Talk to you later lil sis," Bri stated and hung up the phone. Glancing at her watch, Bri realized it was almost 12:30 and she knew for a fact that from 12:30 until 2 Rodrique took his "lunch break" down at the Acadia Men's Club, a club for real gentlemen who just so happened to like other gentlemen.

Rodrique, formerly Roderick, her friend, former classmate, and the most well-known wedding planner this side of the Mason-Dixon. Rodrique had done weddings for CEO's, music, and TV stars, and according to him Flavor Flav asked him to plan his last wedding, but he had to turn him down, because there was no way he was dealing with a grown ass man who still wore a clock around his neck.

At the Acadia Club, Rodrique and other distinguished men of Nashville got pampered like rich spoiled women and participated in "tea parties" where the cakes were always beef and the tea hot and sweet. Bri knew Rodrique was there every Tuesday and Thursday, and he was always in a good mood after being at the club. This was the perfect time to ask him to plan her wedding, especially since she was sure he was more than likely already booked to the max. It would take some real coaxing to get him to squeeze her in, but Bri had the magic touch with all men, straight or gay. Before the day was over, she would have her wedding planner and hopefully her maid of honor, if Evoni ever called her back.

Fifteen minutes later, Bri was getting into her car when her phone rang. Checking the caller I.D., she noticed it was her mother, Bri decided to ignore the call because she was not in the mood for her mother's antics.

As Bri pulled into the parking lot of the Acadia Men's Club, she noticed Rodrique's yellow Benz parked right next to the owner's spot. If nothing else, Rodrique knew how to make a statement with everything he did, including with the car he drove. As she entered the building, Bri couldn't help but marvel at the incredible architecture of the building. It was one of the oldest buildings in Nashville, and story has it, it was built brick by brick by the local black construction workers after they and their wives were denied access to the only social club in Nashville at the time because of, you guessed it, their skin color.

After the degradation and humiliation, all the men got together and decided to build a place more beautiful than the white social club and they did, causing quite a ruckus in Nashville. It was even rumored that the local whites were so jealous they went to the mayor and tried to make him order the men to tear the building down. He tried but was unsuccessful because the men wouldn't budge and the mayor didn't really want a riot on his hands, so he acquiesced, and the building still stood to that day.

Rodrique was easy to spot. He was wearing a bright pink ruffle top with black leather pants and a pink and black fedora; the man was flamboyant to say the least.

Spotting her approach, Rodrique excused himself from his companions and walked over to Bri.

"Hi, darling. How are you? You're looking beautiful as usual, but I detect a slight glow today? What gives? Give me all the juicy details," demanded Rodrique while ushering Bri to a private table in the back of the dining area. Laughing slightly, Bri waited until they were seated before telling Rodrique her good news. "You'll never believe it; the most wonderful thing has happened. I'm so excited and..."

"Wait a minute, sister girl, will you please just spit it out already so I can decide whether it requires a bottle of Dom or some Ripple," Rodrique stated playfully.

"Oh, baby, this is definitely Dom worthy. Harold proposed to me last night. Can you believe it!" exclaimed Bri. "This is what I've been waiting for since I don't remember. Well, aren't you happy for me?"

"Well, darling, if you'll stop jabbering for two seconds, I can congratulate you. I know how much you've wanted this. Let me order us some Dom fa real and hell you can pay for it, you rich bitch," Rodrique chuckled while waving over a young Brad Pitt look alike.

"Rodrique, please I'm not rich yet. Anyway, I also have something to ask you, and I know you'll say yes since we go back like white wall tires on a Cadillac. You're my ace boon coon."

"Bri just spit it out. No need to breakout every known black colloquialism you know. I don't like it when you beat around the bush, sweetie. Give it to me straight with no chaser," Rodrique stated while gazing longingly at the waiter's ass as he swished away to retrieve their Dom Perignon.

"Okay, okay. Well, you see I don't want to wait too long to get married, so I was wondering if the best wedding planner in the world could possibly do me the honor of planning my wedding?" Bri asked while searching Rodrique's face for his answer.

"Bri, you know I don't do weddings on short notice. You know I am normally booked at least a year in advanced. My renowned services are in great demand; especially since I hooked up Lupita Nyong'o's wedding to Michael B. Jordan, shit I made that wedding the event of the century. It made Kim's wedding to Kanye look like a shot gun wedding. Girrrl, I am in high demand so what makes you think I have time to plan your wedding?"

"Please, Rodrique, no one else can do me justice. I need you. I will pay you whatever you ask, just please don't make me plan this thing by myself. I know together we can make this the most talked about event in Tennessee," pleaded Bri.

Not a fan of whining, Rodrique decided to put Bri out of her misery. "Calm down, baby girl, you're in luck. Taylor Swift's wedding to that so called producer has been called off, freeing up my calendar for the next few months. When exactly do you want to have this little soiree? And just so you know, this will cost old Harold a pretty penny. My services do not come cheap, not even to you."

Gleefully, Bri hugged Rodrique. Her wedding was going to be so wonderful. Everyone who was anyone in the business world would be there and all her family and friends and maybe Rodrique could get one of his celebrity clients to sing. Bri's mind was going a mile a minute, and she knew she had a million things to do but with Rodrique by her side, Bri knew it would all come together.

CHAPTER 6

Evoni

The week passed quickly. It was Saturday and Evoni looked forward to seeing her bestie. She and Bri had texted a few times during the week and Bri promised Evoni she had some good news she could only share in person. Evoni wondered what it was. *Had Bri found a never-before-seen Birkin bag*? Evoni thought a little guiltily. She knew she could be hard on Bri for her love of fashion and expensive things. Evoni only did it because she knew Bri didn't care one iota, she was secure in herself and knew Evoni was only needling her because she loved her.

Before Evoni knew it, she was in front of Mama Bee's. She parked and went in, scanning the restaurant for Bri. Then she spotted her over in the corner, looking great as always. She was the best dressed woman this side of the Mason-Dixon Line. Bri was dressed from head to toe in Prada, Evoni imagined even her underwear was name brand. *That is if she's wearing any*, Evoni thought to herself while walking over to the table.

"Hey, girl," Evoni and Bri said in unison while hugging.

"Shoot, it's about time you made it. I am starving. I think I've eaten three baskets of bread already," giggled Bri. "Hell, the waitress has been giving me the evil eye for the last ten minutes, so don't even think about leaving her a tip. "I'll leave her ass a tip," kidded Bri.

"You have issues," laughed Evoni. "Sorry it took me so long to get here. I kept getting interrupted by the damn phone. So how have you been?"

With that, Bri stuck out her left hand. On it was the biggest diamond Evoni had ever seen. "Oh my God, Bri," said Evoni jumping up and running around the table to hug her friend. "Congratulations! I'm so happy for you."

After a moment, Evoni returned to her seat, ignoring the looks from the other patrons. "Tell me everything. I want all the details, don't leave anything out."

Just as Bri was finishing up her proposal story, the waitress who had been eyeing them from across the room came over.

"Are ya'll ready to order yet?" she asked snidely.

Evoni just knew this young girl was not catching attitude with her, not after the week she had just had.

"Do you have a problem with serving us?" snapped Evoni.

The waitress looked over at Evoni with a nasty smirk on her face. "Well, your friend here has been occupying this table since before you arrived without ordering nothin'. Then you show up and ya'll sit here for another ten minutes chit chattin' like ya'll at home. This happens to be the busiest hours of the week for Mama Bee's and ya'll stopping me from making any money since I know ya'll not goin' to leave me no tip; I could tell that from the way your greedy ass friend here ate up all the bread. So yeah, I have a problem serving ya'll."

Oh no this ghetto ass heifa did not just go off on us. It was time to put her in her place.

"Excuse me, let me introduce myself to you, Monesha," said Evoni looking at the girl's name tag. "My name is Evoni Singleton and I just so happen to be the goddaughter of Ms. Lucille Jackson, better known as "Mama Bee." So, I'm going to let your little snide remarks go this one time, because if I wanted to, I could march into that kitchen right now and get your little ass fired. However, since your ignorant ass look like you need every dime you can get your hands on, I will refrain from doing that. But just so you know, don't you ever disrespect me, my friend, or any other customer in this restaurant again. I don't know what projects Mama Bee found you in, but I can assure you that I can have your ass back there waiting on a welfare check with the snap of my fingers. Now how about you apologize to me and my friend and take our orders," Evoni spat out, "before I change my mind?"

Stuttering, the waitress apologized and took Evoni and Bri's orders, then ran off into the kitchen. By this time Bri was dying laughing. "Girl, you know you are something else. I like the way you handled that. I would have had the bitch fired on the spot."

"Yes, but then Mama Bee would be short a server on one of her busiest days of the week and I couldn't put her through that. She's already working too hard by not letting anyone who's not family cook. Right now, it's only her and Cousin Margie cooking all the food and I don't want to add to her problems the task of finding a new server."

"Girl, I love Mama Bee to death, but I do not know why she insists on hiring these young hoochies with no home training. You're her god-daughter why don't you try and get her to hire people with a little more manners and respect?" inquired Bri.

"I have tried so many times, but you know Mama Bee, always trying to save the world one child at a time. She believes that if she can take them out of the ghetto and show them that there is something better, then maybe, just maybe they'll be motivated to do something more with their lives. You know she has had some success stories. Do you remember Tyrone?"

"Oh, yeah. Fine ass Tyrone with the dreads. How could I forget him? I wanted to take him for a test drive, but he disappeared before I got a chance."

"You know you are sick, right?" laughed Evoni. "That boy was only eighteen."

"That is exactly why I wanted him. I could use some young lovin' from time to time."

"You have more issues than *Essence,* you know that right," quipped Evoni. "Anyway, as I was saying. Tyrone disappeared because he was accepted into Dillard University on scholarship. Mama Bee is so proud of him. You know when she hired him at sixteen, he was just getting out of foster care and moving back in with his mother. He was on a road to nowhere; getting mixed up in all kinds of trouble. Mama Bee's influence and her take no prisoner's attitude put him on the straight and narrow."

"Wow, that's great. I'm proud of him. What's he studying at Dillard?"

"Biology. He wants to be a pediatrician."

"Um, damn, a doctor and fine as hell. Girl, does Mama Bee have his number out there?" asked Bri. "I can have my sister fly out there and get him hooked on her chocolate mousse right now. Lord knows she could use a good man. Then by the time he graduates, he'll be ready to make her Mrs. Tyrone...uh. What's his last name?" giggled Bri.

At that moment, Monesha walked over with their food. She placed their food on the table and asked if there was anything else they needed. Not once did she make eye contact. Evoni had clearly scared the young girl.

Monesha really couldn't afford to lose this job. She didn't want to go back on welfare and there was no one else to help her take care of "Peanut" and "Tre-Tre" her five and two-year-old sons by that good for nothin' Ray-Ray, who had left her for someone who was willing to put up with all his bullshit. Now she was working two jobs and trying to save to go back to school. If only she could learn to keep her mouth shut; it had gotten her in more than one bad situation in the past. You would think she had learned, but no, here she goes insulting the god-daughter of the one person who was willing to give a second chance. She felt like a fool.

Looking up at the girl, Evoni began to regret her harsh words. She had a feeling that what she had said earlier had some truth to it. The girl looked petrified, and Evoni felt bad. Evoni decided to talk to Mama Bee and find out the girl's story.

"What are you sitting there daydreaming about when we have all this delicious food in front of us?" quizzed Bri.

Evoni looked down at her plate and smiled. Bri was right, the food did look delicious. Her plate was heaped high with collard greens, fried chicken, macaroni and cheese, and hot water cornbread. Her thighs would suffer the consequences for this meal, but Evoni didn't care at that moment. She just wanted to savor the taste of her godmother's food. "Oh, nothing. Just thinking about a case at work," said Evoni in response to Bri's question. Then they both began to dig into their food.

An hour later, they were both happily devouring Mama Bee's famous peach and blueberry pie topped with vanilla/peach swirl ice cream. They were both stuffed. Evoni didn't even know if she would be able to get up from the table unassisted, let alone make it out to her car.

Bri realized that with all the drama with the waitress and her engagement news, she never got a chance to ask Evoni about the original reason for their lunch date. Bri knew something was wrong. Evoni was doing her best to appear happy, but she could see the sadness in her eyes. Then she had a great idea. "How about we drive over to the park and walk off some of these calories we just inhaled before they go straight to our thighs? You know how beautiful the park is this time of year."

Evoni smiled to herself. She knew exactly what Bri was up to; she wanted to get the scoop on her and Amar. Evoni thought about declining the offer and just going home and crawling into bed but then she realized that she needed to tell someone what happened and who better than her best friend.

"Okay, just let me say good-bye to Mama Bee and pay the bill. I'll follow behind you in my car."

Bri and Evoni both got up from the table. Bri headed towards the door and Evoni towards the kitchen. Fifteen minutes later, they were both walking along the path in the park. Spotting a bench nearby, Bri suggested they sit for a minute.

Soon Evoni had sobbed her way through what happened the previous week, and Bri was trying her best to console her. Bri was livid at Amar for causing her friend so much pain. She hadn't seen Evoni this upset since college when she found out her great-grandmother, Big Mama, had passed. Bri didn't know what to do, but she knew she had to do something to cheer up her friend.

"Girl, you know you probably had Amar peeking out of his window all night with 911 on standby after you threaten to have your brothers come through, joked Bri in an attempt to lighten the mood.

Evoni giggled. Bri was probably right. Her triplet brothers, Devon, Jalon, and Keyshon were all black belts in karate and tae kwon do. Jalon was also an amateur boxer. Standing at 6'3" they were not ones to be messed with and the quickest way to get your butt kicked was to mess with their sister. Although the thought of calling her brothers on Amar did appeal to her, she couldn't do it because, unfortunately, she still loved the bastard, and she didn't want her brothers to hurt him. Love stinks.

Feeling a little better, Evoni told Bri she was ready to go. Unlike Bri, she actually had to work for a living. She had a major custody battle ensuing that would require a lot of long nights and constant use of her espresso machine.

After promising to call Bri the next day, Evoni headed home to the comfort of her favorite chair and to retreat into her thoughts. Listening to the radio on the way home, Evoni heard a news alert that another possible victim of the Music City Murderer had been found. That would make eight women. Depressed enough about her own life, Evoni shut off the radio and sat with her thoughts. As she drove, she reminisced on when she was a kid. Whenever she would go visit her grandmother, Aretha, in Texas, every night before bed, they would sit in her favorite rocking chair, and she would tell her stories about when she met and fell in love with Evoni's grandfather. Her grandparents met when they were fifteen and knew from that first day that they were destined to be together. Story has it; her grandfather got down on one knee and asked her grandmother to marry him that first day. He professed that she was the most vivacious, beautiful girl he had ever laid eyes on, and he wasn't going to allow another man to ever have a chance to experience that same sensation and steal her away. Evoni's grandmother assumed he was joking, so she agreed. She in turn told him that she would marry him on her 18th birthday on the condition that he bring her a rose once a week and always bring chocolate when he came over. Grandpa fulfilled that promise every week for 3 years and on her 18th birthday, Aretha stuck to her word, and they were married. Her grandmother's stories instilled in her a need to one day find that same type of true love, which she believed she had found with Amar only to have him break her heart.

Pulling up in her driveway, Evoni spotted a silver Mercedes Benz SUV and knew that Amar was inside waiting for her. Why the hell didn't she take her keys back that night? This was the last thing she needed. She didn't know if she had the strength to deal with him. When she opened the door, she could smell the aroma of food cooking and she heard Goapele's "First Love" playing from her stereo. What the hell was this fool doing? Did he really think he could get her back by sneaking into her home and cooking up her damn food? She had a good mind to really call her brothers up.

Evoni walked into the kitchen to confront Amar, but he wasn't there. She headed up the stairs to find the triflin' Negro and put him and his food out of her house. When she reached the top of the stairs, there were rose petals leading to her bedroom. She followed the trail and when she reached the entrance, she almost fainted. She couldn't believe her eyes. There were lit candles everywhere and rose petals spelling out the words "Please, forgive me" on the bed and more petals leading to the master bath. It was absolutely beautiful. At that moment, Amar stepped out from behind the door holding a huge teddy bear and a flute of champagne.

When Evoni looked up at Amar, all the emotions from that night washed back over her. "What the hell are you doing in my house?" screamed Evoni. "How dare you bring your triflin' good for nothing ass in my home uninvited, as if everything is just honky dory? Do you have a death wish?"

"Evoni, baby," pleaded Amar, "I just wanted to show you how sorry I am about everything. I never meant for this to happen. Your mother told me she spoke with you and that you were willing to give me another chance. I love you more than anything in the world. I know I failed you, but if you'll just give me another chance, I promise nothing like this will ever happen again."

"You're damn right nothing like this will ever happen again because I refuse to give you another opportunity to hurt me. Amar you were my life. I placed all bets on you, and I lost. I have never felt so betrayed before in my life. Do you know how it makes a woman feel when the man she loves and is supposed to marry cheats on her? It makes her feel like a failure, like she can't please her man. So, maybe this is actually all my fault. Is that what it is, Amar, I wasn't competent enough sexually for you? I mean, did I not blow you well enough or was I not limber enough?" Evoni screamed. "No, no, wait, maybe it was the fact that I wouldn't let you stick it up my ass!!! Is that what it was, did the little bitch let you do her up the ass, huh, Amar?" shrieked Evoni.

"Evoni, stop it! I told you that that didn't matter to me. I love you regardless of that. You know that you have always satisfied me sexually, so stop with all the filthiness. It's so unlike you."

By this time Evoni was crying and just wanted Amar to hurt the same way she was hurting. "So, unlike me? So, fucking some dumb broad is more like you, huh? Well, I hate to break it to you Amar, but you obviously don't know shit about me. Because if you did, then you would know that I'm not the one to be played with. I promise you that you will pay for hurting me this way. Now get the fuck out of my house."

"I'll leave, but this is not over. You know we all make mistakes. All I'm asking for is a second chance, an opportunity to make things right. Evoni, no one's perfect, not even you. Maybe one day you'll wake up and see that. Hopefully, it won't be too late."

Trying to keep it together, Evoni quietly said, "Didn't I tell you to get the hell out? Now leave before I call the cops and have you arrested."

Amar knowing that it was pointless to try and stay, silently left. In his heart he knew that he had most likely lost the only woman he would ever love.

Evoni could not believe the nerve of that asshole. Did he really think that she would just pretend like nothing had happened and her mother,

that witch, was at the bottom of this little failed attempt of reconcili-
ation. Evoni had a good mind to curse her out, as a matter of fact, she
would call her and tell her exactly how she felt.

Seconds later, Evoni was listening to the ringing of her mother's
phone. Then she heard her mother on the other end. "Hi, honey. I'm
surprised to hear from you."

Livid, Evoni snapped. "Why is that, Mother, did you think I would
be busy fucking Amar right now? How dare you interfere in my personal life. The gall of you to send Amar over here after all that he has
done to me. What kind of heartless person are you? I mean I know I
never met your expectations, but do you always have to treat me like I'm
the outsider? I have spent my life trying to please you, but that's over
now, so you can just go to hell," screamed Evoni hanging up the phone
before her mother could respond.

Evoni's resolve broke, and she began to cry uncontrollably. God, how
she wanted to hate her mother for never loving her, but, unfortunately,
she couldn't. She had spent so much time trying to please her, only to
be criticized and put down. All her life she longed to hear praise from
her mother, but to this day she never had. Thank God for her father
and brothers.

Why did bad things always have to happen to her? Evoni knew self-
pity wouldn't help, but she felt the need to wallow in it just the same.
She was so tired of trying to be strong in the face of adversity, whether it
was at work, with her mother, or in her love life. If it weren't for Bri, she
didn't know what she would do. All her life Evoni had felt like a mother-
less child. She remembered once a few years ago, Bri had encouraged her
to ask her mother about counseling. When she approached her mother
with the idea, she just laughed and told Evoni counseling was for fools
and idiots, of which neither she nor any of her children were, instead
she suggested Evoni stop being stubborn and listen to her more often,
insisting that would solve all of Evoni's problems.

Looking back at that conversation, Evoni realized her mother was
certifiable. Seriously, who says things like that except crazy people?
Envisioning her mother in a straitjacket with her hair nappy and no

make-up on while locked in a padded room brought a smile to Evoni's face. It's amazing what a little imaginative thinking could do for one's disposition. Feeling better, Evoni figured there was no use in letting whatever Amar had cooked go to waste. The man was an excellent cook.

After eating and cleaning the kitchen, Evoni meditated for twenty minutes to clear her mind before settling in and doing some work.

After a couple of hours, Evoni was exhausted, physically, and mentally. The brief she was writing could wait until morning, Evoni decided to call it a night and go to bed.

CHAPTER 7

Bri

"Mother, can you please just listen to me?" screamed Bri. "I have told you time and time again I love Harold. I thought we had moved past this? Harold is my everything and nothing you say will ever change that. Now you can accept that or be prepared to lose me as your daughter, it's your choice," Bri snapped and walked out the door.

This was it, her mother could either accept her for who she was and who she loved or lose her. Hopefully, she would make the right choice. Bri walked slowly to her car, hoping her mother would at least come after her, but when she reached her car door and looked back; there was no sign of her mother. Bri drove off furiously in the direction of home, but then she made a quick U-turn longing for the comfort of her best friend. Twenty minutes later, Bri, making it to Evoni's office in record time, sat weeping while her friend attempted to comfort her.

"Come on, Bri, you know how overdramatic your mother is. She'll come to her senses soon enough. She loves you too much to lose you."

"Well, if she loves me so much, why does she seem to go out of her way to make my life a living hell? I have done nothing but love my mother and try to be there for her, despite her many faults. Why can't she do that for me? Sometimes I fucking hate her."

"Bri, you don't mean that, you're just upset right now. Now you know I have the mother from Hell, so I know what it feels like to have a love-hate relationship with your mother. All I'm asking is for you to calm down and focus on the good things in life. I mean damn, girl; you're about to get married while my old maid ass can't even keep a man. Hell, I should be the one upset," Evoni chuckled.

Bri smiled at Evoni's attempt to lighten the mood. Lately, it seemed all they were doing was constantly trying to cheer each other up. What was going on in the universe? "You're right, girl, everything I've been waiting for is finally happening and I refuse to allow my mother to spoil this for me. First your break-up with Amar and now my insane in the membrane mother is causing drama. Maybe we should hire a hit man to take them all out," joked Bri. "That would solve most of our problems."

"Now that sounds like a great idea. You know I still have Sammy the Sandman's number in my phone. I'm sure he'll do it for small fee," quipped Evoni.

"Girl, you are a fool. Stop it. Anyway, thanks for letting me cry on your shoulder. I'd still be a bumbling mess if it weren't for you."

"That's what friends are for. You did the same for me so it's only fitting that I return the favor. Now is the time for tears of joy, not sadness. So, get up and go home to that man of yours and show him how much you appreciate him, Anna Nicole," joked Evoni.

"Hahaha, real funny, Evoni, but you're right. I'm going home to my man. Call me tonight if you get a chance so I can fill you in on the wedding details," said Bri while giving Evoni a hug.

"Will do. I'll talk to you later," Evoni said while walking Bri to the door. "TTFN."

On her way out, Bri spoke briefly with Mari, promising to get together with her soon.

Feeling a bit better, Bri decided to hit her favorite clothing boutique before heading home. Keela's Boutique sold hard to find high-end runway pieces and Keela had texted Bri the previous day to let her know she had something perfect for her. *Nothing like a little retail therapy to brighten one's day*, thought Bri while climbing into her car.

CHAPTER 8

Evoni

Once alone in her office, Evoni sighed heavily. After the drama with Amar and her mother the previous evening, Evoni was mentally and emotionally spent. Evoni checked the clock. It was 12:30, that week's senior associate's meeting was in thirty minutes, and she hadn't even prepared her notes on her case log. The last thing she needed today was to be unprepared; frustrated Evoni began typing notes on her computer. Just then there was a knock on the door, knowing it must be Mari, Evoni just yelled at her to enter. The door eased open slightly and Mari slowly walked in, she sensed her boss had had a long weekend from the cool greeting she had received when she arrived.

"Hi, Ms. Singleton. I just wanted to let you know that I went ahead and typed out your notes for this afternoon's meeting. You seemed to have so much going on today that I wanted to try and ease your load," Mari said with a weak smile.

"Oh my goodness, Mari, you are such a life saver. You have no idea how much this means to me. You are the best secretary here. I will be recommending you for a raise.

In fact, how would you like to join me for a drink after work? I was thinking of planning a bridal shower for Bri, and I know you also think of her as a friend, so maybe you would like to help me? And we can get to know each other a little better."

Mari's face lit up like a Christmas tree at the mention of a wedding. "Of course. I would love to help. I had no idea Bri was getting married. I'm so happy for her. This is fantastic."

"So, it's settled then. We'll go over to Perrier's around 6-ish."

"Yes, ma'am. Well, I'll let you get back to work now and just buzz me if you need anything," Mari stated and turned to leave.

Evoni watched as her secretary of a year left and wondered what Mari's story was. Mari Davies had come to her as a temp and had been so efficient Evoni had campaigned to have her hired as her permanent secretary since her old one had just moved away. Evoni remembered Mari's reaction as being a little over the top. The girl had thanked her like she had offered to give her a kidney and Evoni had wondered then just how badly she needed the job. Somehow, she and Bri had become friends, and Evoni had been meaning to ask Bri about Mari but never got around to doing it. Maybe tonight would shed a little light on her situation.

Evoni glanced at the clock and realized she should head over to the conference room so she could get a good seat next to the senior partner who conducted the weekly meetings. Evoni was trying her best to position herself for advancement. She had been with the firm for 6 years after clerking for a federal judge for two years and knew it was damn time she was elevated to junior partner. She worked her butt off, and it showed with her 90%-win rate. Evoni knew of no reason why she shouldn't be up for partner.

Her seat next to Margo Chapman aka "The Chainsaw" Chapman, safely secured, Evoni's mind raced trying to think of a topic to discuss with her as the other associates began to flow in. Just as an idea popped into her head, over walked the bane of her existence.

"Mrs. Chapman and Ms. Singleton, may I say, you both are looking lovely today. Mrs. Chapman, my mother wanted me to make sure I invited you to a little soirée she's having at the house next weekend for Senator Thomas' campaign. Everyone who is everyone in Tennessee will be there. I hope you can make it."

"I'll check my calendar, it's possible I will be out of town. I'll call your mother and let her know. Now if you'll excuse me, it's time to start the meeting," Mrs. Chapman stated walking to the head of the conference room.

As she walked away, Jeff turned to Evoni and whispered in her ear. "Soon I'll be running this place and if you act right, I may just let you become my secretary and bend over for me." Before Evoni knew what she was doing, she slapped Jeff across his cheek. Startled, Jeff staggered backwards and flopped into his seat. All eyes in the room were on Evoni. If she were lighter, she'd be the color of a tomato. What had she just done? Her natural instinct had taken over and she'd just reacted. "Oh my God, Jeff. I'm so sorry. I don't know what came over me," Evoni gasped.

"Ms. Singleton, I don't know what is going on between you and Mr. Johnson but that type of behavior will not be tolerated here. I suggest you go get yourself together and then come back and act a little more civilized. Mr. Johnson, I don't know what you did or said to cause Ms. Singleton to react so violently, but I assume you will apologize to her for it and keep in mind that despite the fact that your father is a senior partner, I will have you brought before the disciplinary committee, do we understand each other?"

In unison, Evoni and Jeff replied, "Yes, ma'am. It won't happen again."

"Make sure it doesn't. Now if there aren't any more love spats that need to be taken care of, can we please begin the meeting?" A slight chuckle followed and then everyone's attention turned back to the matter at hand.

Evoni sat dumbfounded trying to figure out what had just transpired. *How the hell did I just slap a fellow colleague? That could have been my job. Damn, Jeff. The insensitive bastard could have cost me my job with his chauvinistic remarks. Why did I let him get to me?*

She knew she would have to do some major damage control, since 5 minutes after the meeting let out everyone on the premises, and even some of those not in the office today, would know what happened and the entire scene would most likely be blown out of proportion and end up with some crazy story like she and Jeff were sleeping together and he had just told her he was breaking things off or something else equally ridiculous. *Damn, damn, damn,* Evoni thought. *What the hell am I going to do to fix this?* Feeling like a black man at a KKK meeting, Evoni just wanted to run away as far north as possible.

With a slight almost indiscernible smirk on her face, Mrs. Chapman turned to Evoni. "Ms. Singleton, would you like to fill us in on the progress in your cases?"

Evoni knew she had to put her game face on to save face. "Yes, I will." Gathering her notes, Evoni moved towards the front of the room. Feeling everyone eyeball her, Evoni smiled slightly and launched into her spiel.

Ten minutes later, she believed she had at least partially gained some of her respect back from her colleagues and Mrs. Chapman. She had survived numerous questions from Mrs. Chapman on her current cases and had answered expertly. Feeling a little better, Evoni took her seat and waited anxiously for the meeting to end. Forty-five minutes later, Evoni practically bolted from the conference room. Not sure what to do next, she headed for every woman's safe haven, the ladies' room. Evoni had to regain her composure if she was going to make it through the rest of the day.

Dashing water on her face, Evoni stared at the woman looking back at her and laughed. She knew what she had done could have gotten her fired, but it was so exhilarating to knock the hell out of that S.O.B. Now she would be labeled the "angry black woman" but who gives a damn. Evoni was tired of having to pretend to be something she wasn't. Evoni was tired of having to pretend to be something she wasn't. It was hard coming in day after day, smiling and pretending like everything was just peachy. Evoni hated having to smile all the time for fear that she would be labeled anti-social, unfriendly, or not a team player and most of all she hated ass-kissing She hated it when she was interviewing, and she hated it even more now.

Evoni worked her ass off but knew that if anything ever went down, she would be one of the first ones to go. Hell, the firm only employed three black attorneys and the other two were men and complete assholes. She was trying her best to make partner, but she also was considering opening her own firm. Evoni was so conflicted about so many things, and she didn't have any real answers. What was she going to do?

Glancing at her watch, Evoni realized she needed to get back to her office before her next client arrived. Now more than ever she had to be on point, she couldn't afford to slip up because she knew that by now news had gotten back to the other senior partners of what had transpired, and she would be watched closely. Evoni stepped quickly and quietly from the ladies' room and hurried to her office.

Once inside, Evoni collapsed on her sofa, closed her eyes, and took ten deep breaths. With each breath, Evoni felt herself relax more and more. Evoni wasn't in the mood to deal with her next client.

A divorced mother of three and sister of the mayor, Ms. Colleen Bailey Lee was more than a handful. The woman was known for her theatrics and overbearing personality. On more than one occasion, Evoni had to restrain herself from going off on the woman. She was in a fierce battle with her ex-husband over their 16-year-old daughter and 12-year-old son. It seemed her husband believed Ms. Lee a lush who couldn't properly take care of a frog without the help of a nanny. Her ex-husband was alleging during the twenty years they were married, Ms. Lee never once changed a diaper on her kids, never once gave them a bath or combed their hair. His petition claims she couldn't even remember their names at one point. Evoni feared that this case would put an end to her winning streak and now was not the time to start losing.

Her boss, one of the founding members of the firm, Lenville Craig, had a personal interest in this case, being that he and the mayor were old college buddies and word on the street was that the mayor was thinking of running for governor come next term and Mr. Craig was his top choice for lieutenant governor. Evoni couldn't fathom what would happen to her if she lost this case. Her ass and her boss' ass were on the line, and Evoni knew she would have to perform a few magic tricks to pull it off.

Feeling a little better, Evoni managed to smile sweetly and hopefully sincerely at Ms. Lee as she entered her office. The woman was something to behold. Colleen stood 5'10" in stocking feet, had green eyes and was currently sporting pink hair. Het style of dress was something to behold, it would repulse Stevie Wonder. Today she was dressed provocatively in a purple halter and a yellow and black print skirt that was about two sizes too small. She wore enough makeup to cake the faces of an entire vaudeville show, and she had the audacity to have on four-inch purple heels. Evoni held her breath to keep from laughing out loud. The woman was one of a kind. Evoni wondered how she would convince Ms. Lee to tone down her wardrobe for court proceedings without offending her unique sense of style.

"Ms. Lee, it's wonderful to see you again. How have you been?" quizzed Evoni.

"Well, I'll be much better when this dreadful matter is concluded. Why is this taking so long? Everyone knows I am a great mother. Wayne is just doing this to get back at me for leaving him for Antonio. It's not my fault he couldn't get it up anymore," Ms. Lee rambled.

Not wanting to hear the dirty details of Ms. Lee's sex life, yet again, Evoni interrupted her abruptly. "Uh, Ms. Lee. I'm sure you are right in your assessment of your ex-husband's reasons for this suit, but that is no longer important. What's important is that we prepare thoroughly for your court date next week, so the judge can see that you are fit to raise your children. Now let me ask again if you are sure you want to go through with this? Let me remind you that your ex will more than likely bring up every wrong, deceitful, devious, dirty thing you've ever done in your life. With that being said, is there anything you need to tell me before we go to trial? I don't like surprises," instructed Evoni.

"I've told you everything there is to know about my past and my present. And yes, I am prepared to go forward with this suit. I love my kids, Ms. Singleton, even if I didn't always show it. I've made more than my share of mistakes and I take full responsibility for them all. I am ready to be a mother to my children, and no one will stop that, not even my small penis, peanut brained ex-husband can stop me from doing that," responded Ms. Lee with sincerity coursing through her voice.

Evoni was pleasantly surprised by the strong showing of emotion from Ms. Lee. Never had she seen her client so adamant and apparently sincere about raising her children. That's the kind of response Evoni had longed for from her client. It was hard fighting for someone whose heart wasn't completely committed to doing whatever it would take to keep their kids. Evoni had seen instances where the parent only instituted petition for custody out of spite or greed. Evoni tried to avoid accepting vultures like that as clients and up until now she believed Ms. Lee fit that category like a glove fit a hand. Evoni was happy to see this caring side of her client; it would make her job easier and make her fight just that much harder for Ms. Lee.

"Well, Ms. Lee, I'm glad to hear that. That makes my job just a little easier. Now let's get down to business," stated Evoni with a smile.

After her meeting with Ms. Lee, Evoni's schedule was clear. She was contemplating leaving early just as her cellphone rang. It was her client, Marc French. It must be urgent for him to call her personal number and not the office.

Evoni answered. "Hi, Marc, how's it going?"

"Thank God, you answered. I didn't want to have to leave a message with your secretary. My ex was just here at my house causing a ruckus. Ms. Singleton, she was screaming at the top of her lungs that I was a child molester and trying to sex traffic our kids. All my neighbors heard her. What am I supposed to do?"

Evoni grumbled. Damn this woman. If she were a lesser person, she'd find the bitch and teach her a lesson. Evoni hated what she was doing to her client. "Okay Marc, it's good you called me. Is Jessica still there?"

"No, she left a few minutes ago. One of our neighbors, Jim, came out and talked her down. He managed to get her into a taxi. She was obviously drugged out of her mind," Marc said with disgust.

"Well, thankfully the boys weren't there, right?"

Marc sighed loudly. "No, they are still at school and have soccer practice after that. This is my week to have them, so I'll be picking them up."

"That's good. No need for them to be subjected to Jessica's erratic behavior. Marc, if this happens again, I want you to record the interaction. Episodes like this will only strengthen our case. In fact, I'll have our investigator come by and interview some of your neighbors. It's likely at least one or two of them recorded the scene hoping to post it to social media."

"I can't have this on social media. What would my clients think? That woman is going to literally ruin my entire life," bemoaned Marc.

"Marc, calm down. If anyone has posted the video, I will have my investigator strongly suggest they remove it. The odds of your clients seeing it are slim. I'll try to make sure it's even slimmer."

Marc thanked Evoni for her help and hung up.

Around five forty-five, Evoni emerged from her office with her briefcase. Today had been the day to end all days and all she wanted was to get home to her Jacuzzi tub and a glass of wine. As she rounded the corner, she almost ran into Mari. It hit her at that moment that she had invited her secretary to have a drink after work to discuss Bri's bridal shower. This was the last thing she wanted to do right now.

"Oh, hi, Ms. Singleton. I was just on my way to your office. I knew you didn't have any more clients scheduled for today, so I was coming to ask you what time you wanted to leave for that drink? It looks like you are ready now," Mari said while glancing quizzically at Evoni's briefcase. "You weren't leaving without me, were you?" asked Mari.

"Oh, no. I was actually just coming to look for you. I noticed you weren't at your desk. So, are you ready?"

"Actually, I have to file these papers on the McDouglass case first, but then I'll be ready. Is it okay if I meet you at the bar in say fifteen minutes?"

Grateful for the opportunity for a few minutes along with a glass of wine, Evoni readily agreed. Now she just hoped there was no one at the bar who would bother her. Hurrying out of the building, Evoni practically ran to her car. She couldn't drive fast enough away from her office.

Today had been the day from hell and all Evoni could think about was how normally she would have called Amar for moral support. Thinking of him pissed her off even more, that bastard. Not wanting to get caught up in her thoughts about Amar and ruin the rest of her day even more, Evoni tried to focus on the good things in her life as she pulled into the parking garage across from the bar. She was a successful, attractive, witty, sexy black professional woman with a great support system, excluding her mother, of course. So, what if her fiancé was a cheating asshole and she just barely escaped getting fired for slapping a co-worker? Things could have gone worse, she could have remained in the dark about Amar's wandering penis and married him subjecting herself to greater hurt and she could have gotten fired today, which would have really sucked.

Not wanting to dwell on Amar or her job, Evoni exited her car and walked towards the bar. Perrier's was the hottest professional hangout in the city; many deals were made and broken there. What went on over drinks never ceased to amaze her. Businessmen made 100-million-dollar deals while sharing a bottle of fine cognac, the absurdity of it.

As she entered the building, Evoni couldn't help but smile. Standing with his back to her was none other than Linc, Mr. Bringing Sexy Back himself, her favorite private investigator, and the sexiest man within five states, at the least. As Evoni debated approaching him and speaking, she noticed he was conversing with a really attractive Nia Long look alike. Not wanting to interrupt what appeared to be a very intimate conversation; Evoni turned and went in search for a table. Laughing, Evoni thought to herself that she didn't want to "cockblock," as her brothers used to say when she and her girls stopped them from getting some play. She would speak to Mr. Jacobs later if he was still around after his little "meeting." Evoni located a table and just as she sat her favorite waiter, Walter, appeared from thin air. He was the skinniest man Evoni had ever laid eyes on; he made J.J. from *Good Times* look like Al Roker pre-surgery. Nevertheless, he was the best waiter she had ever had the pleasure of being served by, and he always made her smile.

"Well, well, well. Who do we have here, but the finest lady to ever grace the threshold of Perrier's. When I saw you walk in, I almost fainted from the heat you brought with you. You so hot, I could cook a sirloin on you in five minutes flat," joked Walter. "What a brotha wouldn't give to have a sista as fine as you are waiting for him every night after work. That Amar is a very lucky man."

The mention of Amar turned the smile on Evoni's face upside down, the last thing she wanted to do was explain how she and Amar were no longer together. It was too soon, and she didn't want to deal with it right now.

"Walter, you sure know how to make a girl feel good, if you weren't already taken by Jazzy over there, I would think you were hitting on me." Jazzy was the owner's daughter and Walter's longtime girlfriend of 6 years. Jazzy loved herself some Walter and he her, but they weren't the marrying type, so they chose to keep things simple. Jazzy was the jealous type though, Evoni learned early on when Bri was confronted by her for flirting with Walter. Thankfully she was friends with both Walter and Jazzy and Jazzy understood the dynamics of her relationship with Walter.

Walter chuckled. "I do love my sweet thang, but you are a tall drink of Cristal, and you know I can't resist Cristal."

Evoni couldn't help but laugh along. Her bad mood dissipated. Walter's energy was contagious. "If you don't stop it. You sure are a naughty boy today. Now can you please go get me a glass of wine before I have to spank you?"

Laughing boisterously, Walter hurried off to retrieve Evoni's glass of wine. Evoni's eyes trailed behind him, landing on Linc again. He and his companion were leaning in close whispering. Evoni felt a bit of envy and sadness.

As Walter approached her with her glass of wine, Mari trailed behind him. There went her chance to have a moment alone with a nice glass of wine. Oh well.

"Here's your wine, madam. I also brought a young lady along who claims to be your date for tonight. Is there something you've forgotten to tell me, Ms. Singleton?" Walter teased with a glint of mischief in his eyes.

"Hahaha, very funny, Walter. If ever I switch teams, you won't be the first to know," joked Evoni. "I'm sure you've seen my secretary, Mari, in here before."

"Now you know I never forget a pretty lady. Ms. Mari, what can I get for you this evening?" Evoni smiled thinking how Walter had the uncanny ability to make every woman feel like she was the only one in the room. Evoni was sure he was a ladies' man in his heyday.

Smiling brightly and slightly blushing, Mari gave her order to Walter. Once he was out of ear shot, Evoni turned her full attention to her secretary. Mari stared back at her intently, with a smile plastered on her face. Evoni smiled softly. "So, Mari are you enjoying you work at the office? I wanted to thank you again for all the help you gave me today, you're a lifesaver."

"Oh, Ms. Singleton, it was no problem. I know how stressful your job is, and I want to do whatever I can to help you. You know what they say, a stress-free boss is a happy boss," giggled Mari. "I love working for you. You aren't all stuffy like the other attorneys and you treat me like a real person, not a human word processor."

Evoni laughed lightly. "Please, call me Evoni. We aren't at the office anymore, and I'm happy to know you enjoy working for me. You are an excellent secretary, and your help is invaluable. Hopefully we can get you a raise soon. You're the best secretary in the office."

"Wow, thank you, Ms. Singleton...I mean Evoni. It's always nice to be appreciated. To tell you the truth, all the other secretaries envy me. The stories they tell of the shenanigans pulled by their attorneys are out of this world. So, believe me, working for you is my pleasure. A few more drinks and I may be willing to tell you a few secrets about your colleagues, especially that Jeff Johnson and his father," smirked Mari.

"Ummm, now that seems like some info I may be interested in," snickered Evoni. Her secretary was something else; there was a part of

Evoni that wanted to learn the secrets Mari kept. Maybe she would have to hang out with her more often.

"Oh, it's definitely something you would be interested in, believe me. The things that go on in that office behind closed doors would shock Kim Kardashian," giggled Mari. "I guess now you know at least what type of activities I'm referring to," quipped Mari.

Evoni didn't even want to think of what "activities" Mari was referring to, she didn't want her wine to resurface through her mouth. "Well, let's save that conversation for another day and another environment. Now tell me a bit more about you. You've been with me for over a year, and I feel like I barely know you."

Evoni noticed Mari's hesitation in answering. "You don't have to give me any personal details. I don't want to intrude."

"No, no, it's nothing like that. I'm basically an open book but I have had some personal family drama of late."

Evoni chimed in. "Oh, honey, haven't we all? If it weren't for Bri and copious amounts of red wine, I'm not sure I would have made it through the last couple of weeks."

Mari laughed softly. Feeling a bit more comfortable with her boss, she gave her a quick rundown of her life. "As you know, I'm originally from Texas, Houston to be specific. Both my parents have passed and it's only me, my older brother, and my younger sister. Both of whom are still in Texas. I moved to Nashville to attend college at Tennessee State. After graduating, I got a job as a legal assistant at a small personal injury firm where I worked for a year or so before I left due to sexual harassment by the founding partner. After that I temped up until you hired me on as your secretary. That's the Cliff Notes version."

Evoni smiled lightly. "Very succinct. You'd make a good attorney."

"Thanks."

Walter appeared with Mari's cocktail. "Here you go, madam. A perfectly mixed Old Fashion. In another day and age, I would make an inappropriate joke about how whiskey makes you frisky, but Jazzy would have my head and I quite like it on my shoulders. You ladies enjoy your drinks and I'll be back to check on you shortly."

After Walter walked away. Evoni turned to the reason they were meeting. "I can't tell you how happy I am for my girl, but I must warn you Mari, Bri is a perfectionist and demanding. She won't settle for anything less than the best. She won't even wear panties that costs less than a hundred dollars. So, if you want to back out, now is your one and only chance. After tonight, you're under contract and there's no release clause," joked Evoni.

Mari giggled. "I'm all in. Where do I sign?"

"Great. I really didn't want to have to do this by myself. Bri will plan her engagement party herself, but we will plan the bridal shower and the bachelorette party but expect a lot of input from the bride-to-be. I want these events to be everything Bri could wish for, which basically means it's going to cost me a lot of money," laughed Evoni. "But Bri is my best friend, and she deserves only the best."

"I still can't believe Bri is getting married. I am so thrilled for her. She really has been great to me. She introduced me to my boyfriend one night at the Lennox. She is so outgoing and will approach anyone. I am so envious of her. I wish I had her gumption."

Evoni knew how Mari felt; sometimes she envied her friend's ability to say whatever was on her mind without any thought to consequences. Although it seems like Evoni had been doing a little bit of that lately herself, maybe after all these years, Bri was finally rubbing off on her. "I didn't know Bri introduced you to your boyfriend. She does have the uncanny ability to play matchmaker."

"Yes, she introduced me to Kevin about five months ago and things have been great between us. I think he may even ask me to marry him sometime in the near future. Speaking of weddings and marriage, how are your wedding plans coming along? Isn't it going to be difficult to plan your own wedding and help Bri with hers?" questioned Mari.

Not wanting to disclose her break-up with Amar just yet to anyone, Evoni dodged the question. "Oh, it won't be a problem. I'm pretty good at multitasking. Now let's get to work on Bri's bridal shower," Evoni said while pulling a legal pad from her briefcase. Funny how the roles were reversed, for once she would be the one taking notes.

Two glasses of wine later, Evoni had a comprehensive list of fantastic ideas and themes for Bri's bridal shower. Mari was extremely creative and imaginative; half the things on the list Evoni never would have come up with. Thank goodness she had enlisted her secretary's help; the girl was a natural at planning.

Feeling exhausted, Evoni decided it was time to wrap this meeting up and head home to the comfort of her bed. Tomorrow was another exciting day at the office with more emotionally taxing cases and asshole colleagues, Evoni couldn't wait for Friday.

"Well, Mari, you have been exceptionally wonderful company this evening and your ideas are beyond great. I'm excited about working with you on this. However, I am dead tired after the antics that occurred today, and I am going home to my bed and some Cardi B," joked Evoni. "I suggest you do the same and go home to that man of yours."

"You don't have to tell me twice," laughed Mari. "Mondays are always trying for me. I can't wait to get home to a good meal and a warm bath. I will see you tomorrow, and it was nice talking to you outside the office," stated Mari while rising from her seat. "Goodnight Evoni."

"Goodnight Mari and drive carefully. I'll take care of things here. See you tomorrow."

Evoni paid the check and quickly left the bar. Her bed was calling her name. Today had been a rather eventful day and Evoni was ready for it to end.

Pulling into her driveway twenty minutes later, Evoni practically had to drag her weary body out of her car and to her door. Upon entering her house, Evoni tossed her belongings on the living room table and headed straight for her bed. Any work she had to do would have to wait until tomorrow, tonight she was getting a good night's rest. Evoni did take five minutes to wash the makeup off her face and brush her teeth, but that's all she did. Five minutes after her head touched her pillow, Evoni was in La-La land dreaming of a warm tropical getaway with Morris Chestnut, Shemar Moore and Boris Kodjoe doing all sort of naughty things to her and her enjoying every delectable moment of it.

CHAPTER 9

Bri

It was 6:30 a.m. and Bri couldn't get back to sleep. Her mind was filled with so many thoughts about the wedding, her dress, and her future as Mrs. Harold Williams. Bri knew she wanted to bring Harold the same happiness he brought her but was she capable of being a good wife? Most of her life, Bri had survived by putting herself first and never caring about what anyone else thought. But now she had this beautiful, wonderful man who loved her and always put her first, could she do the same?

Bri silently watched Harold sleeping; he had such a sweet youthful look on his face. It was as if he was in total bliss and peace with the universe. Bri hoped that smile had everything to do with her. For a man who had been so lucky in his professional life, Harold had been extremely unlucky in love.

Bri and Harold had spent many nights in bed after their lovemaking talking into the wee hours of the morning about life, love, their past, the present, and their future together. Harold's candid portrayal of his past often left Bri in tears, the struggles he had known, the trials and tribulations of growing up black in the south back in the late 50's and 60's had to be devastating to any black person's psyche.

Harold was a baby when Emmitt Till was killed but he often told her in vivid detail of the assaults he experienced at the hands of white men and the hanging of many of his friends and loved ones, including his uncle. As a teenager, Harold experienced what most women would call the worst feeling on earth, heartbreak. While attending high school in Birmingham, Harold met and fell in love with Josie Baker. Apparently, she was the most beautiful girl in town, she was light, bright, and damn near white and Harold was completely smitten. Her father was a mortician and one of the more prominent members of the black community while Harold's father was a porter for the local railway company.

Despite their vastly different upbringings, the two fell in love the summer before their senior year of high school. They secretly saw each other every day that summer and the two pledged to run away and marry upon graduation, no matter what. But unfortunately, Josie's father caught wind of their budding romance and decided it was time for him to take his daughter away from temptation. Her father contacted his sister in Philadelphia, who herself was passing for white and working in a law office as a secretary, to see if he could send Josie to live with her. He figured since she could also pass for white, she would have greater opportunities there and he wouldn't have to worry about her getting any fancy ideas about marrying that poor black porter's son.

Back then one didn't disobey one's parents, so Josie informed Harold of her impending departure. Harold suggested they run away that night to New Orleans and get married. He begged and pleaded with Josie not to leave him and her culture behind. After hours of trying to persuade her, she finally agreed to meet him the following night and promised they would leave then.

The following night, Harold waited and waited for Josie to show up and just when he was about to give up, a schoolmate showed up with a note from Josie explaining that she had left that morning for Philadelphia and that although she loved him, she could never hurt her father by marrying him. Harold was completely devastated, knowing that the main reason her father didn't want them to be together was because his family was poor. Her father assumed Harold would stay that way for life. This judgment of his manhood and character fueled Harold's entrepreneurial desire and after graduating high school, he moved to New York City and did everything humanly possible to succeed. And here he is today, damn near a billionaire but still never having experienced true love, but Bri was determined to change that.

Slowly rising from her position in the bed, Bri silently slipped from the room. She wanted to surprise Harold with breakfast in bed, unfortunately she couldn't boil water; so, she would have Maribel, the housekeeper, cook them up a special breakfast. The least she could do was carry it up the stairs to him, maybe even eat a lil' something off Harold, like some strawberries and cream.

After having Maribel fix chicken sausage, eggs, grits, and strawberries with a side of whipped cream for her and Harold, Bri tiptoed back upstairs to where Harold lay still sleeping peacefully. Bri decided he needed a wake-up call, so she gently pulled back the covers and began to kiss Harold lovingly on his eyelids, then his lips, and slowly made her way to his chest. Just when she began kissing his chest, she noticed the slight smile on his face. He had been playing sleep, the sly fox.

"Oh, I see you are awake. It would have been nice of you to let me know before I began my special wake up call," stated Bri teasingly.

"And miss out on the opportunity to have your sexy lips grace my body. Never," exclaimed Harold chuckling lightly. "Now, darling, if you will please grab my robe so I can rise without poking you in your eye," teased Harold. "You know the affect you have on me."

Laughing loudly, Bri rose to get Harold's robe. He was the most amazing man. He was smart, handsome, business savvy, rich, intelligent, loving, kind, and funny. Bri felt like the luckiest woman on earth. It was ironic how one's life could be changed so easily by the one person you least expect. When Bri first met Harold, she had no intentions of really dating him. She just needed a sponsor for her shopping addiction. Working was way overrated, Bri much preferred having rich men grovel at her feet and finance her life. She never stayed with one too long, because she knew how some men wanted to control you when they were basically taking care of you. Bri didn't need a daddy to tell her what to do, so before any of her male friends could reach that point;

she dumped them and moved on to the next sucker. But somehow Harold penetrated all the walls she had in place protecting her heart. He romanced her and made her believe she was the most precious thing on Earth, and he did all that without ever expecting anything in return. He never told her what to do, he let her make her own mistakes, and he was always there to bail her out, literally and figuratively speaking, when she screwed up. Bri still couldn't believe the opportunity she had been given to become the wife of one of the richest men in the country.

As Harold exited the bathroom he gazed lovingly at Bri. "Bria, you are the most beautiful woman I have ever laid eyes on, and I have been around for quite some time, so you know I've seen my share of women. You are absolutely stunning," stated Harold while walking over to where Bri was sitting on the bed. "I am extremely lucky to have you in my life, and I can't wait to make you my wife."

Bri giggled slightly; Harold was such a Romeo. "Hal baby, you have made me the most fortunate woman in the world, and I plan on showing you how much I appreciate that from now until eternity. Now let's eat this wonderful breakfast I so lovingly carried up the stairs, despite my fresh manicure. Afterwards, I plan on giving you a very special treat," Bri teased wickedly.

"In that case, my lady, let's eat because I am ready for my treat. You know you shouldn't keep an old man waiting, the Viagra only last so long," joked Harold.

"Please Hal, you and I both know that you don't need Viagra. You are like the Energizer Bunny, you just keep going and going," laughed Bri. "Now stop being silly and eat."

CHAPTER 10

Evoni

Evoni groaned as her alarm wailed for the second time that morning. She had never been a morning person. And knowing that she had to go face the aftermath of her temporary insanity yesterday just made it even harder to pull herself from the comfort of her bed. Yet, it had to be done. As she headed towards the shower, Evoni glimpsed herself in the mirror. She hadn't even taken the time to tie her hair up last night. She looked like Don King's twin sister. Evoni was not skilled in the art of doing hair and her next hair appointment wasn't until Saturday so for now she would just have to wear the forever faithful bun.

Some days Evoni wished she could just walk out the door without doing her hair and with no makeup, but she had been trained to never leave the house looking anything less than her best since she never knew when she would meet the man of her dreams. *What a crock of bullcrap,* Evoni thought as she maneuvered her body into the shower. *The man of my dreams doesn't care what I look like, but then again, I may never meet that man unless I move to the backwoods hill country where the women are hairy and have no teeth by the age of 35.*

Emerging from the shower feeling refreshed, Evoni glanced at her phone while applying lotion. She had a missed call from Marc. Evoni groaned loudly; it was too early for Jessica's shenanigans.

Evoni listened to the message Marc had left and was surprised but not shocked. Jessica hadn't started another disturbance but instead had asked Marc to keep the boys for longer. Jessica claimed she had something important to do. Marc wanted to know if this was something they could use in the case. Evoni tried calling Marc back but there was no answer, so she left a message telling him to document the date and time of the call along with a summary of what was said. Evoni had a meeting set with Jessica and her attorney for the following week, so any and all ammunition was welcome. Anything to get this case over with and those boys with their father full-time.

Evoni emerged from her house wearing a black Cushnie skirt suit with a pair of red Ferragamo's to die for. She knew she looked fly and her 65-year-old neighbor, Dougie Frazier, confirmed this by dripping a line of drool from his driveway to Memphis. Evoni waved politely at the old horn dog as she climbed into her car. She made sure she didn't raise her leg too high, the last thing she wanted to do was give the old geezer a heart attack.

As Evoni drove, she contemplated the current state of her life. Here she was 35 with no man, no kids, and on the verge of losing her opportunity to make partner. She felt like her life was at a standstill and she didn't know what to do to make things better. She wanted to let loose and have some fun and just relax but her demanding career made that damn near next to impossible. She hadn't even taken her vacation time for the last five years for fear of being labeled lazy even though her white cohorts took off as many days as they could. The more Evoni thought about it, the better the idea of starting her own practice sounded. She vowed at that moment that if she didn't make partner this upcoming selection, she would leave the firm and start her own practice. At least then she would be her own boss and could set her own hours and workload.

Pulling into the firm's parking garage, Evoni spotted one of the senior partners, Ben Merceau, sitting in his Jaguar and from the look of it he was having a heated conversation with someone. His arms were flailing all over the place. Evoni was curious as to who he was yelling at.

After parking, she decided to take the stairs up to the main lobby just so she could try and catch a glimpse. As she slowly rounded the corner, Evoni gasped loudly. The person in the car was Sam Jacobs, the new paralegal for Mr. Merceau. Wow, whatever they were discussing must have been extremely serious because the poor boy looked to be crying. Evoni wondered what was going on. Just then Mr. Merceau glanced up and saw Evoni standing there. He smiled weakly and waved as Sam scrunched down lower in his seat. Evoni waved back as she wondered why the two men were together and why Sam was trying to hide. Not wanting to appear nosey, Evoni quickly walked towards the stairs. Whatever was going on wasn't any of her business. She had enough problems of her own.

When Evoni made it to her office, she was greeted at her door by Ryan Johnson, Jeff's father and senior partner. He did not look happy to see her.

"Mr. Johnson, what brings you down here with us underlings?"

"Well, Ms. Singleton, it has come to my attention that there was a little trouble in the attorney meeting involving you and my son. I would like to speak with you privately about this matter, if you don't mind," Mr. Johnson stated in a voice that suggested he wasn't asking her but telling her.

Evoni faked a pleasant smile. "Of course, if you will follow me into my office, we can discuss this matter further." The last thing she needed was for more people to walk by and see her being scolded like a two-year-old.

Before Evoni could set her briefcase down, Jeff's father was grilling her like a *Law & Order* detective. "Ms. Singleton, could you please explain why you felt the need to put your hands on my son? You know I could have you brought before the disciplinary committee? How dare you act in such a crass manner? I swear you people just don't know how to act," Mr. Johnson snapped.

At the words "you people" Evoni's eyes grew to the size of saucers. "Excuse me, but what do you mean by 'you people?' Because if you are implying "black" people don't know how to act, I have a few things to tell you. First off, before you start mouthing off about someone's manners, perhaps you should speak to your son. He's the one running around here flirting and fucking everything in a skirt with skin darker than a paper bag. And if you must know why I slapped your son; it is because he is a crass, tactless, misogynistic, Neanderthal who made a very inappropriate comment to me yesterday and that wasn't the first time. If you feel the need to bring disciplinary action against me then go ahead but if you do, I swear before God, I will make sure I do the same against your son and he will be disbarred and possibly sued for sexual harassment by the time I'm finished. As for "my people," we have more tact and manners then "your" people have in their little fingers. Maybe that's why you son prefers chocolate to vanilla. Now is there anything else you feel the need to say to me?"

Ryan Johnson stared at Evoni with a look of disgust and hatred. *How dare this, this black bitch talk to me this way*, he thought. Who did she think she was? She did not want him for an enemy. He would make sure he made her life miserable, but for now he would play it cool until he had enough dirt to bury her. "Well, Ms. Singleton, I want you to know that I meant nothing by that statement. I wasn't thinking. I had no idea that Jeff provoked you and I will speak to him about his actions. I'm sorry if I upset you. Just forget I ever said anything. If you'll excuse me, I'll be leaving now."

Ryan Johnson hurried out the door and to the elevators. He had to get as far away from her before he let his real feelings come out and that would only cause more problems. Unfortunately, the managing partner was a God-awful liberal and believed in "equality." He would have to tread carefully. Those people were always more trouble than they were worth, and he would show everyone that in time.

With daggers in her eyes and her blood boiling, Evoni watched Ryan Johnson scurry from her office. She knew there were bigots at the firm, but how dare he be so blatant with her. Evoni cringed at the idea of having to interact with such close-minded people. Feeling a little worn out after her altercation, Evoni decided to call Bri and have her meet her for lunch in a few hours. She needed to vent and who better to do it with than her best friend.

On the third ring, Bri sleepily answered the phone. "This better be good Evoni, you know I need at least ten hours of sleep to keep my skin healthy and beautiful."

Evoni chuckled lightly, only Bri would require ten hours of sleep every day. She was such a little princess. Harold had his hands full. "Stop bitching and wake up. I need you to meet me downtown for lunch around noon; can you do that for your best friend? You know I wouldn't ask if it weren't important."

Bri sucked her teeth and exhaled loudly. "But I just got back to sleep after Harold and I... you know what, never mind. This better be good and worth my lost two hours of beauty sleep. A girl like me can't be seen looking less than my best, so this will cost you. I expect ample compensation for risking being seen in public before two o'clock on a weekday."

"Bri, just shut up and meet me at BJ's at noon and don't be late. I have depositions to take this afternoon, so I only have an hour for lunch. Save the theatrics for Harold and the bedroom and I'll see you in a few," quipped Evoni as she hung up the phone. Bri could be such a diva sometimes.

An hour later, Evoni pulled up to BJ's and as she was stepping out of her car, she heard a honk; it was Bri. Evoni waited patiently for Bri to park her car and fix her make-up. She knew her best friend wouldn't step a foot out of her car unless she was immaculate. A few minutes later Bri walked over to Evoni with the most radiant smile on her face Evoni had ever seen come from her friend. It was at that moment that Evoni realized just how much Bri loved Harold and how happy he made her. Bri had often joked about being in it for the money and perks, but now Evoni saw the love emanating from Bri. Evoni couldn't help but smile, the energy radiating from Bri was potent and contagious.

"Damn, girl, did you get a new pair of Louboutin's or something? I've never seen you smile so hard. You look like you belong to one of those cults where they brainwash everyone into drinking the Kool-Aid," joked Evoni.

"Whatever. You are definitely no Eddie Griffin with your corny jokes. Not even Jim Jones and his Flavor-Aid could make me smile like this. Only my man, I mean my soon to be husband, could ever bring this much joy to me. Girl, the things I did to him this morning. I can't wait to tell you how I was hanging from the chandelier and...."

"Whoa, sista girl. That is way too much information for my virgin ears to hear. The last thing I want ingrained in my memory is an image of you and Harold doing whatever it is that you two do in the bedroom. Please don't spoil my appetite like that."

Bri chuckled lightly. "Damn you, Evoni. Now let's get inside before this place gets packed and we have to wait thirty minutes for a table. Besides you need to explain to me why you dragged me out of my house before two o'clock. This better be good."

After being seated and placing their orders, Evoni unleashed all the pent-up emotions from that morning. When she finished Bri was fuming. How dare some KKK asshole speak to her best friend like that; there was no way Bri was going to allow him to get away with it. Bri had always felt it was her job to protect Evoni. She was always the more ruthless of the two.

"Evoni, how dare he speak to you like that, you should report him. And Jeff deserved that slap. What an asshole. I wish I had been there to see it and possibly get in a hit or two myself."

Evoni laughed. She knew Bri wasn't joking. She would have lit into Jeff. "Ha, report him. No one would ever believe me. He's a partner, and I am just an associate and black to boot. I don't need any more trouble at the firm than I have now. I'll just keep my head low for the time being. You know I've been thinking about leaving the firm and starting my own practice. It's been weighing heavy on my mind and with this last episode, I'm beginning to think now is the time to do that."

"That's my girl. It's about time you leave those assholes behind and start doing your own thing. You are a hundred times more intelligent than 90% of those boneheads. They can't hold a candle to you. Hell, you're the best damn family law attorney in Tennessee and it's time the rest of the world recognized that. Harold and I would be happy to help you get started. I got your back all the way. Now that that has been resolved let's discuss happier things, like my impending nuptials. You know I expect a bangin' bachelorette party. Maybe that fine ass Tyrone can come up from Dillard and strip for me."

"You are such a nutcase, laughed Evoni. "How can you in the same breath discuss your wedding and some young hot tenderoni?"

"Evoni, I'm getting married, not becoming a nun. Besides I just want him to get naked so I can admire that beautiful piece of art he calls a body. Isn't that the whole point of art, for others to admire? And don't ever use the word tenderoni again. It's 2022, not 1988. Girl, you really need to get with it."

"Whatever, I am with it. Just because I don't still shake my ass with twenty-one-year-olds' doesn't mean I'm no longer cool. Anyway, here comes our food and I am starving." Evoni's stomach grumbled as the server placed piping hot baby back ribs, hushpuppies, and fries in front of her. It was too much food to eat in one sitting, but Evoni was sure going to make a go of it.

As the two ladies proceeded to commit gluttony, a young gentleman who looked to be around thirty or so approached their table. Evoni glanced up at the unexpected visitor expecting to see someone who worked at the restaurant but instead laid eyes on a gorgeous light-skinned man with the most beautiful grey eyes she had ever seen. Evoni was staring so hard; she accidentally dropped the fork full of fries she was shoving towards her mouth. Bri sniggered at her friend's inability to hide her lust-struck reaction to the stranger. It was obvious Evoni wasn't going to ask him what he wanted, so Bri took charge.

"Um, can we help you with something?" Bri quizzed the stranger.

"Yes, I have something for Ms. Singleton," the stranger stated while pulling an envelope out of his pocket and placing it on the table.

"What the hell is this and who the hell are you?" snapped Bri. "How dare you interrupt our lunch for some craziness? Evoni, do you know what is going on?"

Putting how fine this man was out of her mind, Evoni focused on what was going on. "What is this and who are you?" asked Evoni. "Is this some kind of joke?"

The stranger chuckled. "Who I am isn't important. The only thing you need to know is that you've been served. You ladies have a blessed day," the stranger retorted as he walked towards the exit.

Bri watched Evoni tear open the envelope. Her eyes became as big as saucers. "Evoni, what is going on? Why have you been served? Does this have something to do with one of your cases?"

"That sonofabitch. That bastard. How dare he do this to me! Oh, it is so on right now. He has no idea who he is fuckin' with," Evoni raged.

"Evoni what the hell is going on? You're scaring me. Who is he? Calm down and tell me what just happened," squealed Bri. She had never seen her friend so angry. Whatever was in that envelope had her ready to kill someone.

Evoni took a few deep breaths to calm herself before relaying to Bri what was in the envelope. "That bastard, Amar, is suing me for wrongful eviction. Can you believe this shit? He's suing me for not allowing him back into my house."

"How the hell is that possible? You two didn't live together and I know you never let him pay your mortgage because you don't roll like that. So how can he be suing you?" Bri questioned.

Could her life get any worse, Evoni asked herself before responding to Bri. This was some low-down triflin' shit and Evoni never imagined being involved in such madness. "Well, under Tennessee law, there are certain factors that a court will look at and decide if a person resided with you, such as, if a person stays with you for a consecutive number of nights over a certain period of time, or has ever received mail at your home, or has a key or paid a bill. These things and other factors will lead a judge to deduce that the person was a member of your household and therefore you can't throw him or her out without going through the legal process."

"Oh, hell no. That law is garbage. What kind of backwards shit is that? There's no way anyone who doesn't pay bills or live with me is going to tell me I can't prevent them from coming into my home when I want. Uh-uh, girl, that shit would never go down, law or no law. What are you going to do? I know you are going to fight this right?"

"Of course, I am. This is just a retaliatory measure. Amar's pissed because I won't take him back and so he is acting out. He just wanted to piss me off, get under my skin and I must admit it worked." Evoni couldn't believe the string of bad luck she was having, how had her life become so topsy-turvy over the course of a few weeks? Just last month she had the man of her dreams, a job she loved, and unbelievable happiness, now all that was gone.

After assuring Bri everything would be fine, Evoni headed back to the office but what she really wanted was to head home, curl up on her sofa with a nice cup of chamomile tea and her favorite blanket and watch trashy reality TV. The last thing she needed was to bump into Jeff or his father at the office.

CHAPTER 11

Bri

Bri couldn't get over the audacity of Amar, not only did he break her best friend's heart, but the bastard was now taking her to court. The nerve of some men. Bri was going to have a talk with Harold about this, perhaps he could help make this situation go away. As for Amar, Bri had plans for him. No one messed with her girl, ever.

Caught up in her contemplations of revenge, Bri ran a red light and the next thing she knew there was a police car behind her with the sirens on. Bri couldn't help but pray the officer was a man; she hated women cops simply because she couldn't talk her way out of trouble with them, unless, of course, it was a lesbian. Immediately after this thought, Bri remembered there was a serial killer in Nashville who the police believed was impersonating an officer to catch his victims. Of course, Bri wasn't the killer's type as far as she knew but just to be safe, she quickly grabbed the pepper spray she kept in her center console.

Bri pulled over to the shoulder of the road and collected her license and registration in preparation for the officer. When the officer approached her car, Bri was pleasantly surprised. Not only was it a male officer, but he was quite handsome in that baby face Denzel Washington way. No way was he a serial killer. Bri decided to play nice and try to get out of this jam.

Bri batted her $300 eyelash extensions at the officer. "Good afternoon, Officer. I know I ran that red light, but I just had so much on my mind. I just got news that a very close friend of mine is having complications with the delivery of her baby, and I was rushing to the hospital to check up on her. You can understand that can't you, Officer?" Bri seductively questioned while putting on her best upset but beautiful face. Halle Berry had nothing on her.

The officer instinctively felt that the young lady wasn't being honest, but he also couldn't help but notice how beautiful she was. *Perhaps we can strike a little bargain*, he thought mischievously. He noticed the huge rock on her left hand, but it made no difference to him. Keeping his serious demeanor, the officer asked Bri for her license and registration. He planned on making her sweat a little bit. He turned and walked back to his car giving her the illusion he was going to run her name and plates.

Bri cussed softly under her breath. Why was this happening? Didn't he think she was cute? Her feelings were hurt, she had never received a ticket from a male officer. Was she losing her touch? As Bri sat in her car stirring and on the verge of tears at the idea that she was losing her sex appeal, the officer approached her car. "Ma'am, I'm going to have to write you a ticket for running that red light. We take very seriously the breaking of any laws here in Nashville."

Bri was visibly upset; there was no way this was happening to her. A male cop giving her a ticket, unbelievable. She figured it must be the huge rock on her hand, although that rarely deterred men.

The officer knew he had her just where he wanted her. He went in for the kill. "Now there is one way we could make this little incident go away," he smiled seductively.

Bri laughed inwardly; she still had it. "Yes, Officer, whatever it takes. I would hate to get a ticket and blemish my perfect driving record. What exactly are you propositioning?" Bri queried with a glint of mischief in her eye.

"Well, Bria, I couldn't help but notice how strikingly beautiful you are and if you would allow me the pleasure of escorting you out, we could possibly make this little situation go away. What do think?"

Bri smiled lightly. Just what she was expecting, another loser guy abusing his authority to try and get laid. How pathetic and unfortunate; he was cute. However, Bri knew she had to play along in order get out this situation.

"Why Officer...it's unfair you know my name, but I don't know yours. But thank you so much for the compliment. A girl never gets tired of hearing she's beautiful. I would love to have dinner with you one day, let me get your name and number and I'll call you next week. For obvious reasons, I can't have you call me," chuckled Bri while wiggling her left-hand ring finger.

"Completely understandable, I hope your fiancé knows what a lovely woman he has. I'm Michael, by the way." The officer reached into his pocket and pulled out the card containing his name and number that he'd prepared back at his patrol car. He had a feeling this would turn out the way he wanted, just another perk of the job. If things went his way, he'd have this young lady tied up in his bedroom screaming for more of Big Mikey real soon.

After leaving the officer, Bri threw his card in her glove compartment with the other 30 or so cards she had from pathetic men just like him. She had no intentions of ever calling him and if she were to get stopped by him again, she would just say she lost his card. Sometimes the simplest lie was the best.

CHAPTER 12

Evoni

Back in the comfort of her own home after sitting through depositions the rest of the afternoon, Evoni tried her best to focus on the love triangle blowing up on her television, but visions of Amar and their ruined relationship kept running through her mind. How did they get to this place? This was the man she was supposed to marry and have babies with. Evoni craved the comfort of his arms, his reassuring words when she had a bad day, the feel of his hands on her body. These were the things she missed most. How was she ever supposed to get over him?

As a tear slowly trickled down her face, Evoni's phone rang. Just what she needed. She hurriedly composed herself and answered with a bit of attitude in her voice. "Hello, this is Evoni Singleton speaking."

"Hi, Ms. Singleton, this is Joe Bradford again from Krispy & Klean, it seems you failed to come pick up the part that's waiting for you, so I wanted to know if there was a problem?"

Shit. Evoni had forgotten about the part again. What the hell was she going to do with it now? "Oh, Mr. Bradford, I'm so sorry for the inconvenience. I've been so busy it completely slipped my mind that I was supposed to come and retrieve the part. I was wondering if it would be possible to send it back?"

Sighing heavily, Joe Bradford answered Evoni. "Ma'am, the part was special order from a car collector in Germany. The sale is final. The part now belongs to you since you already paid for it, so I suggest you come pick it up and then decide what to do with it if you no longer need it. It isn't the job of Krispy & Klean to dispose of unwanted property."

Evoni knew the man was fed up with her antics and so decided not to complicate the matter further. "In that case, Mr. Bradford, I will be in first thing Saturday morning to pick up the part if that is okay with you?"

"That will be just fine Ms. Singleton. Sorry for the hassle, but I have a strict no hold policy for parts ordered not for use in my garage. I hope you understand, and I hope you have a wonderful day." The phone went dead in her ear.

Her day was just getting better and better, all she needed now was a call from her mother. That would be the icing on the cake.

Evoni's phone rang again.

CHAPTER 13

Evoni

The desk sergeant tried to calm the irate woman in front of her but was having no luck. She didn't seem to understand that no matter how much she yelled and screamed, it wasn't going to get her junkie boyfriend out of jail. With a quick glance to her left and a slight nod, the desk sergeant had an officer appear and take the woman away.

Evoni had waited as patiently as she could behind the screaming woman but now that the desk sergeant had turned around to have a laugh at the woman, Evoni's patience had worn thin.

"Excuse me, Sergeant," Evoni said.

The desk sergeant turned around with a grimace on her face ready to berate whoever had the audacity to not wait for acknowledgement. However, when she saw the look on the woman's face, she thought better. No need to get into a pissing contest with what looked to be an attorney. She had three hours left on her shift and a nice bottle of red wine waiting on her at home. No way was she getting into a sparring session with someone who got paid to argue for a living.

"How can I assist you today, ma'am?"

Placing a business card on the desk, Evoni began speaking. "I'm Evoni Singleton, and I am here to see my client, Mr. Marc French."

The desk sergeant sighed heavily and turned to her co-worker. "Alex, can you please let Detective Snow know that the guy's lawyer is here?"

Turning back to Evoni, the desk sergeant stated, "The detective will be out to get you shortly."

Evoni was annoyed but still managed to smile politely and say thank you. But what she really wanted to do was comment on the desk sergeant's unprofessional behavior.

Evoni stood off to the side and checked her emails while waiting for the detective. After about 10 minutes, a middle-aged white guy approached her.

"Ma'am, I'm Detective Snow. Please follow me to see your client."

Evoni followed behind the detective and noticed his ramrod straight posture. Despite the beginnings of a beer belly, it was obvious he was former military and was once in top shape.

He stopped abruptly, and Evoni nearly ran into the man. *Thanks for the heads up.* He opened the door to an interview room and allowed Evoni to enter. "I'll give you a few minutes alone with your client. Is there anything I can get for you, coffee or water?"

"No, thank you, I just need to speak with my client. I will let you know when we are finished."

Detective Snow gave her a half smile with a smirk and closed the door gently. He didn't see any need to piss off the suit just yet, so he'd give her all the time she needed with her client. His mama always told him he'd catch more flies with honey than vinegar and this was one fly he was planning on catching and swatting.

Upon entering the room, Evoni immediately noticed the grey pallor of her client. He looked like death warmed over. She could only imagine how scared he was. She wasn't a criminal attorney but knew being questioned by the police was a frightening experience.

As Evoni took her seat beside Marc, he barely registered her presence. His eyes had the glazed-over look of someone who had lost everything.

Evoni gently touched Marc's shoulder. He turned to her, and she could see the tears he was trying desperately to hold in. "Marc, I'm so sorry this is happening to you. I'll do my best to get you out of here as quickly as possible."

Marc managed a small nod. Evoni eased her way into questioning Marc as to what had transpired between him and the police. After a few beats, Marc slowly began to share the story.

It all happened quickly. Preparing a smoothie after his evening run, Marc was surprised when there was a loud knock on the door. Not expecting anyone, he hurried to the door to find out who it was.

Standing before him were two uniformed police officers, one older white male and a young Hispanic woman. Neither looked very friendly and both had their hands resting on their weapons. Marc asked how he could help the officers, and he was asked if they could come in. Marc invited them in and offered them something to drink. They both declined. The officers were giving him a bad vibe as they looked around his living room like they were searching for something.

Marc again asked the officers how he could help and instead of answering his question, they inquired as to whether there was anyone else in the house. He responded yes; his two sons were home. The officers looked at each other and then back at Marc. The next question confused Marc. They asked him if there was anyone close by that could come stay with his kids.

Marc had no clue what was going on, but he knew it had to be bad. He asked the officers what was going on, but they again ignored his questions and suggested he call someone over to sit with his children. Not knowing what to do, Marc called his neighbor, Kara, and asked her to come over and watch the boys for a bit. Kara was a godsend. She was like a grandmother to the boys and had been there for Marc since the breakup of his marriage.

Without asking any questions, Kara agreed to come right over, although Marc was sure she had seen the police cruiser outside his house. Marc let the officers know someone was coming to stay with the boys.

A few minutes later, the doorbell rang. It was Kara. Not only had she rushed right over, but she was carrying a tray of brownies with her. The woman truly was a gift from the heavens.

Marc thanked her for coming and turned to the officers again to ask what was going on. They continued to ignore his questions and instead asked him if he didn't mind coming back to the station with them. Marc knew he could have declined to do so, but he was curious as to what was going on and he feared it was something that could impact his custody case. He agreed to go.

Marc assured Kara everything was okay, though he had no idea how true that was and told her he would return shortly or at least he hoped so. He asked if he could drive himself to the station and the officers politely insisted he ride with them. He followed the officers to their squad car and got in the back. He'd never been inside a police car, and he didn't like the feeling of being in a cage at all.

Once at the station, Marc was guided to an interview room and told someone would be with him shortly. Marc was nervous and scared. He had no idea what was going on but whatever it was, it had to be bad.

After what seemed like an eternity but was probably only about ten minutes, the door opened, and a guy walked in and introduced himself as Detective Snow. He asked Marc if he wanted anything to drink. Marc declined. The detective took a seat across from Marc and slowly opened a folder. Without saying a word, he slid a picture across the table to Marc.

Marc looked down and gasped loudly. He couldn't believe what he was seeing. It was his ex in a hotel room. She was lying horizontally across the bed. One look at her eyes and Marc knew she was dead. There was no life left there.

Marc was in total shock. He practically hated the woman, but she was still the mother of his children. After a few beats, the detective informed Marc that his ex-wife had been found in the early morning hours by a friend. Marc instinctively assumed this friend had to be a man or hell even a teenage boy but didn't voice those opinions.

The detective went on to explain to him that they were waiting on the final medical examiner determination, but they were operating under the assumption that she had been murdered. Hearing the word murder broke Marc out of his trance. He immediately knew why he was there. They believed he had killed Jessica.

Being a rabid fan of criminal television shows, Marc knew better than to say anything except for the words "I want my lawyer." Marc didn't know any criminal defense attorneys, but he did know one lawyer he could depend on, Evoni.

Now here they sat; lawyer and client; both swimming in unchartered waters. Evoni didn't have much experience with criminal law, but she knew from Marc's story that he had not been read his Miranda rights and so she figured the police didn't have anything to tie him to the crime other than the knowledge that he and Jessica were divorced and engaged in an ugly custody battle. Because in the minds of the officers, it's always the spouse.

Having gotten the details from Marc, Evoni knew it was time to get him out of there. There was no way she was allowing him to speak to the officers and say anything they could possibly use against him.

CHAPTER 14

Evoni

Detective Snow looked over the crime scene photos while waiting to speak to Marc French. Jessica French's death was almost an exact replica of those committed by the person the press had dubbed "The Music City Murderer." All the killer's victims had been white and blonde, like Jessica French, making her a likely candidate. But in the other instances, the killer had left a message with the body, something they had, luckily, been able to keep out of the press. Every woman had been found with a small trinket in her mouth, like that from a charm bracelet. They found no such trinket in Jessica French's mouth or on her body. Nor anywhere in the room where she was discovered.

As much as Snow would love Marc French to be the culprit for the recent serial killings, he didn't see it. What he saw was a man using the recent killings to murder his ex-wife and cast suspicion elsewhere. Snow had no plans on letting him get away with it. Though he doubted the guy was their serial killer, that didn't mean he wouldn't use it to rattle the guy's cage.

Evoni got up from the table and knocked on the door, she had a feeling Detective Snow wasn't far away. Before Evoni could make it back to her seat, the door opened slowly. Detective Snow entered.

"I thought I heard a knock."

"You are correct; great deductive skills," Evoni stated while retaking her seat.

Snow sat across from Evoni and Marc. "Does this mean your client is finally ready to talk to us and help us figure out who could have done this to his wife? I'm sorry, I mean his ex-wife."

"What that knock meant, Detective, was that my client and I are ready to leave. Mr. French has nothing to say to you or anyone else at this point. You and your colleagues have treated him like a criminal; bringing him down here with no explanation as to why and then to spring on him horrific pictures of the mother of his children with no warning or just cause is beyond contemptable. So, no, my client will not be answering any of your questions or providing any statements. What he will be doing is going home to break the news to his sons that their mother is gone."

Detective Snow didn't bat an eye. He was used to slick talking attorneys and their so-called righteous indignation when their clients were brought in for questioning. In Snow's opinion, the only people who called lawyers were guilty people. He knew he'd eventually get his time in the box with Marc French.

"Ms. Singleton, I assure you our intentions are on the up and up. You and I both know that when something like this happens, the first person the police speak with is the spouse. Now, we maybe could have broken the news to your client in his home, but we didn't and for that I will not apologize. Because just like you, I'm trying to do my job as well as I can, and my job just so happens to be catching a killer."

With that Snow opened the two folders he'd laid on the table. "If you and your client will indulge me for just a moment. You client doesn't have to answer, but I'd like to show him a few additional photos."

Evoni looked at Marc who gave her a slight nod. "Fine, Detective, but don't expect any comments from my client. He has and will continue to exercise his right to remain silent."

Snow smiled at Evoni. He didn't need French to say a thing. he just needed to gage his reaction. Snow pulled our several pictures, placing them face down on the table.

Turning one over, Snow eyed Marc. "Mr. French, this is the picture I showed you when we first brought you in. I know it's disturbing but bear with me."

Marc nodded, but Evoni noticed him turning even paler. Evoni glanced at the photo. It was a picture of Jessica laid crossways on what looked to be a hotel bed, there was a tie around her neck and her face was slack. Though still beautiful despite her drug use taking its toll, it was clear from the vacant look in her eyes and the way her tongue slightly jutted out of her mouth that she was dead. Evoni quickly averted her eyes.

"Detective Snow, what is this? Why are you torturing my client with these photos again? Is this some kind of sick joke?"

"Please just bear with me, Miss Singleton. Now, Mr. French, I'm going to show you a second picture." Snow turned over the next picture. It was very similar to that of Jessica, except it clearly wasn't her.

"What is this?" exclaimed Marc. "That's not Jess."

"You're right. That's not your ex-wife but she sure does look like her, doesn't she? Can you see any other similarities between the two photos? You know what, let me point them out to you."

Snow pointed out the many similarities between the two photos but didn't mention the differences. He needed this guy thinking they were coming after him for more than the murder of his ex-wife.

Evoni interrupted Snow's recitation. "Detective, this is clearly some kind of ploy to get to my client and frankly I'm appalled that you'd stoop so low. Are you suggesting my client also killed this young lady, that he's never met?"

Snow turned his full attention on Marc. "I'm sure you've heard of the recent killings in the city. Many have dubbed them the Music City Murders. This young lady is one of the killer's victims. It's quite extraordinary how much the scene and the victim match that of your ex-wife, isn't it?"

"Wait a second. So, now my client not only killed his wife but is a serial killer? This really is preposterous, and my client and I are leaving. I'm sure you have nothing that connects him to the murder of Jessica

French, let alone any of these other women. In fact, perhaps you should be spending more time searching for this serial killer. It may clear up all these murders. Now, if you'll excuse us, we're done here," stated Evoni. "Marc, let's go."

As she turned to leave, Evoni landed one last parting shot. "Detective, in my experience people like Jessica French have more enemies than friends so I'd expand my suspect pool exponentially before the typical cop tunnel vision sets in. You really don't want the arrest of an upstanding, well-connected rich citizen like my client for a crime he didn't commit to make national news." Without giving the detective a chance to respond, Evoni turned and guided Marc out of the station.

Luckily, Evoni recalled Marc's address from her case files because he was still in a state of shock, and she didn't know if he would be able to guide her to his house. Pulling up to Marc's house, Evoni mulled over how to handle the situation. She knew Marc's boys were home with the neighbor and she didn't want them to see their father like this. It would freak them out, and they would have enough to deal with once they found out their mother was gone. The woman was no saint, but she was still their mother so Evoni knew the news would crush the boys.

During the ride from the police station, Marc's demeanor bordered on catatonic; he hadn't said a word and had barely moved a muscle. Not wanting to startle him, Evoni gently touched his shoulder. "Marc, we're at your house. I know your boys are inside and I know you don't want to scare them. What do you say we drive around the block and give your neighbor a call? You can ask her to take the boys to her house just until we get you in and settled."

"Oh God, the boys," Marc cried out startling Evoni. "How am I going to tell them their mother is dead, and their father is the prime suspect? Caleb is only six, he won't understand all of this, and Ashton is already suffering enough with the divorce, this will break him. Why is this happening to me? How do I fix this?"

The sudden outburst took Evoni by surprise. Marc's shoulders sunk and tears peppered his eyes. Evoni didn't have a reassuring answer for Marc, but she knew she had to calm him down. "Marc, I don't know how we are going to fix this...yet, but I do know that you are not a killer. We will get you the best criminal defense counsel in Tennessee. In the meantime, you have two wonderful boys inside your home who will need you more than ever. I need you to pull it together for their sakes. We'll worry about the rest of it later."

Marc visibly straightened and wiped away any remaining tears. "You're right. The most important thing at this moment is making sure my boys are okay. I'll call Kara and ask her to take the boys out the back to her house. There's a small path that leads around the back perimeter that the neighborhood kids use all the time to visit each other."

After placing the call, Evoni and Marc waited roughly fifteen minutes before entering the house, figuring that should be ample time for Kara to get the boys out of the house.

Once inside, Evoni steered Marc to a sunken living room and went in search of the kitchen and hopefully a liquor cabinet. Fifteen minutes later she returned with a steaming cup of black coffee for herself and a nice hot Irish coffee for Marc.

"Marc, drink this," Evoni said while easing the warm mug into his hands. Marc took a gingerly sip and sputtered.

"Is this whiskey?"

"No, it's not whiskey. Tt's an Irish coffee without the whipped cream and heavy on the whiskey," Evoni said smiling. "You looked like you could use it."

Marc gave Evoni a tentative smile and took another sip. The drink did seem to help some. He knew he had to pull it together before Kara brought the boys back.

"Evoni, I don't know how to thank you for all your help. I don't know what I would've done if you hadn't answered my call and came to the police station. I didn't know what to do. It was all so unnerving. The pictures, oh God, the pictures they were awful," Marc lamented. "I can't believe the cops think I did that to Jess. I no longer cared for the woman, but she was still the mother of my children. I know I've said some things in anger, but I would never have hurt her."

"Marc, I know that you are innocent, and you know that you are innocent. Hopefully, the police don't have their heads stuck too far up their own asses and actually investigate this case and find the real culprit. But, on the off chance you are arrested and charged with murder, we have to find you a criminal defense attorney."

"Oh, you're right. But I don't even know where to begin looking for one. I've never been in trouble with the law."

"Don't worry about that. I have someone in mind. I just hope he's available. In the meantime, let's discuss how you want to handle the situation with your boys. Just how much will you tell them? Do you want me to leave before they return so you can do it in private?"

Marc's face turned a slight shade of grey. He had no idea how to handle this situation. Hesitantly he spoke. "I think for the time being I will tell the boys their mother is gone. I won't go into any details but since I try to not lie to them, I won't hide the truth if it comes to that. And I should probably tell them sooner rather than later before the news gets out. I am feeling better, so I'll call Kara and have her bring them home. God, this is going to destroy them. Despite all that she had done, Ashton and Caleb loved Jess unconditionally. I don't know how they are going to get through this."

"I can't even imagine how difficult this will be on you and them. But I am here for whatever you need, no matter what time or when." Evoni gave Marc a light shoulder hug. It's strange how tragedy breeds familiarity. Before today, she would never have believed she would end up hugging and comforting a client outside of a courtroom setting. "I'll leave now, so you can be alone with the boys."

"No, no, no," Marc practically yelled. "Please stay, you have been such a comfort for me, and I don't know how I'm going to get through this conversation. I know you are my attorney but, in this moment, you have been a real friend and I could really use a friend when I break the news."

Evoni was touched but also a little hesitant. She felt like she would be intruding on what should be a private moment but the pleading look on Marc's face won her over. She just hoped her presence didn't make the situation worse.

"Okay, I'll stay, and I'll be here if you need me." Evoni took a seat on the sofa, which felt like she was sitting on feathers and air. It was so comfortable. If it weren't for the current situation, she would have asked Marc where he'd gotten it.

Busy researching how to handle telling children a parent was dead, Evoni failed to hear Marc enter the room with his sons. With a deep breath, Evoni stood and introduced herself. If the boys were confused as to why their father's attorney was in their house so late, they hid it well.

After the brief introductions, Marc asked the boys to take a seat. Sensing the unease of sitting next to a stranger, Evoni moved over to a chair giving Marc and his sons the sofa. With a boy sitting on each side of him, Marc began speaking in a halting voice.

He began by telling the boys he had spent the evening assisting the police with an investigation. Caleb didn't quite grasp the gist of what his father was saying and wanted to know what an investigation was, while Ashton stayed silent. Taking a deep breath Marc continued.

"Caleb, a police investigation is when the police believe a crime has been committed and have to look into it to find the person who committed the crime. It's kind of like your favorite character from Paw Patrol, Chase. You know how he's the police pup and loves searching for clues? That's what an investigation is like; it's a search for clues to find out what happened."

Caleb nodded slowly. He kind of understood. Ashton looked up at his father and asked the question Marc dreaded most. "Dad, what crime is the police investigating?"

Unsuccessfully trying to hold back tears, Marc turned to his sons and wrapped an arm around each of them. "You guys know how much I love you, right?" Both boys nodded.

"I want you to remember that no matter what happens, we are a family, and I will always be there for you. Caleb and Ashton, there's no easy way to say this but your mother has passed away."

"What do you mean passed away?" Caleb asked quizzically.

"That means that your mother is gone; she's in heaven now."

"Like Pop-Pop?" Caleb asked. Pop-Pop was Marc's paternal grandfather and had passed away a little over a year ago at 101 years old.

"Yes, son, like Pop-Pop."

Marc looked over at Ashton, who sat quietly with a resolute look on his face. "Ashton, did you hear what I said?"

Ashton nodded and then suddenly ran from the room.

Watching the interaction between Marc and his sons, Evoni knew she had to do something. She couldn't provide the comfort to them that they needed but she knew someone who could. She quietly slipped from the room as Marc held Caleb close and whispered reassurances in his ear.

After making her call, Evoni decided to give Marc and his son more time alone and headed to the kitchen to get a glass of water and brew some tea. Preferring to wait for her friend to arrive before going back to Marc, Evoni sipped her water slowly and browsed emails on her phone.

Evoni emerged from the kitchen when she heard Marc's doorbell rang. Startled by the intrusive noise, Marc quickly made a move to find out who was interrupting his family at this tragic time. Evoni intercepted him in the hallway. "Marc, let me get the door while you take this tea into the living room. I hope you don't mind, but I've invited a friend over. She's a licensed therapist who specializes in dealing with grief."

Marc looked quizzically at Evoni. He didn't know what to say, it was bold of her to invite a grief counselor to his home without asking and yet he knew she was only trying to help. He could turn her friend away, but he also knew in his heart that he wasn't equipped to help his sons deal with this tragedy. He silently took the tea tray from Evoni and headed back into the living room.

Evoni went to let her friend in and hoped she had done the right thing. She knew it was intrusive and presumptuous, but she couldn't just sit and watch their pain without doing something. Evoni just hoped her intervention didn't backfire on her.

Kanisha Saxton was a force to be reckoned with, standing at 5'11" without heels and rocking her natural hair in an afro that added another three inches, she didn't take any bull from anyone. Yet, Evoni knew, inside that cool, confident, hard exterior was a woman who had survived great tragedy and had the heart of an angel. Kanisha's mother, father and younger brother had all been killed during a fire at the family's small coffee shop when she was only 13. The fire had been set by a disgruntled fired employee. In addition to that loss, she lost her husband of 3 years at age 28, when he was killed by an IED in Afghanistan. She had experienced more than her share of loss, pain, and grief. If anyone could help Marc and his sons through this, Evoni knew it was Kanisha.

"Thank you so much for coming so quickly," Evoni told Kanisha as she ushered her into Marc's home.

"Anything for you, girl, and you know I can't say no to a child in need."

"After the introductions, I think it may be best if I leave," stated Evoni. "There's not much I can do for Marc and his sons here, but I can start looking for him a great defense attorney."

Evoni had filled Kanisha in on the details before inviting her into the situation. She wanted her friend to have all the information before she made a decision on whether to help or not. No one liked the idea of being blindsided with information that they are entering a possible murder suspect's home, but Kanisha had had no qualms about coming over. She had enough faith in Evoni's judgment to trust her when she said she didn't believe her client was guilty.

"I agree. I will stay as long as I am needed. I was planning on taking tomorrow off so my calendar is clear. You go do what you do best, and I'll stay here and do what I do best for this family."

"You have no idea how grateful I am. I owe you big for this. Just name anything you want, and I'll make it happen," Evoni said.

"Oh, I know exactly what you can do to pay me back for this and you're going to hate every second of it," Kanisha quipped. "But for now, let's go help this family."

Evoni escorted Kanisha into the living room where Marc sat with his arm around Caleb holding him closely to his chest. It was obvious the young boy was crying, and Evoni hated to interrupt the moment, but it was necessary. She cleared her throat to alert Marc and Caleb to their presence.

Marc looked up and Caleb slowly turned his head from his father's chest to face the entrance. "Marc, this is my friend, Kanisha Saxton. She's a counselor, and I thought she would be a helpful voice in this trying time."

Marc eased his arm from around Caleb and stood to greet Kanisha. His first impression was that she was a striking woman with a commanding presence. The average man probably cowered in her presence. Marc just hoped she was as good of a counselor as Evoni was an attorney.

Kanisha suggested to Marc that they speak quietly alone. Marc squatted in front of Caleb and gently picked his youngest son up and took him to his room. Caleb didn't make a sound. Upon Marc's return, Evoni let him know she would be leaving but would be in touch soon. Marc thanked her for all her help and gave her a hug. At this point, he figured they were way past handshakes. He would be forever in her debt.

CHAPTER 15

Bri

Bri was livid. She had gotten home after lunch with Evoni to find Harold packing. Bri asked where he was going, and he told her he was going to see that whore, his ex-wife. Bri couldn't believe him. How dare he leave her side to go pay a visit to the bitch who'd broken his heart. The same heart she had worked so hard to mend.

Harold tried explaining to Bri that he only wanted to let his ex-wife know that he'd found her and warn her against ever stepping foot in the state of Tennessee again after what she'd put him through. Bri didn't care. She didn't understand why he needed to get that type of closure. Why not just let the whore live her miserable life out in Nevada with whatever diseases she was bound to catch as a prostitute.

But Harold hadn't listened to Bri, instead he had kissed her and told her not to worry. This was unfinished business, and he never left business unconcluded. Then he'd left for his hangar.

Bri sat in the kitchen nursing a glass of sauvignon blanc, the wine would help her calm down and if she finished the bottle, it would put her fast asleep. She considered calling Evoni, but she knew her girl was going through some major drama, so she didn't feel right bothering her with her issues.

After twenty minutes, Bri decided to screw getting drunk alone and going to bed early. She was going to go out and have some fun. No more sitting around wallowing in self-pity, that had never been her style and she would be damned if she let herself get played out like that.

Now who should she call to go out with her? Her first instinct was Evoni, but Bri knew she would decline. She could call one of her sisters, but she wasn't in the mood for their questions. Who else could she call?

Then it hit Bri, her girl Mari. Evoni's secretary was always down to go out. Bri dialed Mari's number while she stoppered her wine bottle, no use in letting good wine go to waste.

Mari answered on the fifth ring. She was breathing hard and fast, and Bri knew what that meant. *Mari and Kevin had clearly been engaging in a little extracurricular activity*, Bri thought amusingly.

"Hey, girl. I was wondering if you would be down with going out tonight? Harold just left town and I'm bored and wanna have some fun."

Taking a few deep breaths so that she could speak without sounding like she was having an asthma attack, Mari agreed to meet Bri in a few hours at Lights Out, a local lounge that catered to the over 25 crowd.

Bri hung up the phone feeling a little better. Nothing and no one would stop her from having a good time.

Bri realized she had to find something to wear. She had a walk-in closet the size of a bedroom and every inch of it was filled with designer duds. Having so many beautiful things made picking just one outfit extremely hard. Bri knew it would most likely take her the better part of an hour just to find an outfit and another hour to do her hair and make-up, so she had better get started.

True to her estimates, it took Bri over two hours to get ready. Being beautiful was hard work. Bri gave herself one last look before exiting her bedroom. She looked hot as usual. The skin-tight red Versace dress was made for her body and the Alexander McQueen tiger skin pumps were to die for. Feeling a little naughty and knowing she had an appointment with her stylists the next day, Bri put on her sexiest wig, one usually reserved for Harold and the bedroom. She was ready to party.

Lights Out was packed to the hilts with everything from white-collar professionals to blue-collar plumbers. The clientele was very diverse, not only in income level, but also in race. It was a jumping multicultural hot spot. Bri and Mari found a spot at the bar and waited for the bartender to take their drink order. Both women were hoping some poor sap would try to hit on one of them before the bartender made his way over. A lady should never have to buy her own drinks.

Mari was excited to be out. She really enjoyed hanging out with Bri. The two women were a lot alike in personality and both knew they looked good so there was no need to hate on each other. Bri brought excitement to Mari's otherwise dull life. Wherever Bri was there was bound to be excitement or drama.

Just as the bartender was making his way over to the ladies, a guy approached Mari. He was cute in that "boy next door" way but he wasn't Mari's type. However, he should be good for her and Bri a drink.

"Hey, beautiful, my name's Jason. I saw you when you came in and I couldn't help but admire your walk. Are you a supermodel by any chance?" the guy asked.

Mari glanced over at Bri and the two laughed heartedly. "Is that really your best pick-up line, Jason?" Mari asked while trying to keep a straight face. "I've heard better lines at a kindergarten play," Mari quipped.

Looking slightly embarrassed, Jason turned to walk away, but Mari stopped him. "I'm sorry. I hope I didn't hurt your feelings, but I was just being truthful. You are a nice-looking guy. You should just be yourself and say what you really feel instead of trying to use a line; they rarely work. Now why don't you buy me and my girl a drink, while I school you on how to pick up a real woman."

Jason looked shocked to hear a woman speak to him like that, but he quickly took out his wallet and ordered the ladies a drink. Bri moved over a seat to let the guy sit between her and Mari. She figured this lesson Mari was about to teach would be rather entertaining.

"Now," Mari began, "how many times have you used that line on a woman and how many times has it worked?"

Jason glance towards the back of the lounge where there was a group of guys standing and looking in their direction. It was his classmates and their teacher. "Um, actually, I've never used that line before. I don't go out much, and I've never really been bold enough to talk to a beautiful woman."

"What made you do so tonight?" Mari questioned. "Did you take a confidence pill this morning?"

Laughing nervously, Jason again glanced across the room at his classmates who were smiling at him like he had just caught the biggest fish in the sea. "Um-well-see, I saw this course on Eventbrite a couple of weeks ago on teaching guys how to get a date and so I, like, signed up for it and tonight was our first night of practice in the field."

Mari and Bri both almost spit out the swallow of alcohol they had just sipped. They looked at Jason and said simultaneously, "Are you serious?"

Jason was humiliated. He should have known better than to listen to his teacher, Mac. Why would beautiful women like these two give a guy like him a chance? Jason went to get up and leave, he was finished with being ridiculed.

Seeing the humiliation written all over the guy's face, Mari and Bri composed themselves and stopped Jason from leaving. It was obvious he was a nice guy but had been completely scammed by some loser and Bri and Mari wanted to help the poor guy out.

"Jason, my name is Bri, and we are sorry for laughing just now. We aren't laughing at you but at the idea of taking a class on how-to pick-up women. Those classes are a scam, and I'm sure your "teacher" has no clue as to how to get a woman."

Mari said, "For future reference, women don't fall for corny pick-up lines; so just be honest and straightforward. If she doesn't bite, back off. Women are more than their bodies, learn to see us as such. As much as we like to be complimented on our looks, we also like to be treated with respect and as a fully functioning human being with more to offer than ass and tits.

"Women simply want to be treated respectfully. Not ambushed by lecherous men with bad pick-up lines and no interest in us as people. If you see a woman that interests you, simply walk up to her and speak. If she's willing to engage in conversation, great. If not, apologize and move on. And never expect more than conversation the first time out. If or when a woman decides to sleep with you, the decision should be mutual not forced.

"You are a nice-looking guy and polite and courteous, those qualities will go a long way with the right woman. Just be patient and don't try to force it."

"Tell me, which one of those guys over there is your teacher?" Bri inquired.

Jason looked over at the guys waiting for him and told the ladies, "The guy in the red shirt, his name is Mac. He teaches the class, and the other guys are students like me."

Bri and Mari glanced over at Mac, with one look the two women knew this guy was no Casanova. Firstly, he was wearing an outfit that looked like it had come straight off the racks of some discount store. Secondly, he looked like Dudley Do-Right's long-lost twin brother. Bri wondered what lies he could have fed these men to get them to follow him.

The ladies decided to have a little fun with Jason's class. They both leaned in and gave Jason a big kiss on his cheeks and then they both began to caress his body. Jason was in shock; all he could do was sit there and try to keep his mouth closed so he wouldn't slobber all over himself. This was the best night of his life!

Bri and Mari decided to take their game one step further and grabbed Jason and took him to the dance floor. The guy had no moves whatsoever, so Bri took over. She grabbed him by the waist and began to slow wind on him. Jason wasn't prepared for this, and neither was his body. He immediately began to harden upon the touch of Bri and while he was trying to think of anything to stop that from happening and embarrassing him; Mari began to do the same thing behind him. Jason was so out of his depths.

Jason was losing control, and he didn't want either lady to see it. He abruptly ran off the dance floor and towards the men's room. Bri and Mari stared at each other and began to laugh loudly, they both knew what had just happened; the poor guy never stood a chance.

Having had their fun, the two ladies had another drink and then decided to call it a night. Mari had to work the next day, and Bri had a lot of bridal things to do. While exiting the lounge, they spotted Jason's class. The group was hovering over Jason like he was the second coming of Jesus. It seemed their little game had earned Jason star student status.

The ladies hugged and went their separate ways. Bri was slightly annoyed at having to go home to a big empty house. Being alone with so much space was kind of scary at times and Bri watched a lot of thrillers, so she was constantly freaked out about being slaughtered by some psycho mass murderer. Often when Harold had business trips, she would spend the night at Evoni's place, but it was too late to bother her friend. Bri decided to go to the Montreux Hotel. The food from the restaurant there was fantastic, and the kitchen stayed open late for the hotel guests and bar patrons. She could have herself some fries and maybe find someone to chat with to pass the night until she was good and tired and could fall fast asleep as soon as she walked through her door.

The Montreux Hotel had only been in business about a year, but the restaurant attached to it had gotten rave reviews since opening its doors. The head chef was a former Top Chef contestant, and she was a beast in the kitchen. The hotel itself was beautiful. Bri and Harold made it a point to stay there when it first opened and both had been extremely impressed with the décor, the customer service, and the well-appointed rooms. The beds had Egyptian cotton sheets and the mattresses felt like you were sleeping on air.

Bri pulled up to valet park her car. She hated street parking and she hated valet because she didn't fully trust the guys to not take her car for a joy ride. It was the latest Porsche Taycan, fully loaded, who wouldn't be tempted to drive it? But with it being late, Bri decided to use the valet for her own safety, no need in taking unnecessary chances with her life.

Entering through the hotel lobby, Bri walked towards the bar. It was a cozy, intimate setting and Bri wished Harold was there to accompany her. Hopefully, the bartender would be someone she could engage in conversation without him or her hitting on her.

To her surprise, the bar was well occupied. There were a few couples having drinks and what looked like businessmen hovering around a table. There were a couple of guys seated at the bar and a lone woman. Bri decided to sit closer to the woman in hopes that would keep any men at bay.

Bri sat on the stool next to the woman. With a quick glance, Bri could see she was attractive in a Debra Messing kind of way. She was a red head, natural or bottled, Bri couldn't tell, which meant she had spent a lot of money to make it look natural if it wasn't. That was a quality Bri could appreciate in a woman.

The bartender, Raphael, approached Bri. "Good evening, ma'am, can I get you something to drink?"

Bri smiled. The guy was a cutie, and he had an accent. She, like most women, was a sucker for accents. "Hi there yourself, I'll have a Luxurita please," Bri said. A Luxurita was a fabulous drink that had cognac and Patron mixed with the bar's special blend of citrus juices. It was delicious, and Bri also really liked the name.

"Coming right up. Can I bring you the bar food menu while I'm at it?" the bartender asked.

"No, I'm fine, just the drink and an order of fries. Thanks."

Bri was slightly startled when she heard the very feminine sexy voice next to her. "It's a shame you aren't hungrier, the calamari here is devilishly delicious," the woman said with a little wink.

Oh God, Bri thought, *either this woman is hitting on me or she oozes sex whenever she opens her mouth.* Bri hoped it was the latter. "Yes, you are quite right. The calamari here is mouthwatering but if I'm going to have fried food late at night, it's fries. I'm a sucker for potatoes. I can't have both as I would like to continue to fit into my cute little dresses," Bri jested.

"And you do look great in that little dress," the woman said with a hint of amusement. "By the way, my name is Aubrey," she stated while holding her hand out to Bri.

Bri shook her hand gingerly. "Hi, nice to meet you. I'm Bri."

"Bri, that's a lovely name, is it short for anything?"

"Yes, Bria, that's not much longer but I like Bri better."

"Ah, I see. Well, Bri, it's a pleasure to meet you. I was hoping to be joined by someone I could have a decent conversation with without having to worry about their eyes being on my breasts and not my face."

Bri laughed softly; the woman did have nice breasts. She looked like a 38C. "Well, I can assure you I have no interest in your breasts, although they are nice."

Aubrey giggled. "Thank you, they had better be as much as I paid for them."

"Well, it was money well spent," Bri joked.

"You know, Bri, I think I like you. You give off positive energy."

"I try my best to stay positive. There's nothing worse than a bitter, downtrodden woman. Life is hard, and I say when life gives you lemons, sell them to the next sucker for a profit," Bri quipped.

"Oooh, positive and funny, I definitely like you," Aubrey said.

The bartender brought Bri her drink and fries. She took a long sip of her cocktail; it was tasty as usual.

Aubrey leaned over and whispered to Bri. "Isn't that bartender, Raphael, just delectable? I would love to take him up to my room and have him show me his best cock-tail," said Aubrey stringing out the beginning of the word.

Bri laughed. Aubrey was the type of woman she wouldn't mind getting to know better. She seemed to be an uninhibited soul.

"Um, I definitely concur with that assessment, but I am engaged," Bri wiggled her ring finger. "Otherwise, I would definitely take Raphael upstairs and have him serve me up."

"Oh, congratulations on your upcoming nuptials, your next drink is on me in celebration. I'm also married," Aubrey stated while showing Bri the small boulder located on her ring finger. "My husband and I have been together for over fifteen years, but we have an agreement."

An agreement? Did that mean what she thought it meant? "Are you telling me that you and your husband have an agreement to see other people?" Bri asked.

"Yes, but I can assure you it's not what you think. We aren't swingers or into anything freaky. Well, at least, not in that way," Aubrey said with a devilish grin. "Let's just say ours is a marriage of convenience."

Not wanting to appear too curious, Bri took a sip of her drink and tried to figure out Aubrey. She was an interesting character. "So, you're staying at the hotel? I suppose that means you're not from around here?" Bri queried.

"That would be correct. Though if things go well this evening, we may be living here for the short-term. I am in town with my husband so he can complete a business deal. He's a land developer, and he's looking to develop some property here in Nashville."

Bri was perplexed. "Your husband is here too? When you said you would like to take the bartender to your room, did that mean your husband would join in the festivities or watch? Are you guys some type of voyeurs?"

Aubrey laughed loudly, attracting the attention of the men at the bar. "Oh, darling, goodness no! We aren't voyeurs. My husband and I don't share the same taste in men. You see, my husband is gay. We grew up together in Seattle where we lived across the street from each other. From the time we were old enough to walk, our parents were pushing us to be a couple. My husband, Gabe, and I were best friends until high school when we began dating. It was during our senior year that he confessed to me that he was gay. I wasn't shocked. I had my sneaking suspicions; I mean what high school boy doesn't at least try to get into his girlfriend's pants?

"Anyway, Gabe's parents had expressed their dislike of gay people early on when one of Gabe's cousins came out during our freshman year. Gabe was scared to death of his parents finding out and so I agreed to keep seeing him and eventually our parents started pestering us about marriage and so Gabe and I decided to enter an arrangement of sorts. We agreed to marry to keep his secret and in return we both could continue to discreetly see other people and he would take care of me financially."

Bri's mouth hung open. Was this for real? Was she being punked right now? Bri couldn't wait to tell Evoni this juicy tale.

"I can see by your expression that you are a little shocked, but really, it's not that big of a deal. It's really no different than the relationship most women married to professional athletes have, except they usually don't get to play too. What Gabe and I have is genuine love for each other, we just aren't in love with each other. If the world weren't so filled with hate towards homosexuals back then, an arrangement like ours wouldn't have been necessary but it was. Even though times have changed; we both really enjoy each other's company and our relationship and neither one of us wants to end it."

Bri understood Aubrey's point, but it was still a little shocking to say the least. "Okay. I understand why your husband didn't want to come out of the closet to his parents as a teenager but he's an adult now and making his own way in the world, why not just tell them and get it over with?"

"His parents do know now, but they refuse to believe it. They are still waiting on Gabe to become straight and knock me up," stated Aubrey sardonically.

"But what if one of you falls in love, wouldn't you want to be able to be with that person?" Bri asked.

"Gabe and I have an understanding. If either of us ever falls in love, we will discuss our arrangement at that time. To date, neither of us has found a man worthy of destroying our arrangement."

Bri was flummoxed by the conversation but decided to each his own and that it was time for her to make her exit. "Well, Aubrey, you have certainly made this a very interesting night. I don't think I could have made up this conversation if I had wanted to."

"I hope I didn't run you off. I didn't peg you for a prude. I was really enjoying our conversation."

"You're right, I'm no prude. I have quite a few stories of my own that I could tell but it's getting late, and I have a busy day tomorrow. I enjoyed chatting with you. Perhaps we can do lunch before you leave town," Bri said.

"I would love that. Here's my card. Hopefully, I'll be in town for the short-term, call me to set up a time to meet."

Bri took the proffered card. "I'll make sure I do that. You have a lovely night and don't hurt Raphael," Bri quipped while turning to walk away. She needed some fresh air after that conversation.

Twenty minutes later, Bri was home and make-up free, climbing into bed. She was exhausted. She just hoped her subconscious didn't bring any of what she experienced tonight into her dreams.

CHAPTER 16

Evoni

Evoni moaned loudly. Her morning had started off rocky and seemed to be steadily heading downhill. After all the excitement with Marc the previous night, Evoni had gotten very little sleep. She was late for the status hearing for one of her child custody cases and the judge had been none too pleased. He had handed her a verbal spanking before continuing the case until the following week.

After her court appearance, Evoni had to drop off a package to her brother Jalen and on the way got a flat tire. She was now sitting in her car waiting on a tow truck and trying to work on her notes for the National Black Attorneys' Association meeting that afternoon. Evoni was set to give her views on racial diversity in white-shoe firms. It was damn near non-existent in her opinion, no matter if you were in New York or Chicago or any other major American city. Firms were not hiring people of color.

Evoni thought having a symposium on diversity directed towards a group of minorities was pointless, but the NBAA president had personally asked her to participate, and she knew better than to refuse. The NBAA president was a sitting federal judge who was rumored to be on the short list of Supreme Court nominees now that one of the justices was retiring to take care of his ailing wife.

Evoni kept her personal opinion to herself and agreed to be a panelist. She had done a great job in her research. Her facts were unimpeachable. Out of the top twenty firms in the country with over five hundred attorneys, only one had more than a two-percent presence of black attorneys and more than five-percent people of color in total. Evoni believed that was a disgrace to the legal profession. The good ole boy network was still in full force and unless someone with power raised holy hell, things were unlikely to change. Hell, the term "white shoe" was problematic in and of itself.

Evoni got so caught up in her notes that she failed to notice the tow truck come to a stop behind her car. The guy knocked on her window to get her attention. Evoni's heart skipped a beat. He had scared the bejesus out of her.

Evoni stepped out of the car to confer with the technician to see how long this would take, she still had to drop the package off to her brother, and she didn't want to be late for her event. "Hi, Mateo," Evoni said glancing at the patch attached to the guy's shirt. "About how long do you think this will take? I've got a million things to do."

Mateo responded in what had to be one of the sexiest accents Evoni had ever heard. His voice made her moist. "Hola, miss, I'll make this as quick as possible. You have an extra tire, no?"

Focused on the accent and not the words, it took Evoni a second to realize he was waiting for her to answer his question. "Um, yes, there's an extra tire in the trunk."

"Great. I'll have you ready to go in a jiffy, as you Americans say."

Evoni popped the trunk and let Mateo get to work. She debated sitting in the car and waiting or striking up a conversation with Mateo just to hear that sexy voice. She chose the latter. Conversation made everything go quicker.

"Mateo, tell me, where are you from? I hear an accent when you speak."

"I am from Boston, Ms. Singleton."

"You can call me Evoni. I've met my share of people from Boston and that is no Boston accent."

Mateo laughed as he finished jacking up the car. "What, do I not sound like Leo de Caprio in *The Departed*? I kid, I kid. I am from Madrid, Spain. I moved to this country ten years ago to attend Boston University."

"Boston University is a great school. Did you ever run with the bulls?" Evoni asked.

"What is it with you Americans? Is that the only thing you know about Spain, bull running? To answer your question, I grew up running after cattle, so I never had any desire to run from bulls."

Sensing a little attitude, Evoni turned to walk away. She was just trying to be friendly. "I was simply trying to make conversation, but if you are so sensitive then I'll just go sit in my car while you finish up."

"Evoni," Mateo said, "I am sorry. I did not mean to snap at you. I'm just tired of being asked that question about my country. Spain is a beautiful country with so much more to offer than bull running, yet most people never bother to ask me about anything else. It is frustrating."

Evoni could understand that. When people found out she was from Nashville, depending on their race she was asked one of two questions: Have you ever seen Dolly Parton, or do you listen to country music? Nashville was a beautiful cultural city and all people cared to know about it concerned country music. It annoyed Evoni to no end.

"I'm sorry also. I didn't mean to upset you. I would love to travel to Spain and learn about the culture. It's on my bucket list."

"Your bucket list?"

"Yes. You know, a list you make of all the things you want to do before you kick the bucket."

"Kick the bucket?"

Evoni laughed. Apparently, Mateo had failed to pick up on some American slang in his ten years in the country. "Kick the bucket means die."

"Ah, I get it now. Sorry I am not that well-versed in American slang. There is so much of it here."

Evoni noticed that Mateo had finished replacing her flat tire. She was enjoying their conversation and hated for it to end. "Yes, we do use a lot of slang. English can be quite confusing for the non-American."

Mateo stood and walked to where Evoni was standing to place the flat tire in her trunk. They were mere inches apart. Evoni could smell a hint of cologne mixed with the manly smell of hard work. Evoni almost let a moan escape her lips.

Mateo placed the tire in the trunk and closed it. "All finished. You have a great day, Miss Evoni," Mateo said as he turned to walk back to his truck.

Evoni didn't know why, but she didn't want him to go. She was attracted to him physically, but there was something else that intrigued her about him.

"Um, Mateo, do you have a card or something? You know, just in case your tire falls off while I'm on the expressway," Evoni said with a smile.

Mateo chuckled. "You are funny, Evoni. I assure you; I am very good at what I do, but I will gladly provide you with a card," Mateo said and walked back to his truck.

Evoni watched his ass as he walked, the man was fine. Evoni wandered what he was like in bed, was he sensual and fiery?

Mateo returned with the card and handed it to Evoni. Not wanting to appear desperate for conversation Evoni thanked him and returned to her car.

Just as she went to turn on the ignition, Mateo knocked on her window. "Since you got my card, I think it's only fair if you provide me with one of yours also, don't you think?"

Evoni smiled. *He likes me.* "I think you're right Mateo," Evoni said while reaching into her purse and grappling for her business card case. She handed Mateo a card.

Mateo glanced at the card. "You're an attorney; I wasn't expecting that. Most attorneys I have met are white, stuffy, trust fund babies."

"Ha, well I'm none of those things but I am a pretty damn good attorney. So, you should keep that card close and safe, you never know when you'll need to use it," Evoni flirted.

"I'll make sure I do just that," Mateo said. "Well, you have a wonderful day Evoni, and I'll make sure I keep your card close to my heart," Mateo said with a wink and walked away.

Evoni watched him drive away. Had she just flirted with her car repairman? Then she glanced down at the card and saw Owner listed underneath his name. Evoni smiled. She'd love to get the back story on what prompted a Boston University grad to open a car repair service.

Evoni made it to her brother's house without further incident and freshened up while she was there. She had thirty minutes to make it back across town to the convention center, hopefully traffic wouldn't be too bad. Being late was not a good look for a guest panelist.

The traffic fairy honored Evoni's wish; she made it to the convention center with ten minutes to spare. The parking lot was packed. That made Evoni nervous. She had never enjoyed speaking to large crowds. It was extremely daunting to have so many pairs of eyes staring at you. Maybe she should stop by the bar in the lower level before heading in, to calm her nerves.

Ignoring the urge to have a shot, Evoni took ten deep breaths to settle her nerves before heading in to find her seat. As she moved towards the front of the room to the seating for the guest panelists, Evoni felt a tap on her shoulder. She turned and came face to face with Malcolm Leon.

Malcolm's mother and Evoni's mother were old high school friends. For years, they both were intent on Evoni and Malcolm marrying and making them some "pretty grandbabies" as they liked to say every chance they got. Unfortunately, for their plans, during junior year of college they found out something Evoni had known since sophomore year of high school; Malcolm was gay. In fact, he recently married his college sweetheart in Hawaii. Evoni had attended the wedding, which was breathtaking and tear-worthy, but sadly neither of Malcolm's parents had come.

"Malcolm, so good to see you. I didn't know you were in town," Evoni said while leaning in for a quick hug and peck on the cheek.

"Yes, Daniel has a conference in town, and I decided to tag along. It's always good to come home even if you're parents refuse to speak to you," Malcolm said with a little chuckle.

Despite the laugh, Evoni knew not having his parents' support really hurt Malcolm, but he refused to let them or anyone see his pain. "Oooh, you should have called me to let me know you guys were in town. You know how much I love Daniel with his fine Asian ass. That man has me questioning my loyalty to black men," Evoni joked.

Malcolm guffawed.

"Speaking of black men; how's Amar? Now that is one sexy hunk of chocolate, totally worth the calories."

Not ready to tell anyone about her breakup; Evoni was saved by the striking of the gavel on the podium bringing the event to order. Evoni smiled at Malcolm and quickly made her way to her seat. The last thing she needed on her mind before speaking to a room full of legal professionals was Amar.

Despite the hiccups getting to the event, everything went smoothly. All the panelists were great, and the guests had interesting questions and comments. Now all Evoni wanted to do was get home and have a really large glass of wine.

Unfortunately, first things first, Evoni needed to find a good criminal attorney for Marc. She had the perfect person in mind; she only hoped he was available.

CHAPTER 17

Bri

The ringing cellphone jarred Bri awake. Glancing at the clock, Bri wondered who could be calling her this early. All her friends and family knew she didn't wake before 10 a.m. on any day, which is why she would never attend the early morning church service.

Picking up the phone, Bri tapped the decline button. Whoever it was could leave a voicemail. Wanting to fall back to sleep, but knowing the effort would be futile, Bri decided to rise and check to see if Maribel, their housekeeper, had arrived. She wouldn't mind breakfast, since she was awake.

Thinking back on the craziness from the previous night, Bri laughed. Aubrey was certainly an interesting woman; someone Bri could see herself getting to know better. Maybe she'd invite her out to lunch along with Evoni and Mari.

Maribel must have heard Bri moving around, there was a light knock on her door.

"Maribel, come on in."

"Good morning, Miss Bri. I have your breakfast here if you would like it. I have two soft boiled eggs, toast, strawberries, and a glass of pomegranate juice. Shall I set it up in the sitting area?"

"Thank you, Maribel. You are a godsend. That would be perfect."

Bri really was grateful for everything Maribel did for her and Harold. She managed their home better than Bri ever could and she made sure everything was always done to their exact specifications. *Maybe I should ask Harold to give Maribel a raise*, thought Bri. She more than deserved it and Bri knew she had a son going off to college soon.

After Maribel left, Bri ate breakfast while watching a trashy reality show she had previously recorded. Bri didn't believe in watching the news, especially now with all the serial killer coverage. It was depressing and scary. She also found morning talk shows boring or annoying. Reality TV allowed her to escape the craziness of the world and focus on people who were housewives but not wives, had "rap" careers, "modeling" careers, and every other job under the sun that would make someone semi-famous.

Two hours later, Bri was dressed and ready to get her day started. Since she didn't have a job nor anywhere to really be, Bri decided to do the thing she loved most: shopping. Thousands of dollars later, feeling sated, Bri headed to one of her favorite juice bars to reenergize; shopping was tiring.

Fancy Fruit was packed with lithe, tone bodies when Bri arrived; it looked like the spin class from the gym down the street had just gotten out. Bri debated leaving, she really hated to wait. But just then, she spotted a guy she knew from her weekly nail appointments at the head of the line. He was a loyal customer just like her at the salon and no he wasn't gay, he just believed that one was only as good as he looked.

"Braxton," Bri called out while heading towards the front of the line. "There you are, I was looking all over this place for you, why didn't you text me to let me know it was our time to order? I wouldn't have dilly dallied outside," Bri said all this while easing her way next to Braxton in line.

Braxton simply smiled and apologized for not texting. After they had ordered and received their drinks, Braxton and Bri walked out together. As soon as they were outside, Braxton burst out laughing. "You know you're crazy right? Those spin folks are aggressive; you could have caused a riot in there. Only you, Bri, would try something like that."

Bri laughed. "Hey, I knew you would play along. I don't do lines; you were my saving grace."

"I see you, Miss 'I don't do lines.' You owe me a drink for not airing you out and maybe, possibly a hook up with one of your fly friends," Braxton teased.

Bri playfully punched him in the arm. "You are always trying to get me to hook you up with one of my friends. I told you; I don't have any single girlfriends that are your type."

"And I told you, I don't have a type. I just want a well put together woman who isn't afraid to be herself at all times and knows how to work with what she has and use it to her advantage."

"Are you looking for a date or a business partner?" Bri teased.

"Hahaha. You and I both know we are too old to waste time with immature beings that have yet to learn their self-worth and it's too damn exhausting to deal with."

"You're so right, I certainly don't have time for immature men, hence my love bunny, Harold," Bri said with a smile.

"I can't hate on that, hell if I were gay, I'd be jealous," Braxton stated with a chuckle. "Harold is the type of man I hope to one day become."

Bri smiled. "You know you are well on your way to being a huge success and if there is anything Harold or I can do to help your real-estate investment business, just let us know. We are all about helping lift up our people," Bri stated while holding up the black power fist.

Braxton laughed loudly. "You are too crazy. But thank you for the support. Now I need to get out of here and back to work."

"Oh, before you go, text me your address so I can send you a wedding invitation. I'm finally getting my M-R-S degree," joked Bri.

Braxton reached over for a hug. "That's great, Bri. I'm so happy for you. I know from our salon chats there was an issue with the ex holding things up, so you'll have to fill me in during our next meet up."

"You know you will get all the deets soon. Have a blessed day," Bri said with a final hug and kiss on the cheek goodbye.

Bri wondered what Evoni was up to, so she pulled out her cell to give her a call. The call went straight to voicemail. Bri tried calling Evoni's office, but Mari told here Evoni wasn't in. Oh well, she would try again later. For now, she would head to the spa for a massage, carrying her shopping bags had her shoulders hurting.

CHAPTER 18

Evoni

Evoni hoped the attorney she had in mind was available. Tim Blankenship was one of the top criminal defense attorneys in Nashville. In fact, it was rumored he was on the short list for a judgeship. Tim was a second-year associate at Evoni's firm when she came in as a second-year law school intern. He'd been her mentor for the summer. At first Evoni found him to be a bit standoffish and wondered if he had a problem with black people or women. But after a night out with the interns, where Evoni proved she could hold her own, he warmed up to her and they became fast friends. Once Evoni finished her clerkship and came onboard to the firm, Tim was a fifth-year associate on track to becoming a junior partner. Then one day, he abruptly quit. Despite persistent pestering, Tim, to this day, refused to reveal the reason for his leaving.

He'd gone on to join a firm that dealt exclusively in defense work and eventually left there and started his own practice. Though they hadn't spoken in a while, Evoni knew through the legal grapevine that Tim's defense firm was highly successful, and Tim was renowned for his legal acumen and ability to sway a jury. Evoni just hoped he could work his magic for Marc.

Evoni hoped the number she had for Tim still worked. It did. He picked up on the third ring.

"Wow, Mr. Blankenship, who knew fancy high-powered attorneys like you answered their own phones," quipped Evoni.

"Well, well, well...I'd recognize that lovely voice anywhere. How are you, Evoni? What do I owe the pleasure? And just so you know, this high-powered fancy attorney is in between assistants. So, if you know anyone, send them my way," Tim said with a chuckle.

Evoni snickered. "Tim, you rascal, I see you haven't changed a bit. How's the family? Have you managed to convince Tess to have a third one yet?"

"Not even by a long shot. I'm hoping in a year or so, she'll have forgotten how awful the last pregnancy was on her and finally give in to my hopes of having a boy."

"I hate to burst your bubble, Tim, but I don't think Tess will ever forget that. Maybe you should just be happy with two daughters. Girls are better than boys anyway," joked Evoni.

"You're probably right," replied Tim. "Girls are stronger and smarter. So, I know you didn't call me to discuss my hopes of having a boy."

"You are correct, sir. As much as I love you and Tess, I'm actually calling regarding a legal matter. I'm hoping you have room on your busy plate for a referral."

"Well now, that sounds interesting. You are in luck. I just negotiated a sweet plea deal for my last client that saved me at least 2 months of trial work. But before I say yes, I'm assuming this is something serious, not a typical run-of-the-mill white-collar crime. Why me instead of someone at your firm?"

"Tim, you and I both know you can run circles around the criminal attorneys at Jennings and most of Nashville. I suspect that's partly why you started your own firm. And yeah, this is more serious than some asshat rich guy stealing millions from innocent people. Let's just say the words Music City Murderer have been tossed around. But Tim, this guy, I know for a fact, is innocent and he deserves the best representation."

"Wow, thanks for the glowing endorsement. Can I put that on a billboard and attribute it to you?" joked Tim. "But in all seriousness,

I'm honored you think so highly of my skills Evoni. I've always believed you were the best thing to happen to Jennings, even if they can't see it. Though I make no promises, I'd be happy to meet with this guy."

"Thanks, Tim, for the compliment and for agreeing to meet with Marc. After you meet him, I know you'll believe in him as much as I do. He hasn't been formally charged with anything yet but based off what I've seen and the lead detective's attitude, I know the cops are itching to pin this on him."

"That's no surprise, sometimes cops get tunnel vision and try to make the evidence meet that vision instead of following the evidence to where it leads. Have your client call me and I'll set up a meeting."

"Tim, you're a lifesaver. I'll have Marc call you. In the meantime, convey my love to Tess and for goodness sake, give the woman a break from making babies," joked Evoni.

Tim laughed. "I make no promises. Take care, Evoni, and I look forward to hearing from your guy."

CHAPTER 19

Bri

Feeling refreshed after a few hours at the spa, Bri decided to try Evoni again. Maybe she'd be up for dinner later. Although it had only been a few days, it felt like forever since she'd seen her best friend.

The phone rang and rang. Just when Bri went to hang up, Evoni answered. "Hey Bri, I saw your earlier missed call. Today has been crazy. Is everything ok?"

"Yes, girl, everything is great over here, but you sound like you have been put through the wringer. I guess the better question is, is everything okay with you?"

Evoni sighed heavily. "I can't even begin to tell you how crazy my week has been so far and sadly it's not over yet. I have a few urgent matters to attend to then I should be free. How about we meet up later for dinner, I'll give you the 4-1-1 then?"

"You read my mind, that's why I was calling. I'll let you get back to doing what you need to and see you later this evening. How about dinner at Mint? I know how much you love the pastelones there."

"That sounds great. I will see you around 7-7:30ish."

After ending the call, Bri wondered what craziness Evoni was involved in. She knew her friend had a knack for getting pulled into the most unusual situations. Bri remembered in college, how Evoni had become embroiled in a civil suit against the university by a student who said the school failed to protect her free speech rights. The student was removed from the College of Business for starting a smear campaign against the school's biggest donor and a prominent Nashville citizen. Evoni had, by chance, seen the girl in one of the local print stores, printing off flyers with the guy's face on it. She'd reported what she saw to the Dean and had been called to testify in the girl's removal proceeding and eventually in the civil suit. It became a huge deal in Nashville, and Evoni was pestered repeatedly by news reporters for an interview. It had nearly driven her mad.

Bri just hoped whatever this newest debacle was, it didn't end with her friend on the evening news.

With a few more hours to kill before her dinner date with Evoni, Bri decided to check in with her sister, Monique. Monique was still reeling from her former husband's betrayal and had sworn off men. Bri hoped to change her mind. After all, they say the best way to get over a man is to get under a new one.

Bri pulled up to her sister's townhouse twenty minutes later. She knew Monique hated surprise visits, so Bri rummaged through her shopping bags for something to give Monique. No better way to ease her sister's annoyance than with expensive gifts.

Bri made her way to her sister's front door and rang the bell. Monique answered the door with a scowl on her face. Seeing her sister only eased her scowl slightly but before she could launch into a tirade, Monique noticed the "Little Brown Bag" in her sister's hand and her scowl turned into a smile.

"Bri, normally I would be cursing you ten ways to Sunday, but I see you come bearing gifts, so I'll refrain from doing so this one time," Monique stated while widening the opening in the door for her sister to enter.

"Hello to you too, sis. I know how much you hate uninvited guests, but I thought this little nugget would ease your annoyance and it looks like I was right."

"Whatever, Bri, just get in here and let me see what you brought me. It better be something good."

"Dang, girl, hold your horses. Can a sista at least get a glass of wine first? Where's your southern hospitality?"

"It is where I should've left you, on the front doorstep. You know where the kitchen is," Monique retorted while flopping down on her sofa.

Bri chuckled and headed to the kitchen to pour herself a glass of wine. Monique was a fool and a half, that's why she was Bri's favorite.

After getting her glass of wine and getting comfortable on the sofa next to Monique, Bri finally handed over the gift.

"Took you long enough," Monique said while snatching the bag from Bri's hand.

Bri just laughed. Monique was about as patient as a hound around a bitch in heat.

Monique opened the bag and squealed. Inside was a Gucci Diamantissima watch. "I love it! It's gorgeous. I swear I love having a rich big sis," Monique quipped while laughing.

"Harold and I are wealthy, darling, so much better than being just rich," Bri stated with a chuckle.

"Whatever word you wanna use, it works for me as long as I can get gifts I can otherwise not afford."

Bri laughed loudly. It brought her great pleasure to be able to do things for her sister, though her mother couldn't seem to see this upside of Bri falling in love with Harold. "Well, after everything that you've been through, you deserve to find someone just as good to you as Harold is to me."

"Well, I don't know if that's going to happen. I seem to only attract liars, cheats, or assholes. And none of them have had the redeeming quality of being extremely wealthy. Hell, at this point I'll take a man who can only afford to treat me to a Popeye's chicken sandwich as long he's a decent human being."

"Oh, sis. One day you will find the love you deserve and all those assholes that screwed you over, well, let's just say karma will eventually catch up with them. Anyway, enough talk about trash men. Let's discuss something happier, like my upcoming nuptials."

"Cool, let's get Aiden over here. Otherwise, she'll be all up in her feelings once she finds out we discussed things without her. You know how sensitive she can be."

"Very true," replied Bri. "Just make sure you hide that watch well before she gets here. I don't have anything to give her."

A couple of hours later, Bri hugged her sisters goodbye so she could head out to meet Evoni for dinner. Spending time with her sisters was rare, and Bri cherished every moment. Even if she couldn't count on her mother, Bri knew her sisters would always be there for her.

Roughly twenty-five minutes later, Bri pulled into Mint's parking lot. She didn't spot Evoni's car, so she went inside to see if there was a wait for a table. The hostess assured her she would have a table for two available within the next ten minutes. Bri texted Evoni the info and sat in the waiting area.

Evoni entered just as the hostess called Bri's name. "Great timing, I do all the waiting and you stroll in just in time to be seated," joked Bri while giving Evoni a hug.

"You know me; I've always been blessed with impeccable taste and impeccable timing."

Bri and Evoni were seated and quickly ordered cocktails. Bri jumped right to it. "So, do tell. What's going on? It sounds like you have had some juicy drama and you know how much I love other people's drama, so dish."

"Girl, you won't believe me when I tell you, but I recently spent the night at jail."

"What?! Evoni Singleton, please don't tell me you got arrested. Did you do something to Amar? You didn't Lorena Bobbitt him, did you? I mean, he would deserve it but girl you can't do time. You way too bougie for jail. Wait, no it can't be that, otherwise you'd still be in jail."

"Bri," Evoni said while touching her arm, "can you be quiet for just a second?" Bri looked like she wanted to ignore Evoni and launch into another diatribe, but Evoni was saved by their server bringing their drinks.

After placing appetizer and entrée orders, Evoni took a much-needed large gulp of her cocktail. "Bri, I didn't say I was in jail. I said I was at jail. Two totally different things. And, of course, I didn't touch Amar, he's not worth the effort. Now take a sip of your drink and be quiet long enough for me to give you the gist of what happened without divulging any privileged information."

Evoni's story left Bri dumbfounded. Evoni avoided anything related to criminal law the way Bri avoided cheap shoes. To have spent her evening acting as an attorney for a client in a criminal matter was a big deal.

While Evoni was in law school, her favorite cousin was struck by a stray bullet. This wasn't a gang related shooting gone bad or even in a rough neighborhood. Evoni's cousin, Melissa, lived in a nice solidly middle-class neighborhood with her parents while saving for her upcoming wedding. One evening, a neighbor, drinking heavily, got into a physical altercation with his wife. The wife, scared for her life, tried running to get help but the husband chased after her and began shooting. One of the bullets just happened to go through the window of Melissa's childhood bedroom, where she was sitting listening to music and playing a video game. The bullet struck Melissa in the shoulder.

The neighbor was arrested, and Melissa's parents expected him to serve a bit of time in prison. Instead, he was given 6 months in prison and 6 months on parole in exchange for information on a child pornography ring. Meanwhile, the bullet that hit Melissa traveled and ended up near her heart and the doctors deemed it too risky to attempt surgery. So, Evoni's cousin was still walking around with a ticking time bomb inside her.

"Oh gosh, Evoni. That had to be hard for you. I know how much you despise criminal law. And the cops think your client is the Music City Murderer? Are you one hundred percent sure he's innocent?"

"You know what's funny, I didn't mind it too much. Maybe because I wholeheartedly believe my client is innocent and anything I can do to help him, I will. I've spent at least eight months going through every dirty detail of Marc French's life. He may be a lot of things, but I don't think he's a murderer and certainly not a serial killer. You know I don't believe there's any "justice" in our so-called justice system, and I believe it should be completely dismantled and rebuilt based off what the people of this country would want today. I, of course, am not going to continue to represent him, but I have asked Tim Blankenship if he would be willing to do so."

"Wait a minute; you mean Tim, the hottie with the body? The one with the widow's peak? Didn't he leave your firm to strike out on his own?"

"Yes, that Tim. He has made quite a name for himself since leaving Jennings, Kaplan, and Craig. He was voted Rising Star by the American Bar Association last year and was named number five on the list of Best Criminal Defense Attorneys in the US."

"Well damn, sexy and highly successful, maybe you should give him a call not only for your client but for you too. You know what they say, 'the best way to get over one man is to get under another.'"

Evoni laughed loudly. She loved her best friend, but the girl was crazy. "You'll be sad to know that Tim is married with two kids. So, I won't be getting under him or anyone else anytime soon. Although my tow truck driver today was rather tempting," Evoni said coyly.

"Tow truck driver," Bri said incredulously. "Why, Ms. Singleton, do tell. I didn't know you were into blue-collar men."

"Bri, I'm not like you. I like men for who they are, never for how successful they are. But, just so you know, based off the card he gave me, he is the owner of the company, not just a working stiff. And most importantly he's hot with an accent."

"Well, hell, why didn't you lead with that? He could be the Taye Diggs to your Stella, though Taye's fake Jamaican accent needed some work," Bri joked.

"You are just too much," Evoni snickered. "Anywho, it looks like our food is coming."

For the next few minutes, both ladies were quiet as they silently devoured the delicious food. Mint never disappointed.

Bri and Evoni spent the next hour discussing Bri's upcoming nuptials before wrapping up the evening. It had been a long day and both ladies were ready to call it a night.

Evoni

Evoni put in a call to Marc. Surprisingly, Kanisha answered the phone. "Oh, hi Kanisha. Please don't tell me you've been at Marc's all this time? I never meant to take you away from your other work for this long."

"No worries, girl. I just walked in about ten minutes ago. It was rough going with the boys, so I told Marc I'd come by again today to assist."

"You really are the best, you know," stated Evoni.

"Yes, I know. I'm wonderful but these kids are in a lot of pain, so is Marc and I will help them for as long as they need me. Now, I know you're a busy lady and so I will get Marc for you. After this is over, we'll have to do lunch or dinner."

"Girl, just name the date. It'll be my treat."

"I'll hold you to that," snickered Kanisha. "Here's Marc."

"Evoni?" questioned Marc.

"Hi, Marc. How are you holding up today?"

"I'm doing okay, I think. Still kind of numb but your friend Kanisha has been a godsend."

"I'm glad she's been able to help. I'm calling to give you the contact information for a criminal defense attorney. He's one of the best in the country, and he's a personal friend, so you can trust him."

"Do I really need an attorney? I haven't done anything wrong. Surely the police will realize that?" he asked incredulously.

"Marc, I hate to sound callous but when a spouse is killed, the police always think it's the husband. Even without the ludicrous idea of you being the Music City Murderer being tossed around, you are the focus for Jessica's homicide. You are especially interesting because of the contentiousness of the custody battle we were in. You look like a good, marbled steak to the police right now. They are ready to chow down on you and sop up your juices with a buttery roll."

Marc was shaken. He couldn't believe this was his life. "Um, okay. I just thought...honestly, I don't know what I thought. This is all just so overwhelming. How am I a murder suspect?"

"Marc, I know this is a lot to take in. I can only imagine the added anxiety and stress this is adding, but that's why I am giving you the number of a great attorney. He will help ease the stress and hopefully he'll be able to show your innocence sooner rather than later and the police will focus on finding the real culprit. I'm emailing the information right now, and I suggest you give the attorney a call as soon as possible."

Marc took a deep breath. "Thank you for all that you have done for me Evoni. I will never forget the help you have provided. I promise I will give the attorney a call as soon as we hang up."

"Marc, there's no need to thank me just take care of yourself and your sons. I'll be in touch again in a day or two. Take care." Evoni hung up.

With that out of the way, Evoni turned back to her other casework; however, she was having trouble concentrating after speaking with Marc. Evoni wished there was more she could do to help.

Then she remembered she hadn't briefed the partners on this new development that would cost them in billable hours now that the custody matter was moot. They wouldn't be happy, and they'd be really pissed once they reached out and offered to handle the criminal matter and found out Marc was being repped by Tim Blankenship. Evoni realized she had failed to warn Marc not to disclose that she had given him a criminal defense attorney's name, so she shot off a quick text to him.

With that done, she called the managing partner's assistant and requested a meeting on an urgent matter. She was told he had an opening in fifteen minutes.

As Evoni suspected, the managing partner, Steve Whitehall, was not happy about the loss of billables from the French custody battle. However, he seemed mollified when Evoni pointed out that the matter was close to being over anyway based off the overwhelming amount of evidence Linc had gathered against the mother. Evoni also reminded him she had plenty of other matters from equally well-off clients that would provide plenty of billable hours.

He suggested Evoni pass on the names of a few of their top criminal lawyers and Evoni promised she would. A small white lie, but hopefully not one that would come back to bite her.

The rest of Evoni's day was uneventful. She was looking forward to a nice dinner of takeout, a couple of glasses of wine and a nice hot bath.

Bri

Bri's day was anything but uneventful. Her morning started with a silly argument with Harold over cream cheese of all things. Harold being naturally svelte, could eat anything his heart desired and never gain a pound. Bri, on the other hand, only maintained her size 6 figure with vigorous workouts three times a week with a trainer and cycling twice a week along with intermittent fasting and watching her diet. When she came down for breakfast and could only find full fat cream cheese, Bri was annoyed. Maribel knew she only ate fat free, so Bri couldn't understand why she had purchased full fat. Harold thought it was silly she was upset about something so small and told her eating full fat this once wouldn't kill her. Bri knew he was right, but that wasn't the point. Why couldn't Harold see her side of things and appreciate the amount of work she put into looking good?

After their disagreement, Harold left for the office leaving Bri frustrated. Then, to make matters worse, Bri received a call from her hair stylist, Tiana, letting her know she would be out for the next two weeks due to a medical issue. Bri felt bad for her but what was she supposed to do for the next few weeks? Tiana had been Bri's stylist for the last seven years. And everyone knows a black woman's relationship with her stylist is more sacrosanct than that with her pastor. Bri didn't trust anyone else to touch her hair, which meant she would have to don wigs for the next few weeks. Ugh...the indignity.

With her morning properly ruined, Bri decided to spend the rest of the day doing some wedding planning but even that was a disaster as she somehow got locked out of the wedding planning site and it took two hours with customer service before she was able to regain access. At that point, Bri decided to give up on the day and instead have champagne and binge watch old episodes of *Snapped.* When Harold returned that evening, he found Bri sound asleep in the movie theater room with an empty champagne glass, a half full bowl of popcorn and a little line of drool. The TV was still on, showing some type of murder reenactment. Harold didn't want to know what that was about. He gently shook Bri awake and escorted her upstairs to their bedroom where he undressed her and tucked her in for the night.

The next morning when Bri awoke, she didn't feel great, and her teeth felt like fuzzy monsters. Thinking back on the previous day, the last thing Bri remembered was grabbing a bottle of bubbly while she continued her *Snapped* marathon. Champagne on a near empty stomach had certainly not been one of her finest ideas. Harold must've brought her upstairs and undressed her. Too bad he hadn't brushed her teeth for her too or-... "Oh my God!" Bri yelled out while running to the bathroom. Too scared to look in the mirror full on, Bri snuck a small glimpse and inhaled deeply. Her hair was a mess. It was all over the place. She looked like Don King if he had gone three rounds with Mike Tyson.

Bri started to panic, what was she going to do about her hair? With her stylist unavailable, Bri had no choice but to wear a wig. Ugh, she was really hoping to get at least another 3-4 days out of her current styling before having to resort to wigs. Guess that was no longer an option. If Bri weren't so vain, she'd take a picture and send it to Harold so he could finally see why Bri always wore a bonnet and a protective style to bed.

Instead, Bri did her best to tame her hair and wrap it before putting on a wig cap and taking a nice long shower. Feeling better after 20 minutes under her luxurious shower system, Bri got ready for the day. First things first, pick a wig and an outfit to match.

An hour later, Bri emerged from her room dressed to the nines. With Evangeline, her layered long auburn human hair wig on which she'd spent upwards of $2,000, Bri felt like a new woman. Glancing at her Frank Muller diamond watch, Bri decided her first stop would be Spruce, a local luxury shoe boutique, to pick up a pair of limited-edition Louboutin's she'd ordered and afterwards she would head over to Sunshine Manning's house to discuss the upcoming charity gala for Women Helping Women. Sunshine, a multi-millionaire tech wiz, was on the board of directors for the organization and had roped Bri into helping with the gala this year. Women Helping Women came about ten years before when a domestic abuse survivor inherited her abusive husband's millions after he crashed his car in a drunk driving incident. Belinda Waverly, the founder, felt it would be poetic justice to use his money to help other women in similar abusive situations. She hoped her husband was being tortured every day in Hell with the knowledge.

When Bri rang Sunshine's door, she was met by the lady of the house who had a chilled glass of champagne in her hand for Bri. *Now that's the way to greet a guest*, thought Bri with a smile. That's why she loved Sunshine.

Sunshine led Bri into her gorgeous sunken living room where three other ladies were already seated and sipping on bubbly. Bri greeted each lady with a smile but gasped when she came to the third lady. It was none other than Aubrey, from the hotel bar. Bri was shocked but recovered quickly and greeted Aubrey.

Aubrey smiled brightly. "What a wonderful surprise. I didn't think I'd ever see you again."

Sunshine looked between the two ladies confused. "You two know each other?"

"Oh, we met the other night at a hotel bar," said Bri. "If I may ask, how do you two know each other? Aubrey, if I recall correctly, you're not from Nashville."

"That's correct. No, I met Sunshine many years ago through my husband. They are old college friends."

"Oh, that's great. Well, it's nice to see you again. I enjoyed our conversation that evening."

"So did I," said Aubrey with a slight lilt in her voice.

"Oh, this is wonderful. I'm so glad you two already know each other. That'll make what I have to ask so much easier," stated Sunshine with a huge smile.

Oh boy, thought Bri, *what is Sunshine up to now?* Bri located the catered lunch Sunshine had laid out. She wouldn't be repeating her mistake from the previous evening.

"Okay, ladies, if everyone will turn their attention to the handouts I have prepared for this meeting, we can get started."

Bri picked up the handout and perused it. It seemed innocuous enough. Nothing outlandish which made Bri wonder even more what Sunshine had in store for her and Aubrey.

Bri soon found out and complained loudly. "Oh, come on, Sunshine, do you really expect me to do this? Can't I just increase my donation amount? I don't mind giving, but I'm not dying for charity."

"Bri, between you and Aubrey, I know you can do this. Who can say no to either of you? I mean really?"

"Well, that part is true," giggled Bri. "But, Sunshine, this is daring, even for you. Are you sure you want to do this? There may be some blowback. This is still the conservative South."

Aubrey grabbed Sunshine by the shoulders. "I think it's bloody brilliant. To anyone who has a problem with it, you know what I say? Fuck'em," stated Aubrey with a flip of her flaming red hair.

All the ladies laughed and raised their champagne glasses in a toast. "Fuck'em,," they all chanted.

Then the meeting turned to gossip about current events. The Music City Murderer quickly became the main topic of conversation. The ladies speculated as to who the killer could be, Jenny Thompkins, Sunshine' neighbor and owner of multiple locations of a luxury day spa, even went as far as to hint the killer was her sister Bobbie's husband, he was a state trooper and he and Jenny didn't get along. Bri thought about excusing herself, as much as she loved good gossip, she really wanted to get home and relax. But then, one of the ladies mentioned the recent murder of the ex-wife of a wealthy businessman, Marc French, and that stopped Bri. Though Evoni hadn't mentioned her client's name, Bri had a sense that this was the client Evoni had to help with a criminal matter. If there was anyone who had gossip about the French murder, it was these ladies. They knew everything and everyone in upper class Nashville.

Not wanting to give away her connection, Bri stayed quiet and collected interesting tidbits. Sunshine knew Marc and seriously doubted he'd killed his ex, even though she wouldn't begrudge him if he did. The woman belonged in the depths of Hell after what she'd put Marc and their sons through. Sunshine didn't elaborate but simply stated that Jessica French was nothing more than a two-bit gold digger who had taken advantage of a kind, decent man. One of the other ladies, Sandy Bellworth, wife of Tennessee Congressmen, Sean Bellworth, stated she'd heard from a friend of a friend that Jessica French was seen getting out of a green Range Rover on the day she died, and that the driver looked really young. Like teenage young.

They had all heard the rumors about Jessica's predilection for young boys and were appalled but also secretly happy it wasn't any of their sons. Bri figured she'd heard enough. The tidbits were interesting, and she'd pass them along to Evoni, but Bri didn't find any of the gossip earth shattering and particularly helpful to Evoni's client. Then Aubrey spoke up.

"You know, I knew Jessica French. We met many moons ago." Now this Bri found interesting.

"How did you know her?" asked Bri.

Aubrey smiled lightly. "Well, to be completely honest, I didn't know her, know her, but let's just say we had a mutual friend in common and spent an evening together. This was about 10 years ago. She was quite charming back then but also manipulative. I didn't particularly care for her but the evening itself was fun. Of course, I had no idea she was married."

Slightly shocked by what Aubrey was implying, the other ladies were speechless, except for Sunshine and Bri, who knowing a bit about Aubrey, knew she wasn't a prude and didn't care what people thought.

The meeting wrapped up after Aubrey's revelation. Bri was sure the other ladies couldn't wait to get home and spread the gossip. Bri, more interested in who Jessica and Aubrey's mutual friend was, asked Aubrey if she wanted to meet up in a few days to plan out how they would achieve their task. Bri would try to find out the details then.

Leaving the meeting, Bri called up Rodrique to discuss wedding plans. Rodrique, of course, steered the conversation from Bri's wedding to the local gossip mill. By the time Bri extracted herself from the call, she was exhausted. Who knew just listening to the details of other people's tawdry affairs, drug problems and ruined businesses could leave one so tired. *Though the three glasses of champagne at Sunshine's house didn't help*, Bri thought wryly.

Checking her watch, Bri saw she had just enough time for a nice nap before Harold arrived home for dinner.

CHAPTER 22

Evoni

The next few days flew by for Evoni. Bogged down with preparation for the upcoming hearing in Colleen's case, Evoni barely had time to eat; let alone do anything else, like check in with Marc and his situation.

Evoni hoped the situation resolved itself in the form of Marc's ex-wife's killer turning himself or herself in, but Evoni knew that was wishful thinking. Unless some new evidence came to light to exonerate Marc, Evoni knew the cops would continue to focus on him and she fully expected to hear from them regarding the divorce proceedings. Which reminded her; she needed to fill Linc in on what was going on and warn him he'd probably receive a visit from the cops.

By 7 p.m. Evoni was exhausted and decided to head home to finish up the motion she was currently writing. She figured a glass of wine would help her focus, along with sushi from Kireina's, the best and most authentic Japanese restaurant in Nashville.

Half an hour later, Evoni was home and ready to relax for just a bit before getting back to work. Just as Evoni sat down to her sushi and wine, her phone rang. Evoni ignored the ringing, if it was something important the caller would leave a message or call back. Not fifteen seconds later, Evoni's phone rang again. Sighing heavily, Evoni rummaged through her bag until she found the phone. It was Kanisha. Evoni's heartbeat quickened. This couldn't be good.

"Kanisha, what's going on?" Evoni questioned.

Slightly hysterical, Kanisha rushed through her response. "Evoni, you have to come quick. The police are here with a search warrant and won't tell us exactly what they are looking for, but they are destroying Marc's house. Marc tried calling Tim, but he didn't answer. Evoni the boys are here, and they are scared. I'm doing what I can to help but there needs to be someone here with a legal background."

"I'm on my way. I'll try getting in touch with Tim. I think there's some big criminal bar event tonight which would explain why he's not answering his phone. Just keep Marc and the boys as calm as possible and tell them I'll be there as soon as I can."

"Thank you, Evoni. This is a bit too much, even for me. See you soon."

Evoni hung up the phone and hurriedly grabbed her keys and bag. While walking out the door, Evoni called Mari. She answered on the second ring.

"Mari, I need you to call Tim Blankenship, his number should be amongst my contacts. If he doesn't answer, can you find out the location of where they are holding the criminal bar event tonight and have them get Tim? Tell him Marc French needs him at his house stat. I'll fill you in on the details later."

Mari asked no questions and just said she was on it. Backing out of her driveway, Evoni gave herself a mental reminder to work on getting Mari a raise.

Fifteen minutes later, Evoni drove onto Marc's street and was met with flashing lights. The street was lit up like it was the Fourth of July. Evoni let out a curse. This was completely uncalled for; this was a show put on to stress Marc and bring unwanted attention from his neighbors. The bastards were really going out of their way to ruin Marc's life.

Evoni whipped her car into a neighbor's driveway without a second thought. She knew they were most likely peeking out of a window somewhere and saw her, but Evoni didn't care. *Let them call the cops,* she thought sardonically.

Evoni spotted Kanisha, Marc, and the boys off to the left of his property standing under a tree. Evoni was stopped by a uniformed officer. "Ma'am, do you reside here?"

"I do not, but I am Marc French's attorney. So, could you please let me through so I can see to my client?"

"Sorry, ma'am," stated the officer as he moved out of the way.

"No problem," responded Evoni. "And just so you know another attorney will most likely be joining us soon."

"Thank you for the information, ma'am." The officer turned back to face the street while Evoni made her way over to Marc.

Giving Marc a brief hug and Kanisha a slightly longer and tighter hug, Evoni got down to business. "Marc, can I see the warrant? I have my secretary tracking down Tim so, hopefully, he's on his way."

"He's not on his way; he's here," said a voice coming directly from behind Evoni. Evoni turned to find Tim standing behind her looking as handsome as ever in a custom black tux.

"Nice of you to join us."

Tim gave her a small smirk and ignored the jab. He took the comment for what it was, a small joke to try and lighten a tense situation. Tim shook hands with Marc and quickly took over.

"Marc, let me see that warrant." Marc handed the warrant over without saying a word. He and the boys were still shell-shocked. He couldn't believe this was happening.

Tim quickly read through the warrant. It was fairly straightforward, no surprises there. What concerned Tim was what had prompted a judge to grant the warrant. From his limited time on the case, he knew just two days ago the cops had nothing that would warrant a search. What had changed in the last couple of days?

Tim didn't expect the cops to tell him anything, but he had just left the district attorney at the criminal bar event, and he had her number on speed dial. They weren't exactly friends, but they had a mutual respect for each other. She was a straight shooter and Tim didn't think she'd allow any of her attorneys to hide anything from him. He'd give her a call after making sure the officers didn't damage Marc's house further.

Tim walked off to deal with the cops and left Evoni to console the small group under the tree. Evoni couldn't help but notice the closeness that seemed to have developed between Kanisha and Marc. She wondered if they were involved in some way. Evoni made a mental note to find out once things had calmed down.

Evoni remembered passing a small park near Marc's house last time she was there. She suggested they all take a walk over to the park and leave Tim to deal with the cops. Evoni thought being away from the ongoing scene would help ease some of the tension the family was experiencing. Also, Evoni knew reporters would start showing up soon. The last thing Marc needed was a mic shoved in his face by an overzealous reporter asking if he'd killed his ex.

While walking to the park, Evoni texted Tim to let him know where they'd be until the circus was over and asked him to text her once everyone had left. That text didn't come for another hour and a half.

In that time, Evoni carefully observed Kanisha with Marc and the boys. It was clear they were all smitten with her. Kanisha had that effect on a lot of people but rarely seemed to notice; Evoni wondered if the feelings were mutual this time.

Once Evoni received the text from Tim, she and the gang headed back to Marc's. Upon arrival, they were all grateful to see no cop cars or reporters. They located Tim in the family room straightening up; the room looked like it had been struck by a tornado. Evoni figured the police had searched the room before Tim arrived, no way would Tim have allowed them to upend it this way.

Marc sent his boys off to pack an overnight bag. He didn't have the strength to clean up the mess, and he didn't want his sons to have to try and sleep in this chaos. Instead, they would spend the night at a hotel. He'd text the housekeeper, Rosalita, to ask her to arrive early tomorrow and maybe bring an assistant to fix the place up before he returned with the boys. Marc would pay her double her usual rate.

With the boys out of earshot, Tim relayed what he had learned from the D.A. The autopsy report was back, and it appeared Jessica had been strangled to death. There were a couple of fibers found on her neck suggesting the murder weapon was a tie or a similar item. The police had taken all of Marc's ties and anything else in the house that looked like it could be used to strangle someone. They had also taken all laptops, iPads, and any other type of tablet or device that could be used to communicate, including the Alexa. What they expected to find, Tim didn't know. What he did know was there had to be something the D.A. wasn't telling him. They had to have more to get a search warrant.

The autopsy had also confirmed the time of death. It was between 12 and 24 hours before the body was found. Tim asked Marc if he had an alibi for that time. Marc had worked from home that day. The boys were at school during the day, and he had been alone until they returned. He was sure he had spoken with his colleagues and sent out some emails during that time. Unfortunately, because the time of death wasn't narrower, it didn't really help since Jessica could've been killed sometime during the time period and Marc had no alibi. The boys were asleep or at least in their rooms with the doors closed from about eight that evening. Marc was alone from that time until the following morning when the housekeeper arrived.

As of right then, everything was still circumstantial. Unless the police found something incriminating in the items they'd taken from Marc's house or found a witness placing Marc at the scene of the crime, Tim informed Marc, they wouldn't arrest him. One silver lining to finding Jessica was strangled with a tie, it moved Marc lower on the D.A.'s potential serial killer suspect list. The press had gotten word that the Music City Murderer used his hands on his victims.

This was cold comfort to Marc, who looked like he was about to hyperventilate. It was too much. Yes, Marc wanted to be free from Jessica, but he didn't want her dead, even if he had threatened to kill her a time or two during their heated custody battle. Marc loved his sons too much to take their mother away from them.

There wasn't much more to be done that night. Marc and the boys headed to a hotel. Kanisha, Tim, and Evoni headed home. Though Kanisha couldn't be privy to any privileged conversations between the attorneys and their client, it was decided that she was an integral part of the team and Marc wanted her involved; so, she would continue spending time with Marc and the boys and assist in any other way that she could.

By the time Evoni made it home, she was too exhausted to finish her work. The only thing she wanted was her bed. She glanced at the uneaten sushi and half full glass of wine and sighed. It could wait until morning to be cleaned.

After a fretful night, Evoni awoke at 5 a.m. Sleep wasn't in the cards, so she got up and showered and dressed for the office. Before leaving, she cleaned up her forgotten dinner from the night before. While placing the dishes in the dishwasher, her stomach grumbled loudly letting her know it didn't appreciate going so long without nutrients. She'd grab a breakfast sandwich from the little bakery in the firm's building.

At work, Evoni tried focusing on the motion she had to finish and file by that afternoon, but it was proving difficult. Her mind kept going back to Marc and his situation. She wished there was more she could do. After another fruitless twenty minutes, Evoni decided to take a break. She'd have one of the junior associates work on the motion for her. Evoni knew it was something many senior attorneys did, but she usually refrained from using the junior associates as her grunt workers. She remembered being in their position and hated being the work horse for the more senior associates while they went off having boozy lunches and early happy hours. But today she'd have to acquiesce.

After passing the assignment to a third year, Evoni called Mari into her office. She knew her secretary was dying to know why Evoni had her call Tim Blankenship last evening.

Mari entered with a steno pad and sat in her usual spot. "Hi, Mari," started Evoni. "I wanted to thank you for your assistance last night. I really appreciate it. I hope I didn't interrupt anything important with my call?"

"Not unless you find watching re-runs of *Golden Girls* important," laughed Mari. "You know I'm always happy to help out even after hours."

Evoni smiled at Mari. "I know you are. You are absolutely the best legal secretary I've ever had, and I am, as usual, grateful for all that you do for me. I also want you to know I consider you to be more than just an employee. I know you and Bri are friends, but I hope you also know that I consider you a friend."

Mari was a little taken aback. She loved working for Evoni and really liked her as a boss and as a person, but she had never thought of her as a friend. Maybe because she was her boss. Mari wasn't sure, but she was pleased to know Evoni considered her a friend. It meant a lot and she let Evoni know that.

With the heartwarming moment out of the way, Evoni turned back to business. She went on to explain to Mari what was happening with Marc. Mari was shocked. Mr. French had been nothing but a complete gentleman to her every time she'd seen him, that wasn't true for most of the male clients at the firm. Most were lecherous assholes who had a problem controlling their hands. But not Mr. French, he treated her and everyone else with respect. It was hard to believe he could kill anyone, even his horrible ex-wife.

"Wow," stated Mari." "If there's anything else I can do to help, just let me know. I don't believe for a second Mr. French killed his ex. Not saying she didn't deserve it, but I just can't see it."

"I'm glad you think so. It's nice knowing someone else sees things the way I do. You know as well as I do that the divorce between Marc and Jessica was extremely acrimonious and with good reason." Mari knew the facts of the case as well as, if not better, than Evoni.

"The custody battle was even worse, but you entered my notes from my last meeting with Marc, so you know we had all but won the custody battle with the new information Linc had gathered. Marc despised Jessica and all that she had put him and the boys through, but he didn't have a reason to kill her. He was winning."

Mari nodded. She agreed with Evoni. "Do the police know about the custody battle and how bitter it was?"

"I'm sure they do although they haven't tried speaking to me yet. I'm sure they'll also want to speak with you. Just remember everything is privileged, and there's nothing you can tell them other than your personal impressions."

"Of course," Mari said. "They won't get a peep out of me other than letting them know I think they're barking up the wrong tree."

Evoni smiled. "I wouldn't expect anything else. Oh, and I haven't forgotten we still have a bridal shower and bachelorette party to plan. With everything that's been going on, I haven't had a second to sit and think about it."

Mari chuckled. "Believe me, I understand and I'm sure Bri does too. But being the super-efficient, super talented legal secretary that I am, I have already started putting together some options for you to look over. Thankfully Bri has never been shy about what she likes and doesn't like, which makes it a lot easier."

"Mari, you really are the absolute best. I would be lost without you." Evoni quickly glanced at her phone's calendar and noticed she had an opening later that week. "How about you come over to my house on Thursday? We can have dinner, a glass of wine and go over the plans."

"I'd love to. I normally have dance classes on Thursday, but they've been canceled for the next few weeks. My instructor broke her arm rollerblading, go figure."

Evoni smiled weakly. She couldn't help but to think about the dance lessons she and Amar were scheduled to take for their wedding. Just one more thing she would have to cancel. "Sounds good. If things aren't too crazy here, we can leave together. Any preference on food?"

"How about sushi? I've been dying for some sushi, but Kevin refuses to eat it. He says he doesn't eat anything not cooked," Mari said with a shrug and a slight eye roll.

Evoni shook her head and chuckled lightly. If she had a dollar for the number of people she'd heard say something similar; she could buy herself diamonds from Tiffany's. So many southerners hated venturing outside their comfort zones. Hell, many wouldn't even fly. "Sushi it is. In fact, it'll make up for my ill-fated attempt to partake last night."

After a few more minutes chatting with Mari, Evoni turned back to her work. With the draft of her motion pawned off on a junior associate, she could focus on some of her other work. Evoni figured it was a great time to call up some of her clients and give them updates on their cases. Billable hours for the firm and nothing that required reading or writing for her; it was a win-win situation.

Two hours later, Evoni had phoned and spoken to most of her clients. She figured it was a great time for her lunch break.

CHAPTER 23

Bri

Bri's day started off well but went downhill fast, thanks to her mother. Why couldn't she just be happy for Bri, just once? Her entire life, Bri somehow always managed to disappoint her mother, whether it was her grades or extracurricular activities at school, the boys she dated or even the clothes she wore. Her mother always managed to find a reason to chastise or put her down.

At one point, Bri believed they were on the road to a close relationship, but that was before she met Harold. Since then, it was nothing but pointed barbs and cold glares when it came to Bri's life with Harold. It seemed the only time she and her mother got along was when they were discussing her sisters or her grandmother.

That morning Francine called to admonish Bri on her recent engagement, one of her sister's must have let it slip. Francine tried to dissuade her yet again from being with Harold. The conversation ended with Bri's mother hanging up on her.

After that conversation, Bri was in no mood to continue creating her wedding page, which is what she was working on before the disastrous call from her mother. How was she supposed to focus on planning the happiest day of her life when it looked like her own mother wouldn't be attending? Though Bri had been proposed to a few times in the past, she had never said yes to anyone. She never felt ready or enough in love to say yes. Harold was different, and she just wished her mother could see that. Maybe some counseling would help.

Whenever Bri was this upset, she needed to disconnect from everything. Unbeknownst to anyone, other than Harold and Evoni, Bri had a passion for painting. It was her way of venting her frustrations. Bri never showed her work to anyone, except Evoni and Harold whom she knew would never judge her. She was under no mistaken belief that she was a great artist; she was no Picasso or Kehinde Wiley, but the process brought her peace and calm. Bri couldn't handle the idea of strangers judging what she made. Bri giggled quietly thinking she had the fragile ego of an artist, even if she didn't have the talent.

Bri's studio was housed in a separate building on Harold's property. Only the housekeeper was allowed in.

After a few hours in her studio, Bri emerged feeling freer, lighter, inspired and on a natural high. Famished, she headed into the main house for lunch.

The rest of Bri's day was uneventful. That evening while perusing her news feed, she spotted a local story about a suspect in the murder of a female in a hotel having his home searched. Bri clicked on the story. The article stated that the home of Marc French, a prominent Nashville businessman, had been searched the previous evening by the police in connection with the murder case of his ex-wife. Bri contemplated texting Evoni but decided to hold off. If it was Evoni's client, there was a good chance Evoni was stressed and at her wits' end, even if she wasn't representing the guy in the criminal matter. Evoni had a strong sense of loyalty and would do what she could to help.

Bri decided to ask Harold if he had heard anything. Harold and the police commissioner were good friends. Byron Hamsdell, the first black police commissioner in Nashville's history, was working to improve relations between the force and the poor minority citizens of the city. Bryon and the mayor worked together to create an independent oversight board that reviewed all reports of police brutality for validity and punishment recommendations if warranted. Harold was on the board. Since its inception, reports of police brutality had dropped 25%.

Harold's timely arrival preempted any further musings by Bri. After dinner, Bri and Harold retired to the patio area for an after-dinner drink, a Bunnahabhain Islay Single Malt 25-year-old whiskey for Harold and a glass of brandy for Bri. After a few minutes of chit chat, Bri broached the subject of the murder and search. Harold confirmed the home search related to the recent murder of a white female in a hotel. That was enough for Bri to know it was Evoni's client's house that was searched. Bri knew Harold wouldn't tell her anything the police wanted kept private, but he gave her the general strokes of the case. Harold didn't think it looked good for the suspect. Bri inwardly groaned; Evoni would hate to hear that.

Bri quizzed Harold. "Do the police have any other suspects? Isn't it a little premature to focus on just one person? What if it's a setup?"

"Honey, I know you watch a lot of crime shows but things in real life aren't like TV. It's rare the police have the wrong person in sight. You should know from your TV shows that it's usually the spouse or significant other in crimes like this. It was clearly personal."

"I know but maybe this time it is a setup, and the police are wrong. You know it does happen."

Yes, it does happen," stated Harold patiently. "But it's rare. Is there something you know about this case? I know you are a crime buff, but I've never seen you question the handling of a case so intensely."

Bri sighed heavily. "It's Evoni."

"What about Evoni?"

"The suspect, it's her client and Evoni is convinced he's innocent. And you know Evoni, she has great instincts and would never speak out and be involved in a matter like this if she didn't believe the person was telling the truth."

Harold nodded. "I see. I agree with everything you said about Evoni but Bria this doesn't concern you. If Evoni's client is innocent, it will come out. And Evoni is a family law attorney, why is she involved?"

"Now, Harold, you and I know that the justice system doesn't always work, and innocent people do get convicted." Bri went on to explain to Harold why Evoni was involved in the criminal matter.

"Well, Bria, as much as I love Evoni, I'm glad she was able to secure the criminal attorney for her client and hopefully bows out of the whole thing. After years of criticism from the public, especially the poorer constituents, about over-policing in their areas while wealthy areas were left alone and wealthy individuals buying their way out of trouble, the mayor and the police commissioner are both looking to make an example of the person responsible for this crime."

This was information Bri knew she needed to pass on to Evoni. Bri also knew there was no way Evoni would completely remove herself from the case. Evoni believed in her client and knowing the cops had no plans on focusing their attention elsewhere, there was no way Evoni would leave Marc hanging.

The following morning Bri texted Evoni and asked if she had time for lunch or a quick chat. Evoni couldn't do lunch but was available for a few minutes that afternoon to chat with Bri.

CHAPTER 24

Evoni

Evoni wondered what Bri wanted. She hoped it wasn't an update on any maid of honor duties, like planning her shower. Evoni wasn't prepared to deal with the wrath of Bri.

Bri arrived early afternoon. After a quick chat with Mari, Bri knocked softly on Evoni's door.

"Come in."

Bri entered and found Evoni hunched over her laptop typing furiously. With a quick glance Evoni invited Bri in. "Just give me two minutes."

"Take your time, girl, it's not like I have a set schedule," remarked Bri.

A couple of minutes later, Evoni finished typing and sighed heavily. "Thanks for waiting, I had to fire off an email to the managing partner. The last thing I need is to do something else to land me on his bad side."

"Please, they should be kissing your feet. You're the best attorney in this place. If it weren't for you, Harold certainly wouldn't have them on retainer."

Evoni laughed. "Maybe I should bring that up next time I'm being chastised. Anyway, girl, what brings you by?"

Bri hated to ruin the mood but forged ahead and told Evoni everything she had gleaned from Harold.

By the time Bri finished, Evoni was livid. She wanted to throw something. How dare they use this as a case to prove to the poor minority residents that they weren't classist and prejudiced. They didn't care whether Marc was innocent or guilty; he was just convenient. Evoni was all for treating everyone equally, from the corner boy to the mayor's son but Evoni also knew that if the suspect was the mayor's son the police would do everything in their power to try and prove it wasn't him or that he deserved leniency. This was so unfair to Marc. He didn't deserve to be the lamb led to slaughter to satisfy the mayor and police commissioner. Evoni knew she had to do something.

Bri could see the frustration on her friend's face and wished there was something she could do to help.

After a few more moments of silence, Evoni finally spoke. "Thanks for bringing me this information, Bri. Though it makes me mad as hell, it also lets me know we can't count on the police to find the real killer. I'll relay everything you've told me to Tim."

Bri knew her friend, no way she would tell Tim and let this go. "So, what else are we going to do to right this wrong?"

"We?" questioned Evoni with a raised eyebrow.

"Yes, we. I know you Evoni better than anyone else and I know there's no way you are going to just sit back and allow this travesty to occur. And if you're in, I'm in."

Evoni rubbed her forehead. She could feel a headache coming on. "Bri, I can't let you get involved in this. This is not your battle."

Waving Evoni's objections away, Bri stood. "You aren't letting me do anything. This is something I want to do. Evoni, you are my sister, and I will never leave you out here alone. I'm your ride or die, no matter what. Also, I want to be helpful. Let me do something worthwhile."

Evoni knew arguing with Bri was pointless. Once she made up her mind, there was no changing it.

Bri waited patiently for Evoni to come around to seeing things her way. It didn't take long.

"Fine, Bri. Just don't tell Harold. I don't want him coming after me. For now, I am going to give Tim a heads up. Maybe try and set up a meeting with Marc."

Bri smiled widely. Being the huge true crime buff she was, this was exciting. She could help to find a killer and keep an innocent man out of prison. If the case wasn't personal to her best friend, Bri would be jumping for joy. "Thanks, Evoni. I know you're only trying to protect me, but I'm a big girl and if you remember, I was the badass in college." Bri giggled thinking of the many times she'd stood up to guys who were harassing women on campus and in bars.

Evoni couldn't help but to laugh too. Bri was right, she was a badass in college. At one point, their friends started referring to her as Coffy, after Pam Grier's 70's vigilante movie character. "Okay, Coffy. I'll let you know the next steps after I've spoken to Tim and Marc. Now if Marc objects to your involvement, there won't be anything I can do about that. This is his life, and he has final decision."

"Yeah, yeah," Bri said waving away Evoni's objections. "Coffy doesn't get told no; he'll be on board." With that she walked over to Evoni, gave her a hug, and told her to call her as soon as she heard something.

Evoni watched her fabulous friend leave and couldn't help but smile. Bri was the sister she never had and just knowing she had her in her corner, eased some of Evoni's anxiety. Now to call Tim and relay this latest news.

As Evoni expected, Tim cussed up a storm and vowed to crush the entire Nashville police department and the mayor. He even threatened to run for mayor in the next election to get back at them. Once he finished ranting, Tim hung up to call Marc and set up a meeting.

He called back minutes later, asking Evoni if she could meet that evening at his office. She agreed and hung up.

The rest of Evoni's day went by rapidly. Work kept her mind off Marc. By the time she finished up, it was roughly fifteen minutes before she was due at Tim's. Luckily his office was only about a ten-minute drive. Packing up her bag, Evoni hurried from her office. She didn't want to chance anyone stopping by.

Evoni pulled up to the tall glass building housing Tim's office. Thankfully there was street parking a block away. Evoni parked and hustled inside the building. At security she gave her name and was ushered into an elevator that placed her outside Tim's office right on time.

Tim's receptionist spotted Evoni and buzzed her in. The offices were quite opulent. It was clear Tim and his partners were doing pretty well for themselves.

The receptionist escorted Evoni to a conference room where she found Marc and Tim sitting, both with a tumbler of brown liquid. Evoni doubted it was tea.

Tim got up and greeted Evoni with a hug. "Evoni, glad you could make it. I was just catching Marc up on what's happened since we last spoke. Would you like something to drink? I can have Manny bring you water, tea, coffee, wine or what we're having."

"After a day like today, I think I'll have a glass of what you're having."

"Good, that means Manny can work on getting the food order in. I hope you don't mind Mama Bee's. That woman's food is like manna from heaven."

Evoni laughed. Should she tell Tim Mama Bee was her godmother? *Nah. I'll wait until some other time and treat him to a meal there and surprise him.* "I love Mama Bee's."

"Great. Manny, please take care of that and afterwards you can leave for the evening."

"Yes, Mr. Blankenship. I'll inform security to escort the delivery person up when they arrive. Goodnight, everyone," stated Manny as he closed the conference room door.

After Manny's departure, Tim brought Evoni up to speed on what information he'd provided Marc. Marc sat quietly during the exchange but spoke up soon after.

"First off, I want to thank you both for what you are doing for me and for believing in me. Since this whole saga began, I've been pretty much shell-shocked and barely able to function. That ends here tonight. I refuse to be the scapegoat for a crime I didn't commit and risk losing my children, my livelihood, and my freedom. Screw that. Whatever I can do to get out of this mess and back to my life, tell me and I'll do it."

Evoni and Tim looked at Marc and smiled. It was good to see Marc ready to fight back. He'd need every bit of that fight to win this battle.

They worked on strategy until they were interrupted by the door buzzer. It was the delivery man with dinner. While Tim went to collect the food, Evoni asked Marc how his boys were doing.

"You know, Evoni, my boys have shown me what it means to be strong. Though they are hurting over the loss of their mother and trying to come to grips with the idea that they may lose their father; they have been my rocks. Without them I don't think I would be able to do this. Of course, Kanisha has been a blessing. The boys have come quite attached to her and to be honest so have I in a way."

Evoni noticed Marc's eyes light up when he mentioned Kanisha. *So, I was right*, thought Evoni. There was something there. Evoni just hoped they waited until this mess was over before pursuing it.

"That's great to hear Marc. You'll need all the support you can get during this time. In fact, my good friend, Bri, who brought me the information regarding the motivation of the police, is interested in helping in any way she can. You have a lot of people in your corner."

Tim walked in with the food at that moment. "I couldn't help but to hear the last part of that. Your friend Bri, she's in a relationship with Harold Williams, right?"

"Yes."

"Well, in that case, Marc, I say let her help. Harold is a powerful man in Nashville, hell one of the most powerful in the country. Having his resources and network at our disposal would be beneficial."

"Well, I don't know how much of Harold's assistance we'll have but Bri is smart and resourceful even without Harold's connections and money; though they could come in handy."

"Evoni, I am just grateful your friend wants to help. I will take all the assistance I can get. After all, this is my life we're talking about."

"That's settled then, Bri is now part of the team. Now, Evoni, I don't have to remind you she can't be privy to any attorney-client privileged communications."

"Of course not. You know me better than that. I would never jeopardize a client."

"I know, but it always bears repeating. Now that that is out of the way, let's dig into this food and then get back to strategizing. I'm expecting an arrest warrant to come out soon, and I want to be prepared."

For the next two hours, they ate and worked. Feeling sleep coming on, Evoni decided it was time to wrap up. Tim and Marc agreed. There wasn't too much more they could do anyway, not until they had a better idea of the evidence the D.A.'s office had against Marc and whether he'd be arrested. Because it was looking more and more likely, an arrest would take place. Tim suggested Marc have a relative come to town to stay with the boys. Marc agreed to call his Aunt Abby, who lived in Memphis and have her come up the following day.

Evoni made it home twenty-five minutes later and found herself too wired to sleep; she texted Bri and let her know she was now a part of the Save Marc team. Evoni told her to meet her at her apartment Thursday evening to discuss next steps. Then she went to take a shower.

Emerging from the shower, Evoni felt refreshed and decided to get some work done. Taking a quick glance at her phone, she saw Bri had texted back. Bri was all in and joked that she never imagined she'd be the one doing the saving, she thought that was for captains and hos. Evoni chuckled, leave it to Bri to find the humor in this situation.

The next two days went by quickly, fortunately no arrest warrant was issued but Evoni figured it was imminent. By the end of the day on Thursday, Evoni was more than ready to go. As rewarding as family law was, it was also mentally and emotionally draining. Some days Evoni wanted to give up, but she knew she would miss it.

There was a knock on Evoni's office door. "Hey, Ms. Singleton. You about ready to head out? If so, I can place the order for the sushi."

"Oh Mari, I almost forgot. Bri will be coming over tonight." Evoni quickly filled Mari in on what she'd learned from Bri regarding the police's motivation for going after Marc. "So, if you'd rather we reschedule, I'm okay with that. Though I'm sure Bri will have quite a few thoughts on what she wants for a shower and bachelorette party."

Mari spoke up. "If you don't mind, I would still like to come over. We can go ahead and run some ideas by Bri, and I'd really like to help Marc out anyway I can."

"Are you sure? You know this isn't a firm case, so you are under no obligation to assist," stated Evoni.

"Yes, I'm sure. I told you; I don't believe Marc killed Jessica and I would love to help prove that he didn't."

"Okay, we can use all the help we can get, and you have a great legal mind. You could give a few of the lawyers around here a run for their money."

Mari smiled brightly. She looked up to Evoni and aspired to be like her, so such high praise meant a lot to Mari. "It's settled then. I will place the order for the sushi and then head out. I'm thinking of getting a variety of rolls and nigiri, miso soup and maybe a bottle of sake."

"That works for me. Just make sure you get eel and red snapper. Bri will be joining us tonight and those are the only types of sushi she eats. Oh, and add a bottle of sparkling sake."

Mari laughed. "It'll be great to see Bri. I'll make sure I get those in both nigiri and rolls. See you in a few," stated Mari while closing Evoni's door.

Evoni quickly packed up her stuff. She texted Bri to let her know she was heading out and would be home within forty-five minutes. Bri responded she was on her way and would meet her at her house.

Roughly fifty minutes later, Evoni spotted Bri's car parked on the street in front of her house. Evoni pushed the button to raise her garage and pulled in. Once her car was in, both Bri and Mari pulled into her driveway and parked.

Bri jumped out of her car and hugged Mari. "Mari, I didn't know you would be here. You're part of the team too? This is awesome. I can't wait to solve this mystery." Mari laughed and hugged Bri back. Bri's enthusiasm was contagious, and Mari found herself getting excited.

"Alright, Velma and Daphne, can you both get in here so we can eat and get down to business? I'd like to get to bed at a respectable hour tonight and I'm starving."

Both ladies laughed and headed into the house. Both knew Evoni could be mean when she was hangry.

Once in the house, Evoni got out plates and glasses. Once everyone had food and a drink, they got down to business, with the first order being discussion of Bri's engagement party, bachelorette party and bridal shower. Better to take care of the fun stuff first before digging into murder.

After an hour and a half of discussing flower arrangements, décor and acceptable catering options, Evoni decided to steer the conversation to Marc's dilemma. "Ok ladies, now that we have Bri's marching orders on how to plan the perfect wedding events for her, let's talk about Marc. Let's brainstorm ways to assist in getting him out of this predicament."

With that announcement, Bri reached into her bag. Evoni and Mari burst out laughing.

"What in the world is that?" questioned Evoni.

"What's so funny?" retorted Bri. "Every great detective wears one of these. You ladies would know that if you watched crime and mystery shows like me," stated Bri while placing her fedora on her head.

It took Mari and Evoni another minute to stop laughing. Bri was just too much. She was the definition of extra, but that's why they loved her. "Okay, Dick Tracy. Now can we get started?" quipped Evoni.

"Make fun all you want but when I solve this case, you'll be apologizing for doubting the luck of the fedora."

"I'm sure we will," said Mari with a grin. "Now, Evoni, what can we do to help?"

Evoni went on to fill in Mari on the recent developments. Mari was livid. "How dare they not even look for another suspect?" she squawked. "I know they think they have a good case against Marc but whatever happened to not having tunnel vision and seeking the truth?"

Evoni and Bri looked at each other. It was good to see Mari's outrage but they both knew just how unjust the so-called justice system could be. They'd watch countless videos of unarmed black men and women being killed by the police and the police suffering no consequences. They'd seen innocent black men exonerated after spending decades in prison for a crime they hadn't committed. They knew not every cop was bad, but doing nothing to stop the corrupt, bad cops made them complicit.

"That's why we're here, Mari, to stop this travesty from happening. Jails and prisons may not be packed with innocent men, but we do know there are times when there are such miscarriages of justice. We are here to make sure that doesn't happen to Marc."

Mari sighed loudly. "I'm sorry for my outburst. I know this isn't the first time nor will it be the last time an innocent man will face prison. I also know this isn't new or even the worst thing the police have done. As a bi-racial black woman who can pass for white dating a black man, I know the injustices he faces on a daily basis. I'm not naïve, but I guess I just hadn't thought about just how broken our justice system is. I never imagined they'd do the same to a wealthy white man."

"Believe me when I say we get it. It's never easy to see that the people who are supposed to serve and protect have no interest in actually doing that," stated Bri. "Marc is lucky. He has the means to hire a good attorney and he has a team of people with access to money and resources fighting for him. Most people aren't so lucky. Maybe after we clear Marc, we can all work together to keep this from happening to others. We can call ourselves *The Justice Sisters*," Bri said with a smile.

"I like that," stated Mari. "Okay, Evoni, you're our fearless leader, tell us what we can do to help."

"Well, Tim, Marc and I discussed the best course of action; something that will hopefully not end with us in handcuffs. First off, Bri, unlike Mari who has privileged status due to working with me on Marc's custody case, you aren't covered by attorney-client privilege. I can only discuss generalities with you as of right now."

"You know, I've seen on TV where, the lawyer hires a third party as a private detective, thus giving them privilege protection, can't we do that here?"

"Bri, I don't watch much TV but I'm sure those people are licensed private detectives and last I looked, you only have a hat, not a license."

Bri rolled her eyes. "Whatever, I was just asking."

"I know you were," said Evoni. "But for now, this is the way things have to be to protect Marc."

"I know, I know and I'm sorry for being a baby. Okay, so what are we going to do?"

Evoni looked between Mari and Bri. She really hoped nothing they found out would put either of them in danger. She would never forgive herself. "So, I was thinking, since you have the gift of gab, Bri, that we could pay a visit to the motel where Jessica was found and see if anyone saw anything."

"Oooh, I like it. I can see it now- I'll sweet talk the creepy motel manager and try to get a peek at the guestbook and maybe a key to the room where Jessica was found. This is going to be fun." Bri's eyes lit up like Times Square.

Evoni laughed lightly. "I'd like to say that's not what we're going to do because you look way too excited about it, but it is. We need to see if anyone else was at the motel that could be a suspect."

"What if the motel manager isn't a creepy man?" questioned Mari.

Thinking out loud, Bri stated, "If it's a woman, I bet she'll take a bribe. If she's working at a motel, I'm sure she could use a little extra cash or maybe a cute Burberry bag. What woman would say no to that?"

"Whoa, I can't be a part of any bribery scheme, so let's put that on the backburner. Mari, if it's a woman, we'll try to appeal to her emotional, maternal side. If that doesn't work, well, we could always club her over the head and steal the key," joked Evoni.

"Isn't that grand, you denounce bribery but are okay with battery. I'm beginning to rethink how good of a lawyer you are," teased Bri.

Evoni leaned over and playfully punched Bri in the shoulder. "Whatever, dork, you know I was joking. We'll improvise once we see what we're working with."

"Okay," piped in Mari. "What happens if we find out there was someone else suspicious at the motel? Are we going to tell the police?"

"No," stated Evoni. "Tim and I discussed this, and we think it's best we keep our investigation as secret as possible. Just because we find someone else who could be a suspect, it doesn't mean the police will listen to us or investigate and it won't clear Marc. No, to do that, we will have to find direct proof that someone else is responsible. I wanna stress, this could get a little tricky. I don't anticipate any danger as I have no interest in confronting a potential murderer, but there is an off chance the real killer could be watching to make sure he or she gets away. We need to be extra vigilant and careful. And feel free to back out now, I'll understand."

Both Bri and Mari stared at Evoni. Neither had really given much consideration to the potential of danger, even though they were looking to solve a murder.

Bri spoke first. "Coffy doesn't back out or run from anyone. I'm still in and I have a concealed carry license."

Evoni smiled and squeezed Bri's hand. There was never any doubt in her mind Bri friend would be all in. Nothing scared her. But Evoni feared what Harold would do if he found out Bri was out investigating a murder. She'd have to have a talk with Bri about that once they were alone.

"I'm also still in," stated Mari. "I'm no Coffy, whoever that is, but I have a mean left hook and a stiletto my grandma left me that I carry everywhere with me."

"Well, I guess that settles it. *The Justice Sisters* are official. And Mari, when this is over, we're sitting you down to watch some blaxploitation films." All three ladies lifted their wine glasses and toasted to *The Justice Sisters*.

Deciding to visit the Sunny Day Motel Saturday morning, instead of the following night as they expected it to be busy with patrons on a Friday night; the ladies broke out the sparkling sake and continued discussing strategies for getting information from the motel manager and housekeeping.

CHAPTER 25

Bri

Bri awoke with a start on Saturday morning. Today was the day. With Harold out of town on business, she wouldn't have to fib to him about where she was heading.

Bri's first order of business was finding the right outfit. What would a lady version of Sherlock Holmes wear?

After twenty minutes in her closet, Bri had the perfect outfit. A black hi-low zippered blazer jacket by Cushnie, with a pair of black Re/Done High Rise Ankle Crop Jeans along with her red Giuseppe Zanotti zippered boots. A girl had to have a little color.

Once dressed, Bri quickly ate a yogurt and a banana...breakfast of champions. Bri felt something rare as she ate...nervous. She hoped they learned something to help Marc and she really, really hoped she didn't screw up her part of the mission.

The ladies agreed to meet at Evoni's house and take one car to the motel. Bri hoped Evoni had coffee, because she didn't have time to stop for a cup if she didn't want to be late.

When Bri arrived, she noticed Mari's car already parked in Evoni's driveway. She pulled in beside her. As she was exiting, Evoni and Mari came out of Evoni's house. Bri noticed the coffee in Evoni's hand and smiled.

"I knew I could count on you," Bri said while reaching for one of the cups in Evoni's hands."

"Dang, can I get a good morning and a hug first?" joked Evoni.

"Girl, I am in need of this. I was running a bit late this morning and didn't have time to stop to grab a cup but because you are the bestest friend ever, I just knew you would have coffee for me, and I was right."

"Because you recognize how awesome of a best friend I am, you are forgiven. Now take your coffee and let's go. By the way, I will be borrowing those boots at some point, just an FYI."

Bri laughed. "You know you are welcome to anything in my closet just as long as you sign the contract."

Mari looked at Bri quizzically. "What kind of contract?"

"Girl, Bri had me draft a wardrobe borrowing contract years ago. It basically states that if you stain, ruin, lose or don't return any garment borrowed, you will either replace said garment or reimburse Bri the purchase price."

"I guess I won't be asking to borrow anything from you. I know I can't afford to replace anything in your closet," joked Mari. "I'll just stick to buying knock-off designs at Zara."

All three ladies laughed.

"Hey, before I had Evoni draw up the contract, I had a lot of girlfriends who developed amnesia and forgot my phone number and address when it came time to return items. And I'm not running a charity for cheap bitches."

"Okay, ladies, let's get this show on the road. Who knows what time this 'No-Tel Motel' gets busy. I'd prefer not to be seen there by anyone who knows me," stated Evoni.

"Girl, if you run into anyone who knows you at this place, believe me, they won't be sharing that information with anyone. From what I read online; the customers are the type who rent rooms by the hour," remarked Bri.

"Be that as it may, I would still prefer not to be seen anywhere near the place, lest people think I'm engaged in nefarious activity. I may not get along with my mother, but I don't want to give her a heart attack."

"Oooh boy, yes, Mrs. Gloria would keel right over. Maybe you should wear a disguise," Bri jested.

"Believe me, I thought about it. Anyway, let's get going. Mari, do you mind if we take your car?"

Mari saw no problem with that, and the ladies piled in and headed off. The drive to the motel took about twenty minutes. Once there, Evoni asked Mari to park as close as possible to the entrance. No need to risk any unnecessary exposure.

Once parked, the ladies exited the car and headed towards the entrance. The building was a typical two-story motel layout. Though surprisingly, it didn't look as decrepit on the outside as Evoni had imagined. However, she could see it resembling the hang out of drug addicts within the next year or two if the owner didn't spruce things up.

The lobby, if you could call it a lobby, consisted of the registration desk, one lone chair with torn fabric, and a coffee machine that looked like it hadn't been washed since 1975. Looking around, they failed to notice anyone behind the registration desk. Because the lobby was so small, Evoni suggested she and Mari wait outside while Bri tried to get information from the attendant, whomever it may be. If she didn't succeed, either Evoni or Mari would try.

Wishing Bri good luck, Evoni and Mari left and went back to the car where they scanned the area for any unsavory characters.

Once they were gone, Bri took a deep breath and mumbled to herself, "Showtime." Bri rang the bell on the desk and waited for someone to come out. Thirty seconds later, Bri was shocked and speechless. Standing in front of her, was a real deal drag queen.

"Don't look so shocked honey. If you keep looking at me like that, it may start affecting my self-esteem and have me second guessing this little number," she said while twirling.

With that, Bri couldn't help but to laugh. "Honey, you are fabulous. You just took me by surprise."

"Good. For a second there I figured you'd never seen a man in a dress. This is Nashville after all."

"Oh no, I love a good drag queen. I'm a *RuPaul's Drag Race* superfan. And may I say, you look like you should be auditioning for the show. Baby, you are everything. The hair, the makeup, the dress, all of it makes me feel less than a woman," jested Bri.

"Oh, baby girl, even in that simple outfit, you're a ten. And I am loving those boots. Balenciaga?"

"No, Giuseppe."

"Yes, queen," she said with three snaps. "I suppose we should introduce ourselves. I'm Cinnamon Bunz, with a Z."

"Nice to meet you, Cinnamon. I'm Bri." Bri stuck her hand out for a handshake.

"Forgive me if I don't shake your hand, I'm a bit of a germaphobe. Of course, you can't tell with me working in this dump, but I am."

"No worries, I'm not the biggest fan of touching or being touched by strangers."

"Now, I know you aren't at this dump for a room. So, what can I do for you?"

"You are correct, I am most definitely not here for a room. I was actually looking to speak to someone regarding the murder that took place here recently."

"You a reporter or something? I know you're not a cop."

"I could lie to you and say yes, but I like you and you seem like a straight shooter, so I'll tell you truth. Hopefully you'll be inclined to help me."

Bri launched into the story on Marc as a suspect in the murder. Finishing up, she waited for Cinnamon's reaction. She didn't have to wait long.

"Ooohhh, girl. You are out here living a real-life episode of *Jessica Jones*. How exciting. Because you were straight with me and because I think you are fabulous, I'll keep it real with you."

Bri held up her finger. "Before you continue, I have friends waiting outside. Do you mind if they come in and hear what you have to say?"

"Not at all. Honey, this way you won't have to play a game of telephone, and everyone can hear it straight from the horse's- or rather the queen's mouth."

Bri hurried outside to find Evoni and Mari. Within minutes, all three were huddled around Cinnamon. Once Evoni and Mari got over the initial shock of seeing a drag queen standing in front of them, Cinnamon launched into her story.

She left them all speechless. Jessica French was a frequent visitor to the motel. Cinnamon remembered at least six occasions where she had checked her and a gentleman in. The same gentleman. The gentleman was a stocky older white guy with a small gap between his front teeth. He was known to all the ladies from his ridiculous commercials. The gentleman was none other than Hank Dupree, owner of three local used car dealerships. Anyone that owns a television has seen his obnoxious commercials. He's loud, brash, and cocky. And more importantly, he's the son of Nashville's oldest city councilman, George Dupree.

"Why would someone like Hank Dupree come here?" asked Mari. "No offense, Cinnamon."

"None taken, girl. I know this place ain't much. The only reason I work here is because it's owned by my uncle, and he lets me work whatever hours I want which allows for me to do shows locally and out of state. But to answer your question, I think it's precisely that reason why people like Hank come here. Most people who stay here are either visitors or not so upstanding residents. It's a place where no one wants to be noticed and everyone tends to mind their own business. You'd be surprised just how many so-called upstanding citizens frequent this motel and others like it. It affords them the anonymity that the local more upscale hotels can't."

"I think the better question is what was he doing with Jessica French? Was it an extra-marital affair or something else?" pondered Evoni.

"Funny, you should ask that. Though they came here frequently, I didn't really get the vibe they were sleeping together."

"This gets curiouser and curiouser," stated Bri.

"You're right about that," said Evoni. "Cinnamon, you're sure Jessica was here with Hank the night she was murdered?"

"Yep," affirmed Cinnamon. "I remember because they checked in right as my shift was ending and my replacement, Taylor, was running late, which annoyed me because I had a show to get ready for. I will say when they arrived, the lady, Jessica, didn't seem herself. She's usually upbeat and smiling, but that day she was rather subdued and had a look of defeat about her. I remember thinking maybe she had lost a loved one because she looked really, really sad."

"Did you tell the police any of this?" queried Evoni.

"I wasn't here when they initially interviewed everyone, but a young patrol officer followed up with me the following day. I tried to tell him, but he wasn't really interested. He just showed me a picture of another man and kept asking me if I'd seen him here at any point. I told him I hadn't."

Evoni pulled out her phone and pulled up Marc's company's website. Is this the man the officer showed you?"

"Yes, that him. I'm guessing he's the ex? Cops always have a hard-on for the spouse or ex."

"You'd guess right," stated Evoni.

"When's Taylor set to work next? Do you think she would speak with us?" queried Evoni.

Cinnamon responded. "Taylor is set to work this evening and Monday morning. But she's not the most reliable person. She often calls in sick, and someone else has to cover her shift. To be honest, I think she may be on something, but my uncle refuses to believe me. He thinks she's just searching for herself," stated Cinnamon with air quotes. "She's a grown ass woman over the age of thirty."

"Hmm, okay, so she's flaky and a possible addict of some kind. That's good to know. I know you can't give out employee information, but maybe you can give us a call next time she's here?"

"That I can do."

After picking Cinnamon's brain for any additional details, Bri asked if it was possible to see the room where Jessica's demise occurred.

Cinnamon warned them that the room had since been cleaned, though she wasn't sure how thoroughly, as the maid service was questionable at best. She went and retrieved the room key and directed the ladies to the room. Before they left, Cinnamon informed them that the room hadn't been rented out since the murder. Firstly, because it was a crime scene and then because apparently no one wanted to sleep in a bed where someone had been murdered, or rather knowingly murdered.

When they reached the room, there was still a piece of crime scene tape floating on the railing. Even with the knowledge that the room was empty, they still were a little unnerved entering a room where someone had been killed. Even though there would be no obvious signs, it was still a bit much.

The room looked exactly like every other cheap motel room they'd seen on TV. Bri was a little disappointed. The carpet was brown shag. There was one double bed with an atrocious brown and green comforter, a nightstand with a lamp and an old clock radio. Across from the bed was a console holding an ancient television. A door to the left of the bed contained a minimalist bathroom with a tub/shower combo, a toilet, and a sink with a mirror over it. It all looked so...ordinary.

Bri and Evoni caught Mari staring at the bed. It seemed it was finally hitting her that someone had died there. It was a sobering thought. After a few more seconds of silence, Evoni got them into action. "Bri, you take the nightstand and console. Mari, you take the bathroom and I'll take the bedroom floor and bed. Let's see if we can find anything."

Bri took one look at the furnishings and wished she'd brought disposable gloves. Thank God she was up to date on her tetanus shot.

After about ten minutes of fruitless searching, they gave up. It was clear there was nothing in the room that would help them.

Feeling a little disappointed, they headed back to Mari's car. Bri stopped and asked them to wait a quick second. She hurried into the office and returned a few minutes later.

As they were leaving, Mari asked her why she'd gone back to the office.

"Well, for one I wanted to thank Cinnamon for her help again and I also wanted to get her drag show schedule. I would love to attend a show. Maybe even bring Harold along. I think he'd get a kick out of it."

"I can picture Harold now, looking every bit the conservative older gentleman, whooping and hollering and making it rain on drag queens," clowned Evoni. They all laughed at that image.

Mari spoke up. "Well, if you do go, let me know. I've never seen a drag show and would love to go."

"Me too," said Evoni. "I love *RuPaul's Drag Race,* but I've never seen a drag show live."

"It's settled then, once we catch the psycho that killed Jessica and save Marc, the first order of business will be a drag show."

For the duration of the ride back to Evoni's, the ladies discussed next steps. They all agreed they needed to speak with Hank. He could be the killer or the last person to see Jessica alive. The question was how best to approach him.

By the time they pulled into Evoni's driveway, Bri had an idea. The Annual Nashville Chamber of Commerce business leaders' event was happening in a couple of days; no way would a schmoozing, used car salesman miss it. Bri was sure she could still get tickets as Harold was invited every year but rarely attended. She'd call the Chamber of Commerce Monday morning and inquire.

With a next step in place, the three ladies bid adieu and headed their respective ways. Evoni had work to do. Mari was meeting Kevin for a late lunch and Bri was going had a spa date with her sister Aiden.

CHAPTER 26

Evoni

Evoni was startled awake; her cellphone was ringing incessantly. Reaching over and grabbing it off the nightstand, she answered groggily.

"What assholes!" Evoni screamed into the phone. On the phone was Tim, the police had arrested Marc earlier that morning. And by early, he meant around 3 am. Thankfully Marc's aunt had arrived and was there to look after the boys who were hysterical.

"They knew exactly what they were doing. They knew with it being the weekend, there was no way Marc would be eligible to go before a judge and request bail before Monday."

"Evoni, we both knew this was most likely coming and I'm mad as hell, too. Right now, I'm leaving the jail. I've spoken with Marc and surprisingly, he's doing okay. I think we really prepared him for this over the last few weeks. He followed our instructions and didn't speak to the detectives without me. I've told him in no way should he say anything to any other inmates. Hopefully, he follows that instruction."

Evoni silently agreed with Tim. Too often, the accused were informed on by jailhouse snitches looking for a break in their own cases, whether what they said was true or made up, the prosecutor rarely asked or cared. As long as it helped them get a conviction.

Tim asked Evoni to swing by and check on Marc's house. Evoni agreed. There wasn't much they could do for Marc on a Sunday.

Luckily, Marc was a wealthy man, so if they could get bail, there wouldn't be an issue paying.

Evoni got dressed and headed out. Upon reaching Marc's house, she noticed a never-before-seen car in the drive; must be Marc's Aunt Abby's. When she reached the door, she could hear yelling coming from inside. Evoni hesitated to ring the bell, unsure if she wanted to walk into what sounded like World War Three.

Startling Evoni, the door opened suddenly and out stormed Marc's oldest son, Ashton. Evoni quickly moved out of the way to avoid being run over. Before the door could close, Evoni stepped into the house. The yelling had stopped and now it was eerily quiet. Evoni looked around and didn't see anyone. Not wanting to startle anyone, she called out. "Hello, anyone home? It's Evoni Singleton, one of Marc's attorneys."

A few seconds later, Evoni heard a reply. "Coming."

Emerging from upstairs was an older woman. Evoni assumed she was Marc's Aunt Abby.

"Hello, dear. Did I hear you say you're a lawyer? I'm Abby, Marc's aunt on his mother's side."

"Hi, nice to meet you. Yes, I'm Evoni Singleton. I was Marc's family law attorney and now I'm assisting his criminal defense attorney with this current matter," Evoni stated while holding out her hand.

Abby ignored her offered hand and came in for a hug, taking Evoni by surprise but she gave her a quick hug back.

"Sorry, I'm a hugger and anyone who's trying to help my Marc is family to me."

Abby steered Evoni towards the kitchen and asked if she'd like anything to drink. "Though I'm not familiar with some of these gadgets. What happened to good old-fashioned teapots and coffee makers? Now everything has a million buttons and requires a degree in computers to understand," complained Abby.

Evoni smiled at the small rant. She was used to hearing older people complain about new gadgets, her father was one of the worst. "How about I fix us both a cup of tea? I know Marc has a delicious ginger turmeric blend."

"That would be wonderful. Thank you," replied Abby. "I know I sound like an old fart complaining about gadgets but some days I just want simplicity."

"Believe me, I understand," said Evoni. "All the new technology which is constantly changing can be a bit much. There's software at the office that I can't seem to grasp no matter how many times the IT guy shows me how to use it."

"Well, that makes me feel a little better," Abby stated with a slight chuckle.

While Evoni prepared the tea, Abby asked her why she had stopped by.

"Tim, Marc's criminal attorney, called me and told me about the arrest. Though I am Marc's family law attorney, I've been involved in this criminal matter since it began. I thought I'd stop by and check on Marc's sons and you, see how you were holding up. I hope that isn't an issue?"

"Oh, of course not. I'm glad you stopped by. I'm not sure if you heard the yelling or saw Ashton storm out of here, but it has been a rather trying morning. It would be good to talk to someone who's involved."

"I did see Ashton leave. He seemed very upset."

"Yes, he's been yelling and throwing things since his father's arrest. He's angry, which I don't blame him for, and that anger has manifested itself in a temper tantrum of sorts. He became extremely upset when I told him we had to wait until his father was arraigned and a bail set before he could be brought home and that that wouldn't happen until Monday at the earliest. On top of that, I think he blames himself for what happened to his mother."

"What? Why would he think he played a part in what happened to her? It's sad to say, but Jessica was a deeply disturbed woman with demons she hadn't conquered. Ashton shouldn't feel like any of this is his fault because it isn't."

"Ms. Singleton, I've spent a lot of time around children. Though I never had any of my own, I helped my sister raise Marc after his father passed away and later took him in when his she passed. I've spent well over twenty years volunteering at various homeless shelters for teens. And one thing I can tell you is that they always blame themselves when there's an issue in the home. Kids are tough and resilient, but they also internalize their emotions and hide their pain. Jessica's drug use and abandonment for days at a time are harrowing experiences, even for a fourteen-year-old."

Evoni stayed quiet. Abby was right, that was a lot for a teenager to deal with. Evoni knew from researching Jessica for the custody hearing, that she often left the boys alone and that Ashton covered for her instead of telling Marc. Keeping secrets like that and watching his mother spiral out of control was enough trauma for years of therapy.

The two ladies sat quietly sipping their tea for a few minutes. "Ms. Singleton, may I call you Evoni?"

"Of course, yes."

"Thank you and feel free to call me Abby. Evoni, be completely honest with me. What are the odds Marc will be convicted for killing Jessica? She was a despicable human being, even in the beginning, I knew she was no good for him. But Marc loved her and despite all that has happened and all the hell she put him through, I know with all my heart that he would never hurt her. Marc's a gentle soul."

"Abby, I can tell you I believe with every fiber of my being that Marc is innocent, and we are doing everything we can to make sure he doesn't end up in prison for something he didn't do. With that being said, it won't be easy. We have our work cut out for us. With no accurate time of death, it's almost impossible to give Marc an alibi, and the cops are convinced they have their man. They aren't going to look for anyone else. We will have to find another viable suspect and bring it out at trial, or we will have to prove unequivocally that Marc couldn't be the killer."

Abby sighed loudly. "It sounds like we've got our work cut out for us. Tell me, what can I do to help? And don't ask me to sit idly by while my nephew, who's more like a son to me, is railroaded and carted off to prison."

Evoni couldn't help but think that if she ever got into trouble, she hoped she'd have as many people wanting to help her. Marc was a lucky man.

"Abby, you can help right now by giving me a bit more background on Jessica and Marc's relationship, there may be something useful."

"I don't know where to start. As Marc's attorney, I'm sure you know the basics and how they got together."

"Yes, but I'd like to get your impressions of Jessica and their relationship. It seems you didn't like her from the beginning, why was that?"

"Well, I'm sure you know, Jessica didn't come from the most stable home life."

Evoni debated telling Abby what she had learned about Jessica. Including the fact, that she wasn't an orphan, but she had been a suspect in the untimely demise of her family in a fire. Evoni decided to hold that information back for now.

Abby continued. "When Marc first brought Jessica round, we tried to give her a chance and by that, I mean his grandmother, Dorothy, and I. But Jessica was hard to like. I could see why Marc took a liking to her. She was gorgeous and a few years younger than Marc. She would put on a good show for Marc when he was in the room, the sweet, gentle southern girl but the minute Marc turned his back she either ignored us or made snide comments. Neither Marc's grandmother nor I thought the relationship would last, so we didn't say anything to Marc. Unfortunately, we were wrong, not six months after they began dating, Marc proposed. We were livid."

"Did you ever tell Marc about Jessica's behavior?"

"No, we didn't. I wanted to, badly, but Dorothy was afraid of losing Marc. She could see how smitten he was and wasn't sure he'd take our word over Jessica's. We held our tongues and let things progress. Only now, I wish I had said something and then Marc wouldn't be in this situation," stated Abby, her voice thick with emotion.

"You can't blame yourself. You did what you believed was right at the time. You had no way of knowing what a tragic outcome there would ultimately be."

"Dear, my rational mind knows you're right, but my conscience won't let me stop thinking it."

Evoni understood the feeling. That internal conflict within all of us, even when we know we had no control over a situation, it doesn't stop us from wondering "what if."

"Is there anything else you remember about Jessica?"

"There's not much that sticks out. After the wedding, I rarely saw her. Either she refused to come visit us, or Marc could sense we didn't particularly care for her, because we only saw her a few times after that. Marc would visit us alone or with the boys after they were born, but never with Jessica. We were grateful."

"Did Marc ever mention any problems he and Jessica were having?"

"Not in detail, there were a few occasions where he made a few offhand comments that gave me the impression things weren't great. But he never explicitly went into any problems. In the last year or so before the divorce, Marc began coming down more frequently, sometimes with the boys, others without. Sometimes he'd stay as long as a week, when in the past it was never more than a weekend."

Evoni wondered if that was when Jessica's drug problem first began. Though Marc said he never knew about the drugs prior to the divorce; otherwise, he would never have allowed Jessica custody. Maybe he was in denial or maybe it wasn't drugs at that time but something else. Evoni made a mental note to check into Jessica's friends and acquaintances from around that time.

The two women paused conversation when they heard a noise. They heard a door open and then feet running up the stairs. "I guess Ashton is back. I suppose I should go check on him and Caleb. Caleb was napping but could be awake by now."

Evoni took that as her cue to leave. It seemed Abby had everything under control. But Evoni would give Kanisha a call and ask her to stop by and check in on Ashton.

After leaving Marc's house, Evoni decided to stop by her parent's place. She was hoping her mother was still at church. Evoni wasn't in the mood for another lecture on her love life. She just really needed to see her father. It had been a few weeks and Evoni missed him. She was a daddy's girl through and through.

To her surprise, when Evoni pulled up to her parent's house, she spotted her brothers' cars. Evoni was excited to see them but knew she would be in for a lecture, as she hadn't spoken to them since before the breakup with Amar and Evoni knew there was no way her mother hadn't told them about the breakup.

As expected, as soon as she walked through the door, she was accosted by her brothers.

"Okay, before we get into the Spanish Inquisition, can I say hello to our father?" Evoni queried.

"Fine," said Devon, the oldest of the three triplets by mere minutes. "But we expect a full accounting of what happened with you and Amar. We got Mom's version, but we know she has a bias as she's always loved Amar. We want to hear what happened from you. And then we'll decide if we need to give him a good old fashioned beatdown."

Evoni shook her head and rolled her eyes slightly. "Devon, no one is giving anyone any type of beatdown, no matter how tempting it sounds. I will meet you guys in the back by the pool but first let me talk to Daddy."

Evoni found her father in the kitchen cooking up a storm.

"Um, it sure does smell good in here."

Evoni's father turned around with a big grin on his face. "There's my baby girl. Come on over here and give your father a hug. It seems like it's been forever since I laid eyes on you."

Feeling guilty, Evoni gave her father a big, long hug. She would have to work on being a better daughter. Of course, she'd stop by more if her mother wasn't such a pain. But that was no excuse for not coming to see her father.

"I'm sorry, Daddy. I know it's been a while since I stopped by. There's no excuse, I'll try to do better."

Wrapping his thick arms around her, Evoni's father gave her a kiss on the forehead. "Baby girl, I know you're busy with work and your relationship with your mother isn't the best. I'm not trying to make you feel guilty, I just miss you, that's all."

"I know, Daddy, but I promise to try and do better. Speaking of my mother, she's not here, right?"

"No, she's still at the church helping the First Lady plan an upcoming Women in Ministry event. Why do you think I'm in here cooking lunch?"

Evoni laughed. "Oh, Daddy, please, you and I both know my mother doesn't like to cook. Speaking of cooking, where is Rosa Lee?"

Rosa Lee had been the family's cook-cum-maid for years. She was like a second mother to Evoni and one she liked a helluva lot more than the real one.

"She has the week off. She's gone off to California to visit her son and her grandkids."

"That's wonderful. I know it's hard for her being so far from her son."

"Enough about Rosa Lee, how are you?" questioned her father. I'm sure it's been hard after what that scum, Amar, put you through."

Surprisingly, because she'd been so busy with Marc's case, Evoni hadn't thought of Amar very much over the last couple of weeks.

"Daddy, I'm fine. I'm just glad I found out Amar wasn't the man for me before I married him. I can say I dodged a bullet."

"Damn straight you did. And if I ever see the bastard, I have a few words for him and maybe a few other things too," her father said emphatically.

Uh-oh, thought Evoni, fearing a hike in her father's blood pressure, she quickly changed the subject. "So, what you got cooking? It smells delicious."

Her father was an excellent cook, having gotten his start in the military. He'd taken numerous classes over the years and often created new recipes with Mama Bee.

Evoni went to raise the top on a pot and felt her hand being slapped away. "No peeking. You'll have to stay for lunch to see what culinary delights I've whipped up. Now go talk to your brothers. They've been steaming since they found out about you and Amar. Hopefully, you can set them at ease or give them a good reason to kick his no-good butt. Honestly, either works for me."

Evoni laughed and threw a dish towel at her father. "Daddy, stop it. You are the most non-violent person I know. You won't even kill a spider."

"I may not be willing to kill a spider, but I damn sure will shoot a snake. Now, scoot."

Evoni laughed and went to find her brothers.

Evoni located the triplets lounging by the pool, discussing the only thing on the mind of twenty-five-year-olds...women.

Startling her brothers, Evoni spoke up. "I hope those names are of women you guys are dating and not doing drive-bys on."

"Drive-bys? What do you know about drive-bys?" questioned Keyshon.

"Don't get it twisted little brother, your sister isn't as old as you think I am. Now who are these young ladies you guys were just referring to as hotter than the desert on a summer day?"

All three triplets looked shame-faced and quickly changed the subject. Devon spoke up first. "None of that is important, what is important is what that punk Amar did to you. We need details, sis."

"Yeah," piped in Keyshon and Jalon. "We need details, so we can know what kind of beatdown he deserves."

"As previously stated, no one is giving anyone a beat down. This is between me and Amar. Now, as far as details, all you need to know is that I found out Amar wasn't being faithful and decided to end things. Nothing more, nothing less."

"That low-down dirty snake," growled Jalon. "See that's why I hate pretty boys; they think they have the right to treat women any kind of way and get away with it."

Evoni looked at her three brothers, who all could qualify as pretty boys by many women's standard, but she knew they were good men, her father had made sure of that. "I'm just glad he showed me his character before I walked down the aisle. Take this as a lesson to always treat women the way you expect other men to treat your sister and the way Daddy treats Mama."

"All the time, sis," piped up Devon. "Daddy taught us how to treat women and we would never use or abuse any of our black queens. Now some Beckys," joked her brother without finishing that sentence.

"Ha-ha, Devon, you know you were raised to treat all women the same."

"We know that sis, Devon was just joking," stated Keyshon. "We would never disrespect a woman."

With that out of the way, the four siblings caught up on other family gossip and Evoni pried into her brothers' dating lives. It seemed both Keyshon and Devon were involved with women whom they were getting serious about and Jalon, ever the playboy, was single and loving it.

The four continued talking until they heard their father yell that lunch was ready. They filed into the house and out onto the back patio, where their father had set up a feast fit for royalty.

There was his famous Nashville hot chicken, salad, mac n' cheese, sweet cornbread, Louisiana shrimp étouffée and of course cold sweet tea. Just looking at the food, Evoni felt her thighs getting bigger. She really needed to get to the gym. Of course, that wouldn't stop her from partaking in her father's delicious food. She also planned on taking a plate to go.

"Daddy, this looks delicious. This is enough food to feed a small army," stated Evoni while taking a seat.

"Well, your brothers eat like a small army," joked her father.

Everyone laughed.

"Hey, we are growing boys," quipped Jalon.

"No, you are grown men," stated Evoni. "You stopped growing years ago, ya'll just greedy."

Jalon hit her with his napkin while everyone laughed. Evoni was thankful her mother wasn't there. It would have changed the whole mood.

The lunch was the best meal Evoni had had in a while and just spending time with her family had brightened her mood. It felt good spending time not having to think about work or Marc's case.

After lunch, Evoni spent some time watching her father and brothers play dominoes and then decided it was time to say adieu, before her mother returned. She didn't want to push her luck.

Evoni said her goodbyes and headed out. It was a great afternoon, but all that rich food gave her the "itis" and she could really use a nap.

Upon returning home, Evoni climbed into bed and napped until the early evening, then she woke up and heated up leftovers from lunch before turning to work.

CHAPTER 27

Evoni

Marc was granted a bail of 1,000,000 dollars. The prosecutor attempted to paint Marc as a flight risk, but the judge didn't buy it. By midday Monday, Marc was home with his sons.

Tim decided to give him the rest of the day to spend with his sons, but he wanted everyone to meet the following day around noon. Everyone included anyone helping with the case.

Tuesday found everyone seated in Tim's conference room enjoying lunch and discussing next steps in Marc's case. Because Bri and Aunt Abby were present, nothing that could be considered privileged was discussed.

Tim brought the meeting to order. "We knew Marc's arrest was inevitable and it's good to no longer have that threat hanging over our heads and we can focus on proving Marc's innocence. On the bright side, the cops aren't complete imbeciles. They are no longer accusing Marc of being the Music City Murderer. On the other hand, this also means that the police force wants to focus all their resources on catching this serial killer and they have every incentive to get this matter wrapped up as soon as possible, even if it means railroading an innocent man.

"But we can't focus on that, we must stay the course and continue to conduct our own investigation. Do our Charlie's Angels have anything to share?"

Evoni, Bri, and Mari laid out for the rest of the team what they had learned from Cinnamon.

"Hmm," said Tim. "That may be useful, and we may need to call Cinnamon as a witness. Now, if only we could get to Hank and get his whereabouts for the time period that the coroner thinks the death occurred."

"Well," piped in Bri. "We have an idea." Bri went on to tell everyone about the upcoming Chamber of Commerce event and how she expected Hank to be there.

Tim liked the idea. "I knew having the fiancé of the great Harold Williams would pay off," joked Tim.

"Okay team. Evoni, Bri, and Mari will try and get any information they can from Hank. In the meantime, I've hired a private investigator who will join us in a bit. We'll have him investigate Jessica's whereabouts on the days leading up to her death. Maybe he'll find something useful."

Marc spoke up. "What should I do?"

"Marc, your only job is to stay away from the media and take care of your boys. Let the rest of us handle the investigating."

"And me?" questioned Abby.

Tim turned to Abby and smiled. "You, ma'am, will be a great character witness for Marc if this goes to trial and you can help him out with the boys and keep him in check."

"Well, that doesn't seem like much," stated Abby while crossing her arms with a slight pout.

Tim laughed gently. "Ma'am, it may not seem like much, but it is. In cases like these, keeping the accused calm is crucial. We have to make sure Marc doesn't do anything to draw any more attention to him or do anything that could hurt his case. And every trial needs good character witnesses and no one else here knows Marc like you."

This seemed to appease Abby. There was a knock and the door slowly opened. Bri gasped. In walked Jackson, the private investigator hired by Harold to find his ex.

Jackson looked amused at Bri's reactions. "Good afternoon, ma'am, it's nice to see you again. How's Mr. Williams?"

Everyone turned and looked at Bri. Bri simply shrugged. There was no point in bringing up how she vaguely knew the man. Tim arched an eyebrow at the awkward exchange and then moved on to introducing Jackson to the group.

Marc and Tim brought Jackson up to speed and Evoni provided him a copy of Linc's report from the custody investigation. After posing several questions to Marc including asking about any old acquaintances from Murfreesboro Marc knew about, Jackson felt he had enough to start his investigation and promised to provide an update within the week. With that, he left.

The meeting broke up soon after, with everyone assigned a task.

After the meeting, Mari and Evoni headed back to the office. With the Chamber of Commerce event taking place that Thursday evening, Bri had offered to pull some looks for Evoni and Mari. They made plans to stop by her house later that evening to try on gowns.

CHAPTER 28

Bri

Bri spent the rest of the afternoon pulling gowns for her, Evoni and Mari and had them along with matching shoes and clutches transported to her house.

That evening, Evoni and Mari arrived at Bri's around 7:30. Bri was excited to show them the gowns.

Both ladies were dumbfounded. The gowns Bri had chosen were beautiful and fitted their personalities. Those for Evoni were elegant but classy and for Mari classy but sexy.

They spent the next two hours drinking wine and trying on dresses; eventually, all three ladies found a gown they loved.

Evoni settled on an orangey gold gown with a short side split and a sparkling neckline that complemented her medium brown skin-tone. Mari fell in love with an emerald green gown with a thigh high split and simple spaghetti straps. Bri, of course, went with a red gown covered in Swarovski crystals with a plunging neckline.

They agreed to all get dressed at Bri's the night of and head out from there. With that decided, Mari and Evoni said goodbye to Bri and headed home.

Bri finished putting together the looks for Mari and Evoni and then headed to bed. It had been an exhausting day.

With meetings with Rodrique on wedding plans and working on Sunshine's event, the next two days went quickly for Bri.

Before she knew it, it was Thursday and Evoni, and Mari were knocking at her door. Thankfully, Bri had the forethought to set up hair and makeup, so each lady would look like a million bucks.

While they were getting ready, Evoni finally got around to quizzing Bri on Jackson. It was clear Evoni was interested as she was extremely curious as to whether Jackson had a girlfriend, as she hadn't seen a ring indicating he was married.

"Evoni, I love you, girl, but if you ask me one more question about Jackson, I'm going to snap. For goodness sake, I only saw the man once and briefly, I don't know anything about his personal life."

"Okay," said Evoni putting up her hands in surrender. "I'm sorry, it's just that he's fine as hell and you know things have been drier than the Sahara over here since Amar. I was hoping he could come water me," joked Evoni.

Bri and Mari laughed.

"This is why I told you to always keep a pair and a spare around just in case, but did you listen?" queried Bri.

"A pair and a spare?" asked Mari curiously.

Bri and Evoni shared a look and giggled. "So, my grandmother gave me this sage advice after a difficult breakup in my twenties. She told me I should always keep a main man, a pair, and a spare, just in case."

"Your grandmother told you to keep at least four men on the hook at the same time?" inquired Mari.

"Yep," said Bri. "That way you always have a backup. I tried imparting this wisdom to Evoni, but she refused to listen."

"Whatever, I don't have time to deal with more than one man at a time. It's too exhausting," said Evoni.

"And that's why you're drier than the desert."

Evoni laughed and lightly tapped Bri. "Ha-ha, I don't see you taking your own advice, Miss Thing."

"With Harold there's no need. I knew after the first time we slept together I had him hooked. This punanny is one of a kind," joked Bri.

All three ladies laughed. It was clear the conversation was just as amusing to their stylists as they were shaking with silent laughter.

"Well, I think I'll stick to just one," stated Mari. "But I'll keep that little note in the back of my mind, just in case Kevin forgets what he has."

"Amen to that," said Evoni and Bri in unison.

Once they were fully glamourized, the three ladies headed out. Bri had hired a limo for the evening. When they arrived at the event, it was obvious the who's who of Nashville's business elite were in abundant attendance. There were even some country music stars, which excited Mari to no end.

Once they were seated at their table, the three decided to split up and look for Hank. Whoever found him first would text the others. While on the hunt for Hank, Evoni ran into a few of her colleagues and judges. Not wanting to be rude, she made small talk and quickly extracted herself.

Not spotting Hank, Evoni went looking for Bri and Mari. Evoni stopped in her tracks, standing at the bar chatting up a beautiful brunette was none other than Mateo, the hot tow truck guy. Evoni wondered if she should go over and speak but decided it would be rude to interrupt, besides she was there on a mission not to flirt.

After twenty minutes of mingling, Mari spotted Hank out on the hotel's balcony. He was with a young woman who looked young enough to be his daughter. Mari hoped that was the case, otherwise, the alternative was unpleasant to think about.

Mari texted Evoni and Bri to meet her by the balcony. They arrived within a few minutes. Unfortunately for Mari, it was clear the woman was not Hank's daughter. His hands were wandering, and it looked like she wanted to get away but wasn't sure how. Bri decided to intervene.

"Hank Dupree. is that you? Oh, my God, guys, it is him. It's Hank Dupree from the commercials," stated Bri turning to Evoni and Mari with a look of mock excitement on her face.

Hank looked up and spotted the beautiful woman calling his name. The young woman used this moment to escape Hank's clutches and hurried back inside. Hank, his current conquest lost, turned to Bri with his patented salesman smile.

"Why, hi there beautiful. I see you know ole Hank, but I don't think we've had the pleasure of meeting."

Bri stepped forward for a handshake with Evoni and Mari hovering at her back. "Hello, I'm Bria Montgomery and these two ladies are Evoni Singleton and Mari Davies."

"Well, well, three beautiful ladies. I must say I am a lucky man to be blessed with this much beauty."

Evoni smirked. He wouldn't feel so blessed once he found out why they had sought him out.

Evoni let Bri do what she did best, flirt and get Hank at ease. They noticed within the first ten minutes of conversation; Hank was already on his second whiskey. Evoni figured one more and he should be good and primed for questioning.

By the time Hank finished his third whiskey, his hand had made numerous attempts to ease on to Bri's thigh but each time she slapped it away in what appeared to be a playful manner, but Evoni could tell Bri was losing her patience.

Deciding to take charge and get this over with, Evoni turned to Hank. "Mr. Dupree, I'm curious, are you familiar with the Sunny Day Motel?"

For a quick second, Evoni noticed a look of alarm in Hank's eyes, but he quickly recovered. "I can't say that I am. I'm not much for motels. I'm more of a Ritz-Carlton type of guy," he said with a sleazy smile.

"Hmm, that's strange because we were told you are a regular there with a certain lady who was recently found murdered. It would be a shame to have to pass this information on to the press," said Evoni.

"Now, you just wait a minute," Hank stammered. "Just who the hell do you think you are? How dare you try to impugn my good character!"

Evoni, Bri, and Mari laughed. "A used car salesman with good character. That's a good one Hank," snickered Bri.

"Just who the hell are you ladies? You know it doesn't matter; I think this conversation is over." Hank made to leave.

"I wouldn't do that Hank," stated Evoni with steel in her voice. "You really don't want to piss us off, and I really will go to the press with information on your sordid relationship with Jessica French. I bet being involved in a murder scandal wouldn't be good for business or sit well with dear old dad."

Hank sighed loudly. "You've got it all wrong. I was not sexually involved with Jessica French. She was just a friend."

Evoni gave Hank a questioning look. "What kind of friends go to seedy motels to hang out?"

Hank began pulling at his shirt collar and a light bead of sweat formed on his brow. "Where the hell is the damn server? I need another whiskey."

Mari offered to go to the bar and grab a whiskey. "Okay, Hank, we know you were at the motel with Jessica the day she died. If you two weren't sleeping together, what were you doing?" asked Bri.

Hank knew there was no point in denying anything else or lying. These ladies clearly knew what was what. "Okay, okay, I'll tell you about my relationship with Jessica."

"I met Jessica about a year ago at a bar. She tried to hit on me, but she was a little too long in the tooth for me."

"Right, because you're more fond of jailbait," interrupted Bri.

Hank shot her a glare and ignored the comment. "Because I was bored, I bought her a couple of drinks and we got to talking. We hung out until the bar closed. Once the bar closed, Jessica asked me if I wanted to continue partying. She said she knew a place that stayed open all night. I figured, what the hell. I didn't have anything better to do and I wasn't ready to go home. Anyway, we ended up at this big house out in Brentwood. I don't know whose house it was, but Jessica seemed to know everyone there. We continued drinking and then at some point party favors were brought out."

Evoni and Bri gave each other a knowing look. Party favors was a euphemism for drugs.

Mari returned with Hank's whiskey, and he took a big gulp before continuing. "So, yeah, I've never been one to do any drugs other than a little weed every now and again to help me relax, but these were hard core. At first, I declined, but Jessica and her friends kept pressuring me until I finally decided to do some Molly." A look of euphoria came over Hank's face.

"I had never felt anything like it. It was like the whole world opened up and everything was just so much better, more intense, more pleasurable. After that, things get a little blurry and I just remember waking up around 7 a.m. on the floor of the kitchen with no idea how I got there."

"Let me get this straight, you did Molly and then you don't remember anything else after that?" questioned Evoni.

"Yes, for the most part. I vaguely remember going to a bedroom with a young lady," said Hank with a sheepish look. "But that's truthfully about it."

"Okay, so what happened after you woke up?" asked Mari.

"I looked around for Jessica but didn't see her, so I got in my car and drove home. I didn't hear from her again until a few weeks later when she showed up at one of my dealerships looking for me. My general manager called me and let me know she was looking for me and I had him put her on the phone. I asked her what she wanted, and she said she just wanted to see if I was interested in hanging out again. I was hesitant but agreed to meet her that evening at a bar downtown. From there we began to kind of meet up once a week or so and we always ended up back at the big house in Brentwood. I hate to admit it, but I really got into the party favors."

"So, you did more than Molly?" asked Bri.

"Um, yeah. You gotta understand when you're around people doing a bunch of different drugs, it's hard to say no. Eventually Jessica and I were meeting up around once a week just to do drugs. That's why we were at the Sunny Day Motel. Not because we were sleeping together, but to party. We'd been going there for a few months. I figured it was a safe enough location, where no one would recognize me."

The ladies had not been expecting Hank to admit he was practically a junkie. He certainly didn't look like one.

"Okay," said Evoni. "Let's get to the night Jessica died. How long were you with her at the motel? Did you kill her?"

Hank's nostrils flared and his eyes stared daggers at Evoni. "Hell no, I didn't kill her! Jessica was very much alive when I left her. We were setting up to party when I got a call from my old man saying that my mother had been rushed to the emergency room. My mother has a bad ticker, so he was alarmed and asked me to meet him at the hospital. I rushed out and left Jessica in the room."

Evoni knew there was no easy way to prove Hank's story without violating HIPAA laws or outing Hank to his father; but maybe she'd have Tim ask Jackson to stop by and sweet talk a nurse or two to try and get verification. But Evoni didn't think Hank was so much of an asshole to lie on his sick mother. This was a dead end.

After peppering Hank with a few more questions, the ladies excused themselves. "Well, that was a bust," stated Mari.

"Hank may have been a bust, but we did get some useful information," said Bri. "We know they partied out in Brentwood and Hank remembered the house was unique and it was located on Lexington Drive at the end of a cul-de-sac. Maybe someone who goes to those parties will have some useful information."

"Bri's right," stated Evoni. "That is another lead to check out. But maybe let's not go to the actual party just yet. I'd prefer not to spend my night hanging out with people high on drugs."

"Amen to that," stated Bri.

They agreed to stake out the house in the daytime and maybe gather some information on who lived in the house. With their inquiry over, the ladies headed out. No need to stick around for the rubber chicken dinner. They'd stop by a drive thru on the way home and grab something.

CHAPTER 29

Evoni

The next morning Evoni began searching for the house Hank had described. Unique didn't quite capture the design. Evoni was able to locate the house via Google and obtain the address. The house sat on a full acre and looked like it had been designed by a child playing with Legos. Using LexisNexis, she ran the address. The search returned the owner of the residence as a John Berkenshire, a very wealthy real estate developer in Tennessee. Mr. Berkenshire owned well over twenty properties in the area. Evoni wondered if this was his home or just an investment property. Evoni performed a search on John Berkenshire, and the number of hits were in the thousands. It seemed he was a philanthropist, known for donating to worthy causes on a local and national level. About ten years prior, he had run for mayor of Belle Meade, the wealthiest town in Tennessee. Unfortunately for him, he lost.

After perusing a few more articles on John Berkenshire, Evoni compiled everything she found in an email and sent it off to Bri and Mari. With that done, Evoni called Kanisha. After Marc's arrest, they had spoken once briefly, and Kanisha had assured Evoni that the boys were in good hands between her and Abby. She hadn't spoken to her since Marc's release.

Kanisha answered on the third ring. "Ms. Singleton, what can I do for you today?"

"You know, sometimes I hate caller ID," joked Evoni.

"It's a godsend, makes it so easy to ignore people you have no desire to talk to. But you, my friend, can see you are definitely on my calls to answer list."

"Aww, that's so sweet, it gave me diabetes. It feels good to be loved."

Kanisha guffawed. "You are still silly, and that's why I love you. Anyway, girl, I'm sure I know why you're calling. Everyone in the French household is doing well. In fact, I'm heading over later today to spend a little time with the boys."

"I'm so glad to hear that, K. You are an angel. You have been such a big help to Marc and the boys."

"You're right, I am an angel. A gorgeous, sexy, kickass black angel and don't you ever forget it," quipped Kanisha. "But, on a serious note, having their Aunt Abby around has really helped. I think the boys need to be surrounded by as much love as possible right now. After Marc's release and some long talks between father and son, Ashton settled down. Caleb is rather subdued but overall seems to be handling things well."

"I'm sure that's thanks to you, my brilliant therapist friend."

"Well, what can I say," stated Kanisha with a hint of false modesty. "You know a girl could get used to all these compliments, great for the self-esteem. I guess I should call you whenever I need an ego boost."

"Now don't go getting a bighead, with that afro you may just float away."

Evoni and Kanisha chatted for a little while longer before agreeing to meet up for lunch soon.

The rest of Evoni's week was typical, and the days flew by. The only hiccup was the restraining order issued against one of her clients after she keyed her soon to be ex's brand-new Range Rover. He made the mistake of taking his new girlfriend to one of their old haunts and Evoni's client just happened to be there. With family law, the drama was never ending.

The weekend arrived and with it, major storms. Evoni spent all day Saturday at home cuddled up on her couch binge-watching her favorite tv shows. By Sunday, she was ready to venture out. Checking the time, Evoni realized she hadn't been to church in what seemed like forever and today she didn't have an excuse. Evoni quickly texted Bri to see if she was up for the afternoon service and then headed to shower. By the time she emerged, Bri had texted back and agreed to meet her at church. Of course, a text from Bri was never that straight forward. She told Evoni she was simply coming along to make sure Evoni asked for absolution for lusting over Jackson. Evoni responded in emojis- a laughing devil, an eggplant, and a shrug. She tossed the phone back on her nightstand and got dressed.

Church service was food for Evoni's soul. She emerged feeling lighter and happier. Afterwards she and Bri headed to their usual after church spot, Mama Bee's, for a late lunch/early dinner.

As always, the perk of being Mama Bee's goddaughter worked in Evoni's favor. They didn't have to wait in the long line for a table. Once they were seated and drink orders place, Evoni looked around for the waitress from her last visit. She never did get around to finding out her story from Mama Bee. She gave herself a mental reminder to set up lunch with Mama Bee.

Bri commented on how Evoni looked more energetic and content after church. Bri realized it had been a while since she checked in on her friend and on how she was handling the breakup with Amar. Bri felt guilty that they'd spent so much time discussing her upcoming marriage while Evoni was dealing with the loss of a fiancé, a good for nothing, lowdown dirty fiancé, but still, a fiancé.

"Tell me, how are you, really? I know things have been crazy with work and Marc's case but how are you holding up?"

"Honestly, Bri, I think I'm okay. It seems Amar's little retaliatory antics have ceased. My attorney called me a few days ago and let me know the wrongful eviction suit had been dropped. I guess Amar came to his senses and realized he wouldn't get the reaction he was hoping for.

"Lord knows I loved Amar, probably always will, but I can see now that he was unworthy of that love. I gave that man all of me and it still wasn't enough. I don't wish him harm, but I do hope one day he sees what it feels like to have the one you love betray you. Of course, if my mother had it her way, I'd just forgive him and sweep it under the rug."

"Evoni, girl, I hate to tell you this, but our mothers are both batshit crazy. Excuse me for cursing on a Sunday," Bri said while looking heavenward.

"You are right about that. They're both certifiable. Yours doesn't want you to marry the man you love, and mine wants me to marry a cheating dog. What genetic lottery did we win?" questioned Evoni while laughing.

"Shoot, if I didn't look so much like my sisters and my grandmother, I'd be convinced I was switched at birth," said Bri.

"I hear you. I've secretly considered getting a DNA test," joked Evoni. "So, your mother still hasn't come around on you and Harold getting married?"

Before Bri could answer, their food arrived, and it was delivered by none other than Mama Bee herself. Both Evoni and Bri jumped up to give her a hug and kiss after the plates were sat down.

Mama Bee dropped down in the empty seat next to Evoni. "How are my two favorite beautiful black women?"

"Fine," they replied in unison.

"Evoni, it feels like it's been forever since I laid eyes on my one and only goddaughter."

Feeling guilty, Evoni quickly apologized.

Mama Bee playfully swatted Evoni. "You know I'm just joking, sweetie. I know you're busy being a successful high-powered lawyer. But I do want you to know your mother called me about Amar."

Evoni groaned. Bri ducked into her food.

"Mama Bee, don't listen to Mother. You know she's always disagreed with every decision I've made. When I first began seeing Amar, she was against it but then she warmed up to him after he constantly praised her and bought her gifts every time we visited."

"Now, honey, you know I love your mother like a sister, but you know Gloria's words don't hold sway with me. That woman is still stuck in 1950 with her mindset. Maurice has always treated her like a queen so I'm not sure where she gets off asking you to put up with less. As for Amar, I never told you this, but I never really cared for him. Too slick and pretty for me. But he did look like he was good in bed. I bet it was the sex that hooked you, wasn't it?"

Evoni and Bri almost choked on the food they were chewing. "What? Just because I'm old you ladies think Mama Bee don't still got it?"

"Mama Bee, TMI," exclaimed Evoni. "Especially while we're eating."

"Don't tell me you two don't discuss your sex lives while you eat, you just don't wanna hear an old woman. On that note, I gotta get back to the kitchen and make sure these young'uns aren't sending out subpar food. Evoni call me to set up lunch and make sure it's at an acceptable restaurant. In fact, I'll send you a list." With that Mama Bee kissed Evoni and Bri goodbye.

"Girl, Mama Bee is too much. I hope I still have my groove when I'm her age."

"I hate to break it to you B, but we aren't that far off these days. I get a new ache and pain on a weekly basis. It's been all downhill since hitting thirty."

"Whoo, girl, you don't have to tell me," said Bri. "A few days ago, I woke up feeling like I had gone three rounds with Mayweather when all I'd done was sleep. Aging sucks but at least we look good doing it."

Evoni laughed and clinked glasses with Bri. "Thank God for good genes, jacuzzi tubs and Epsom salt."

After their delicious meal, Bri and Evoni opted to take dessert to go. Both ladies left with a hefty slice of Mama Bee's prizewinning sweet potato cheesecake. With Harold returning that evening from an out-of-town trip, Bri wanted to get home and wait for her man, she vowed to even try and save him a sliver of her cheesecake, but no promises.

CHAPTER 30

Evoni

With no plans, Evoni decided to go for a walk in the park and clear her head. Having to talk about Amar brought her feelings to the surface. Overall, she was doing okay but occasionally, the pain in her heart ached; though Evoni knew she hid it well. Truth be told, she missed him. The way he could make her laugh, the way he massaged her feet after 12 hours in heels, how he always knew when she needed cheering up, his smell, that gorgeous smile and body.

It seemed he had finally gotten the message that she wasn't forgiving him, as he hadn't called in the last couple of weeks. For a second, Evoni wondered if he was with the hussy he cheated on her with. Not wanting to dwell on that, Evoni switched her thoughts to Marc and his case. She didn't know if she, Bri, and Mari playing Charlie's Angels would discover anything to help but she hoped so. If Evoni was honest with herself, she had to admit investigating was thrilling. Sure, there could be boring parts, but just being in the thick of things and not sitting on the sidelines waiting for information to be trafficked to her, gave Evoni a jolt.

Would Linc be proud of my investigative skills? Evoni thought with a chuckle. Speaking of sexy investigators, Evoni wondered if Jackson had found anything useful. She'd have to give Tim a call for an update and maybe get Jackson's number from him while she was at it.

Evoni walked amongst the many trails, letting her thoughts wonder aimlessly. Time passed quickly. Checking her watch, Evoni realized she'd been walking for a couple of hours.

Heading back to her car, she felt a little lighter. Her love life may be DOA, but she'd be damned if her client would end up the same way.

Evoni called Tim while driving home. Tim answered and before Evoni could ask for an update, Tim asked her to stop by. Jackson would be arriving shortly with an update, and this way Tim wouldn't have to play telephone. Besides, he informed Evoni, since Tess found out they were working on a matter together, she'd been hounding Tim to have her over. Evoni agreed and relished her good luck, not only would she get a case update, but she'd get to see that fine-ass Jackson.

Pulling up to Tim's house, Evoni couldn't help but to admire the landscaping, it was clear Tim paid good money to make his yard look this good. Evoni would have to ask him for a recommendation.

Evoni rang the bell and was greeted at the door by Tess, Tim's gorgeous wife. Tess gave her a hug and a kiss on the cheek. "Evoni, I was so excited when Tim said you would be stopping by. It's been ages since I've seen you. How are you? Oh, look at me blathering on, and I haven't even let you step foot in the house yet."

"Hi, Tess. It's great to see you too. It has been too long. How are the girls? I know they must be getting big by now."

Tess answered Evoni while escorting her down the hallway. "The girls are great. Abby is nine now and sassy like her mother," Tess said with a snicker. "Cori is eight going on eighty. She has to be the most serious child I've ever seen. If my grandmother wasn't still alive, I'd think Cori was her reincarnated." By this time, they were standing outside Tim's office.

"I'll be in the kitchen finishing up dinner, stop by and see me before you leave, and we can continue catching up."

"You got it," said Evoni. With that Tess headed back down the hall and Evoni lightly knocked on Tim's door.

"Come in."

Evoni entered and found Tim sitting behind his desk with a pile of legal pads in front of him and his laptop pushed off to the side.

Tim noticed her gaze. "Sometimes it's good to go old school and actually write out my thoughts. Something about putting pen to paper makes the work feel more important and reminds me to think things through thoroughly."

"Believe me, I get it. It's something about writing by hand that makes the job seem more than just something anyone with a laptop could do."

"Yes, yes. You get it. I knew there was a reason why we work so well together. Tell me, when are you going to leave that hell hole where you work and come join me?" said Tim with a questioning gaze. "You know my firm does more than criminal law, though after we get Marc off, you may reconsider your stance on that issue."

Before Evoni could answer, there was a knock on the door and Jackson entered. God, just looking at him took Evoni's breath away. The man was a walking talking orgasm waiting to happen. With the body of Jason Momoa, the silky chocolate skin of Morris Chestnut and the face of a god, Evoni couldn't imagine him being single.

"Jackson, perfect timing. You saved Evoni from having to turn down my job offer," Tim said with a wink at Evoni.

Jackson gave Evoni a small smile. "Nice to see you again, Ms. Singleton."

"Evoni, please. Don't make me feel any older than I already am. It's nice to see you again, also."

"My apologies, Evoni. That's a unique beautiful name, and I must say you don't look a day over twenty-five to me."

"Okay, okay enough flirting you two. We have work to do. Jackson, save the pickup lines for when you're off the clock."

If it weren't for her buttery brown skin, both men would have seen Evoni blush. *God, am I flirting?* How embarrassing.

Jackson gave her another smile and sat in the chair next to her.

"Now," said Tim. "Jackson, I'm really hoping you have something juicy to report."

Jackson cleared his throat and launched into his report. "First, I want to thank Evoni for a summary of the work her firm's investigator did in preparation for the custody battle. That saved me a lot of legwork. I spent some time down in Murfreesboro where I ran into a sweet old lady who had just returned from three months in Europe, which is why your investigator missed her. It was a stroke of good luck and timing."

"What did this lady have to say?" questioned Tim. "Did she know Jessica and her family?"

"Well, it seems prior to the death of Jessica's parents, her mother, Susan, worked for Mrs. Dunlevy, that's the lady I spoke with. Mrs. Dunlevy hired Jessica's mother on as part-time help at one of stores. She owns a string of liquor stores inherited from her parents. Anyway, Jessica's mother worked three days a week in one of her Murfreesboro stores for about eight months. It seems this was around the time Jessica was fourteen or fifteen."

"How old is Mrs. Dunlevy, she seems to have a great memory for an old timer?" asked Tim.

"She's eighty-five, looks seventy-five and has the memory of a thirty-year-old," said Jackson. "Believe me, I tested it."

"Okay," said Evoni jumping in. "We know Jessica's mother worked for her. What did she have to say about Jessica? Knowing her mother's work history doesn't seem all that relevant."

"Well," said Jackson slightly exaggerating the word. "I was just getting to the relevant part. That was just the foreplay."

"Get a room already you two," said Tim. "What did the old lady have to say that was juicy?"

"When I asked her if she ever met Susan's daughters, Mrs. Dunlevy said yes. Apparently, there were a few times when Susan also did a little housecleaning for Mrs. Dunlevy and on those occasions, she would bring her daughters, Jessica or Jessie as she was called back then and Jennifer or Jenni. Mrs. Dunlevy remembered them being quiet girls who barely made a peep while their mother worked. She basically had to force them to even take a snack or a drink. Anyway, this went on for about four months, when suddenly Susan stopped bringing Jessica around. Mrs. Dunlevy inquired and was told that Jessie was sick and needed a break from the Memphis heat, so she'd sent her to stay with her sister out in Colorado."

"What was wrong with Jessica?" asked Evoni.

"Mrs. Dunlevy didn't know and found Susan's explanation questionable as she refused to ever provide an actual condition Jessica was suffering from. After that I dug into Susan's background and found that she was an only child. She never had a sister."

"So why did she lie and where the hell was Jessica?" queried Tim.

"Susan only worked for Mrs. Dunlevy for another few months after that before quitting with no explanation. But she remembered seeing Susan while out and about roughly a year later. Susan didn't notice her. But Mrs. Dunlevy did notice both girls were now with their mother, so Jessica was back from wherever she had been."

"Hmm," said Evoni. "Are you guys thinking what I'm thinking?"

"I'm not," said Tim exasperatedly. "Am I missing something?"

"I believe what Evoni is thinking is that even to this day when families send teenage girls away for long periods of time, it's usually due to a pregnancy," stated Jackson while looking at Evoni for confirmation.

"That's exactly what I was thinking. It makes total sense. Somehow Jessica found herself knocked up and Susan wasn't looking for another mouth to feed or that type of embarrassment, so she sent Jessica away to have the baby and gave it up for adoption or to an orphanage."

"God," said Tim while wiping his face. "Do people still do that? This would have been what- the late 90's? Teenage pregnancy wasn't nearly as stigmatized then as it was in the 70's. And it's not like the family had a reputation to protect, from what I've heard they weren't exactly pillars of the community."

"Who knows what the reason was, but I'm willing to bet that is exactly what happened. Can we find out anything about this child?" probed Evoni.

"That's what I've been working on the last couple of days. With Jessica's family dead, it's almost impossible to know where they sent her off to but I'm trying to track down people who went to school with her and hopefully, I'll find someone Jessica confided in."

"So, this kid, if he or she exists, would be about how old?" Tim asked.

"Well, if she gave birth when she was fifteen or sixteen, that would put the kid around twenty-five," stated Jackson.

Evoni voiced what everyone was thinking. "What if this kid found Jessica and confronted her about abandoning him or her all those years ago? What if they saw Ashton and Caleb living the life they should've had? That could be enough to push someone over the edge. Especially if when confronted, Jessica didn't feel any remorse."

"That's a great theory and one I'd love to pan out. But it's just that right now, a theory. We don't even know for sure there ever was a baby. Let's focus on finding some evidence that proves this child exists and then go from there," Tim said ending that line of query.

Tim then turned to Evoni and asked her to relay to Jackson what she had learned from Hank Dupree. Evoni gave Jackson a brief overview of the meeting with Hank.

"So, the used car king is a druggie, why am I not surprised? Do you guys really think someone from one of these parties may have killed Jessica?" inquired Jackson.

Evoni shrugged. "I think it's at least worth checking out. Jessica could have seen or heard something at one of these little drug soirees that she wasn't supposed to. Just based off the zip code, you know the people involved are movers and shakers, not your typical riff raff. I'm sure they are all people with something to lose."

"Okay, here's what we are going to do," indicated Tim. "Jackson, you'll keep digging into Jessica's past and into whether she had a child. If you find out she did, you'll try to locate said child. In the meantime, Evoni and her band of beauties will stay on the drug party angle and see what, if anything, comes of it. I don't have to tell either of you this, but I will anyway, be careful and don't take any unnecessary risks."

"Aye, aye, Captain," said Evoni and Jackson in unison. All three laughed.

"Alright you two, get out of here and enjoy the rest of your Sunday. I'm going to pour myself a stiff drink and relay what we've learned to our client. God, I really hate this job sometimes."

Evoni didn't envy Tim at all. With all that he'd been through, they just seemed to keep adding more and more misery to Marc's plate. Evoni just hoped the weight of it all didn't crush him.

Evoni and Jackson said goodbye to Tim and headed out. As much as Evoni would have loved to follow Jackson out of the house and maybe engage in a little small talk, she needed to see Tess before leaving like she'd promised.

Evoni bid Jackson goodbye and headed to the kitchen where she found Tess with her head in the oven. "Smells good in here."

Tess jumped slightly and pulled her head out. "Oh, Evoni, you scared me. I didn't expect you all to be done so soon. Here, let me pour you a glass of wine and let's catch up while the roast finishes up."

Evoni, always in the mood for a glass of wine, took a seat at the kitchen island. She spent the next fifteen minutes catching up with Tess. Tess brought up the recent serial killings, but Evoni deflected. She was tired of talking about murder. Instead, she steered the conversation to every good mother's favorite topic, their kids. They laughed over stories about Tim's and Tess' daughters' shenanigans and how they had Tim wrapped around their little fingers. Feeling a little worn out, Evoni decided to call it a night and promised Tess they'd do lunch soon.

By the time Evoni made it home, she just wanted to shower and go to bed. Her cheesecake would have to wait until the next day.

CHAPTER 31

Bri

Bri, Mari, and Evoni discussed surveilling the house in Brentwood. They decided Monday morning would be a good time to catch the owner or resident of the home, and since Bri was the only Real House-wife of Nashville, she got to do the honor. Which for Bri meant getting up at the ass crack of dawn, something she never did. To keep Harold from questioning why she was up only an hour or so after him, Bri told a little fib. She told him she had lost a bet with her sister and now had to attend one of her tortuous 6:30 a.m. cycling classes. Harold found this very amusing.

Bri not so much. Why would anyone be up at this ungodly hour? She dragged herself out of bed and into workout clothes, for Harold's benefit. Thankfully, her soon to be hubby had coffee ready to go. Bri gave Harold a kiss goodbye and headed out. This was going to be awful.

When Bri arrived at the house, she gave a silent thankful prayer that there were cars parked on the street. It was a major point they had overlooked. If street parking weren't allowed, there would be no way to stakeout the house. The cars parked on the street were mid-level sedans for the most part. Bri figured they were either cars of workers in the homes or the kids of the families that resided there. Bri was glad she'd taken the Acura that Maribel drove to run errands instead of one of the more expensive cars. The Acura would be less conspicuous.

Bri found a spot to park not far from the party house. It really was an interesting home; the design was slightly garish, but the uniqueness also piqued one's interest. Bri wouldn't mind a look inside. Bri settled in for a long wait. Much to her surprise one of the three garage doors open not ten minutes later. Someone was an early riser. Bri spotted a young blond lady get into a silver Mercedes G-Wagon.

Bri faced a dilemma, should she follow the car or stay watching the house. Not being trained in the art of following someone nor in the mood to be yelled at by Evoni, Bri was decidedly in favor of continuing to watch the house.

Taking out her cellphone, Bri quickly snapped pictures of the car's license plate and a couple of the woman as she pulled out of the driveway. Maybe Jackson could run the plate number and find out who it was registered to.

Once the car left, there was no further activity in the house for at least another hour. Just as Bri was starting to daydream about her bed, a red Honda Civic pulled into the driveway and parked behind the garage door the silver Mercedes had exited from. Bri assumed this was the cook or housekeeper. Bri watched the lady input the garage code and enter once the door opened. Bri also took a picture of her license plate, just in case.

Less than fifteen minutes later, the middle garage door opened. Bri quickly took a picture of the license plate on the black Range Rover and held her phone up waiting to snap a picture of the driver. The driver was a man, around forty, ash blond hair, relatively attractive, in a Ryan Gosling kind of way. Bri quickly snapped a picture.

After the car left, there was no further activity at the house for the next hour. Bri figured she'd done her job. Pulling out to leave, Bri almost crashed into the silver Mercedes that had left earlier. The Mercedes driver flipped her off and continued on. *How rude.*

Before heading home, Bri stopped and grabbed a bottle of water. If she arrived at the house and saw Harold's car, she'd splash some on her shirt and face. Bri was nothing if not thorough with her lies.

Harold's car was gone, and Bri didn't have to intentionally wet herself. With her job complete, Bri decided she deserved a nap. Afterwards, she'd give Evoni and Mari an update.

Waking from the best nap ever, Bri checked the time. It was still only 11:30 a.m. She wondered how adults could function all day without a nap when they woke up before 8:00 a.m. Hopefully, she'd never have to find out.

Bri showered and headed downstairs. Maribel had arrived and offered to make her a quick lunch. Bri thanked her and headed into her Lady Lair, the only room in the house off limits to Harold. It's where she cried when she was sad, mad, or frustrated. It's where she kept her vision boards and her journals; where she meditated and daydreamed. This was Bri's sanctuary.

Bri sat at her desk and signed into her laptop. Her iPhone and Mac were synced so it was relatively easy to locate the pictures she'd taken that morning and email them to Evoni and Mari, along with her thoughts. With that done, Bri turned her attention to her wedding vision board. She'd first created it three months after moving in with Harold. Over time, she'd added and removed items as trends and fashion changed. Now Bri gave it a good long look and liked what she saw. She had impeccable taste. Bri snapped a picture and sent it off to Rodrique. He'd know exactly what to do. Not a minute later she received a reply. It was only one word…YESSSS!!!! Bri smiled.

Checking her email, Bri saw a response from Evoni, with Mari copied.

Hi Bri,

These are great. I can't believe you actually woke up early enough to get these. I'll pass them along to Tim and Jackson. Hopefully, we'll have some names soon. I met with Tim and Jackson last night and found out some interesting information on our victim. Busy right now but I'll shoot you an email with the deets later. I'll call you and Mari this evening to discuss. You aren't going to believe it. Talk to you later. Xoxo

Evoni

Well damn, thought Bri, *why couldn't she just tell us what the information was? Now I'll have to spend all day wondering about it.*

Knowing her ability to obsess, Bri decided to find something to keep her mind occupied for the next few hours. Stopping by the kitchen to tell Maribel where to bring her lunch, Bri headed to her studio. Bri had been working on a piece centered around the 1921 Tulsa Race Massacre and was hoping inspiration hit her and she would finish it. It was the first piece she'd created that had not only a cultural meaning to her but also a deeply personal one. Her great-grandfather had owned a small grocery store in Tulsa at the time. It was burned to the ground and he and her great-grandmother were attacked and almost killed.

Hearing the stories over the years about the racial violence her people experienced instilled in Bri not only anger but a sense of pride. A pride in her people for surviving and thriving, despite everything being against them. Bri knew she was blessed. Harold's wealth shielded them from the brunt of racism experienced by minorities in this country to a certain extent. They were less likely to be accosted by the police or accused of stealing from a high-end store or degraded publicly for how they dressed, walked, or talked. It was a privilege she didn't take lightly. Especially considering the spate of recent high-profile police murders of black and brown people and the resulting protests.

Bri spent the next few hours in a zone. The piece wasn't perfect, but it was coming together. Feeling like she'd accomplished her goal, Bri decided to reward herself with a glass of rosé.

Taking her wine to her Lady Lair, Bri sipped and wasted time reading a popular black blog and posting cute selfies to Instagram. Evoni didn't understand what Bri got out of Instagram, but Bri, like most people, liked the validation that she received from her followers. It was a curse most people were stricken with, the need to be liked. Unlike Evoni, who didn't care what people thought of her, a quality Bri greatly admired in her friend; Bri wasn't so lucky. Despite all that she had, Bri still craved acknowledgement and validation from others. She wished she was secure in herself. Bri blamed her mother.

Checking her messages for the hundredth time, Bri smiled. Evoni had finally emailed. Bri began reading and almost spit out her wine. She couldn't believe what she was reading. This was a plot right out of a Harlan Coben novel. A secret abandoned child who could possibly be the murderer. Sometimes truth could be stranger than fiction.

Bri fired off a quick email to Evoni consisting of nothing but emojis. She didn't have words that would express her shock and glee in finding out such a juicy tidbit. Being a crime buff, Bri couldn't help but to create scenarios in her head; each with a different culprit and reason for the murder.

Not wanting to waste her creativity, Bri wrote each scenario down. You never know if one would turn out to be accurate; and if so, Bri wanted proof for when she rubbed it into everyone's face. Besides, it was inevitable that Harold would find out she was involved. If things turn out well, it will go a long way in appeasing him.

With nothing more to do until Harold arrived home, Bri texted Aubrey to check in and see when she wanted to get together to figure out the best approach to achieving their task for Sunshine. Aubrey replied quickly. She suggested they meet the following day for lunch at Nicky Doll's Bistro, a cute little French place in Franklin, a suburb of Nashville.

Bri agreed to meet her there the following day at noon-ish. That would give Bri enough time to put together a fabulous outfit because from the little she knew of Aubrey; she knew she would be dressed to the nines.

Harold arrived about an hour later. For dinner, Maribel prepared lamb steaks, Mediterranean couscous and bacon maple glazed green beans. Harold collected a nice bottle of red wine from the wine cellar and he and Bri sat down to a wonderful meal. Bri loved how intelligent Harold was and the thought-provoking conversations he often engaged her in. It showed the level of respect he had for her, most men treated her like she was just something pretty to look at, all show and no substance. Harold, unlike those others, listened to her and valued her opinion. He even solicited her opinion on business affairs from time to time. That was one of the numerous reasons why Bri loved him.

With dinner finished, they retired to the sitting room and continued their conversation. Bri made sure not to mention anything regarding what she had been up to lately. She wanted to keep that a secret for as long as possible.

CHAPTER 32

Evoni

Unlike Bri, Evoni spent her evening going over briefs and motions while shoving down a take-out salad. She didn't make it to bed until well after midnight.

The following morning, she awoke with a crook in her neck and a pain in her wrist; she had clearly slept in a bad position. She made a mental note to book a full body massage as soon as she had the time.

Evoni was due in court that morning for a hearing on the mayor's sister's case. The last hearing hadn't gone as well as Evoni would've liked. In today's hearing, the judge would rule on the last motion submitted by Evoni to dismiss the ex-husband's petition. If the judge denied her request, then Colleen's two kids would have to testify. It was a scenario Evoni tried to prevent as often as possible. Making a child choose between parents and pay the toll for the demise of a relationship they had no control or say so over was something Evoni would never get used to. It was wrong on so many levels. Yet so many parents couldn't see past their own anger and need for revenge to see the effect their behavior had on their children.

Arriving at the courthouse, Evoni spotted her client sitting outside smoking a cigarette. Evoni sent a silent thank you heavenwards that Colleen had listened to her and gotten rid of the pink hair. Her hair was now a mousy brown. Colleen was also dressed fairly conservatively, for her. Her skirt was still a little too short but was a nice conservative blue. Evoni wished appearances didn't matter, but the reality was, they did, particularly for women. Judging the worth of a woman based off her looks was a tale as old as time.

Evoni greeted Colleen and waited for her to finish her cigarette before going over what she expected to happen today. "If the judge rules against us, are the kids here and ready to testify?" questioned Evoni.

"Yeah, I brought 'em. They're hanging out at the café across the street with my niece, Shawna. I gotta tell you though, I don't like this one bit. How dare that damn Johnny call me an unfit mother just because I like a little tipple every now and again. Claiming I was never there for the kids when he can't even remember the kids' birthdays and don't get me started on the number of important events he's missed. Asshole."

"Well, you haven't been drinking lately, and you're attending the AA meetings, right?" asked Evoni.

"Yeah, I'm clean three months, and I'm attending those damn meetings with all those sad sacks. I tell ya, I've never heard so many people complain so much about life. You sometimes wonder why they don't just end it if they're that miserable."

Evoni silently groaned. Thank God the judge didn't see this side of Colleen; they'd be dead in the water if he did. "Good to hear you're sticking with it. That'll score us some points with the judge if this thing doesn't end today. Let's head in," stated Evoni while getting up from the bench where they were sitting. Colleen followed her, still complaining about her no-good ex.

The judge didn't dismiss the case, so Evoni was forced to put Colleen's kids, Bailey and Brian, on the stand. Bailey held up fine under questioning and expressed her desire to live with both her parents. When opposing counsel pressed her to choose, she chose Colleen. But Evoni knew she would be scarred for life. Brian didn't hold up as well. Within minutes of being questioned, he began to cry. Evoni knew as a pre-teen boy that this was beyond embarrassing for him. Brian shut down not able or willing to respond to any more questions. The judge ordered a recess until after lunch. Colleen tried to comfort Brian, but he was inconsolable.

During the recess, Evoni approached Colleen's ex and his attorney. Expressing dismay over what had occurred on the stand with Brian, Evoni asked Johnny if he was willing to reconsider his current petition for full custody and instead try and work something out with Colleen for joint custody. Johnny became belligerent and refused to engage. He wanted full custody, no if, and or buts. His attorney gave Evoni a look and a shrug, there was only so much he could do.

Evoni returned to where Colleen was attempting to console Brian. Colleen looked at Evoni and asked if it would be necessary to put Brian back on the stand. Evoni told her the decision wasn't hers to make and that it would be up to the judge.

"I can do it, Mom," Brian said while wiping away remnants of his tears. "I just don't want you or Dad mad at me."

Colleen turned to her son and gave him a tight squeeze. "Oh, honey poo, nothin' you say up there will make me or your dad mad. We both just want what's best for you and the judge wants to know how you feel. I know you don't wanna choose between us, and that's okay. You don't have to, does he Ms. Singleton?" asked Colleen causing Brian to look at Evoni for an answer.

"Your Mom is right, Brian. If you can't choose, just tell the judge that. He'll understand. He knows how hard this is on you and your sister and no one in that room wants either of you to be hurt or upset."

"See," said Colleen. "So, when we go back in, just answer the questions asked with your truth, no matter what that is. Okay?"

"Okay," said Brian, taking a final swipe at his tear-stained face.

With that resolved, Colleen took Brian and Bailey to lunch. Evoni grabbed a sandwich and a water from a food truck and headed back into court to prepare for the afternoon session.

The afternoon session went well. Brain completed his testimony and so did Colleen's AA sponsor and several other character witnesses. The judge decided to take a few days to think over his decision. A hearing was scheduled for the following week. The judge would announce his decision as to who would get custody of the children.

Evoni was exhausted by the end of the day. Dealing with family drama and trauma was mentally, physically, and emotionally taxing. Sometimes Evoni considered changing to a less stressful area of the law, like tax. However, she knew she'd be bored to tears, and Evoni loved what she did.

Helping people brought her joy, especially those who were less fortunate. That was the one upside of working at a large white shoe firm, it allowed Evoni to utilize their expansive resources for her pro bono work. Helping those who couldn't afford to otherwise engage in custody battles, seek child support or domestic violence protection orders were the reasons why she put up with the large law firm culture. However, Evoni knew she would soon have to decide whether to continue her career at her firm or leave. If she didn't make partner, she'd have to weigh her options, which now included the possibility of working at Tim's firm. It was good to have options.

Her ringing phone brought Evoni out of her musings. Rummaging through her bottomless pit of a bag, Evoni found the phone just as it stopped ringing. She debated just throwing it back into her bag and waiting until she got home to check to see who it was, but her conscience wouldn't let her. Evoni checked her screen and noticed the call was from Jeff Johnson. She groaned loudly. *What the hell does he want?* Evoni didn't have the energy for any of Jeff's gaslighting and micro-aggressions today. Knowing she couldn't ignore the call; Evoni pressed the button to listen to the voicemail he'd left.

The voicemail was cryptic and didn't give Evoni any indication of what Jeff wanted, he just asked for her to return the call. He sounded like an adult and not a child with no lewd jokes or rude comments. Someone of authority must've been sitting next to him.

Evoni hit the button to return the call. "Hi, Jeff this is Evoni returning your call."

"Evoni, thanks for calling me back. Do you have a few minutes to chat?"

Staring at her phone, Evoni was confused. Was this Jeff Johnson being polite, wonders never ceased. "Sure, I have a few minutes, just leaving court. What can I do for you?"

"Um, I hate to ask, but I need some assistance with a pro bono client."

Thinking about how coincidental it was that she was just thinking about her pro bono work, Evoni took her time responding. What trouble could Jeff have caused? "What do you mean by you need some assistance? Is this one of the Sheila's House clients?"

Both Evoni and Jeff provided pro bono legal services at Sheila's House, a non-profit safe haven for women who have been recently released from prison and try to rebuild their lives. Evoni provided legal services related to any family law needs and Jeff for any lingering issues related to their criminal actions. Evoni hated to admit it to herself, but Jeff had proved a valuable asset and seemed to have a way with the ladies, though that part wasn't surprising.

"Yes, it involves one of the Sheila's House clients. I'd prefer to discuss in person, can you meet me at Coffee Grind in about fifteen minutes? It's not that far from the courthouse.

Evoni sighed. The last thing she needed today was to deal with Jeff but if it involved a client, Evoni figured she should see what he had to say. "I suppose I can but Jeff this better be important. I've had a very trying day in court, and I don't have time for any of your shenanigans," stated Evoni emphatically.

"Thanks, Evoni. I promise this is important. I wouldn't bother you if it wasn't. See you in fifteen," Jeff said and hung up.

Getting into her car, Evoni wished she had a shot of vodka to fortify her for this meeting. Dealing with Jeff was like dealing with a petulant child at times.

Pulling into the parking lot of Coffee Grind, Evoni noticed Jeff's Grey Graphite BMW M4 in the lot, she knew it was his because of the vanity plates which read BG JHNSN.

Evoni spotted Jeff at a corner table. Funny, from afar, he looked like a decent guy. Jeff looked up as she was approaching and hurried around and pulled her chair out. This was getting very weird. Last time they interacted, Evoni slapped Jeff and now here he was playing the gentlemen. Evoni began to wonder just how bad Jeff needed her help.

Once they were both seated and their drink orders taken, Evoni got down to business. She wanted to get this over with. "So, Jeff, what can I do for you?"

Jeff cleared his throat and took a big gulp from a glass of water. "Evoni, first off, I want to apologize for my behavior, especially the last time we interacted. I deserved the slap you gave me. I want you to know that I've told Chapman that I provoked you. There won't be any kind of disciplinary action against you."

Evoni was shocked into silence. Jeff Johnson doing the right thing, who would've thunk it? Evoni was unsure how to respond. "Thank you. I appreciate that but I have to ask what brought about this change of attitude? You and I have never gotten along, and you have frequently made it known that you don't consider me an equal."

Jeff embarrassed, looked straight at Evoni. "You're right. I've been an ass to you, and I'd question this sudden change in character, too. But, Evoni, I never disliked you. I hate to admit it, but I've always been jealous of you. You and I both know I only have my job because my father is a named partner; otherwise, I would've never been hired. It's nepotism at its finest."

Evoni didn't even try to argue with that statement. She was just surprised Jeff was openly admitting it.

Jeff continued. "Anyway, my realization of how awful my actions have been towards you and other women at the firm, hell in the city, coincides with why I've asked you here." Jeff noticed Evoni's raised eyebrow. "Just bear with me and you'll understand."

They were interrupted by the server bringing their drink orders, a ginger peach turmeric tea for Evoni and a vanilla mocha latte for Jeff, along with a slice of cinnamon rum coffee cake.

After the server left, Jeff continued. "So, you know our work at Sheila's House has really opened my eyes to a lot of things that I never considered before. Helping the women and hearing their stories has shown me the injustices in our criminal justice system and society as a whole. It also has highlighted my white privilege. I'm ashamed to say, before I never gave much credence to the idea that the plight of black and brown people was so much worse simply because of race. I was taught that everyone had the same chances in life, and it was their own fault when they didn't succeed. No one ever taught me about systemic and institutional racism, and I never thought to look outside my own upper-class bubble to see the plight of people who weren't afforded the same privileges I was."

Well damn. Where the hell did all this come from? Suddenly Jeff Johnson is woke? Am I being pranked? Evoni took a sip of tea and cleared her throat. "Well, Jeff, I have to say I'm shocked. I never dreamed I'd hear the words white privilege and systemic racism come out of your mouth, at least not in a way I'd appreciate it. I welcome your changing worldview, but what brought about this epiphany?"

Jeff looked down at his coffee and began fiddling with the coaster underneath. Not answering Evoni's question directly, Jeff spoke "The reason why I asked to see you is I need for you to take over a case for me. I don't know if you know Cassidy Travers from Sheila's House but she's one of my clients and I can no longer represent her. You see Cassidy and I have been seeing each other."

"Say what," Evoni practically screamed and looked around to see if anyone noticed. "You know you can't date a client. That is unethical."

"I know, which is why I'm asking you to help me out. It's not something I planned. It just happened. I've been helping her with getting her record expunged, and we got to talking during our meetings and one thing led to another."

"One thing led to another?" Evoni asked incredulously. "What is this an act from a bad movie? Things don't just happen in real life, Jeff. Things happen because of our actions. You obviously overstepped boundaries and need to take ownership of that."

Jeff sighed heavily. "You're right. I knew exactly what I was doing. But, Evoni, it was never intentional. I was drawn to her. I've never felt this way about anyone before. Cassidy has opened my eyes and changed my heart. She's shown me how much of a misogynistic, sometimes racist asshole I was. She's the best thing that's ever happened to me."

"Jeff, I don't mean to sound callous, but you've screwed a lot of black women. What makes this one different?"

"Well, for one, we haven't slept together. We're waiting and just getting to know each other. Evoni, this is serious. I think I'm in love."

Evoni stared hard at Jeff. Looking into his eyes, she saw sincerity. This fool really had gone and fallen in love with a black woman. *Whoo chile, how is Daddy Johnson going to respond to this?*

"Okay, I'll take over Cassidy's case for you. And Jeff, I really hope you have changed. The microaggressions and gaslighting you've engaged in toward women, particularly women of color, aren't okay. You have a lot of work to do if you want to be an ally. It's not going to be easy, and it will be uncomfortable. Have you taken the time to think about how your family will react to your relationship? I hate to say it, but your father is a world-class racist prick."

"To answer your questions, yes, I've thought about how my family will react and I've decided I don't care. It's a not so well-kept family secret that my father, the man who berates minorities every chance he can get, has been sleeping with our Afro-Latina housekeeper for years. I don't want to be like my father. Even though I have done and said some questionable things that scream racist with a black woman fetish, I don't want to be that. I want to be a better man and human. I am willing to go up against my family for Cassidy, if it comes to that."

"That's all well and good, but you must be willing to go against your family and call them out not just for Cassidy but for all the people they discriminate against and make racial, transphobic, homophobic slurs and comments towards. Are you willing to stand up against the very system you were raised in?" Evoni asked pointedly.

"I am prepared to do whatever it takes to be an ally. So, yes, if that means calling out my family and friends and risking being disowned, then so be it. Evoni, I'm tired and I want to do better, hell just be a better person; not just for Cassidy but for myself."

Being a black woman in America, Evoni knew how hard it was to find true allyship from white America. She hoped Jeff was sincere and willing to see his privilege and use it to help people of color. Of course, only time would tell. But for now, she'd give him the benefit of the doubt.

"Jeff, I'll take your words as being sincere, but real change only comes through actions. We'll see what happens. In the meantime, send me Cassidy's file and I'll take a look."

"Thank you, Evoni. This means a lot to me. Once you meet Cassidy, you'll see why I fell in love with her. And I want you and all the other people I've hurt to see the change. Hopefully one day we can even be friends," stated Jeff wholeheartedly.

"Only time will tell, Jeff, only time will tell." With that Evoni got up from the table, put down money for her drink and a tip and left.

To say the day was interesting was an understatement. Evoni called Bri from her car and filled her in on Jeff's newfound epiphany. Bri cracked up. "You mean to tell me this woman turned Jeff from a Tucker Carlson to a Jon Stewart without even giving him the punanny? Hell, once he gets a taste, he may start paying out reparations from his own trust fund."

Evoni roared. "Girl, you are too much. I'm dead. Just take me away now Jesus."

Bri laughed. "You know I'm right. I want some of what she has. Maybe we can bottle it and sell it. Hell, we could singlehandedly cure racism."

"Okay, Al Sharpton, slow your roll. We'll see if Jeff's newfound wokeness lasts, especially if things don't work out between him and this woman. And he has yet to face his family, that's the real test."

"Right you are. There's nothing like good old-money racism; that's a battle I don't envy. His father may as well be Strom Thurman, hates black people but loves black vagina."

Evoni laughed so hard she started to cry. "Okay, I'm hanging up now because you are going to cause me to wreck. I will call you back later."

Bri giggled. "I'm just speaking the truth. Anyway, call me later. Bye."

After hanging up with Bri, Evoni managed to make it home in one piece. Deciding a nice long bubble bath and a glass of wine were in store, Evoni grabbed a bottle of red and headed toward the master bath. It was time to soak away the day.

The next couple of days were uneventful. Evoni was able to catch up on work and do some research on the names Jackson had provided from the license plate numbers she'd provided. As expected, the man residing at the home was not John Berkenshire but Chad Timmons, who was John's sister's only son. The lady in the Mercedes was his girl-friend, Cherry Monroe, and yes that was her legal name. The Honda driver was indeed the maid. Her name was Rocio Hernandez.

Thank God for social media. Both Cherry and Chad were heavy users. And their profiles were public, which made it very easy to take a deep dive into their daily lives. It appeared Cherry was a former beauty queen turned realtor who really wanted to make it onto reality TV. The girl's Instagram page was basically one big audition tape. Chad's social media revealed he was a true playboy. It looked like he changed girl-friends every six months to a year. Evoni guessed Cherry's time would be up soon. Chad was your typical rich frat boy; except he was a forty-four-year-old man; which would explain the crazy drug parties at the house. For a job, Chad listed business consultant, which could many anything. Consultant was the most overused bullshit job title ever. Literally anyone could say they were a consultant.

Evoni figured it meant he was a trust fund baby, and his "job" was just something to keep Mommy and Daddy happy and the wallet open.

Rocio Hernandez was a different story. There were at least three in the vicinity and only one had social media accounts. She was a twenty-four-year-old nursing student. Evoni didn't think she was right one. Evoni found the addresses of all three and decided she, Bri and Mari could go to each of the addresses and see if they spotted the Red Honda. One thing Evoni knew for a fact is that rich people tend to forget the help is around and will say and do things they wouldn't want anyone else to know about in front of them. Rich people rarely see poor people, especially old-money rich people who grew up with help.

Evoni emailed Mari and Bri her note on the residents of the house and her plan to figure out which of the three Rocio's was the correct one. They would each take one address and check it out. Finding Rocio and getting her to talk and staking out that Saturday night's party were the plan for the next couple of days.

It turned out the Rocio they were looking for resided at the address given to Bri, located in a lower middle-class neighborhood in Antioch. Like a lot of larger southern cities, there had been an influx of more well-off northerners moving there for the better weather and cheaper housing. This in turn pushed out a lot of the less fortunate longtime residents to the outer suburbs. It was happening all over the south from the Carolinas to Texas.

With Rocio's address confirmed, the ladies decided to try and catch her at home the following evening before their stakeout began in Brentwood.

CHAPTER 33

Evoni

On Saturday, the ladies met up at Mari's condo since it was in the direction they needed to travel. Evoni and Bri rode over together. Mari was allotted only one visitor's parking pass. Bri having been to Mari's before, drove while Evoni fiddled with the DSR camera she had brought along; in case they needed to get some good pictures out in Brentwood.

'Do you even know how to use that thing?" questioned Bri.

"Yes, I do, thank you very much. I took some photography classes with Amar. It was supposed to be a hobby that we would do together. We even joked about becoming wedding photographers on the side."

"Humph, good, you at least got something out of that relationship," remarked Bri. Bri looked over at Evoni. "Too soon?" she asked.

"Yes, too soon, heifa," said Evoni who then laughed.

Bri joined in. "Sorry, girl, but you know how I am."

"That I do, which is why I didn't smack you."

"Hey, hey, now no violence. I'm too pretty to be out here in the streets pulling hair, and I don't have any Vaseline in the car."

Evoni snickered. "Ain't that the truth."

Soon they arrived at Mari's and Bri pushed the button to be buzzed through the gates. "This gate sure is taking a long time, isn't it?" inquired Bri.

"It is, I wonder if it's broken," said Evoni. Just then a security guard approached from a partially hidden little hut.

He approached the driver side window. "How can I help ya'll today?"

"We're here to see Mari Davies."

"May I see some ID, ma'am?"

"ID?" asked Bri. "Is that necessary?"

"Yes, ma'am. It's policy."

"Ok," said Bri reaching into her bag for her wallet. She handed over her license. The guard took it and went back into his hut and made a call.

He returned a few minutes later. "I'm sorry, but I can't let you in. I don't see your name on the list of approved visitors, and Ms. Davies isn't answering the phone to verify your admittance."

Wanting to cause a scene but also not wanting to cause a scene as Bri knew how Nashville PD operated. She asked Evoni to give Mari a call.

"Ma'am, I'm going to need you to back out and leave the premises until you can provide verification that you are an approved guest."

"My friend is calling Mari right now. I'm sure she'll be able to confirm for you in a minute."

"That's all well and good ma'am but again I'm going to need you to vacate the premises until that time," stated the guard in a harsh tone.

"Is that necessary? I assure you we aren't interlopers. In fact, the last few times I was here, we didn't have to show ID at all. We just want to get in to see our friend. How about I pull over to the side?"

"Ma'am, I'm not going to ask you again. Please move your car or I will be forced to call the police. You people never listen," he finished under his breath, but Bri heard him.

"Excuse me, what did you just say? Who are 'you people?' In fact, Larry," said Bri reading his name tag, "don't bother answering that. I'll let your supervisor find out the answer for me. People like you are the reason this country is stuck in the past and can never truly move forward. I pity you."

Before the guard could spout off a retort, Evoni intervened holding the phone out. "I have Ms. Davies on the line, would you like to speak with her?"

"You can put it on speaker," stated the guard. Evoni did so and Mari affirmed that they were her guests. Without another word, the guard pushed the buzzer for the gate to open, turned away and walked back to his hut.

Bri was livid. Living in the south, she was used to the racism, but it never ceased to incense her. When would they learn, she and people like her weren't going anywhere and the good ole days were gone? They either needed to get with the times or be ready for the consequences of their actions. Bri knew she'd be having a conversation real soon with Larry's boss. He'd be on the unemployment line if she had anything to say about it.

Mari met them at the car with the visitor's parking pass. "I'm sorry ya'll. I was in the kitchen and left my phone in the bedroom. I didn't get the first call from the security guard."

Bri didn't respond. She was still trying to get her temper under control. Mari sensed the tension. "Did something happen?"

Evoni explained the situation with the guard. Mari was pissed. "You know what ladies, I'm on the fifth floor, number 12. Please go on up, the door is unlocked. I'll meet you up there." And with that Mari walked away and headed in the direction of the security hut.

Evoni and Bri shared a glance and quickly followed Mari...no way they were missing this.

Mari approached the guard hut and knocked. Larry opened the small window on the side and grinned at Mari. "Hello, ma'am. How can I help you?"

Mari glared at Larry. "You can help me by not being a racist prick to my guests. How dare you ask for ID. You know that isn't a visitor requirement but because they're black you assumed you could just play your little game with them and go on a power trip, huh? But I tell you what, Larry," Mari practically spit out, "I'm going to show you who has the power. You can expect to hear from your employer and building management within 24 hours. If they don't do anything, I will make it my mission to let the whole of the internet know what kind of asshole you are, and I know you've seen the power of social media."

Larry was speechless. He'd never been spoken to that way, and in defense of a couple of jiggaboos at that. Larry was seething at this race traitor but needed this job. Bobby Jo was pregnant with their fourth kid, and she had hinted she wanted to stay home full-time. "Ma'am, I don't know what your friends told you," said Larry through gritted teeth, "but I don't have a racist bone in my body. I simply asked to see ID because...."

"Because what?" jumped in Bri. "Because you weren't used to seeing two black women in a Maserati, a car you couldn't afford in this lifetime? Or because you are so insecure as a man that the only way you can feel good about yourself is by harassing black people? Which is it, Larry?" Bri asked with a sneer.

Evoni chimed in. "Yes, Larry, please enlighten us. What possible reason could you have to go against management policy?"

Instead of answering, Larry slammed his small window shut. *Screw this job*, he thought, *no way am I explaining myself to a pair of black bitches. I got too much white pride for that.*

But Larry also knew the odds of keeping his job were slim. His employer was one of those liberal douchebags, who was always going on about equality and diversity and inclusion as if these mutts deserved to be on the same level as someone like him.

Bri, Mari, and Evoni turned to walk away but suddenly Mari walked back over to Larry's guard shack and knocked on the window. Larry refused to open it, but she knew he could still hear her. "By the way asshole, I'm black," Mari said while giving Larry the finger.

Once they were inside, Mari apologized profusely. Evoni and Bri assured her she had nothing to apologize for and let her know they appreciated her doing what was right.

"Let's not waste any more time on Larry, other than to get him fired bright and early Monday morning," said Bri.

"You got that right," said Mari. "I relish making that call. If I was a vengeful person, I'd make an anonymous call suggesting he's the Music City Murderer and make his life a living hell for a few days. But I'm saved and better than that. Larry will get his comeuppance the good old fashion way, through karma."

"I know that's right," said Evoni and Bri while giving Mari a high-five.

Are you ladies ready to go see Rocio?" asked Evoni. "Hopefully, she'll have some information on Jessica, though I doubt she sticks around for the parties. If not on Jessica, at least she'll be able to give us more insight on Cherry and Chad."

"Let's roll," said Bri. "Needless to say, we will be taking my car; I don't trust old Larry to not vandalize it. And then I'd end up in jail and Evoni you'd have a second criminal case to work on."

"And that is definitely something I don't want," said Evoni laughing.

The ladies headed out. When they reached the gate, Larry quickly buzzed them out without even glancing in their direction. He was clearly still upset.

They pulled up at the address for Rocio twenty minutes later. Thankfully, the red Honda was parked in the driveway.

"Okay, how should we approach her?" asked Mari. "I don't think we initially want to mention anything about a criminal matter, we don't want to make her suspicious and think it has anything to do with her."

"Agreed," said Bri and Evoni in unison. "Three people confronting her could also scare her," said Bri. "How about Evoni go up to the door and if Rocio is in and amenable to speaking with us, if so, she can ask to invite us in?"

Evoni agreed. She stepped out of the car and looked around. Though you could tell the neighborhood wasn't the greatest, you could see where the residents showed pride in their homes. There were a couple of what looked to be empty houses a few doors down from Rocio's that would quickly fall into disrepair unless someone moved in soon or performed some upkeep. Evoni spotted two little black girls jumping rope in front of the house across from Rocio's. It warmed her heart. Not only to see two beautiful smiling little black girls but also to see them derive joy from something so simple as jumping rope in this day of social media, online games, and Netflix.

Evoni rang the doorbell at Rocio's house. She could hear laughter coming from inside and Spanish music. The door opened, and Evoni didn't see anyone. Then she heard a small voice. "Hello."

Evoni looked down and saw a cute little Hispanic boy, who looked to be about six.

"Carlo," said a voice. "Que te dijen acerca de abrir la puerta?"

The owner of the voice, a petite Hispanic woman with the largest doe eyes Evoni had ever seen appeared in the doorway. "Yes, how can I help you?"

Evoni smiled at the young lady and said "My name is Evoni Singleton. I'm looking for Rocio Hernandez. I am an attorney and I'd like to speak with her about a private matter. Nothing to be alarmed about," Evoni said hoping to put the young lady at ease.

"Abuela, there's someone at the door for you," yelled the young lady.

From what must have been the kitchen, appeared an older Hispanic lady holding a spoon and wearing an apron. She looked like the lady in the picture Bri had snapped.

"Sí, how can I help you?" Evoni repeated what she'd told the younger lady.

"What is this private matter? I have done nothing wrong," Rocio said with a defiant glare in her eyes. "I have my papers. I am legal."

"No, no, no. It's nothing like that," stated Evoni. "I just have a couple of questions about the couple living in the house you work at in Brentwood."

'Mr. Chad and his girlfriend, what have they done? I don't want any trouble."

"I promise you they haven't done anything, and there's no trouble. May I come in and explain?" asked Evoni.

Rocio sighed heavily and stepped aside to let Evoni in. Evoni followed Rocio towards the room she had exited earlier. It was indeed the kitchen, and the most heavenly smell was emanating from the pots on the stove.

Rocio pointed to a chair at the table and Evoni sat while Rocio tended to her pots. "That smells delicious," said Evoni. "Que es?" she asked in Spanish. Evoni knew about five phrases and that was one of them.

"It is for Chiles en Nogada. Which is a traditional Mexican dish. It is made with chiles or peppers as you Americans say with picadillo. Have you heard of picadillo?" queried Rocio.

"In fact, I have," said Evoni. "My father loves to cook, and he once took me, my mother, and my brothers to Mexico to explore the cuisine. We visited many cities and sampled many delicious dishes. It was a memorable experience."

This anecdote seemed to put Rocio a little more at ease. Taking a seat across from Evoni, Rocio asked Evoni what it was she wanted to know. "My English isn't great, but I imagine it's better than your Spanish," said Rocio with a slight smile.

Evoni laughed. "I imagine it is. First, thank you for speaking with me. As I mentioned at the door, I'm Evoni. I know you work for Chad Timmons, and I just wanted to ask you a few questions about him."

Rocio's face screwed up with a look of disgust at the mention of Chad's name, clearly, she wasn't a fan. "You may ask your questions, but I will not say I will answer them," said Rocio.

"That's fair," responded Evoni. "I don't want you to do or say anything that will make you feel uncomfortable. Any information you can provide will be greatly appreciated. But before we get started, I have a couple of friends waiting outside, do you mind if I invite them in?"

Rocio's eyes narrowed. "Who are these friends?"

"Just two girlfriends who drove over with me. I promise you we won't impose on too much of your time."

"I suppose it is okay," Rocio said resignedly.

"Thank you," said Evoni while quickly shooting off a text to Bri. Within a minute the doorbell rang. Rocio went to answer and returned with Bri and Mari in tow.

Taking a seat on either side of Evoni, both Bri and Mari exclaimed how delicious the food smelled. Rocio gave them a brief explainer on what she was cooking. The attention and praise helped loosen Rocio up more. "What questions do you have?" asked Rocio looking at Evoni.

"Firstly, how long have you worked for Chad?"

"I do not work for Chad. I work for Mr. Berkenshire. He pays me to keep the house clean even when no one is staying there. He is a good man. He give my son a job at his business in Austin."

"How long have you looked after the house in Brentwood for Mr. Berkenshire?"

"It has been seven years."

"How long has Chad lived at the house?"

"About a year. Mr. Berkenshire tell me Mr. Chad is a loser, but he is his sister's son so he must help him."

Bri jumped in. "Does Mr. Berkenshire ever come to the house?"

"No, he has not been to the house since Mr. Chad move in. He not really like him."

"What do you think of Chad and Cherry?" asked Evoni.

Rocio got up and checked her pots. Evoni figured it was a delaying tactic and that Rocio wanted to think about how to answer the question.

Roxio returned to her seat. "I am sorry. I have been so rude. Can I offer any of you ladies something to drink?"

Rocio was delaying. Evoni wondered why. "I think we're fine but thank you," she said.

"I think you were about to tell us how you feel about Chad and Cherry," said Mari.

Rocio sighed heavily. "Mr. Chad is a mal hombre, a bad man. He is mean to Cherry and the girl before her. I see bruise on her face one day. Only bad men hit women."

Everyone nodded in agreement. Any man who hit a woman was a coward and indeed a bad man.

Rocio continued. "He, Mr. Chad, never speak to me unless he is yelling at me for not doing something the way he likes. Once he yell at me because I didn't clean his bathroom quickly enough. I do not like working when he is in the house. I try to wait until he leave for work but sometimes, he stay in all day. Just sit around the house eating, drinking, and doing drugos."

"You've seen Mr. Chad do drugs?" questioned Evoni.

"Sí, and it's not marijuana. He snort something up his nose."

Evoni, Bri, and Mari looked at each other, now they were getting somewhere.

"What about Cherry?"

"Cherry no problem. She is okay. She only mean when Mr. Chad mean to her. Then she take it out on me. She does not know about the new young lady Mr. Chad bring around when she gone."

It sounded like Cherry's time was almost up. Not wanting to take up too much of Rocio's time, Evoni wanted to get to why they were there. "Rocio, do you know anything about parties Mr. Chad has at the house...parties with drugs?"

Rocio shook her head. "I do not see any parties, but I have come to clean and found the house trashed, basura everywhere. It is disgusting. Also, people everywhere, on the floor, the couch, by the pool, everywhere. Mr. Berkenshire would not be happy."

"So, you have never told Mr. Berkenshire about Chad's parties or rather the state of the house?"

"No," said Rocio shaking her head. "I do not want to come in between family, not my business."

Evoni pulled out her phone and pulled up a picture of Jessica. "Have you ever seen this lady at the house?"

Rocio brought her face close to the phone squinting. "Sí, I see her many times. One time I see her sleeping on the grass. Oh, and one time I see her argue with Mr. Chad and another woman. She very upset. She throw glass at Mr. Chad, then run off."

Interesting, thought Evoni, *what could they have been arguing about?* She hoped to find out later.

They asked a few more questions, but Rocio didn't have much more to offer. Evoni, Mari, and Bri thanked Rocio for her time.

"Please, before you go, let me give you some food. My food the best," said Rocio with pride in her voice.

The three looked at each other and quickly agreed. No way were they passing up food that smelled that good. They left with arms loaded with plates of Chiles en Nogada, homemade tortillas, guacamole, and rice and beans. While figuring out how to place the food in the car without anything wasting, they heard Rocio call out.

Rocio approached the car. "I just remember something about the lady. One morning when I was pulling into the driveway, I see her arguing with a young woman, a gringo, by a black car. The other woman slap her and then get in car and drive away."

"When was this?" asked Evoni.

"Maybe four weeks ago," said Rocio hesitantly. "I'm not exactly sure."

"Do you know what kind of car the other lady was driving?"

Rocio shook her head. "I'm not good with cars, but it was a big one...an SUV."

"This is great Rocio," said Bri. "Thank you so much for your help and for the delicious food."

Rocio smiled. "It is my pleasure. You are lovely ladies. I am glad to help. Buenas noches," she said and headed back to her house where the young lady who answered the door for Evoni was standing watching.

Checking the time, the ladies decided it was a good time to head to the house in Brentwood. Hopefully, Chad didn't disappoint and held a party tonight. The last thing they wanted was to do this all over again. And thanks to Rocio, tonight they had delicious stakeout food.

CHAPTER 34

Bri

Driving onto the street of Chad's house, Bri was lucky enough to find a parking spot almost exactly where she'd parked previously.

They parked and looked over at the house. There were lights on inside but didn't look like there was much activity going on. Bri hoped this was because they were early, and people hadn't begun arriving yet and not because the party wasn't happening.

The smell of Rocio's food wafting from the to-go plates was a reminder that it was past dinner time. Bri, Mari, and Evoni figured it was a good time to sample Rocio's cuisine before guests began arriving and they were otherwise occupied.

The food tasted even better than it smelled if that was possible. Not wanting to overeat and become sleepy, each lady ate a small portion and put the food away but not without longing glances at that still waiting to be devoured.

Feeling satiated, the ladies sat back and waited for some action. They didn't have to wait long. Within minutes of each other, three luxury rideshare cars arrived. Ready with her camera, Evoni began snapping pictures as the riders exited. Two of the arrivals were young women, who looked like they may have been the evening's entertainment.

The third rider was a man, about fortyish, sandy blonde hair, medium height, and build; nothing exciting except Mari recognized him as Taylor Sanders, the owner of at least two prominent Nashville area restaurants.

All three guests walked right in. It was clear Chad left the door unlocked for his guests. Soon thereafter, more and more people began to arrive. The ladies recognized many of them, including at least one sitting judge, a celebrity stylist, and a local country singer who was poised to make it big. It was a regular who's who of Nashville.

After about an hour of arrivals, it seemed all the guests had arrived or at least those that were going to be on time. With photos of everyone, the ladies began discussing the merits of going into the party.

"I say we go in and check things out. For all we know they could be playing board games and sipping sweet tea," said Bri.

"Or re-enacting *Get Out*," stated Evoni. "And I'm not trying to be on the auction block."

"I vote for going in," chimed in Mari. "We really should confirm Hank's story and maybe once everyone is knackered, we can get some information about Jessica."

Bri and Evoni chuckled. "Mari, your white girl is showing. I don't think I've ever heard anyone use the word knackered," laughed Bri.

Mari joined in. "Hahaha...whatever. Make fun of my word choice, but you know I'm right."

"You know I'm all for going in," stated Bri while looking straight at Evoni. "She's the one who needs convincing."

Evoni knew they were right but really didn't want to go into that den of inequity. But she was outvoted so she acquiesced. "Fine, we'll go in but if I see anyone with a teacup, I'm out of there and you two are on your own."

With that settled, they decided to wait a bit longer before venturing in. They wanted Chad and his guests to have imbibed and loosened up before barging in unannounced.

After another forty-five minutes, they decided enough time had passed. No other guests had arrived during that time, so they didn't think they'd miss any new arrivals.

Though they couldn't hear any noise from the street, once they reached the door, they could hear the music playing loudly. There was a lot of laughter coming from inside.

"Here goes nothing," said Bri as she pushed the door open. Thankfully no one was in the foyer, and they were able to walk in without being seen.

"Okay," said Evoni taking charge. "We're sticking together. I'm not asking, I'm telling. We don't know what we are dealing with, and we don't know what drugs these people are on. I'm not taking any chances."

"No argument here," said Bri. "I'm not trying to be alone in a room with crackheads, cokeheads, methheads, or anything in between."

"Ditto for me;" stated Mari.

"Good," said Evoni. "Let's start in the living room and work our way back. God, I hope we don't walk in on an orgy."

The scene in the living room was more mellow than expected. Sitting around in a circle on the carpeted floor were two men and three women; all, thankfully, still fully dressed. They were taking turns smoking from a bong. Spotting them standing in the doorway, one of the women, a strawberry blond with a cute pixie cut, invited them in.

Bri, Mari, and Evoni inched their way into the room and took a seat on the sofa. One of the men tried passing them the bong, they declined. He just shrugged, took a hit, and passed it on.

The woman who'd invited them in got up from the circle and came and sat in front of them on the floor. "So, you ladies clearly haven't been here before. I'd remember you if you had been."

"You're right," remarked Bri. "This is our first time. Guess we're popping our cherry, so to speak."

The woman laughed. "I'm Tracy. I'm glad to be here for your first time. Welcome to 'The Awakening.'"

Evoni, Bri, and Mari looked at each other. Was this some kind of Jim Jones cult they'd walked in on?

"What is 'The Awakening?'" asked Evoni. "The person who invited us didn't mention this was a group. Please don't let this be some kind of cult."

Tracy laughed. "Sorry, I should explain. It's not a group or a cult. Chad is a bit pretentious and a walking talking wannabe philosopher. He deemed these little get-togethers 'The Awakening.' He claims the drugs he procures are sourced only from shaman and priest and priestesses; thereby when you partake your third eye is 'awakened' and you can finally see the world clearly and your purpose in it.

"It's all horseshit. Though there are a few people here who seem to have bought into it but most of us are just here to get high and party. And when the drugs are free, no reason to not play along.

"But you ladies don't really look like the party types, no offense."

What the hell, thought Evoni. Tracy seemed to be a straight shooter. "You're right. We aren't exactly party girls. We're here about a friend." Evoni pulled out her phone and showed Tracy a picture of Jessica. "She told us she came here often, and we're just trying to find anyone who knows her."

"Wait, that's Juicy. She was a regular here, but I heard she's dead."

"That's right, she was found dead in a motel. Someone strangled her to death," stated Bri.

"Oh, crap. I didn't know how she died. That sucks something major. Have the cops found who did it? I hope you don't think it was anyone here," said Tracy while clutching at her non-existent pearls.

"No, no, no," said Evoni working to reassure Tracy and keep her talking. "We're just trying to find people who knew her in a way we didn't. You know trying to find some closure."

Visibly relaxing, Tracy reached out for the bong that was passing by and took a hit. "Juicy was a mainstay around here. She'd been coming to Chad's parties for as long as he's been having them. Everyone here knew her. She was the life of the party. The girl never met a drug she didn't like. Unfortunately, that also meant she sometimes got on the wrong side of a few people."

"Like who?" questioned Mari.

"Oh, just a few people here and there. Juicy had a bad habit of bringing in new people and spilling secrets. I don't know if you've looked around, but many people here are pretty well-known in Nashville society. What we do here is a pretty well-kept open secret amongst us; kind of a 'what happens in the house, stays in the house' understanding. But Juicy would bring in newbies and introduce them around making certain high-profile people uncomfortable which in turn led to a few dustups."

"Anyone in particular?" questioned Evoni.

"As much as I'd like to help you ladies, I can't name names. Sorry, but these little parties only work when there's a pact between the attendees to not reveal their secrets. I'm sorry. But, hey, since you're here you may run into someone she had issues with, but I can't be the one to tell you. Again sorry," said Tracy while moving back to her circle.

Evoni, Mari, and Bri left the living room and continued exploring the house. There were a handful of people in the dining room engaged in what looked to be strip Twister. They decided to avoid that little orgy waiting to happen. They headed downstairs. The finished basement contained a movie theater, a wine cellar, and a game room. They entered the game room which contained a mix of men and women, including Chad and Cherry, all hanging around a pool table. The center of the pool table contained an assortment of drugs and drug paraphernalia; none of which the ladies recognized.

There was no way they were partaking in any drugs, but they needed to speak with Chad and Cherry; preferably separately. They decided to pretend to engage in a game of foosball while waiting for an opportunity to present itself. They each grabbed a beer in an attempt to somewhat fit in.

They didn't have to wait long. Cherry excused herself and headed towards the theater room, it looked like she was taking a call. They waited a few minutes and then followed her. They found her sitting at the front of the theater in a corner whispering into her phone. Though they couldn't hear what she said, her demeanor led them to believe the conversation wasn't a friendly one. Waiting in the shadows until Cherry ended the call, they emerged as she hung up. Evoni laughed loudly to announce their presence, they didn't want Cherry to know they'd been spying on her.

Cherry looked up and made to leave. Bri approached her. "Oh my God, can I just say how much I love your dress. What is it, Gucci?"

Cherry smiled lightly. "It's actually Stella McCartney. Please excuse me," she said attempting to maneuver around Bri.

Bri stepped in her path. "You're Cherry, right--Chad's girlfriend? I gotta say, this party is great. It's our first time here," said Bri gesturing towards Evoni and Mari. "We're friends of Juicy. She invited us here a couple of months back, but we were never able to make it. So sad what happened to her, huh?"

Cherry nodded. "Yes, tragic but really I have to get back to the party."

"Before you go," said Evoni jumping in. "Can you just give us a few minutes of your time? We are trying to find out if you ever saw anyone fighting with Juicy?"

"Why would anyone fight with Juicy?" asked Cherry quizzically. "She got along with everyone as far as I know. She was the life of the party. I can't say she was a friend, as most of the people out there now aren't. They show up for the free booze and party favors."

"So, you don't recall her having any disagreements with anyone who comes to these parties?" Bri asked.

"I mean, there were a few times where a couple of the guys became upset when Juicy brought in new people, but no one ever got mad enough to want to kill her."

"What about Chad, did he have any issues with her?"

Cherry stared at Evoni like she had horns growing out of head. "Why would Chad have issues with Juicy? She was just another hanger on. Chad is the most laidback easygoing guy. He likes to party and doesn't like drama. He and Juicy were friendly acquaintances, nothing more."

Evoni considered what Rocio had said about Chad. Cherry was clearly hiding Chad's true character.

At that moment, they all heard someone calling Cherry's name. "That's Chad, I better go. Look I really hope they find the person who killed Juicy, but I can assure you it wasn't anyone here. Now if you'll excuse me," stated Cherry while pushing past them.

They followed Cherry out of the theater room where they bumped into Chad questioning Cherry as to why she was gone for so long. Yep, he seemed like he was Mr. Easygoing...not.

Chad spotted them and turned to Cherry. "Who are they? I've never seen them before?"

Cherry answered. "They're friends of Juicy. They say she told them about the party, and they just got around to checking it out."

Turning to stare at Bri, Evoni and Mari, Chad remarked, "Is that right? So, you just happen to show up here after Juicy has bit the dust? How convenient."

"That's right," said Bri challenging Chad. "Is there a problem with that? Juicy was a good friend of ours. We would all go to Vegas together. She knew how much we liked a good party and so she gave us this address a while back."

"Hmm," said Chad. "That does sound like Juicy. She gave out my address to every Tom, Dick, and Hannah apparently," he said looking directly at Mari. "But as I always say, the more the merrier. Just don't cause any trouble and don't blab anything about what you see here."

Chad then turned and walked off. So much for talking to the man of the house. After walking around for a bit more, they were ready to leave. Everyone they spoke to knew Juicy or Jessica and didn't have a bad word to say about her other than her constantly bringing in new people. Apparently, no one there had any idea why anyone would want to kill her and didn't even know she had children and was engaged in a bitter custody battle. Jessica was clearly living two different lives, and Evoni wondered how Linc had missed this one in his investigation.

With nothing more to glean, they exited the house. After being inside, they all craved a hot shower and a nice glass of wine, hold the party favors. Bri drove back to Mari's, where Larry had been replaced by Troy, who recognized Mari and waved them through the entrance. After dropping Mari off, Bri drove to Evoni's. They chatted in the car for a few minutes and then said goodbye. It had been an eventful day and they hoped something they had learned would be helpful to Marc.

CHAPTER 35

Evoni

Marc's pre-trial hearing was set for that upcoming Wednesday. During the hearing, the D.A. would present his case and evidence. Tim would get a chance to cross-examine any witnesses. Also, the judge would rule on any pre-trial motions that had been submitted. The team decided to meet Monday evening to discuss strategy and new developments.

Monday evening found everyone gathered around the conference room table in Tim's office. Most were enjoying the catered dinner from Jack's Tackle, a local seafood place with to die for crab cakes and lobster rolls. While eating, everyone shared their findings. Jackson went first. His report was short and succinct. He thought he'd found the town where Jessica had been shipped off to but was still waiting on confirmation. Once he could confirm Jessica had given birth, he could then work on tracking down the whereabouts of the child. It was slow going but necessary.

Next, Tim informed everyone about the upcoming preliminary hearing. "I expect the state has some evidence we don't know about as they were able to get an arrest warrant, despite the tie fibers found around Jessica's neck not matching any ties found at Marc's. The good thing about this hearing is we get to see first-hand the prosecutor's case against you which will help us prepare for trial, if it comes to that."

Evoni looked at Marc. He didn't look like he'd slept in a week. His skin was pale, his eyes red and he looked like he had lost weight. This was weighing on him, and it showed. Evoni reached out and took his hand. "Marc, are you okay? I know it sounds silly, but we need you to take care of yourself, for your kids' sake and for court. Unfortunately, appearances matter in court. So, we need you to look put together and confident."

"Evoni's right," said Tim. "I know this is a difficult situation, but you must try and get some rest. Have you seen a doctor about maybe getting some sleeping pills?" asked Tim.

Marc shook his head. "I don't believe in taking any pharmaceuticals unless absolutely medically necessary. But I know you're right and Aunt Abby has been trying to get me to take some of her herbal remedies for sleep. I suppose I should take her up on the offer. It's just so hard to rest knowing your life hangs in the balance and you have no control or say so. All of you are working hard on my behalf, and I appreciate it. I just wish there was more I could do to help myself."

Everyone at the table understood Marc's feeling of impotence. They were all doers, people who were decisive and acted. They got the frustration of being sidelined in your own life.

"I think I'm going to get some fresh air," said Marc looking at Tim.

"I think that's a great idea. Go clear your head, we can continue without you."

Evoni and Tim shared a look. It would be easier to relate what they'd learn about "Juicy" without Marc in the room. He didn't need another reminder of just how little he knew the woman he'd been married to and had children with.

Once Marc left, Evoni, Bri and Mari relayed the information they'd gleaned from Rocio and Chad's party. It wasn't much, but it gave them something to work with. If they could get Rocio to remember exactly when she'd seen Jessica arguing with the other lady, Jackson could, with some inside help, search traffic cameras from the area and try to locate the other woman. She was a suspect until ruled out.

By the time Marc returned, the meeting was breaking up. Everyone said their goodbyes and Evoni assured Marc she'd try to make it to the hearing on Wednesday.

When Wednesday arrived, Evoni stopped into the office to check in with Mari. Thankfully she had nothing pressing on her calendar, so Mari was able to reschedule her meetings. On her way out of the office, she bumped into Linc in the elevator. "Ms. Singleton, it's been a while. I almost forgot you work here," joked Linc.

"Hahaha," said Evoni. "I've been busy, but I am glad I ran into you. Are you busy right now or can you walk with me for a few minutes? I'm heading to the courthouse," stated Evoni.

"For you, I can make time."

Evoni blushed slightly. Why did the man have to be so damn fine? Was it a requirement for being a PI, she wondered thinking of the other fine-ass PI she was working with. "Thanks," she said.

As they exited the elevator, Linc held the door for Evoni to exit and it took all her willpower not to moan while walking past him, he smelled so good. Once they were out of the building, Evoni began talking. "Firstly, I want to thank you for all the work you've put in on my cases. You've been a tremendous help."

Linc smiled. "Thanks. There's nothing a man loves hearing more than he was useful. It happens so rarely," he said with a chuckle.

Evoni laughed along. "Well, your gender isn't exactly known for being helpful, considerate, and thoughtful, so...."

"Believe me, I get it. Men suck. I'll take the compliment."

Evoni smiled. Linc was extremely charming; Evoni wondered why some woman hadn't snatched him up yet. "The other thing I wanted to speak to you about is the investigation into Jessica French you conducted. We've found out some additional information about her and wanted to know if you came across anything relating to it while you were investigating."

Evoni shared with Linc the amateur investigating she and her friends were doing on Marc's behalf.

Linc listened intently and waited until she finished before responding. "Well, it looks like someone is coming for my job," he joked. "But on a serious tip, I do recall following Jessica to a house in Brentwood, but I had no idea all of that was going on inside. I apologize for not including it in my report. I figured she was visiting a friend. I guess I screwed up on that front, but I really didn't want to hang out in that neighborhood for too long. A big black man sitting in his car would draw a lot of unwanted attention and the last thing I needed was a Karen or Chad calling the cops on me."

Evoni nodded her head in agreement. Linc was right. In today's climate, a black man or, for that matter, a black woman could never be too careful. There seemed to be a never-ending supply of Karens and Chads just itching to call the cops on a black person for any reason. "No need to apologize. I totally understand not wanting to hang around in Brentwood. I just wanted to make sure there was nothing we missed."

"So, you're playing private eye for your client. Need any help?" asked Linc.

"As much as I'd love to say yes, because God knows we have no idea what we're doing, I can't involve you in this. If the firm finds out I'm involved, there will be blowback and I don't want you getting caught in the crosshairs. Also, Marc's actual defense attorney has a contract private investigator, Jackson Jameson, who's working on this."

"I know Jackson, he's a good guy. He and I are both members of a couple of the same organizations. You're in good hands. But, Evoni," said Linc while looking into her eyes, "you never have to worry about anything you do blowing back on me. Everything I do is because I want to do it and I'm always ready to take any repercussions for my actions; no matter what they are."

Evoni broke away from his look. She couldn't handle this man looking at her like he'd do anything to protect her. Too bad she hadn't met him before Amar or before they began working together. Sometimes the universe was just cruel. "Understood, but if I were to play any role in you getting in trouble, I wouldn't be able to live with myself."

"Okay, okay. I'll stay out of it but remember I've always got your back."

"I'll write it down, take a picture and post it on Instagram," joked Evoni.

Linc laughed. "You do that; whatever it takes to keep me on your mind," Linc said with a wink.

"Whew," stated Evoni. "It's getting a little toasty out here." They had reached the courthouse. "Let me get inside before I sweat out this hairstyle I just paid way too much for."

Linc shook his head. "I swear I will never understand women. You guys spend a lot of money on aesthetics, but I think you all are most beautiful when you aren't made up and trying to impress. I want to see the natural you."

"That's a sweet sentiment but you do know women look good for other women," Evoni said with a laugh. "We're all in silent competition with each other. We couldn't care less about ya'll."

Laughing loudly, Linc quipped, "I wish I had known that when I was dropping money on a weekly basis for hair and nail appointments. Thanks for the heads up."

"You're welcome. Feel free to come to me for advice on women, I'll give you the friends and family discount."

"I'll keep that in mind, Ms. Singleton. I'll let you go, good luck in court." Linc gave her one last smile and turned and walked away. Evoni stood there a few extra seconds, watching him from behind. Lord, that man made her mind act out scenes from a Zane novel. Evoni shook her head to clear her lustful thoughts and headed inside.

She found Tim and Marc in the hallway conferencing. Evoni decided to wait a beat instead of interrupting. After about five minutes, Tim excused himself to take a call and Evoni approached Marc.

Marc glanced up at her. "Oh, Evoni, you made it. Thanks so much, I know you probably have a million other things to do."

"Morning, Marc, of course I made it. I told you I will be with you throughout this process. Do you mind if I sit?" asked Evoni.

Marc moved over. "Of course, of course, I'm sorry. Where are my manners? Can I get you a coffee while we wait? There's a vending machine down the hall. Though the coffee is barely above drinkable."

"I'm fine," said Evoni. "I find that all courthouse coffee is atrocious. I tend to avoid it at all costs. How are you, Marc? How are the kids and Abby?"

"The kids are doing okay considering everything that's happened. Kanisha has been doing individual sessions with Ashton, and they really seem to be helping him come to grips with everything. Thankfully Caleb is young, so he doesn't fully understand what is going on and Aunt Abby is well. She likes you, you know, a lot. She says you have spunk and gumption. She's been a godsend. Just having her in the house eases the tension and gives me room to breathe, you know?"

"That's good. You need to be able to find some time to breathe and step away from all the craziness. I like your aunt, too. She's a firecracker," Evoni said with a smile.

Marc laughed. "That she is. I remember as a kid, after my mom passed and I went to live with Aunt Abby, getting into trouble at school for cheating. I hadn't, but the teacher refused to believe me and so she sent a note home with me for Aunt Abby. I explained to Aunt Abby that I hadn't cheated and if anything, the other student had copied off me. Well, the next day Aunt Abby marched into the school and demanded to see the teacher and the principal. She refused to leave until it happened.

"Once everyone was gathered, she asked me to tell them what I had told her. I recounted my story and after I finished Aunt Abby grilled the teacher as to how she had decided that I was the one who cheated. She reminded her I had As in every class, was a student tutor and had never once been accused of cheating so why would she automatically assume I was the cheater. The teacher had no rebuttal, she stuttered and stammered until the principal came to her rescue and assured Aunt Abby, he would handle it. The following day, the teacher apologized to me. I never had any more trouble out of her or anyone else after that."

Evoni chuckled. "I love it. Every kid deserves an advocate like that. We all need someone to fight for us when we can't and Marc," Evoni said while touching his sleeve, "right now 'those someones' for you are me, Tim, and the rest of the gang. We will get you through this and get to the truth."

Marc smiled at Evoni. She could see the gratitude in his eyes. "Evoni, I appreciate so much all that you guys are doing for me. I'm basically a stranger but you are working to keep me free like I'm family. I don't think there are words to express just how much that means to me. I will never forget this," finished Marc.

Tim walked up. "What'd I miss? It looks like you two were having a heart to heart without me. If I had feelings, I think they'd be hurt."

Everyone laughed. "You ready to head in?" asked Tim.

"As ready as I'm going to get," replied Marc while standing. The trio went inside, and Tim and Marc set up at the defense table. The prosecutor was already sitting at his table, reviewing his notes. It was Reed Hastings, an up-and-coming hotshot in the DA's office. Tim had never gone up against him but heard he was skilled and that juries loved him. This didn't bother Tim. Juries loved him too.

Because she wasn't an official part of the legal team, Evoni took a seat in the first row behind the defense table. She was there for moral support and to see first-hand how the prosecutor's case would stack up.

At 10:00 a.m. on the dot, the bailiff called court to session. The judge, Walter Bentley, was known amongst the legal community as Judge Walter Waffle. He tended to change his mind on his own calls during trial. It was frustrating for everyone involved and often led to confusion amongst the jury. There was no way to know how this would play out for Marc.

Once everyone was seated, the judge addressed pending motions before the court. First was Tim's Motion to Dismiss, which was summarily denied but that wasn't unexpected. The second and final motion was also from Tim. It was a Motion for Discovery. In essence, Tim was requesting that the state turn over all evidence they had against his client. And any exculpatory evidence the D.A. office had. If there was exculpatory evidence that would explain why Hastings was so slow to turn it over. He wouldn't want to provide time any ammunition to get the charges dismissed. The judge quizzed the A.D.A.

"Mr. Hastings, has the state not turned over all evidence to the defense?"

"Um, Your Honor, we are working on that as we speak. Mr. Blankenship should have a copy of everything we have by the end of the day."

"Good, let's make sure that happens. I don't want to hear otherwise. With that being said, I'll reserve ruling on this motion. Mr. Blankenship, please let the court know tomorrow morning if all evidence has been received."

"Yes, Your Honor," replied Tim.

With that out of the way, the judge began the hearing. Hastings called his first witness, Tamra Westbrook. Westbrook had been part of the Nashville Medical Examiner's Office for five years and had a reputation of being one of the best MEs in the country. She testified as to the cause of Jessica's death and the time frame. Tim had no questions for her.

Next up was Homicide Detective William Snow who shot a smug look across at the defense on his way to take the stand. Hastings took him through the crime scene, then on to his investigatory findings. Snow explained why they had latched on to Marc as a prime suspect. They were aware of the ongoing bitter custody battle, which provided motive. After their initial interview with Marc, where Marc had been unable to provide a solid alibi, the detectives decided to investigate him further.

Hastings asked Snow what happened after they began investigating Marc. "Well, sir, first we obtained the location data for his cellphone which showed it was in the vicinity of the defendant's home for the time frame in question."

"But that doesn't prove anything does it?" questioned Hastings who knew the answer just like anyone else who lived in the twenty-first century.

"No sir, it doesn't. It just means the phone was at the residence but not necessarily Mr. French."

"Okay, so you were able to confirm Mr. French's phone was at his home but not Mr. French, correct?"

"That's correct. Mr. French had no way of proving he was home or otherwise engaged during the time of the murder."

"At what point did you request a search warrant for the defendant's home?"

Snow answered. "We were able to obtain a search warrant for Mr. French's home and electronics after a positive identification by a patron of the motel where Jessica French was killed."

"What," yelled Marc. "That's a lie. I've never been to that motel. I don't even know where it is."

The judge banged his gavel. "Mr. Blankenship, please get your client under control. I will not tolerate such outbursts in my court. If he does it again, I will have him jailed for contempt. Do I make myself clear?" asked Judge Bentley almost at a near shout.

"Yes, Your Honor. It won't happen again." Tim turned to Marc and whispered to him.

"Mr. Hastings, you may continue," stated Judge Bentley.

"Thank you, Your Honor. Now, Detective Snow you were explaining you found a witness."

Snow picked up where he had left off. "That's correct. With the witness identification and the absence of an alibi, we were able to get a search warrant."

"Did you find anything incriminating during your search?" asked Hastings with a slight smile. It was clear he was enjoying this and knew exactly what Snow would say.

"We did. We found several ties made by the same company as the fibers found on the body of Jessica French. We also found nasty emails between the deceased and the defendant, some in which he threatened to kill her if she didn't stop lying about him."

"Anything else?" probed Hastings.

"Yes, we also found a key from Sunny Day Motel in the residence," answered Snow who turned and stared at Marc with a feral smile on his face.

And at this point, you felt you had enough to arrest Mr. French?" queried Hastings.

"Yes, we reached out to your office and received approval for an arrest warrant."

"Thank you, Detective Snow. No further questions, Your Honor," Hastings stated and headed back to his seat.

"Mr. Blankenship, do you have any questions for this witness?" asked Judge Bentley.

"Yes, Your Honor, but may we have a five-minute recess? I need to confer with my client," stated Tim.

The judge glanced at the clock. "Okay, Mr. Blankenship, I'll be generous and give you ten. Everyone back here in ten minutes, court adjourned until then." Everyone rose for the judge. After his exit, Tim ushered Marc out of the courtroom and Evoni followed.

Needing a quiet place to talk, Tim directed them to follow him. They found themselves in an unused outer office in the Clerk of Court's office space. Tim was a close friend of the clerk, and she allowed him to use the unused space when needed in exchange for a $200 bottle of wine.

Marc spoke first. "You have to believe me; I've never been to that motel. I didn't even know it existed until Jessica's death. Whoever this witness is, he or she is lying through their teeth," Marc stated angrily.

Tim interrupted him. "Marc, we believe you, but this is a problem. I'm less concerned with this so-called witness and more so with the key card. Any idea how it got into your house?" asked Tim.

"None," stated Marc emphatically. "Maybe Jessica left it there once. She has been in the house since we split to see the boys a few times. Sometimes they'd leave something they needed at her place, and she'd bring it by for them. That's the only explanation I can think of, because I promise you, I have never been to that place."

"Okay," said Tim blowing out air. "I can work with that but let's hope we solve this thing before it goes to trial. Because there's no doubt in my mind the judge will hold this over for trial and I'd prefer not to have to try and convince a jury that Jessica happened to leave the key card in your house. People like simple explanations and the simplest explanation would be that the card belonged to you."

Before heading back, Tim cautioned Marc on any more outbursts. "No matter what anyone gets up and there and says, you must control yourself. I'm sure this so-called witness will be up next, and his lies will infuriate you, but you have to stay in control," stated Tim.

"I promise no more outburst. I was just unprepared for the lies."

"Okay, let's head back."

Back in the courtroom, Judge Bentley called court back into session and Tim began his cross-examination of Detective Snow. Snow held up well. Nothing seemed to rattle him. He had an explanation for everything.

"Detective, this so-called witness you found. Did he or she seek you out or did you find them?"

"She came to us. She said she'd seen the murder on the news and knew the deceased. The witness told us she'd seen the deceased's ex-husband that same evening at the motel."

"Let me make sure I have this straight. You're telling me this witness just happened to be at the same motel as Jessica French and just so happened to see my client there?" scoffed Tim.

"That's exactly what I'm saying," stated Snow. "You know sometimes coincidences do happen."

"Moving on, this key card you claim to have found in my client's house, where exactly did you find it?"

"I'd have to consult my case notes, but I believe the key card was found by an officer in the defendant's kitchen."

"So, it wasn't found in an area only my client has access to?" probed Tim.

"That's correct."

"Were there any indications as to how long the key card had been in the kitchen?"

"Not to my knowledge."

"Were my client's fingerprints found on the card?"

"No. There were no prints found on the card, it had been conveniently wiped clean."

"So, it's possible the key card had been there for months and could've been placed there by someone else?" questioned Tim.

"I suppose that's possible."

"What if I told you, Jessica French had been back in the house since the divorce on numerous occasions and that she could have easily left behind the key card?"

"You could tell me that, but can you prove it? As far as I'm concerned, your client is the one who had that key card unless he's saying one of his kids visits motels," stated Snow with a smirk.

"No further questions, Your Honor," said Tim from his seat.

The judge excused the detective and asked Hastings to call his next witness. He called Jaime Bullock-Jefferson.

Jaime Bullock-Jefferson was a sight to behold. Her hair was a color red not found in nature, with brunette roots. Her skin was sallow, much like a jaundiced newborn. Evoni was taught to never judge a book by its cover but this one time she felt comfortable in her assessment that Jaime was a drug user.

Tim looked over at Marc as Jaime took the stand. Marc shook his head. He had no idea who the woman was.

Once Jaime was sworn in, Hastings began by asking her to explain how she knew Jessica French. "Jess and I go way back. She and I worked together years ago as shampoo girls," answered Jaime while trying to discreetly scratch at her arm.

"And did you and the deceased stay in touch over the years?" questioned Hastings.

"Um, not really. After Jess moved away, she kinda forgot about the people she knew before she became a rich man's wife. But I didn't blame her, I would've done the same thing, but I never got that lucky."

Hastings continued. "So, Miss Bullock-Jefferson, when did you reconnect with Jessica French?"

"Oh, about six months ago. You see, I moved here about eight months ago from San Antonio, TX, where I'd been shacking up with my no-good boyfriend Dwayne for the last few years. I finally left him after I caught him in bed with the upstairs neighbor, that tramp Lisa. You know---"

Hastings interrupted his witness to get her back on topic. "So, you became reacquainted with Jessica French when you moved to town. How often would you say you two hung out?"

"You see, I ran into Jess one day at Munchie's Gas Depot, we were both getting gas. We exchanged numbers, and we hung out from time to time after that."

"During the times you hung out with Ms. French, did she show you any pictures of her ex-husband?"

"Oh, yeah. Jess showed me lots of pictures of her two boys and in some of them were her ex. Whenever she happened across a picture with him in it, boy she'd cuss up a storm."

"So, you were familiar with how Jessica French's ex-husband looked?"

"For sure. Though Jess hated his guts, she couldn't help but to brag about how hot he was. She'd rub it in my face from time to time about how I could never get a man that looked like that and had money to marry me. It kinda made me mad, but I usually let it go. Jess always was the type to rub things in somebody's face."

"Thank you, Miss Bullock-Jefferson. Can you now explain to the court how you came to be at the Sunny Day Motel on the evening of Jessica French's death?" requested Hastings.

Jaime looked scared for a minute. It was obvious she didn't want to say anything that would get her in trouble. "Um, well, Jess called me up and told me she was hanging there and needed someone to party with because her friend had bailed on her. So, I agreed to come and hang."

"Did you and the deceased hang?" queried Hastings.
"Yeah, we did. Around midnight I got a call from a friend who needed a ride so that's when I left."

"And what did you see as you were leaving?"

"While walking to my car, I spotted a man getting out of a dark colored Mercedes. He looked familiar. I was near a pole in the lot, so I hid behind it and waited for the man to get closer. I just had a feeling, you know, that I needed to see who this man was."

Hastings ready to seal the deal, asked, "And did you recognize this man once he was closer?"

"Oh yeah, it was Jess' ex, the hottie."

"Miss Bullock-Jefferson, do you see that man here today?" asked Hastings.

"Um, yeah that's him sitting right over there. Even though he killed Jess, he's still easy on the eyes."

Tim jumped up. "Objection, Your Honor, speculation. The witness does not have first-hand knowledge of who killed the deceased."

The judge sighed loudly. "Sustained. Mr. Hastings, please keep your witness from making speculatory comments."

Hastings, trying to appear contrite but failing as his glee over his witness' testimony was glaringly obvious, assured the judge it wouldn't happen again as he was finished with the witness.

Tim stood. "May I approach the witness, Your Honor?"

"Yes, you may proceed," responded Judge Bentley.

Tim walked across the room to the witness stand. He smiled at Jaime. "Good afternoon, Miss Bullock-Jefferson. I just have a few questions for you if that's all right?"

Jaime nodded and the judge instructed her that she needed to speak for the record. "Oh, um, yeah, I guess that's okay."

"Wonderful," stated Tim. "So, on that evening at the hotel, you say the deceased called you and asked you to come party. What exactly did she mean by party?" probed Tim.

Jaime began to look uncomfortable and stole glances at Hastings, who gave her a subtle nod. "Well, like, you know. We were just hanging out and listening to music, talking, that kind of stuff," said Jaime glancing up without meeting Tim's eyes.

"Interesting. So, there was no drinking or drug use Miss Bullock-Jefferson? And just to remind you, you are under oath and have sworn to tell the truth. If you do not, you can be found guilty of perjury," Tim stated forcefully.

Jaime squirmed in her seat. "Um, yeah, we did a little bit of drinking, but just beer you know, nothing heavy."

"And drugs?" quizzed Tim. "Did you and the deceased partake in any pharmaceuticals?"

Jaime looked down and didn't answer. "Can you please instruct the witness to answer?" Tim asked the judge.

"Miss Bullock-Jefferson, can you please answer the question before the court?"

Jaime looked up at the judge and gave a slight nod and then put her head back down. "Yeah, we did a few party favors. It was Jess' idea. She liked to do the hard stuff, but I normally only do a little weed."

"What drugs did you take that evening, Miss Bullock-Jefferson?"

"I might've done a little Molly."

"Molly," Tim said questioningly. "That's the street name for MDMA, correct?"

"Yeah."

Tim went in for the kill. "Miss Bullock-Jefferson, do you know that MDMA or Molly as you refer to it, causes distorted vision, hearing, and sense of time? If you in fact did partake in Molly before leaving the motel, how can you be so sure the person you saw was my client when you were drugged and had only seen a picture of him?" prodded Tim.

Jaime wasn't sure how to answer and just stared at Hastings looking for some help; none was provided. Hastings looked down at his legal pad and began scribbling. Finally, Jaime responded. "All I know is what I saw."

Tim left it at that. This wasn't trial so there was no need to hammer home his point. Hastings had no further questions, and Jaime was released. She scurried from the courtroom with her head hanging.

Hastings didn't call anymore witnesses and as suspected the judge found there to be sufficient evidence to hold the case over for trial. Judge Bentley set the trial to begin six weeks out.

While packing up to leave, Hastings approached Tim. "I have a one-time offer for your client. Plead guilty and we'll drop the charge to manslaughter and only ask for ten years."

Tim laughed loudly. "Hastings, you are clearly in the wrong line of work. You missed your calling as a comedian. No way is my client pleading guilty to something he didn't do; your case is weak, and you know it."

Hastings smiled at Tim. "We'll see about that. See you in court," he said and strolled away.

Tim called after him. "Just make sure that discovery is at my office by 5:00 p.m. today. Don't wanna piss off the judge now do we?"

Hastings turned and glared but didn't respond.

Evoni, Tim, and Marc left the building. Tim asked that they meet up again later that evening. He wanted to get going on disproving the testimony given today while it was still fresh. Evoni agreed. They'd meet that evening at Tim's home since it would just be the three of them and Jackson.

CHAPTER 36

Bri

Sitting across the table from Aubrey at Café Bouchon, Bri laughed so hard tears streamed from her eyes. Bri thought she led an eventful life, but hers paled in comparison to Aubrey's.

Aubrey and her husband were true jetsetters. They'd set foot on every continent and hundreds of countries. It was an enviable lifestyle, particularly when both parties got to play with hot men in every locale. By the time Aubrey finished her tale, Bri was practically snorting. Aubrey's story involved her, twins, and a bizarre accident in a hot tub. Thankfully all parties involved survived, though not everyone's egos.

After regaining her composure, Bri and Aubrey discussed their game plan. They were tasked with procuring at least one painting from John Grunell, one of the most renowned artists in the world, who just so happened to reside outside of Nashville in a secluded cabin. He was also famous for being two things conservatives hated: a homosexual and a Marxist. Bri wasn't sure if any of it was true, but Nashville was still a heavily conservative leaning city and the conservatives were still a force to reckon with, with both power and money.

In his younger years, John Grunell made a name for himself in the art world and in Hollywood circles. Due to his newfound fame, he became the face of the small but influential Marxist movement advocating for the overthrow of our current capitalistic government structure and calling for a revolution led by the working class. Though this garnered his artwork a lot of attention and drove up the prices; it also put a bullseye on his back and there were rumors of multiple failed assassination attempts.

Then one day Grunell simply disappeared from the public eye. No one knew where he was until about two years previous when a snooping blogger found out he was living outside Nashville and posted an article online.

It was rumored that after his whereabouts were discovered, Grunell set up booby traps on his property and kept a large collection of guns and attack dogs. This worried Bri. But Sunshine assured them that the stories they'd heard were exaggerations. Having a tenuous connection to Grunell through friends of friends, Sunshine assured Bri and Aubrey that John Grunell was curmudgeonly and a handful but not mean and threatening. Bri wasn't so sure.

"So, let's head out to Grunell's cabin tomorrow, say around 11? It's fairly secluded but I think I know where to find it."

Bri hesitated. "Are you sure about this Aubrey? Because I'm not."

"Honestly, Bri, I get where you're coming from. I'm not overly enthusiastic about approaching a gun-toting recluse who knows how to make bombs. I did ask around and the few people I came across who know him assured me he wasn't what the media painted him to be. But if you feel uncomfortable, I'll do the initial approach."

"Thanks Aubrey. That'd be great. If he still hates the rich, he's more likely to think you're the rich one and shoot you. That way I can make a break for it," joked Bri.

Aubrey laughed loudly drawing looks from the other patrons. "Bri, don't get us kicked out."

"You know if we do pull this off, it will be a coup. His work is extraordinary. No one has been able to purchase a Grunell in over ten years. His paintings are worth a mint. We'd surely raise a ton of money by auctioning off one of his works. The few I've seen online were perfect depictions of working-class individuals. It's like you could feel the sacrifices the people were willing to make just to survive but still sense the pride they had." Bri had a twinkle in her eyes that Aubrey had never seen before.

"I take it you are either a collector or an artist. Your eyes lit up when you began talking about Grunell's work," observed Aubrey.

Bri laughed lightly. "I'm no Grunell, but I do paint. It's cathartic to me. It's my version of self-care."

"I'd love to see some of your work sometime."

"Well, I'm private when it comes to my work. In fact, only the two people I trust most in this world have seen it."

Aubrey smiled. "I guess I'll just have to wait until you trust me, because Bri, I like you. I know we haven't known each other long but you have a very sincere and authentic vibe about you. Being who I am and living the life I lead, there aren't many people who I find to be their authentic selves when around me. They usually want something or want to please me."

Bri blushed. "Thank you, Aubrey. I like you too, and I sincerely hope we get a chance to get to know each other better. But I gotta tell you, I feel like I should give you a rose or a clock or something to signify that I'm keeping you around for another episode."

Aubrey laughed so hard she snorted. "Oh God, did you just reference *The Bachelor* and *Flavor of Love*?"

Bri giggled. "Hey, Flavor Flav is the original king of love reality shows, you have to recognize that. And by the way, I love that you got that reference. No offense, but not a lot of white people would."

"I have a small secret. I love trashy reality TV, especially all the so-called finding love shows. I've seen them all, *Flavor of Love, Rock of Love, Love is Blind, Temptation Island, For the Love of Ray J, The Bachelor,* and *The Bachelorette*; you name it, I've watched it."

"I love it. Trashy reality TV is good TV. There's nothing like watching train wrecks on screen. Though a lot of it is scripted nowadays, it's still very entertaining."

Bonding, Bri and Aubrey spent the next thirty minutes discussing their favorite reality television moments. By the end of the conversation, they were both in stitches. "Oh, gosh, look at the time," said Bri. "I have a nail appointment to get to."

Aubrey checked her phone. "Time sure does fly when you're in good company. So, I'll see you tomorrow. Shall we meet at my rental or your home?"

"Why don't we meet at my house? I'd love for Harold to meet you, and tomorrow is a rare day when he'll be home."

"Wonderful," said Aubrey as they both got up from the table. "Hopefully, you'll get to meet Gabe soon. He's going to love you."

"I can't wait to meet him," stated Bri while giving Aubrey a quick hug. "I'll see you tomorrow, say around ten thirty? I just messaged you my address."

Aubrey looked at her phone. "Got it, see you then."

CHAPTER 37

Evoni

Evoni, Tim, and Marc along with Jackson sat around a conference table in Tim's office going over the testimony from earlier that day. Tim and Evoni reassured Marc the testimony wasn't as damning as it seemed. It would be easy to discredit a drug addict in front of a jury, but what would be even better is finding a way to prove her story false.

"How can we prove it wasn't me? I don't have an alibi for that night, and I do own a silver Mercedes, even though I rarely drive it."

"You know we still haven't spoken to the motel clerk who was on duty that night," stated Evoni. "She's been rather elusive. Jackson, if you could locate her and speak with her, she may be able to tell if she saw the person in the Mercedes. We know it wasn't Marc, but it had to have been a man, one who closely resembled Marc. We just have to find out who."

"Right," said Tim. "And if we find the man, we may have our killer, especially if we can prove he also bought ties from the same shop as Marc. Our biggest problem is the key card. We need to find a reasonable alternative for it being found in your house."

Marc sighed. "As I said earlier, the only explanation I can think of is that Jessica left it there sometime in the past."

They spent the next fifteen minutes coming up with any and every possibly plausible scenario to refute the key card evidence. None seemed particularly convincing, and Tim hoped new information would come to light before trial.

"Okay, Jackson, please tell me you have some useful information on Jessica's potential child and/or the person the housekeeper saw Jessica arguing with? I really need some good news today," stated Tim.

Jackson smiled. "Oh, you're going to love this, and I'm thinking you'll feel like giving me a big ole' bonus."

Evoni intrigued, urged Jackson on. "Jackson, I'm dying of anticipation here. Don't drag it out. I promise, if the information is good, I'll make sure Tim gives you a really big bonus."

"Hey," exclaimed Tim.

Evoni put her fingers to her lip and made the shushing motion. Tim laughed.

"Okay, let's start with the child. Firstly, there was, in fact, a baby. A little girl born to Jessica at the age of fifteen. It seems Jessica's mother made her give up the baby to a distant cousin who was having trouble conceiving."

"Wait, how did you find this out?" questioned Evoni.

"I kept digging into Jessica's mother's background and family and eventually found the daughter of one of the mother's first cousins. She was more than willing to spill some family secrets after I promised her $500, which I will be expensing," said Jackson looking at Tim.

"Of course, of course. Go on. Where's the daughter now? Did you find that out?"

"I'm not considered the best PI this side of the Mississippi for nothing. Of course, I found out her whereabouts. In fact, she is currently here in Nashville or at least she was as of a few weeks ago," stated Jackson smugly. "I believe the young lady the housekeeper found arguing with Jessica was none other than her daughter, a Kimberly McFarland. Here's a picture I got from the cousin."

Evoni, Marc, and Tim were all shocked. This could be huge for the defense. If the daughter was in Nashville and confronted Jessica, it was more than possible that she could have also killed her.

"So, we don't know where the daughter is now?" asked Tim.

Jackson shook his head. "I haven't been able to locate her yet. I ran a check on her name and got a hit for a rental car, but it was turned in about two weeks ago and she didn't rent another. So, either she found other transportation, or she's left town. I've put a bug in the ear of a couple of my patrol buddies and asked them to let me know if they come across anyone fitting her description. Other than that, I'll keep checking hotels to see if anyone recognizes her."

Once Jackson finished, they all turned to look at Marc who appeared shellshocked. He hadn't spoken since Jackson mentioned finding the daughter.

Evoni patted him on the shoulder. "Marc, are you okay? I know that was a lot to take in."

Mark simply shook his head and left the room. He had no words. He truly knew nothing about the woman he had married and fathered children with and now his sons had a half-sister out there who could possibly be a killer. It was all too much.

They waited around for another ten minutes to see if Marc would return, he didn't. They called it a night.

After the meeting ended, Evoni headed home. On the way, her phone rang. Evoni's Bluetooth announced the caller as her mother. There was no way Evoni was talking to her. She didn't have the time or patience for Gloria.

The following day, Evoni arrived at work and was immediately summoned to the managing partner's office. This couldn't be good. Evoni figured either she was being let go or her not referring Marc to an in-house criminal attorney had come to light.

It was the latter. Steve Whitehall looked none too pleased when Evoni was ushered into his office. He didn't even offer her a seat.

"Ms. Singleton, it has come to my attention that your client Marc French is being represented by Tim Blankenship. Would you care to explain how that happened? I distinctly recall giving you the names of our top criminal defense litigators to pass along to Mr. French."

Evoni knew she had no choice but to lie. "Yes, sir, I did pass along those names to Mr. French. He told me he would consider them. I had no idea he'd settled on Tim Blankenship. I just assumed he'd gone with one of our attorneys. I'm sorry I didn't follow up."

Whitehall sighed heavily. "I must tell you, Ms. Singleton, you are a good attorney, but you aren't making any friends here on the top floor. I know you've been itching to make partner. However, if you can't even get your own clients to hire us for other matters, I'm not sure that will happen. Especially after the little incident with Jeff Johnson a few weeks ago. You are walking on a rather thin line right now."

Evoni didn't know how to respond. The fed-up black woman in her wanted to let him have it but the professional woman who valued her career knew that wouldn't help the situation. "You're right, sir. It won't happen again."

"See that it doesn't." With that Whitehall dismissed Evoni. Evoni breathed a sigh of relief but knew she wasn't off the hook just yet. If it came out that she was helping Tim informally, she would be out on her ass. *Though*, Evoni thought, *maybe that wouldn't be the worst thing in the world. Hell, I have options.*

After her meeting with Whitehall, Evoni spent the rest of the day on client matters. The judge in Colleen's case had ruled for temporary joint custody between the parents to be revisited in six months. Neither parent was particularly happy with that but they both understood they each could've lost custody altogether. Now her attention was focused on two upcoming divorce hearings. Evoni knew she had to focus, but her mind kept going back to Marc's case and the mystery man Jessica's friend-cum-drug buddy had seen. Evoni didn't believe for a second it was Marc, so who could it be? Jessica French was a druggie and a floozy; it really could've been anyone. But who wanted her dead?

Unable to concentrate, Evoni phoned Jackson to see if he'd spoken with the motel clerk. Just her luck, he didn't answer. Evoni sent him a quick text. She decided to update Mari and Bri. With her neck already on the line, Evoni decided it would be best not to do it at the office. She instead group messaged Mari and Bri asking them if they were available for a quick drink at Perrier's.

With that done, Evoni slipped out of her office while no one was looking and headed to her favorite place to decompress, the lake in the park across from her favorite coffee shop, which luckily was a short walk from the office.

Sitting by the lake, Evoni's mind wandered to Amar and her mother, the two people she loved but who clearly didn't love her. Was her mother the reason she gravitated to men like Amar? Thinking back on the men she'd dated; Evoni saw a pattern emerge. They had all been men who came off as caregivers when she first met them. They catered to her. They listened to her and gave her compliments on a regular basis on everything from her looks to her cooking. They gave her everything she craved from her mother; Evoni realized. That is until she was fully committed to them, then things changed and they either cheated or became assholes or both.

Evoni wondered why it had taken so long for her to realize this. The revelation made Evoni feel better. Now she, at least, knew what she was doing and could hopefully stop and find the right man for her. Having solved at least one thing in her life, Evoni checked the time and realized she needed to leave if she were going to arrive on time to meet with Bri and Mari.

Evoni beat Mari and Bri to Perrier's and had just settled down with a glass of red when they arrived. Once everyone had a drink, the girlfriend check-in began. Bri told Mari and Evoni about her meeting with the reclusive artist, Grunell. Both women were shocked and a bit jealous at Bri's good fortune of scoring a painting.

Mari provided an update on her relationship and on the nasty security guard from her building. Apparently, his company wasn't happy with his performance even before Mari complained. Her complaint was just the final nail in his coffin. The three ladies toasted to that. Racism, overt or subtle, shouldn't be tolerated.

With the feel-good news over, Evoni provided an update on Marc's case. Feeling the ladies in on the previous day's hearing angered Evoni all over again. It was clear Marc was being railroaded and Evoni was beginning to feel like there was nothing they could do to stop it.

"I should talk to this so-called witness," stated Bri. "Maybe I can get more information out of her."

Evoni shook her head no. "I don't think that's a good idea. Let's leave that to Jackson."

"Why?" questioned Bri. "No offense to Jackson but he looks like a cop. A super-hot cop, but a cop, nevertheless. I, on the other hand, look like a fabulous wealthy woman who this druggie will think she can score some cash off."

"She does have a point," said Mari backing up Bri. "Maybe she'll be able to get more information. Though the woman is a drug addict so there's probably not much more she can remember."

Evoni took a moment to consider Bri's suggestion. "How about this? We give Jackson a chance to talk to the D.A.'s witness and if he gets nowhere, you can talk to her. Because she's a witness for the prosecution at trial, I'd like to keep everything as above board and uncomplicated as possible."

"I suppose I can see the logic in that," stated Bri who was disappointed. She was truly enjoying playing detective.

The conversation moved to the upcoming charity gala for Women Helping Women. With Amar no longer in her life, Evoni needed a new plus one, so she asked Mari if she'd like to be her date.

"Are you serious? I would love to go. The gala is the most talked about event in Nashville every year. Anyone who is anyone is in attendance. And the work they do is beyond worthy. I never thought I'd get a chance to attend," gushed Mari.

Evoni smiled at her secretary. "Mari, it's my pleasure. I'm glad you can join us. Believe me, going with you is better than showing up alone. At least I'll have someone to chat with while Bri and Harold are schmoozed by everyone in attendance."

Bri laughed. Evoni was right. Every year those in attendance tried to network with Harold or ask for investments in their businesses. It was exhausting.

"Then it's settled," said Bri. "You both can get dressed at my place, and we can all ride over together in the limo. I'm sure Harold will be smiling like the cat who ate the canary when he walks in with three of the baddest women in Nashville."

With that settled, Evoni took care of the bill and the ladies parted ways.

Over the next few days, Evoni found herself immersed in case work with little time to focus on herself or Marc's case. She did hear from Tim that Jackson had finally located the elusive hotel clerk. She had upped and moved to Savannah, Georgia, without telling her employer or anyone else. Jackson caught up with her and she had nothing helpful to add. Sure, she'd seen the silver luxury car, but she didn't see who got out and didn't see when it left. She hadn't seen or heard anything during her shift. Since it seemed she didn't have a reason to lie, there wasn't much more to be done with her.

CHAPTER 38

Bri

The following day Aubrey pulled up to Bri's house in a late model red four door Maserati Levante. Bri invited her in and offered her a drink. "A glass of champs if you have it. I need fortification for the task at hand."

Bri responded, "You haven't said anything but a word. One glass of champs coming up. I think I'll need something a little stronger."

Bri popped the cork on a bottle of Perrier Jouet Blanc de Blanc and poured herself a shot of tequila. Handing Aubrey her champagne glass, Bri proposed a toast. "Here's to securing at least one Grunell and not getting shot in the process."

"Cheers to that," said Aubrey as they clinked glasses. "Where's your future husband? I can't wait to meet him. When I mentioned his name to Gabe, he about wet his pants. Your fiancé certainly is quite renowned in the great state of Tennessee."

Bri laughed heartily. "Well, Harold is a man about town. He knows everyone who is worth knowing around these parts, so I wouldn't be surprised if he hasn't at least heard of your husband. Anyway, he's in the library. I'll go grab him. Make yourself comfortable in the living room."

Aubrey headed to the living room to wait. Bri arrived a few minutes later with a distinguished looking older gentleman. He gave off Billy Dee Williams vibes. Aubrey could see why Bri was attracted to him. He carried himself like a man twenty-years younger and didn't look a day over fifty.

Harold approached Aubrey with his arms out for a hug. "Aubrey, so nice to meet you. Bria says you're one of kind. I'm a hugger. I hope you don't mind."

Aubrey leaned in for the hug. "I certainly do not. Who would refuse a hug from the great Harold Williams. I was just telling Bri how excited my husband was when I mentioned I'd be meeting you today."

Harold smiled. "May I ask your husband's name?"

"Gabe Drummond. He's a real estate developer."

"Ah, young Mr. Drummond. He's making waves around town I hear. I haven't had the pleasure of meeting him, but I am aware of his work. I know you ladies have plans, so I won't keep you but please let's get together soon."

"We'd love to. Gabe will be beyond thrilled. This might get me out of buying Christmas and birthday gifts for the next year," joked Aubrey.

Bri and Harold laughed. Bri smiled admiringly at Harold. He really was something special. God, she couldn't wait to be his wife.

Harold said his goodbyes and left the ladies alone. Aubrey finished up her champagne. "Ready?" she asked.

"As ready as I'm going to be. Let's roll."

During the drive to Grunell's, Bri took the time to quiz Aubrey on her knowledge of Jessica French.

"Really, I only met her that one time. I was in Montgomery, Alabama, on a work trip. While there I visited a local upscale lounge where I met a stunning bartender named Justin. God was he gorgeous. While chatting him up, this cute blonde walked up to the bar and began flirting with him right in front of me, like she was trying to outdo me. I found it amusing and decided to play her little game. By the end of the night, we were all laughing and drinking together. Then one thing led to another and that was that."

"So, you didn't talk about anything personal?"

"No, we were too busy flirting at the bar and once we left, there wasn't much talking. I didn't even know she was married; she wasn't wearing a ring."

Bri mulled over what Aubrey had just told her. The information wasn't useful to Marc's case, but it added even more color to the picture of Jessica.

After a time, Bri and Aubrey entered an isolated area. It was eerily quiet, as if no other creatures were around, human, or otherwise.

"This looks like a setting for a horror movie. Are you sure you want to do this?" joked Bri.

Aubrey giggled. "Heck, you're the one in trouble. Everyone knows the black person dies first in every horror movie."

Bri laughed loudly. "You are so right. But you know in real life, we are the first ones to run, and we never go into dark rooms or woods. That's for you white people."

"Touché," stated Aubrey. "We do always seem to enter dark spaces and call out hello," Aubrey said while laughing. "Why is that? Like, who walks into a room and doesn't turn on a light, especially when it's creepy? Not even blondes are that dumb," quipped Aubrey.

Bri and Aubrey burst into laughter. It felt good to lighten the mood while driving into the unknown.

After a few more minutes of driving, they reached what had to be Grunell's cabin. Though it was a cabin only in name; it was essentially a mansion. "Wow, this is really something;" stated Bri. "It's nothing like I imagined. A cabin is supposed to be rustic and small; this place is palatial. Doesn't look much like the home of someone who despises the bourgeoisie."

"Indeed, it is," stated Aubrey. "Mr. Grunell, though a recluse, clearly likes the finer things in life. There's no way there's not at least a wine cellar in there."

Bri agreed. Aubrey parked along the circular drive and hopped out. "Wish me luck."

"Good luck and may the force be with you," quipped Bri.

Aubrey approached the front door filled with excitement but also trepidation. She was finally about to meet the great Grunell and hopefully not get shot doing so. Standing at the door, Aubrey looked for a doorbell but failed to see one. She knocked loudly.

From inside came loud barking, Grunell clearly had dogs. Aubrey wasn't sure if this was a good thing or not. She gave a backwards glance at Bri and smiled to reassure her. Aubrey waited a few beats, but no one appeared. So, she knocked again and again the dogs barked loudly. Maybe he wasn't home.

As Aubrey turned to go back to the car, she heard a creak. Turning back around she came face to face with a man, about sixty in appearance, with grey hair thinning on the sides, glasses and clean-shaven. The man was wearing camo shorts and a soccer jersey for Manchester United. *What an interesting combination*, Aubrey mused.

The man in the door didn't say anything he just stared at Aubrey. He was holding the leashes of two giant German Shepherds. They were beautiful. Guessing the man was waiting for her to speak, Aubrey rushed out words. "Ah, my name is Aubrey Drummond, and I'm looking for John Grunell."

The man gave her the once over. "Why are you looking for him?" he asked.

"Um, I am here as a representative of a non-profit called Women Helping Women. We are hosting a charity event and my friend and I," stated Aubrey looking back at Bri, "would like to speak with Mr. Grunell regarding a donation."

The man in the door smirked. "Why's your friend sitting in the car, scared Grunell will bite?"

Aubrey didn't know how to respond as she wasn't sure who the man in the doorway was or if he and his dogs really did bite.

The man gave her a break. "John doesn't like visitors but since it's two pretty ladies he may be willing to see you. Wait here for a minute and tell you friend she can get out of the car."

The man turned and went back in the house closing the door on Aubrey who motioned for Bri to get out of the car.

Bri reluctantly got out and met Aubrey at the steps. "What just happened? Was that Grunell?"

"Um, I don't think so. But maybe one of us should text someone our location and let them know where we are exactly, just in case. That guy weirded me out a little."

"Good idea." Bri quickly sent her location details to Evoni. Bri really hoped Grunell wasn't a psychopath but had her gun in her bag. She never left home without it.

Bri and Aubrey stood on the front porch for a few more minutes before the front door opened back up. Standing in the door was the same man from before minus the dogs.

"Ya'll can come on in. He's agreed to see you." The man looked down at their feet. "He doesn't allow shoes in the house; slippers will be provided."

Bri and Aubrey exchanged glances. They were both wearing cute, very expensive shoes. Sunshine would owe them big for this.

After removing their shoes, they were handed disposable slippers like those given out at nail salons. Bri and Aubrey slipped them on and followed the man into the house. Bri was uncertain. She felt like the silly girl in every horror movie who runs towards the danger.

They were escorted into an all-white living room; it was devoid of any other color. Guess that explained why no shoes were allowed.

The man who escorted them in finally introduced himself as Julian, Grunell's property manager and let them know Grunell would be down shortly. "Would you ladies like anything to drink while you wait?" asked Julian. "Perhaps coffee or tea?"

Aubrey and Bri declined. Julian left them, and they used the wait time to look around the room. The first thing they noticed was the absence of artwork in the room; the walls were bare.

"I bet you're surprised, aren't you," said a voice startling both Bri and Aubrey. They were confronted with the appearance of a man who clearly hadn't aged well. Grunell was supposedly around fifty but the man in front of them looked not a day younger than sixty-five. "You'd think an artist would display his own work, but I never have. I find it a bit pretentious and self-indulgent. Besides, I find my own work to be a little derivative to be honest, but my agent somehow convinced the world it was poignant and moving," said Grunell with a shrug.

Bri and Aubrey were at a loss for words. The man in front of them was nothing like they expected.

"Well, don't just stand there. Have a seat and tell me what you want. I don't get a lot of visitors, and that's the way I like it. But I'm sure Julian told you I love the company of beautiful ladies and you two are striking. No offense."

Bri and Aubrey smiled lightly. "None taken and thank you," stated Bri as she and Aubrey took a seat on the loveseat.

"Well, now, what can I help you ladies with? I'm sure you've heard quite a few stories about me. Some of them may even be true, but I promise you most are not. Yes, I was involved in Marxism back in day, but I was not involved in any bombings or attempts to assassinate the president. If I had been, I'd be either in jail or hell right now."

Bri spoke up. "I have to say, you are nothing like I was expecting. I'm thrilled to know you're not a raging bombmaking nutjob."

Grunell cackled. "You and I both, young lady. Now I still don't like our current form of government, but I'm not insane. I'm not above enjoying the finer things that life has afforded me. You see, I grew up poor in a small backwater's town in California. Everyone thinks California is the land of sunshine, beauty, and liberalism but it's far from it once you're outside the major cities. It was even worse back then. There were the rich white people, poor white people like my family and poor black and Hispanic people. You'd think all of us poor people would work together but as you can still see today, we keep allowing ourselves to be divided and preyed upon.

"Anyway, to make a long story short, my family and others like us were treated like trash by the rich until it came time to go up against the blacks or Hispanics. Then, they came and tried to cajole us and lean on our allegiance to our whiteness. It sickened me then and still does today. Once I was old enough, I got out of there as fast as possible. I ended up in Oakland for a spell which is where I first ran into a small band of communist sympathizers. It was there where my artwork was first discovered and sold. I was making a bit of money and a name for myself but felt guilty as hell about it. That's why I got into Marxism. I'd seen how the rich treat the poor, and I didn't want to become just like them.

"Anyway, enough about me. How about you two beautiful ladies tell me who you are and why you're here," stated Grunell.

Bri and Aubrey introduced themselves and explained the reason for their visit. Grunell didn't respond instead he turned and left the room. When he reached the hallway, he turned around and said, "Are you two going to just sit there or are you going to follow me?"

Bri and Aubrey looked at each other and shrugged. Hopefully he wasn't leading them to their kidnapping and brutal mutilation. Was he about to string Bri and Aubrey up in his basement and have his way with them and sale the recordings on the dark web? Bri's imagination was running wild with scenarios, all ending with her dead before getting a chance to say I do.

A few doors down the hallway, Grunell stopped and unlocked a door. He ushered Bri and Aubrey inside. Both were speechless. The room contained dozens of paintings sitting on easels, leaning against the wall, sitting in chairs. There were so many, they didn't know where to look first.

"These are amazing," Bri said with awe. "I can't believe I'm in a room full of original Grunell's. I think I just orgasmed."

Aubrey and Grunell laughed. "I'll take that as the highest of compliments, young lady," stated Grunell.

For the next twenty minutes, Bri and Aubrey perused Grunell's collection, stopping and gasping at those they found extremely moving. "These are beautiful," exclaimed Bri. "The sheer artistry, the detail, the composition." Bri stood in front of a painting that seemed to capture the essence of a woman. "Are you open to selling this one?"

Grunell shook his head. "I no longer sale my work. I see no need to profit any further from a gift I was bestowed and have used to give myself a good life."

Bri disappointed, smiled. "I get it and that's admirable."

Grunell smiled at her. "But for you two pretty ladies, I am willing to give you each the painting of your choice."

Bri and Aubrey gasped. "Are you serious?" they exclaimed.

"I am. I like you two and I don't like many people. Also, I get a sense you both will truly take care of my work."

"Oh, we will," they stated in unison. "This is incredible. I don't know what to say. I feel like thank you isn't enough. Is there anything we can do for you?" asked Bri.

"Just enjoy my work and I truly hope whatever painting you auction off brings in plenty of money for your charity."

Bri and Aubrey selected their three paintings and spent a few more minutes chatting with Grunell who extended them an open invitation to return. Bri left feeling honored and excited.

The following week flew by. Bri was so busy with her responsibilities for the gala that she was barely able to focus on anything else. Before she knew it, it was Saturday morning, the day of the gala.

Bri awoke to a beautiful, sunny day. Groaning loudly, Bri threw back the covers. She had been up until 2 am with Sunshine and the rest of the ladies working on final details for the gala. They went through a few of bottles of wine which Bri knew was the source of her pounding head. What was she thinking?

"Hey, Sleepyhead. Rise and shine," said Harold while leaning over to kiss Bri on the forehead. He'd been waiting for her to awaken but dared not disturb her. Harold liked being amongst the living.

"Do I have to?" muttered Bri. "Can't I just stay here in this spot for the next two days?"

"Bria, you know you would never forgive yourself if you missed out on seeing all your hard work come to fruition. Also, need I remind you, we paid thirty thousand dollars for a table and five thousand for your dress. There's no way you don't want to show it off."

"Ugh, I wish you didn't know me so well," said Bri while climbing out of bed and into Harold's arms.

Harold chuckled and directed Bri towards her bathroom. "You'll feel much better after we get a mimosa and some food into you."

"Did you say mimosa? You should've led with that. But let's make it straight champagne. I can't afford the orange juice calories today." Bri stumbled into the bathroom to wash her face and brush her teeth. Feeling slightly more awake, she followed Harold to the kitchen where Maribel had laid out some of Bri's favorite breakfast foods. There were pineapples and strawberries, scrambled eggs with chorizo, and mini cinnamon French toast sticks. Bri groaned, she knew she should probably stick to the fruit with the day being the gala, but the food smelled amazing, and her hungover stomach could use the nutrients. She figured she'd do a two-hour workout after breakfast and burn off the calories.

After two glasses of champagne and her fill of Maribel's delicious food, Bri texted Evoni to see if she would like to join her for a CrossFit workout. Evoni begrudgingly agreed after Bri reminded her she also had to get into a rather form-fitting dress that evening.

CrossFit was torture but Evoni and Bri survived, barely. "Why did I let you talk me into this?" questioned Evoni while wiping sweat from her face.

"Because you love me and you want to look snatched tonight," said Bri chuckling.

Evoni laughed. "This is true. And now that I'm single again, I need to look snatched at all times so I can find some new prospects."

"Girl, please. You can walk out of your house in sweats, no makeup and a bonnet and you'd still have a hundred pairs of eyes on you. You are drop dead gorgeous. So much so that I almost didn't befriend you back in the day. I didn't want the competition."

Evoni sniggered and swatted Bri playfully. "I'll take the compliment but chick we were always going to be friends. It was destiny."

"You right," said Bri linking arms with Evoni. "You're the Pam to my Gina."

They both laughed and silently thought about how great it was to have such a wonderful person as a best friend. They knew without a doubt they would be friends until the day they died.

The next few hours passed quickly. By five, Evoni and Mari had both arrived at Bri's. There the ladies got their makeup done and donned their gowns. Bri stepped out in a gorgeous gun metal body hugging b michael couture gown while Evoni opted for an equally gorgeous Christian Siriano gown in a golden yellow hue and a plunging neckline. Mari, having to find a gown last minute, settled on a beautiful forest green sequined Halston gown.

Harold sprinkled the ladies with praise and was giddy with excitement over the honor of escorting not one but three gorgeous ladies for the evening. "If I weren't the picture of health, I'd be scared of dying from a heart attack being surrounded by such beauty," joked Harold making Mari and Evoni blush.

Bri playfully swatted at Harold. "Don't even play about something like that. I need you around for a really, long time. But you're right, we are gorgeous," stated Bri with a wink.

With that, the foursome exited the house and climbed into the waiting limo. The gala was being held at the esteemed Viceroy Hotel located in downtown Nashville. The scene out front would make the uninitiated think this was the Oscars. There would be paparazzi everywhere along the entrance and blue carpet.

CHAPTER 39

Evoni

Everyone from Congress people to Dolly Parton were amongst the chosen few to attend the gala. Evoni joked that the politicians were there for donations or votes.

After having their pictures taken, the foursome made their way inside. The hotel ballroom looked like an enchanted forest, that year's theme. Bri spotted Sunshine immediately, huddled with the planner finalizing last minute details. Bri would catch up with her later. More pressing was finding Aubrey and making sure the painting was there and not damaged in any way. It would be bid on during the live auction. No one outside the planning committee knew it existed. Bri hoped the painting would fetch a pretty sum.

Harold guided the ladies to their table where a couple of Harold's oldest friends and their wives were already seated. There was Lewis Freeman, whom Harold had met decades ago in New York shortly after arriving from Alabama. Lewis was president of the only Black owned bank in Nashville and then there was Melvin Lawson, Harold's cousin and closest friend since they were five. Melvin was a real estate developer and on his fourth marriage. He loved money and women, in that order.

Bri knew once Harold began catching up with his friends, he'd be lost to her for at least the next hour. So, after exchanging pleasantries with the wives, the threesome went off to mingle.

After grabbing glasses of champagne, Bri spotted Aubrey off in a corner chatting with a tall, good-looking blonde man. *That must be Gabe*, thought Bri.

Bri dragged Evoni and Mari over to where Aubrey was standing. Bri was excited to finally meet the mystery husband.

Aubrey spotted Bri as she approached and smiled brightly. "Bri, I'm so glad to see you. Gabe has been dying to meet you and Harold."

Bri quickly introduced herself to Gabe. "Aubrey, Gabe, this is my best friend Evoni and my other friend Mari."

Evoni and Mari exchanged handshakes with the couple. Evoni thought they made a striking pair. Aware of their unorthodox marriage, Evoni couldn't help but to think about Malcolm and his strained relationship with his parents because of his sexuality. Evoni wondered if it was better to live openly like Malcolm and lose the relationship with one's parents or hide to protect that relationship like Gabe. It was a tough choice either way.

Gabe excused himself after Bri alerted him to Harold's whereabouts, leaving the ladies to chat. Aubrey assured Bri the painting was safe and secure. In fact, it was being guarded by security by direct order of Sunshine.

Satisfied, Bri suggested they find a place to sit and chat. Her five-inch Louboutin's were killing her feet. Needing a refill on their drinks, the ladies made their way to the closest bar without a line, which just so happened to be near the outside patio area.

After grabbing their drinks, the ladies meandered outside where they were lucky enough to find four seats.

"Evoni, Bri told me you are a lawyer. Family law, right?" asked Aubrey.

"Yes, family law. It's time-consuming, challenging and can be heartbreaking, but also fulfilling. And it pays the bills," joked Evoni. "Mari is my lifesaver. She's my legal secretary. I'd be lost without her," stated Evoni smiling at Mari.

Mari smiled brightly. Evoni's praise meant a lot to her. One day soon, she'd have to tell Evoni that she'd inspired her to go to law school. Mari had secretly taken the LSAT and applied to a few local universities. She was waiting to hear back.

The conversation quickly turned to Bri's upcoming wedding, reminding Evoni she really needed to get to work on the shower and bachelorette party.

Out of the corner of her eyes, Evoni spotted Hank Dupree talking with an older distinguished looking gentleman. Evoni recognized him. He was Hanks' father, and it didn't look like he was too pleased with Hank at the moment. Maybe his predilection for party favors had finally caught up with him.

Looking inside the ballroom, Evoni spotted Tim and Cassie. She excused herself and went to speak. Though Cassie was excited to see Evoni, she knew Tim had something to tell her, so she quickly begged off to the bar for a refill on her drink.

Tim updated Evoni on Jackson's progress on the missing daughter. In short, there was none. So far, there had been no further sightings of the daughter or any information on her current whereabouts. He'd also been unable to locate any footage of the motel parking lot so there was no way of finding out who the man in the silver car was. Evoni saw their chance of ending this thing before trial slowly slipping away.

Soon it was time to head in and sit for dinner, speeches, and the auction. Back inside the ladies headed to Bri's table where Aubrey collected Gabe. Evoni felt an urge in her bladder and excused herself to the Ladies' room. She would hate to get up in the middle of someone's speech. That would be embarrassing.

The first bathroom had a rather long line. Evoni spotted a server and asked if there was a bathroom she could use with a shorter line. The server pointed her in the direction of the employee's area. She said the bathroom was nothing fancy but there would be no line. That worked for Evoni.

The employee area looked like a basic office setup. No frills and fuss. Evoni spotted the sign for the bathroom further down the corridor. As Evoni approached the bathroom, she heard voices coming from a darkened hallway to her left. One of the voices sounded vaguely familiar.

But with her bladder calling, Evoni ignored them and went into the bathroom. After finishing up, the same voices were still whispering. The whispers were getting louder as it seemed one of the two, a female, was getting angrier.

Curiosity piqued, Evoni slipped off her heels and tiptoed to the corner of the hallway where the two walls met and pressed her back against the wall, hoping to stay hidden.

As the two continued speaking, Evoni gasped and quickly placed her hand over her mouth, hoping they hadn't heard her. The man had referred to the woman as Cherry. It was Cherry Monroe arguing with the man. Then she heard the mention of Jessica. Now Evoni had to stick around. They could be talking about Jessica's murder. Were they the killers?

Evoni fumbled in her evening bag and retrieved her phone, pressing record. Hopefully the mic would pick up the voices. At that moment one of her shoes slipped out of her hand and fell to the floor with a thud. Evoni quickly stored her phone in her bag and reached for the shoe, planning on running. There was no way the sound wasn't heard.

CHAPTER 40

Bri

Bri wondered what was taking Evoni so long. She knew the lines at these things could be lengthy but unless Evoni had the bladder of a horse, she should be back by now. Dinner was being served and soon Sunshine would make her way up to the stage to start the program. Bri wondered if she should go looking for Evoni. Asking Harold, he assured her Evoni was probably fine and had just been waylaid by someone she knew.

Bri sat back and waited, but she wasn't happy about it.

CHAPTER 41

Evoni

As Evoni hurried down the hallway, she heard footsteps behind her and suddenly felt a tug on her arm. "Hey, you. Stop right there. Why were you eavesdropping on our conversation?" asked the male voice.

"Well, well, well, if it isn't the party crasher. You sure do have a knack for being somewhere you aren't supposed to. Unfortunately, this time, you've made a fatal mistake," said Cherry while approaching Evoni with a small knife in her hand.

Who the hell brings a knife to a charity gala? "Cherry, so nice to see you again. Who's your friend? Did he kill Jessica for you?"

Cherry laughed. "So, you did overhear us? That's too bad, Emoni. I guess you'll just have to join Jessica."

"It's Evoni, you psycho bitch."

"Emoni, Evoni, Ebony. Who cares, soon you'll be just another dead black bitch. Jake let's take her to the basement. I happen to know there's a nice quiet isolated room down there where we can dispatch this nosey bitch."

Evoni sensed Jake's hesitation. Was he not onboard with killing her? Maybe he wasn't the one who killed Jessica. Maybe she could use that to her advantage.

"Jake, is it? You know you look a little bit like my client. Let me guess, Cherry sent you to the motel so someone could see you and think it was

Marc? Did you also strangle Jessica for her? What's she giving you that's worth going to hell or jail for life?" asked Evoni trying to buy time.

"I didn't kill anyone," Jake yelped.

"Shut up, you idiot. We don't have time for this. You don't need to explain anything to her."

Evoni needed to get Jake and Cherry to lose focus on her and give her a chance to make a run for it. She doubted anyone would think to come look for her in the dark recesses of the hotel employee area.

"Jake, what are you, her puppet, her whipping boy? Why are you doing this? Did she promise to leave Chad for you? I can tell you that's not going to happen. I hate to say it, but you just don't look like her type."

Jake laughed nervously. "Nah, Cherry and I go way back. She's like a little sister to me."

"Didn't I tell you to shut up?" Cherry angrily hissed at Jake.

"Why, what's wrong with her knowing if you're just going to kill her? What can it hurt? No one will ever know it was me at the hotel in a car similar to the ex-husbands."

Cherry sighed loudly. "Of course, no one will ever know Jake but that doesn't mean we owe this bitch an explanation."

"You're right. You don't owe me an explanation, but Jake is also right. What's the harm in satisfying my curiosity before I die? I mean, we never even suspected you. Why'd you do it, Cherry? Was it your idea or Jake's to stage the scene to make it look like the Music City Murderer did it?"

Cherry sighed heavily. "You really don't quit, do you? Fine if that's your dying wish. Juicy was an annoying drug-addicted bitch who had the nerve to try and blackmail me. She found out I was having an affair with Chad's best friend, Aiman," Cherry snapped. "So, I began following her, looking for a chance to get her alone. I followed her to the motel with Hank. I called Jake to meet me just in case I needed backup but then Hank left. Then some other junkie whore showed up and almost ruined my plans. But she didn't stay too long and the perfect opportunity presented itself. The drugged-out whore was wasted by the time I knocked on the door. It took very little effort to put the bitch out of her misery and out of my life.

"Her looking like a victim of that serial killer was simply a coincidence or maybe my subconscious. Either way it wasn't intentional, but it did have the added benefit of making sure the cops never looked my way."

"Wow, so you're a ho and a murderer. You are quite the renaissance woman," quipped Evoni.

Cherry went to slap Evoni. Instinct kicked in and Evoni dropped her shoes and grabbed Cherry's hand.

"Let go of me, you bitch," hissed Cherry. Jake reached out and forced Evoni's hand from around Cherry's. "Keep on and instead of the knife, I'll strangle you like I did that junkie, Juicy."

CHAPTER 42

Bri

Back in the ballroom, Bri was beyond worried. She knew something had to be wrong. Evoni had been gone for over half an hour. Bri tried texting but didn't receive a response. The latest speaker seemed to be wrapping up. As soon as she did, Bri was going to look for Evoni. She slipped her phone out of her bag and texted her plan to Mari.

CHAPTER 43

Evoni

Not getting a chance to make a run for it, Evoni with Cherry's knife to her back, slowly began walking towards a service elevator. There was no way Evoni could let them get her into the bowels of the hotel. She'd die down there, and it could take days for them to find her.

Stalling, Evoni quizzed Cherry. "Why were you cheating with Chad's best friend? Does Chad walk tall but carry a small stick?"

Cherry poked Evoni with the point of the knife. "Ha-ha. You do know I have a knife to your back, right? Chad is a loser. He tends to allow his hands to do the talking for him when he gets upset."

So, Rocio was right. Chad is the abusive type. What a prick. And how fitting that this conversation is taking place at an event for domestic violence survivors. "Why do you stay?" asked Evoni genuinely curious.

"I need Chad's access to his uncle. Plain and simple, I plan on taking that family for everything they have. You don't need to know the details, but I plan on being very rich, very soon and I couldn't let Juicy mess that up. And Aiman, well he was just a sweet treat. A girl needs to feel good from time to time."

"Now, no more questions or I may just stab you right here."

They were approaching the service elevator, and Evoni knew she had to make her move then. "Just one more and I'll be the bestest captive ever," Evoni said sardonically. "Did you mother actually name you Cherry and do you have sisters named Strawberry and Raspberry?"

Annoyed, Cherry pushed Evoni with her free hand. Pretending to stumble forward, Evoni launched herself into Jake who was walking in front of her, pushing him to the side. Evoni made a run for it, turning down the first dark corridor she found. She could hear Cherry and Jake giving chase.

Spotting an open door, Evoni hurried inside and quietly closed the door. With the door closed, the room was pitch black. Evoni didn't want to risk using her cellphone flashlight, so she held out her hands to find the closest solid object. Her hand hit what seemed to be a shelf of sorts. Maybe this was a janitor's closet, if so, there would be potential weapons, if needed.

"How could you let her get away? God, I swear sometimes you are useless," excoriated Cherry.

"Hey, it's not my fault," exclaimed Jake. "You're the one who had the knife to her. From where I'm standing, you're the useless one. If you had just paid the druggie chick off, we wouldn't even be in this situation. I only agreed to help you because you promised me a huge payday. You never said anything about murder. And now I'm up to my neck in this, so I do believe we will have to renegotiate my cut."

Cherry sighed. She really did like Jake, but it was clear he was becoming a liability. She would have to cut ties with him sooner than planned. "Fine, we can discuss your cut later. First, we need to find that black bitch and take care of her."

Evoni heard all of this as she hovered in the closet. She needed a plan. At that moment, she remembered her cellphone and took it out. She never stopped recording. She had everything on tape. Because all her photos and videos were automatically saved to the cloud, the moment Evoni hit the stop button she knew she had them. Now to get some help.

CHAPTER 44

Bri

Bri's phone chimed as she and Mari were exiting the ballroom. It was a text from Evoni. She was trapped in a closet and being hunted by Cherry and some guy named Jake.

Bri showed the text to Mari and took off running. She had to find her friend quickly. Bri searched the hallways near the closest bathroom but didn't see any door that looked like a closet.

Bri spotted a server carrying a tray of food. "Hey you," she shouted. "Are there any other bathrooms on this level?"

The server looked at her strangely and then shrugged. "Not for the public. There's an employee bathroom in the back."

"Which direction?" quizzed Bri.

The server pointed to his left and walked away.

Bri and Mari hurried in the direction indicated by the server. Before they reached the next corridor, they heard voices. Bri grabbed Mari and took a few steps back. It had to be Cherry and the Jake guy. She could almost recognize Cherry's nasally voice.

Tiptoeing backwards Bri and Mari hurried back the way they had come. They needed a distraction to get Cherry and Jake away from that corridor.

"I have an idea," said Mari. "They don't know anyone else is down here, so if I were to make some noise in the opposite direction, they would think it's Evoni."

"Yeah, but that gets Evoni out of danger and you in danger," pointed out Bri.

"I saw an exit sign back there. I'll get their attention and then make a run for it. I'll be on the next floor before they even know what happened."

Bri looked at Mari. "Are you sure you want to do that? This is dangerous, and I don't want you getting hurt. I wouldn't be able to forgive myself, neither would Evoni."

Mari squeezed Bri's arm. "I promise you; I'll be fine. You know I was a track star in high school and college. I can outrun them even in a fancy ball gown."

"Okay," Bri acquiesced. "Just be careful and text me when you're safe."

With that, Mari took off in the opposite direction. Not long after, Bri heard a clanging sound and then footsteps hurrying away from her direction.

Bri quickly sent off a text to Evoni telling her the coast was clear and scurried down the hallway. Moments later, Evoni emerged from her hiding spot and ran into Bri.

"Oh, thank God, you're okay," stated Bri while wrapping her best friend in a big hug. "Now tell me what the hell happened? Is this usually how your bathroom trips end when you're alone?"

"Hahaha," said Evoni. "Let's get the hell out of here. I have to speak to Tim right now."

Bri's phone chimed. It was a text from Mari. She was safely back in the ballroom at her seat. She didn't know where Cherry and her friend were.

Bri relayed the message to Evoni. "Mari is definitely getting a raise. I don't know what the going rate is for risking your life to save your boss, but she deserves it and I'm going to make damn sure she gets it, even if it has to come out of my own pocket," Evoni said emphatically.

CHAPTER 45

Evoni

By the time they made it back to the ballroom, the auction was in full swing. Evoni needed to speak with Tim right away. Cherry and Jake didn't know she had a recording, but Evoni was sure they'd still try to run since they hadn't succeeded in killing her.

Evoni texted Tim while sweeping the room with her eyes hoping to spot him. Her phone buzzed. It was Tim. He would meet her in the hotel lobby bar in ten minutes.

Bri texted Harold to let him know where she was and that she had found Evoni. She didn't want him to worry.

Evoni's adrenaline was wearing off, and she needed a drink. The realization that she could've been killed was setting in.

Tim arrived as the ladies were downing their second shot of tequila.

"Well damn, it looks like this is where the party is," Tim joked. "Is this why you needed to see me so urgently?"

Tim noticed the glazed look on Evoni's face and knew something was wrong. "Why don't we move to an area that's a little more private?" he suggested.

Once they were seated at a quiet booth in the back, Tim questioned Evoni. "Are you okay? You look like you've been rode hard and put away wet."

Instead of responding, Evoni queued up the recording on her phone and handed it to Tim. Tim raised an eyebrow at her but took the phone.

Once the recording ended, Tim cursed loudly. "Those sons of bitches. I can't believe it. Are you okay?" he asked Evoni. "I can't believe what you've been through. Thank God, you're okay."

Evoni shrugged lightly and gulped down another shot of tequila. She would have a major hangover the next day. "Physically, I'm fine. Mentally and emotionally, I'll have to get back to you on that. What's most important now is getting that recording to the police."

"I agree," stated Tim. "Thankfully Tennessee is a one-party consent state, and since you are a party to the recording, it should stand up in court."

Recording conversations or accessing another's email or texts were a frequent occurrence in family court, so Evoni was well-versed on Tennessee's one-party consent law.

"It just so happens that D.A. Raynor is here tonight and sitting two tables from me. I'll be right back."

While waiting for Tim to return, Bri texted Mari to meet them in the bar. This way Evoni would only have to tell her story twice tonight. Once to them and the D.A and later to the cops.

Once they were all gathered back in the bar, Evoni conveyed what happened to Raynor and allowed her to listen to the recording.

Afterwards, Raynor stood without saying a word and walked out.

The group looked at each other. Tim spoke. "She's pissed off. I know that look. She knows her office screwed up and now they'll have to admit it in open court. I bet you a hundred bucks she's tearing the Chief of Detectives a new one right now."

Raynor returned a few minutes later. She looked at Evoni. "Can you please forward a copy of that recording to my email? As for your phone, unfortunately, the police will have to take it as evidence once they arrive, but I expect you'll have it returned to you sooner rather than later."

The group watched Raynor walk away. "Would it have killed her to at least pretend to care about your well-being?" remarked Bri.

"She didn't earn the nickname "Ratchet Raynor" for nothing. The woman is as cold as ice and as hard," declared Tim.

CHAPTER 46

Evoni—Two months later

Things moved quickly once the police had the recording in hand. Cherry and Jake were apprehended at the airport. Unbeknownst to Chad, Cherry had been stealing expensive items from the Brentwood house and selling them. She had amassed quite a windfall.

It turned out Cherry and Jake were neighbors growing up. They were friends throughout high school and then lost touch. When they re-connected through social media a few years later, it seemed both had turned to a life of crime. They both were con artists. One more successful than the other. Cherry had never gotten caught and knew how to fleece rich men. Jake, on the other hand, had done two six-month stints in jail for grifting.

It was Chad's bad luck that he ran into Cherry in a club one night. Once she knew who his uncle was, she planned to use him to take the family fortune. She refused to reveal the exact details of her plan to Jake or the cops. But whatever it was, it was worth getting abused by Chad.

Once Cherry and Jake were in custody, the D.A. agreed to drop all charges against Marc.

Knowing who had killed Jessica did nothing to ease his children's pain, but at least Marc could now focus on helping them heal and on his burgeoning relationship with Kanisha.

As for Jessica's missing daughter, Marc hired Jackson to continue looking for her. It looked like she had fled Nashville and Jackson was following her trail across the Midwest. He had a lead on her current location and was hoping to get there before she skipped town. They didn't know who or what she was running from, but it had to be serious.

Thankfully, Evoni's firm never found out about her involvement in Marc's case. Needless to say, the police and D.A. Raynor had no interest in naming her as the person who had obtained the evidence against the real culprits.

After winning big in the divorce proceedings for a multi-millionaire country music star, Evoni was offered partnership. But she turned it down. She decided instead to start her own firm slash detective agency with Bri and Mari. They were currently looking for an office space and trying to decide on a name. They were also planning on poaching the two hottest private investigators they knew.

The Women Helping Women auction went off without a hitch. They had taken in the largest amount of money in the organization's history, mainly due to the huge bid on the Grunell painting. The winning bid was made by Harold's cousin, Melvin. After everything died down, Harold confided in Evoni that Melvin had, in fact, purchased the painting for him as a wedding gift for Bri. Evoni knew her bestie would be ecstatic.

The Nashville Police Department was still on the hunt for the Music City Murderer, he'd claimed two more victims. Hope of solving the case was growing dimmer with each passing day and the mayor was calling for the Chief of Police's head. But all that was a worry for another day.

For now, the most pressing issue on Evoni's plate was what scandalous outfit to wear to Bri's bachelorette party. The theme was Hookers, Hos, and Hags. Trust her friend to have a theme like no other.

Just as Evoni was leaving the house, her phone rang. She didn't recognize the number but decided to answer anyway.

"This is Evoni."

"Ms. Singleton, this is Joe from Krispy and Klean....

Lekecia Barclay is a first-time author with more books in the works. Born in Ruston, Louisiana, Lekecia fell in love with books and writing at an early age. A Political Science major and English minor in college, Lekecia dreamt of writing novels but first had to fulfill her goal of becoming a lawyer. She has now rekindled her passion for writing and is looking forward to crafting future novels in this series and others.